—Praise for *Deborah's Gift*

"In a style as clear, eloquent, and evocative as the paintings of its heroine, Lois Ann Abraham's historical novel follows the life of a woman fiercely committed to overcoming the suffocating social restrictions of her times as she pursues her dreams. Deborah careens from one tragic turn to the next, but despite a world of heartache, she never wavers from her conviction that the creative act is its own form of salvation. Abraham's novel reminds us that to live is to love, lose, and endure, but to live well requires the unwavering courage to be true to one's self."

—Michael Spurgeon, Director, Borchard Foundation
Center on Literary Arts

"In deliciously descriptive and delightful prose, Lois Ann Abraham tells a coming-of-age story set mostly in America—though important things happen on the French island of Martinique—as the 19th century hastens into the 20th, into the modern age. Deborah, the spirited child who becomes a determined young woman and disciplined artist, once describes her life in fairy tale terms, but it's a grim, sometimes-terrifying story beneath the shiny castles and princesses of her coded tale. Her artistic gift helps her see and make sense of that fractured world.

"There are many kinds of gifts in this novel, beginning with the Statue of Liberty, given by the people of France to the people of America, a gift that sets in motion the plot of *Deborah's Gift*. And for those who delight in language, there are little, wrapped surprises on nearly every page."

—Gary Thompson, author of *Broken by Water:*
Salish Sea Years

"Lois Ann Abraham is at the top of her game in *Deborah's Gift*. This book is escapism at its finest, and I devoured it with a knife and fork—I couldn't put it down—and still I am hungry for more. I can't wait to tell everyone I know—you must read this book."

—Jodi Angel, author of *You Only Get Letters From Jail*

"Beginning just after the Civil War and ending in the 1920s, *Deborah's Gift* unfolds one woman's struggle against becoming an "empty, blind, compliant doll." Overcoming obstacle after obstacle and defeat after defeat, Deborah succeeds in freeing herself from "the damage of social constriction" to emerge as a successful painter. From St. Louis to Martinique, Manhattan to New Mexico, Deborah leads us through the unexpected turns her life takes. A satisfying novel that is especially refreshing in these times when women's rights are again being challenged. I couldn't put it down."

—Cynthia Linville, author of *The Lost Thing*

"*Deborah's Gift* took me on a wild, lush, and tempestuous journey from Saint Louis to New York City and across the ocean to the island of Martinique, the Pearl of the West Indies. The same adjectives are apt ones for Deborah—a born artist, whose unquenchable passion for art and life make her unsuitable for the roles relegated to women in the high society into which she was born at the turn of the last century.

"Abraham's prose is fluid, visual, and sensual. She brings an artist's impressions of the world to life, not only of paintings but of the observed world—Deborah's unique, passionate, laser-like lens and focus on what she observes, wants and needs are very much evident on these pages."

—Dorothy Rice, author of *The Reluctant Artist*

"Lois Ann Abraham has created a fully-realized fascinating character in Deborah. We see the world and its disasters and delights through Abraham's sensory prose and Deborah's artistic eyes. I could smell the turpentine and feel the paint under her nails. Deborah appreciates what she calls the "luxury of being a single woman who makes enough from her art to cover expenses and then some" during a time when women's options were limited to what men told them what they were allowed to dream. A compelling and important story."

—Mary Camarillo, author of *The Lockhart Women*

DEBORAH'S GIFT

A NOVEL

Lois Ann Abraham

New Wind Publishing
Sacramento, California

New Wind Publishing
Copyright © 2022 by Lois Ann Abraham.

Although the author has drawn on actual places, where real-life historical persons appear, the situations, incidents, and dialogues concerning those persons are entirely fictional.

"Why Wasn't Brently Mallard on That Train?" first published in the Spring 2014 issue of *Inside English*. The first chapter of *Deborah's Gift*, "Iris in the Garden," is included in *Circus Girl & Other Stories* (Ad Lumen Press, 2014).

Library of Congress Control Number: 2022907637

ISBN 978-1-929777-26-6 (paperback)
ISBN 978-1-929777-28-0 (ebook)

Cover design by Karen Phillips, Phillips Covers

Deborah's Gift / Lois Ann Abraham. -- 1st ed.

New Wind Publishing
Sacramento, California 95819
www.newwindpublishing.com

In memory of

Zona Ellen Smith, artist

1890-1976

Prologue

Deborah waits to hear the front door click shut as her lover slips out to make his guilty way home to an invalid wife. He has lingered too long, poor fellow; Brently Mallard will miss his train. She enjoys the round, warm, rosy feeling of her body, enjoying it even more now that she is alone again in her refuge where she keeps rendezvous with a passion that has nothing to do with erring husbands.

The sparsely furnished little room is in disarray. Her paints and brushes fill packing crates; her papers and canvases are piled high along one wall. Her palette, smeared with green and brown, her untidy paint tubes, a drying canvas on the easel, and a finished painting on the wall are left to pack. Everything else has been boxed and packaged for weeks, dreaming in the darkness of escape. Deborah is waiting for the death of her great-aunt, *Tante* Charity, the French form of address the old lady insists on, waiting for her to pass from this life to what Deborah devoutly hopes will be a blankness, a disappearance, utter annihilation with no possible return, not even a ripple, a breath, an echo, please God, not a dream.

With an occasional dalliance when it pleases her, she is poised to return to Martinique when the fetters keeping her in St. Louis are finally removed. Deborah has just enough money to rent her small studio on Jefferson Street, to pay for paint and canvas and unobstructed room to work. She has created a sweet oasis to help her endure the harsh, dry desert of respectability, where she has sequestered her heart and steeled her nerves. Here she works in privacy, uninterrupted by expectations or obligations, unjudged and free. Only Katy, her childhood nurse, knows where to find her.

Deborah steps to the easel in the middle of the room to have another look at her latest attempt to capture the dream, another picture of Mt. Pelée. Too much red on the flank of the mountain? To balance it with blue in the valleys? To let the brightness in or to contain it? To infuse the piece with the tenderness of a mother brooding over her first-born child, to reveal the suffering of such love denied in the steepness and the harsh challenge of its reach into the sky. She will paint this scene again and again until the impulse has been satisfied and replaced with another compelling directive. But for now, darkness lurks behind the cloudy sky, anger waits in the heart of the mountain. The red streak stays.

The most recently completed—and because most recent, her favorite—piece still hangs on the wall, a sweet, bright landscape of Mt. Pelée in repose—the dark gorges and their rivers waving down the slope to the sea, blue as only this sea is blue, a blue into which the eye must sink and rise and sink again, depth and surface, solid, liquid flashing blue.

This painting is her dreamscape, a portrait of the adopted homeland where, as a girl, she stepped into her own life and suffered for it. There, her son, the baby she has seen once and lost, was taken from her arms; there, he still grows and plays and becomes himself. She has tried to capture in charcoal, in pastels, the face she remembers from the night of his birth. At last, she will see her baby again, touch him, and reclaim him after Tante Charity finally, finally dies.

Deborah floats becalmed in the lapping waves of the future, between tides, waiting to inherit the family fortune and lucrative holdings in the Indies, on Martinique, at the beautiful estate of Sans Douleur. Deborah's heart threatens to break into song after being silenced for so long; she will return to the island of flowers, where dreams and pleasures mingle in the hot green shade, where return is inevitable, where her little one waits. She knows her life of deception has taken its toll. Deborah is ready to heal.

She remembers the feel of Martinique, the sun on her skin, how the heat hovering even in the shade warmed her flesh, then her bones, then something deeper, making her into a single being instead of the amalgam of parts she has created to survive in a blind midwestern life of pleasing others. Her bags and trunks are packed with just enough clothing to get her from St. Louis to New York, then to ports of call in the Antilles. At last her ship will dock in St. Pierre, and she can set aside the tight waists and corsets that constrict her in this maddeningly stuffy American city. Once more in the lush embrace of Sans Douleur, she can spend all day in her wrapper if she wishes, eating mangos and letting the juice run down her chin, painting the bright bougainvillea as it flames against the white walls, listening to the shouts of the beautiful black children, the happy laughter of her own, still unknown, son.

Gianni is seven, almost eight now; she pictures him as a coffee-and-cream colored boy, strong like his father, but kind, she hopes. The only news she has received since he was taken from her arms is a crumpled note in nearly illiterate French saying, "l'enfan et bien ici." The child is well here. Villette, who was there at his birth, is looking after him until Deborah returns to Martinique, once Katy comes to tell her the old dragon has finally died, and the treasure and the keys to Sans Douleur are hers. She has earned them.

Once there, she will try again to paint the moods of Mt. Pelée, whose green velvet invites the hand to stroke it.

The steep mountain looms over Sans Douleur like a mother or a goddess, beautiful and impassive, sometimes bold and sometimes concealed in a shroud of mist. When she paints the mountain now from memory, she has the impression of slaving over the portrait of a lost lover rather than a landscape, hoping to capture its beguiling ambiguity on the canvas.

As Deborah paints, she is reminded of rumors relayed to her in tantalizing bits, by lamplight, in the darkness when the servants whispered to each other. Hidden away, they say, in the deep crevasses and in the highest jungles of the mountain are wild men, the *marrons*, coal-black Africans from the very first shipment of slaves to the Indies who escaped before they could be sold, used, beaten, and robbed of their power. The first night, so the story goes, the marrons were the ones who broke out of the pens where the people had been herded like livestock. They fled into the dark river valleys of Mt. Pelée, not knowing if they were still alive or if they had died in the hellish misery of the ship's hold and had arrived in the kingdom of devils.

Their lives are the subject of folktales and superstition. No one claims to have seen them, yet everyone knows they are there. One might see a patch of black in the deepest shade of the trees, so black it is almost purple, and then it is gone. What has been almost seen is likely a marron. It is the marrons who are responsible for the small thefts and mischiefs that plague the plantation owners, marrons who commit the major crimes of trampling cane, breaking machinery or poisoning horses. The marrons exist to curse the rich white owners and to punish their unwild black brothers and sisters who have accepted the heavy chains and lived to endure the lash. The picture of Mt. Pelée would be incomplete without their invisible presence.

She wants to paint the stifling green heat of the small garden house where she stayed and waited for her time to come, sketching the shapes of the world and dreaming of how the world might change. She wants to capture the joy and misery of the people of St. Pierre, golden, yellow, brown, umber, and black—the harsh, desperate gaiety of their clothing on Sunday and market day and their music, frantic, beautiful, and unbearably sad, even on days of celebration. She leaves it for the *békés,* the white people, the owners, to paint each other. They mean nothing to her. She paints what she has seen and her paintings teach her to look more deeply.

She wishes now that she had spent more time just looking. But she was young then, only sixteen. And she was distracted by the novel pleasures and impulses of her changing body. Now, as she looks back and longs for the brief freedom that had been hers, she realizes how important it is to know Pelée intimately, to gaze into its face as she had gazed at the sleeping lover who lay beside her in the hot Martinique afternoons while her great-aunt dozed in her impeccably French bedroom, her nose pointed imperiously at the whitewashed ceiling overhead.

Soon Sans Douleur will belong to Deborah and no one can take it away no matter how she chooses to live. She has kept her side of the painful bargain; there has been no scandal. The honor of the Millais family—risen on the tide of sugar and slavery to a social position beyond reproach—that honor is intact, in spite of Deborah's horrifying indiscretion.

Deborah sets aside her unfinished Mt. Pelée painting and replaces it with a blank canvas. As she waits for an image to form in her mind, she gazes through the window at a patch of pale lavender-blue sky just edging into the first hints of dusk. She imagines the new life quivering in the buds on tree branches in the little square, emerging or soon to emerge in leafy crowds in abundant proof of the changing season. She wonders what will come to her out of the bright promise of spring.

A knock on the door, now, coming as it must in time.

"She's gone, miss," Katy says, her eyes sparkling with the enormity of the moment. "God have mercy on her, as it's mercy she'll be needing in the next life. You'd best make yourself decent and get to the house."

Deborah feels a joy rising up from the core of her, a hope she has cherished that now floods her body. She will reclaim her son. She will embody the longed-for return of her own mother. She will no longer be the absent mother whose loss leaves only the smell of perfume or ashes behind. She will be the mother who returns.

After a moment, she assumes the blank face of mourning that will be expected of her as she buries the old lady and accepts the conventional condolences of respectable society.

"You'd best come now, as that Richards is already there, all over the house and asking for you. Do come, Miss Deborah!"

"Of course, Katy," she says. "Just help me find my things and I'll be there straight away." And inside her heart is satisfaction; a whispered word resonates there as though it is hers alone, waiting for this moment to deliver its meaning. *Free. Body and soul, free.*

1

~ *Iris in the Garden* ~

Deborah remembered very little about her parents. Such great care had been taken to shield her from a grief too heavy for a child of six to bear that it was some time before she realized they had died and were not coming back. She had been told they were going to New York, and then everyone was crying and trying to be brave. She was not surprised that Grandma Gussie was sad that they were gone; Grandma Gussie loved them all. That's why she had come to stay while they were away, to take care of her. But it surprised her that the servants, even her nurse Katy, would miss them so much.

In the morning of the day they left, her father looking as clean and trim as a nutcracker, her mother flustered like a peony in the wind, there had been bustling and last-minute reminders to lock up the gates, to watch out for the wobbly club chair in the foyer, frantic searches to find misplaced luggage, a reminder to Grandma Gussie to call Dr. Foster if Deborah's cough returned, last hugs, just one more thing, hugs again, and they were off. The house had seemed very quiet then, and darker; Deborah wished she had been taken in the carriage to catch the train to New York to see the new statue, taller than the courthouse, the tallest building in St. Louis, instead of being left at home, being minded.

After lunch, there had been messengers, shocked voices, and worried looks. Katy had taken her to the park for a second time, even though it was time for her rest and they had been to the park that very morning. She had already fed the ducks and skipped around the pond once each direction, so she had been petulant, pulling at Katy's arm, teasing her to go home, expecting sharp words and the hot little sparks that flew out of Katy's eyes when she was annoyed, but Katy was gentle and patient with her and bought her a little wind-up duck from a sidewalk vendor to occupy her, a delightful novelty until it foundered and sank sideways into the water, too far out of reach to retrieve.

That night, as she ate supper with Katy in the nursery, with jam butties for a special treat, she again heard hushed voices and doors closing, but Katy started telling fairy stories about princesses and enchantments and magical stones and talking birds. Katy usually rationed out her stories one at a time when she was in a good mood or Deborah was sick. She heard her parents' door close and expected for just a moment that her mother would come in for a nighttime kiss, but her parents, she remembered, were gone. Instead, Dr. Foster had come in to see her, though her cough was only a tiny itch now. She felt him exchange a look over her head with Katy, who tucked her in and climbed the narrow stairs to her narrow bed, taking the candle and leaving Deborah with only moonlight to mark her way. But a lamp had been left burning in the hallway outside her parents' bedroom. Had they come back after all?

Ordinarily she was barred from her parents' room, though she was allowed to enter on Christmas and birthday mornings, spreading out the gifts and treats on the eiderdown and nestling into the warm space between them, reveling in her mother's flowery smell, petting her father's scratchy face and her mother's soft one, snuggling close. She thought now that she would just open their door a crack and see if they had returned. She would be quiet as a mouse.

She carefully pushed the door open. A beam of light from the hall shone on her mother lying very still, alone in the middle of the big bed. Deborah took a few steps into the room, holding her breath. The light seemed to be streaming out of her mother's white face, but then the hall lamp went out, and Deborah felt her way back through the dark room, cracking her face against the doorframe, and that was why she cried once she had regained her bed.

"My poor dear child," Grandma Gussie said in the morning. Her face looked more creased than yesterday, like a toy bear that had lost some of its stuffing. "Your parents, your father and your mother...your parents...I'm so sorry, my darling." Her voice cracked, and she shook herself to try again. "They're gone. But I will be here to look after you."

"I know," Deborah said. That arrangement had already been explained to her. "They've gone to New York to see the new statue."

Grandma Gussie turned her head, but Deborah could tell she was crying by the way her shoulders moved as she walked out with her hands to her face, bent forward as though battling a strong wind. Then Katy was sent to clear things up.

Katy sat on the low chair by the fireplace and took Deborah onto her lap, although she had said the last time that Deborah was grown too big to cosset. Her own little sisters had been doing the washing up to help their mother by the time they were her age.

"Your parents are not in New York, Deborah. They've gone to heaven to be with God."

"Why? Why not New York?"

Katy set her face the way she did when she wanted to do one thing and had to do another instead. "There was a terrible carriage accident on the way to the train station. They died, my dear. Your father was gone, was dead in an instant. Your dear mother was so badly hurt—there was nothing the doctors could do for her. The priest came to give her the last rites, and she died in the night." Katy crossed herself. "Do you understand now?"

"When are they coming back?" Deborah knew what dead meant, but she needed Katy to tell her for sure. There could still be a mistake.

"They won't be coming back to this world, that's certain. But if you're a good Catholic and lead a good life, then you will join them in heaven."

"When?"

"When you are a very old lady with gray hair and grandchildren of your own and the good Lord calls you away. Until then, you've just to say your prayers and be a good girl."

Deborah wriggled off Katy's lap and looked out the nursery window. The air outside cooled the glass against Deborah's hot forehead. The garden seemed farther away than it had the day before. She wondered if she had grown taller to make everything seem so small. The sunlight pouring out of the throats of the irises below seemed to blur, retreat, and disappear. In the dark space inside her chest, she felt that when the light came back, it would be darker, tinged with the flavor of tears. Morning would come again, but she was alone in a new way, and the next morning would follow and the next until all the light was lost.

~~~~~~~

A few months later, Deborah tried to paint the irises in the garden, the fuzzy purple, speckled brown petals and the fierce onslaught of gold that came from their throats. Ever since she could remember, she had made pictures. Hidden under the nursery table, shielded by the drooping tablecloth, she drew horses and princesses, the hair of both curled into fantastical shapes, their expressions haughty and grand, but the garden began to attract her attention as spring came and the iris bloomed bravely among the bobbing peonies.

With Grandma Gussie's permission, she took her paint box and pencils outside before lunchtime and drew from life for the first time. She found that the path from her eye to her hand passed through her singing heart. The first picture wasn't right, it wasn't quite what she saw, but the next one was better as she planned where to place the stems, how to put one blossom in front of another. When her best picture was finished, she took it shyly to give Grandma Gussie, who was fond of flowers and had many a still life on the walls of her bedroom, but those were dark pictures, their only bright spots the shine from a distant window on the curve of a teapot or the eye of a dead pheasant laid beside the fruit.

"Oh my, very strong," Grandma Gussie said. "Very strong and very...warm." Her kind face furrowed as she studied the purple petals, which faded onto the page, and the light pouring from the golden hearts of the flowers. "Very strong, indeed." Her voice sounded troubled, as though alarmed by the revelation that the light shining for Deborah was so warm, so strong. Surely the child had not intended to invest the flowers with such bold physicality.

"Shall I make one for Tante Charity?" Deborah dreaded Tante Charity's yearly visits, but such a gift of living light would please anyone, even someone whose fierce gray eyes seemed to see only what needed to be corrected. Irises don't need fixing.

"I'll put this away with my treasures," Grandma Gussie said. "It's too fine to put up where it could get ruined." She carefully laid the picture in the crease of her book and closed it cautiously.

The picture Grandma Gussie didn't see, the one that would have troubled her even more, was of Katy's arm. Katy had leaned on the windowsill, her sleeves rolled up high, revealing her round, rosy, speckled arms with pink dimpled skin on the sides that met the sun and a creamy white on their inner curves. She was looking out to see if the apothecary's boy was coming along the street. If he was, she would turn her head away and ignore him, even if he whistled at her. Impudent scamp. She wasn't going to be tempted from her duties by a feckless lad, not when her job could be lost, and her sickly mother and three younger sisters back home counting on her wages to get by. Katy glanced down to see Deborah on the floor, pastels next to her, tablet on her lap, peering at Katy and changing the color of her chalk rapidly, tongue caught between her teeth.

"Good heavens! You've made me all fat and speckledy! How could you be so naughty? You're a wicked child, you are!"

"You are speckledy, Katy. That's what your arm is like to me." Deborah threw herself at Katy, wrapping her arms tightly around the speckledy, soft, vital arm that she loved to watch lifting the kettle from the hob, and wringing out the washcloth to wash her face after supper. "I love your arm." And she kissed Katy's arm over and over to show it was so.

"Please, Miss Deborah, leave off. You're like a crazy whelp, you are. Leave off! What would your grandma say to see you acting so?"

Deborah left off but kept the picture in her folder. And

to make up with Katy, who seemed affronted, she drew a painstaking picture of Katy's new hat, a gorgeous black straw creation trimmed with grosgrain ribbon in an elegant bow, chiffon draping, shiny red berries, a curling white feather, and a knot of cunning white silk roses. This was the picture Deborah showed Tante Charity on her next visit. Since Tante Charity wore an elaborate hat every time she left the house, whether for church, shopping, or visiting, she would appreciate the beauty of this beautiful portrait of Katy's beautiful hat.

"It's a picture of Katy's hat, Tante Charity. I made it for you."

"Indeed!" was all Tante Charity said, studying Deborah's work and then turning her punishing eye around the room as if to seek out the offending headpiece.

"Augusta!" she ordered and, as always, Grandma Gussie hurried to answer, following a lifelong pattern of concern for the needs of her older sister.

"Yes, Charity. What is the matter?"

"We must speak of this . . . hat." Tante Charity turned her eye to Deborah and then swept Grandma Gussie out into the hall and down the stairs for a private conference, the picture held between fastidious finger and thumb. Deborah didn't know what she had done, but she knew it must have been wrong. There was no pleasing Tante Charity unless one presented her with a face as cold and placid and unchanging as a painted china plate, the face that grown-up women wore, a face she was learning to copy.

That night, Katy took her hat off the bureau and wrapped it in tissue to store in its box. She slid the box under the bureau and turned away. Her eyes were red, and her lips twisted as though to hold back hot words.

"Won't you want to wear it to Mass tomorrow?" Deborah asked.

"No, miss, I won't. Evidently, it's too good for the likes of me." Katy left the room without her usual kind good-night, and Deborah puzzled about it as she went to sleep.

The sorrow of losing her mother and father colored her dreams: a carriage lay on its side, one wheel spinning; darkness crept down the hall like a fog, and a heartless woman as tall as a building crushed her way through St. Louis, sowing tears. In her waking hours, Deborah imagined clinging to the two of them, not letting them get into the carriage, insisting on going with them, but she hadn't known there would be an accident. No one had known.

She had grieved that early loss until it was part of her, a secret organ tucked inside her body, ticking away. Every morning, she took out the locket Grandma Gussie gave her the first Christmas after her parents died. Inside the heart-shaped case were miniature pictures of their faces, and she kissed each one, studying their expressions, sometimes thinking that they were sad without her, sometimes seeming pleased at her attentions, though she knew their faces didn't really change. People who were already dead were beyond the reach of those still living. People who were dead were safe.

But now, she had caused something bad to happen to Katy, and it was different than an accident like the one that had taken her parents. She had made a mistake. Deborah realized for the first time how much caution even a peaceful life, a small gesture, a generous impulse required, how dangerous to love something and let it show.

~~~~~~~

Grandma Gussie, always concerned about her grand-daughter's health, held Deborah back two years from starting school, preferring to teach her at home. Gussie remembered her own schooldays, the nuns' vigilance, their punishments, and the way Charity, two grades ahead, incited her friends to pick on the younger girls, including her little sister. Deborah would be particularly vulnerable with her recent bereavement. She could already read and write, add and subtract, so it seemed reasonable to put off her enrollment in St. Agnes School for Girls until she turned eight. Unfortunately, the various school cliques and cabals formed in the first year had solidified by the third. Deborah, her social skills learned from a life with adults, wasn't very interested in classroom intrigues or playground games. The other girls found her calm silence mysterious and unnerving. No one knew what she might do if provoked. Better to occupy themselves with the childhood business of playing, competing, and squabbling with known friends and enemies. Deborah remained an outsider.

She was excited that the third-grade curriculum included an art class every Tuesday and Friday during the last period of the day. She could hardly wait for that precious hour in the art room and the class, taught not by one of the sisters, but by a real art teacher from outside who would answer Deborah's questions and teach her how to make wonderful pictures.

Her hopes were dashed at the first class. Miss Thrash brought in a basket of autumn leaves, paper, and paste. The object of the lesson was to attach the leaves to the paper with the paste. Then an inscription in one's best penmanship: "Enjoy the season!" and "Happy Autumn!" were suggested as appropriate messages, taking special care to spell "autumn" correctly. These works would be displayed at the Open House in November and then returned to the students to take home to their families.

Deborah, astounded and dismayed, sat staring at the

three leaves, the bit of paste, and the blank white paper on the table in front of her. It seemed like a project designed for idiots. She crumbled the leaves, first out of frustration; then, as she caught fire, she worked out a design from the fragments of red and gold, pasting some leaves onto the branches of a tree hastily drawn on the left margin, and posing others in mid-air. The rest piled on the ground, spilling across the card. In the center, in her best penmanship, she wrote: "Be Happy."

When sharing time arrived, the girls took turns in front of the class, showing their work and reading their inscriptions aloud. Miss Thrash said, "Good work!" or "Nicely done!" and pinned the paper to the bulletin board. She ignored the occasional "Autunm" that showed up, not wishing to deflate the girls' pride, especially at the first class. Deborah was surprised when her classmates met her offering with silence, then a spate of nervous giggling. Miss Thrash pinned it up without comment.

It's good work, Deborah thought. *It's nicely done!*

When the bell rang, marking the end of class, Miss Thrash drew Deborah aside.

"Deborah, I know you tried, and that's good. But it's really important to Follow Directions, do you understand? Do you think you Followed Directions with this project?"

"I put the leaves on the paper."

"I want to give you another chance, Deborah, so here: I'm giving you three more leaves, a sheet of paper, and a little dab of paste all in this little packet. I want you to go home and think about Following Directions. And then do the project over. Can you do that, Deborah, for Friday's class?"

"No, Miss Thrash," Deborah said, starting to cry a little. "I don't think I can." She left the packet on Miss Thrash's desk, unpinned her work from the board, and ran home to Grandma Gussie. Deborah was adamant that she couldn't study with Miss Thrash. Although bewildered by her granddaughter's distress, Grandma Gussie spoke to the headmistress and negotiated an early release on Tuesdays and Fridays. Deborah was to have real art lessons at home. She was too young to bear up under the exacting scrutiny of a male tutor, whose focus would necessarily be on ambitious works of art and the techniques of greatness. Such serious demands would be too strenuous for a little girl. Instead, a suitable, less expensive, female teacher would be found with a milder approach that would encourage an eight-year-old's talents to bloom. So every Tuesday and Friday, when Deborah ran home from St. Agnes School for Girls, she dashed up the stairs to set up her easel, palette, pencils, and paints to be ready for the arrival of Miss Jean Singleton, her art teacher.

At their first meeting, Deborah was afraid of Miss Singleton's stiff back, her expressionless face, and the suffering in her eyes. She didn't want to learn to suffer. She wanted to learn how to make real horses—horses that ran, horses as real as flowers with real faces, real hair. But once she showed Miss Singleton some of her pictures—irises, Katy's arm, a second sadder version of Katy's hat, a particularly nice pretend horse—Miss Singleton seemed to soften and looked at her kindly.

"These are very good, Deborah. This lets me know where to start." Miss Singleton set up a pomegranate, a blue vase with white flowers drooping down its sides, and a pair of Deborah's white gloves draped together in the foreground.

"What do you see, Deborah? I think some of your pictures are what you imagine. But to paint accurately, we must first use our eyes. Then, and only then, are we ready to draw. And some day to paint."

Deborah stared at the still life. She squinted. She tilted her head to one side and then the other. At first, she only wanted to see what she was supposed to see to please this new uncertain but promising ally.

"I see finger marks on the vase so that it's mostly shiny but with dull spots. I see the rough part on the glove where I chew on it when I'm bored during Mass. And blue streaks in the pomegranate like the veins in my arm. The flowers look desperate. Did you put water in the vase for them?" Miss Singleton rose silently and carried the water pitcher from beside Deborah's bed over to the vase and carefully poured. "Now?"

"In a while," Deborah said. "They're just starting to drink. I don't want to draw sad flowers."

They sat together studying the simple tableau set up to challenge the little student. Then Deborah, looking sideways at Miss Singleton for her permission, picked up her special art pencil and began to draw.

Their first lesson set the tone for their times together. They were content in each other's company but never merry, sharing nothing but the look of things and the way outlines could communicate shape and perspective could communicate distance. Small colors could blend into large, glorious spaces. At first, Deborah tried to Follow Directions, but as the lessons became more familiar, as she came to know Miss Singleton and the breadth and limits of her vision, the student began to push against those limits. Sometimes they argued.

"You're not drawing what you see today, Deborah. Use your eyes, not your imagination. Then you'll be ready to add color."

"You want me to draw what everyone else sees so that they can recognize it and say, 'Oh, what a lovely tree!' I just want to paint what I see, a tree that is always growing and waiting and hard, not lovely at all, but strong and determined. Then it makes sense to me."

"Do it both ways," Miss Singleton suggested. "One for everyone else, and one just for yourself."

They worked together in amicable silence, with pencil, charcoal, crayons, or watercolors, creating many versions of a little sapling in the garden. This pear tree, too young to bear fruit, inspired them to draw and paint it in various ways, standing resolute, vulnerable, untried, doomed, a study in line, tender colors or bold, an interruption of the ground and sky, a slash, a springing line, a pear tree in all seasons.

When Deborah painted in secret, just for herself, the pictures were not the still-life arrangements or garden scenes of her lessons, but private images pulled out of her dreams: lurid, indistinct, twisted figures that rose out of oceans of color—flying trees, a red wheel spinning through the sky, the faces of witches, the stars on fire. She would never call on Miss Singleton to appraise and correct these unorthodox pieces. Grandma Gussie would never be distressed by the hot, gyrating world of Deborah's unfettered imagination.

~~~~~~~

For Deborah's tenth birthday, Miss Singleton received permission to take her to the Corot Exhibit at Forest Park, skipping a whole day of school to ride the streetcar to the museum and see the paintings without the interference and noise of the inevitable weekend crowd. They stood side by side at each painting like true votaries, exploring, discovering, accepting, and sometimes floating away into the cool atmosphere of a lake scene with a gray-green willow and its gray reflection in the water. Then a few short steps to the next station and the next haunting landscape. Deborah knew she was supposed to be passive in the face of such greatness. Grandma Gussie had somehow made this clear when announcing the outing. She seemed to encourage Deborah's worship of the great paintings and to discourage her from seeing herself as a fellow artist.

They came to a dark composition, a cart and mill-pond with black branches streaming over the water, mirrored in ripples under a deep gray sky.

"This one isn't real," Deborah said. "It's not coming through the same eyes. It's not the same as the others."

"Perhaps not," Miss Singleton said. "I rather like it, though."

After the long morning, Deborah's eyes were tired and full of images. She needed a rest, a chance to breathe her own breath, to find herself. They stopped at the teashop for a quick tea and a sugar bun for lunch.

"Can you see what a great master Corot is? A genius, a truly great painter! It's such a fine opportunity for you to see paintings from famous collections." Miss Singleton was saying what Grandma Gussie had said, and her voice had changed to a teacher's. "What did you learn from Corot today?"

"I want to use oil paints like he does."

"And so you shall, someday. Best to start with easier materials, pencil, pastels, watercolors. But what else did you learn, Deborah, about his painting?"

"He paints light like it's water, all drippy," Deborah said. "And water like it's mud." She could see from Miss Singleton's expression that she had said the wrong thing. "Shiny mud," she amended, hoping to make it right. Though she couldn't find the right words, seeing the melting substances, light like water, the soft surfaces, the serene lines, all of that had been important.

Miss Singleton laughed and set her cup down in the saucer; this was the first time Deborah had seen her face lose its caution long enough to brighten, "Let's walk down to the lagoon, shall we? Bring your crumbs to feed the ducks. We can look at some water that *is* water."

That night as a tired, satisfied Deborah laid her head on her pillow, the paintings were still there, dancing and tumbling in gentle colors behind her closed eyes. And she hoped as she fell asleep that she would live to be an old lady, as Katy had almost promised, so she would have time to paint everything in the world, everything she could imagine, everything that mattered. And in time, when she was grown up and could go wherever she wanted, she would go and paint the monstrous face of the statue that had stolen her mother and father, the cold, indifferent giant woman set on an island in New York to lure people to their deaths.

~~~~~~~

When Grandma Gussie died three years later, everything in the world changed again. The warmth left the gray stone house where Deborah had always lived. A black carriage came to the house and took away Grandma Gussie's empty little body laid out in her coffin, clothed in her favorite lavender satin dress and covered in lilies. Deborah was left alone until a different carriage, almost as dark, opened its maw and Tante Charity emerged: first her gloved hand gripping the door handle, then the sharp toe of her shiny black shoe and the quivering black leaves and ribbons on the top of her monstrous, floating black turban.

For the rest of her life, Deborah would remember the look on Tante Charity's gray face. Perhaps she had wept in private over the loss of her sweet little sister, but if so, her sorrow left no trace, and now her face burned with the dark chill of victory.

Gussie was gone, Gussie whose softness had always, always, been rewarded. Gussie, the gentle daughter who, so innocently, effortlessly outshone her elder sister, the favorite of their tyrannical, capricious father. Charity could not compete, having starch rather than sugar as the main element in her temperament. So she appealed to her father's pride by embracing the family's French heritage and cultivating a Francophile attitude that colored every aspect of her life. This affectation, adopted as an adolescent, became a permanent fixture of her character, a source of pride and a platform for contempt, a defense against the humiliation of being less valued than her happy little sister.

She never forgave Gussie for marrying William Baird, sweet William, after Charity refused him. He had no fortune, no standing in the community. All he had was a heart-shaped face, a soft pink mouth like a cherub's, and a kiss that Charity would never forget, stolen on the verandah at the Christmas Ball when she was nineteen. When she rejected his marriage proposal a few months later, William was disappointed but not as crushed as she thought he would be. By the following autumn, he was engaged to Gussie; a year later, they married. He went off to the War like the rest of the young men, lost his left arm on the battlefield at Bull Run, and came home to establish a factory that turned a pretty profit keeping the Union army provisioned with uniforms and shrouds. After the War, timely investments in West Virginia coal made him very wealthy indeed.

Then Gussie had produced the baby, Deborah's mother, and William and Gussie moved into a fine house near the doting grandfather. Charity removed to an establishment of her own in New Orleans where she would no longer have to endure happy family dinners and admire the baby. In New Orleans, no one would compare her to anyone else. And there she had lived, with only occasional visits to St. Louis to preserve the illusion of family attachment.

Now Deborah would be her ward until she reached her majority or married well, which event Tante Charity assumed would follow in due time once her formidable French mind had settled on a suitable husband. She would take the girl in hand in the intervening years to correct the bad habits Gussie had no doubt allowed to flourish.

Tante Charity began her regime by eliminating Deborah's private art lessons as expensive, unnecessary, and inappropriate. Miss Singleton was dismissed summarily, never to come again, no chance to give her student a last word, no gift of paint or brushes, no good-bye at all. Deborah wept bitterly but to no avail. On Tuesdays and Fridays, instead of private drawing lessons, she could choose from the electives offered by St. Agnes School for Girls: Art, French, and Latin. Deborah avoided Miss Thrash's version of art by choosing French; she would continue to make pictures one way or another at home with pencil and watercolors. Tante Charity welcomed her choice as the first sign of good sense and proper values she had discerned in the girl.

Deborah did her best to pay attention in Sister Bernadette's French class, but she found it tedious. She whiled away the hour by drawing tiny little scenes of places she would rather be—under the sea, in bed, in a tree—once producing a flaming hellscape with Sister Bernadette as Satan, a picture that gained her a degree of popularity when it was shown around after school. Sometimes she joined in the clandestine note-passing game of devising insults out of the limited vocabulary of first-year French: *fils de jamon gros, chien avec la tête de fromage, le cochon de ma tante, visage du blanchissage.* Son of a fat ham, dog with a head of cheese, the pig of my aunt, laundry face.

Deborah proved to be a harder project than Tante Charity had anticipated. There was an air of carelessness, a look of passion about her, as though she deliberately pushed the calm, pleasant mask of femininity aside and gazed at the world open and uncovered. It was no doubt a trick of feature, the penetrating brown eyes, the wide lips that communicated an invitation which surely could not arise from a young girl's innocent heart, however misleading her expression might be. She was quiet, as a young girl should be, but she had a look too intellectual, too critical. She appeared forward, even when she was silent, as though she were about to speak or act in some unexpected way. To Tante Charity, she seemed poised to spring into some unaccountable action, some *outré* gesture, some unrecoverable *bêtise.* She had none of the blind sweetness one prized in the young female. Uncomfortable child!

~~~~~~~

Deborah had been flattered to be included in the invitation to Horace Norbuckle's soirée, but she was bored by the dinner-party conversation and the drawn-out serving of various courses in their appropriate order. The dim light in the dining room obscured the paintings, and up and down the table, various faces floated out of the darkness and then vanished back into the gloom before she could really see them. As the ladies rose to withdraw to the withdrawing room, Deborah murmured a request to be excused and escaped.

Richards met this lovely girl on the stairs and took the

opportunity to ask her, as an art lover, if she would care to see the paintings in their host's private gallery. Deborah was grateful for the opportunity, as she had been refused permission to visit local exhibits since the paintings might include images her great-aunt found objectionable, and she was starved for conversation about something that mattered.

Richards was delighted with this chance encounter; the evening now offered more than he had hoped. He ushered her eagerly past a discreet, leather-padded door into the presence of a series of paintings: Venus and Cupid (very fine flesh tones), a harem scene, a woman at her bath, a Madonna with baby at her painstakingly detailed breast, a large, imposingly framed painting of a semi-nude woman looking in a mirror and brushing her golden hair. Deborah studied each one carefully.

"And how does my little artist like what she sees?" Richards asked with a roguish smile, enjoying her puzzled expression.

"May I ask a question?"

"Of course," he said, wondering how she would manage to ask the obvious question about the nudity of the subjects. He began rehearsing his answer about the divine beauty of the female form, expecting to eye her sweet young body, wax warm, and enjoy the shy confusion he would cause in her bonny little bosom.

"Well," Deborah began. "Why are all the women blind? Everyone can see them, but they don't look like they can see anything."

Richards goggled, his ability to speak impaired. The answer to a different question was blocking his mental pathway and refusing to be called back. His confusion was compounded when Tante Charity appeared in the hallway, interrupting what might have been a prelude to seduction.

Clearly, Richards was harboring guilty intentions. It was written all over his face. It announced itself. What she saw was a layer of guilt partially masked by a quickly assumed assurance as befits a man of the world. Behind that, a baffled, nonplussed expression predated the guilt by mere seconds.

"Uriah Richards," the formidable Charity Millais intoned, as though reading his name from a roster of the damned. She nodded, repeated her pronouncement, and glared at him with a murderous look that shredded his composure by adding a layer of fear over the guilt, which still covered the sensation of having been prepared for a titillating eventuality that did not occur. He was left a bit uncertain as to which female scared him more—the fantastical niece or the terrifying old lady. He promised himself a stiff brandy with the other men to help him recover his self-possession.

Charity would need to take great pains to keep Deborah out of the reach of wicked men who might try to take advantage of her as she entered the dangerous waters of womanhood. She resolved that while they would inevitably meet socially and Richards would continue as their family attorney and man of business, he was never to enter her house as a guest, and certainly not have access to the girl. As a result of the sinister encounter she had witnessed, as well as others she imagined, she decided to take Deborah with her to the estate in Martinique the next time there was business there. It was simply out of the question to leave the stupid girl at home. She would be ruined.

2

~ *Still Life with Birds* ~

G rowing up in St. Louis, Deborah had seen the muddy Mississippi River many times. As a St. Louis resident, she had been taught to feel pride in it, its significance to the nation, the mighty King of Rivers, the flowing heart of a proud republic. But its turgid brown expanse, crawling with ships and boats, lined with working docks, had not prepared her for the enchantments of a sea voyage to the tropics and the intoxication of such living blue water, a blue that deepened and brightened with every morning's dawn, with every day's noontime, that faded to black at night when only the reflections of moon and stars lit its surface.

Tante Charity believed the three-week voyage would suffice to drill Deborah in the French she would need to socialize effectively in Martinique's major city of St. Pierre. She sat her great-niece down every day in the ship saloon or in a deck chair as far from the water as possible to quiz her on irregular verbs and the vocabulary of *politesse* and drawing room conversation.

For Deborah, it was torture to be constrained from hanging over the ship's railing to drink in the dazzling blue of the water below. It stretched blue and bluer to the horizon, where sky and ocean met and sometimes spilled into each other; at other times, the sky showed pale against the hot blue-green of the water. Every day the piercingly white clouds piled up, or passed by, or fanned out into fishbones in the sky, and every day, the grim old woman attempted to train her restless great-niece into caring about the niceties of French colonial society. Still, Charity needed her afternoon naps, which left Deborah free to explore.

Of the passengers aboard, the majority had no interest in a sixteen-year-old girl, whose role was to look sweet and keep her peace. The same majority did not merit Deborah's attention either, except for an occasional irregular feature—a jowl, a long earlobe, a particularly delicate or hairy hand—which she recorded privately in her sketchbook, being careful not to stare and thus offend. A small group of Belgian missionaries, clothed in righteousness and black serge, seemed exotic at first, but they remained aloof from all the other passengers and held their unnaturally subdued offspring close, away from the edge of the deck, away from drowning, safe from being lost, presumably lost for eternity. Deborah thought of painting them, then realized that spilling black ink on white paper would capture them in one featureless blob.

The Americans on board—men seeking to find their fortunes or at least subsistence—spent most of their time in the lounge huddled over ledgers and brochures for patent medicines, insurance schemes, and shipping businesses. Their doughy faces were reddish or sallow or pale, dotted with shrubs of moustache or beard to match their carefully arranged, tonic-drenched hair. They looked like men who traveled on the trolley in St. Louis, and she had seen them before.

The captain was courteous and formal, always tipping his captain hat and wishing her good morning or day or evening, greetings Deborah interpreted accurately as dismissal rather than invitation. The sailors in their sea-faded colors were fascinating to watch as they went about their mysterious tasks, but they were always busy and spoke a language of their own, one Deborah couldn't follow at all. She drew them at the beginning of the trip because she thought she should, then set down her pencils to look and look as the enormity of the sea and sky pulled at her. She longed to show Miss Singleton this water that was *even more* than water. Deborah's only interesting conversations were chats with the first mate, Mr. Short, who took a shine to her right away. She reminded him of his fiancée, Bryonie, who had passed away from consumption many years ago when he was off in the army fighting for Mr. Lincoln. She had the same eagerness, the same bright eyes and tendency to ask questions, then drop into reverie. Their first conversation began conventionally enough, with his inquiring whether she was enjoying her first sea voyage. He asked the same question with a little variation of each passenger, always listening politely to their answers and concerns about accommodations, mealtimes, and safety.

"It's so blue," Deborah replied. "If I took a glass of this water, would it be blue? Or would the blue disappear? Could you paint with it?"

"Oh, in a glass, it would show clear as anything," he assured her. "This is just the color of the sea in the tropics. It will be bluer yet before we dock in St. Pierre."

"No one told me," she said. "They just said I would be sick, but I'm not."

"You're a good sailor, then."

"Can you swim?" she asked.

Mr. Short was surprised to find himself flooded unaccountably with the memory of a warm night and the warm body of an island woman, wet and satiny, swimming, then turning and sliding against him in the rocking surf, grasping him with her strong legs and opening to him, her face bathed in the light of the huge moon as the sea hissed around them, black and shiny.

"Can you?" Deborah asked again, and he realized he

was holding his breath.

"I can," he said, exhaling and then pausing to take out his tobacco pouch, "I can swim, which is unusual for a sea-going man. Most of these fellows would sink like a stone. But then I came to sailing late in life after the war." He tamped the dark tobacco leaves down in the bowl of his pipe, glad to look at something in his hands. "I was raised a farm boy in Connecticut, and we learned to swim in the pond almost as soon as we learned to walk."

"I can't swim," Deborah admitted. "My great-aunt says it's not proper for a lady. I don't care at home, but I would like to . . . " she made a quick wave at the blue " . . . like to swim in this ocean." They leaned against the rail companionably and looked out at the ocean until some sailor's shout or a subtle movement of the hull brought Mr. Short out of the moment, and he returned to his duty. It was the beginning of a pattern that marked the days for Deborah, a quick chat about the sea with Mr. Short while Tante Charity sought refreshment in the darkness of her afternoon nap.

Except for these brief passages, Deborah spent most of her precious free time devouring and memorizing the shifting blue water, the white scalloped lines of froth, and the occasional ragged lines of seabirds skimming its surface. The increasingly wild sheen of the colors seemed to promise that their destination, the mysterious Martinique, where she would live while Tante Charity's business was conducted, must be the heart of color itself, a place where all colors begin, and the thought made her wild inside. She would never paint another rainbow without knowing how white its colors were, colors mixed with air, reflections of color rather than the colors themselves as she could now imagine them, a red as red as this sea was blue, a yellow as deep.

When it was time for her French lesson, her eyes and mind were so dazzled and full that she had a hard time paying attention to the sounds of French that were required. Mr. Short heard a few bits of these lessons and suggested that French was said to be the language of love. He looked away as he said it and soon left the deck for other duties, abashed at his nerve in speaking to a young girl in this way, though he meant no harm. To Deborah, French was the language of constriction and judgment, an arena where mistakes were made and corrected, the tongue of imprisonment. In Tante Charity's mouth, the language of love was chopped and swallowed, minced, pronounced through gritted teeth and pursed lips. Deborah thought Mr. Short's kind words were closer to the true language of love, suggesting a kind of love that was open and natural, offered and accepted freely, or offered and easily refused.

~~~~~~~

Mt. Pelée was first visible as a smudge on the horizon, but Mr. Short assured Deborah that it was the major mountain on the island, and they were only a day out of port. Even Tante Charity stood at the railing to watch as their destination emerged over the hours from obscurity and haze into a miniature toy set, then became a believable island. None of the other passengers drawn to the railing were as eager to land as Deborah, who was giddy with the notion of a new world to paint. After such a slow approach, the ship arrived all of a sudden, and there were farewells and scurrying around for misplaced bags and tripping over thoughtlessly placed luggage. It was already late afternoon, and the passengers were anxious to attain their resting places before dark, to enjoy the comfort of friends and family, hot dinners, cool drinks, and soft feather beds on solid ground.

Tante Charity kept a tight hold on Deborah's arm, but Deborah freed herself to thank Mr. Short for all his kindness. He had once expressed admiration when he looked on as Deborah did a quick sketch of the ship's deck. She now presented it to him as a good-bye gift, having added a figure to the scene: Mr. Short's sturdy body and browned face, his cap and pipe. The portrait would have troubled her great-aunt with its spirited attention to detail, the strong suggestion of vigor and energy. Then Deborah was pulled away and propelled down the gangplank to the wooden pier and into a low building for customs.

Of course, Deborah had seen colored people in St. Louis, where workers plodded along the gutters barefoot or in dusty old shoes, to pick up or deliver orders, labor in the gardens and packing plants that belonged to white people. She knew the war had freed them from slavery and that they were poor. She knew Big Cleo, who took away the soiled laundry, and Cleo's son Ramsey who brought it back clean and folded, smelling of starch. She had seen strong black men hauling freight on the docks along the Mississippi, bent under the weight. She had not realized how slowly they moved.

In this new place, Deborah scanned the faces of the people—black, brown, yellow, and mahogany—and their bright clothing and odd headwear, their darting movements so unexpected as they grouped and dispersed like a flower shattering into a hundred butterflies. The speed of these St. Pierre people, along with the shouts and laughter around her on the boardwalk, filled her with an excitement bordering on alarm, a sense of how many kinds of freedom there might be for the emancipated. She was overwhelmed by the clattering business of the harbor, the chips of swirling color and sound. The smell of ripe and rotting fruit, of bodies, burning sugar, coconut, salt, and fish added to the confusion of her senses. The sky was beginning to show the deeper light of late afternoon, with gray clouds promising to widen into a peach-colored band across the horizon, then open to a black spangled sky. But there was no time to stand and gawk. Before Deborah could make sense of the scene, she was whisked away and thrust into a waiting carriage to drive to the town home of Tante Charity's second cousin, M. Emile de Rognac, and his family. They were to stay only a few days before traveling up the side of the mountain to Sans Douleur. Charity expected the housekeeper, Villette, had made the house ready for them. One wished to take care of the business at hand without delay and then return to the more moderate climate of St. Louis in safety.

Deborah was formally introduced to the de Rognac family, the parents and their four almost-grown children, all in formal dress—Papa and two sons in black and white with fancifully knotted bright silk cravats, Mama and daughters in lacy white, their hair elaborately dressed with white feathers and flowers. They stood bolt upright for the ceremonies of introduction, then draped themselves elegantly over the ice-blue satin-covered furniture in the salon. They all spoke French with a swallowed accent Deborah did not understand, though she tried to respond appropriately and politely under the watchful eye of Tante Charity. The gentlemen found her wide-eyed efforts to communicate entirely *charmante*; Madame and her daughters secretly considered her a trifle *gauche*. But then, American.

Charity was glad to excuse an exhausted Deborah from the family dinner party. The event was intended, after all, to welcome her back to this island she and her sister had visited so often as children. She sent her niece off to bed accompanied by one of the maids, who also brought a warm milky soup for supper and asked if the young lady wished her to sing to her until she fell asleep. Deborah immediately accepted this surprising offer, and the sturdy young woman planted herself on a straight chair next to the bed, letting the yellow and blue ruffles of her skirt pile up around her so that she rose like the black center of a strange flower.

The lamplight gleamed across her broad face as she opened her wide mouth even wider and sang a wild, sad song. The passionate and melancholy tune sounded like a warning with strange foreign words that could not have been about the safety of sleeping children or the sweetness of dreams or the protective power of mother love. Her soup finished, Deborah closed her eyes to listen more intently and fell asleep.

After a long breakfast the next morning, she quizzed Henri, the elder de Rognac son, about the servant who had sung her to sleep, but once he finally understood what she was asking in her halting, wooden French, he seemed offended. It was not for him to keep track of the women servants.

"Perhaps," he suggested gruffly, "it was Cassandre."

Deborah found an opportunity to ask young Henriette de Rognac which of the servants was Cassandre, but the woman she pointed out was long and tall, mulatto rather than black, dressed in black and white, her red turban topped with sharp points like a fox's ears. Deborah continued to search, even asking Cassandre and another older servant, but they mistook her halting question for a request for more soup, and—what a pity—there was no more soup. With luncheon, however, would be a spicy *crevettes chaudrées*, very tasty, that the young lady would like very much.

At luncheon, over the promised dish which proved almost too spicy to eat, Deborah interrupted the murmured conversation she could not follow, asking her question in French carefully prepared and memorized beforehand. On being addressed, the hostess inclined her beautifully coifed head and listened politely.

"We have many servants," Mme. de Rognac assured her, as though this were an answer. "Perhaps twenty, twenty-one. They come and go. *Et ici tout le monde chante.* Here everyone sings." She brought her glance back to the guests at her table and looked up to greet the entrance of the *boulettes de porc* piled high on one gleaming tray, three different sauces in china pitchers on another. Everything charming, everything as it should be.

Evidently, no one could or would say who the nighttime singer had been or what the lullaby might have meant. Deborah had to content herself with the memory, but she continued to study the women servants' faces and feel as though something important had slipped away from her, lost in the space between a song and a dream.

The next day was spent touring the city of St. Pierre with M. Rognac, who required them to admire the white, red-roofed government buildings, the church, and the theatre overlooking a busy harbor. The visitors must all drink from the little fountain that sparkled in front of the theatre and remark on the sweetness of the water there. Perhaps on their next stay in St. Pierre, they could attend a dramatic performance. It would be without doubt world-class, European, most sophisticated, and elegant. Only the white families and a few highly distinguished colored people would attend.

Deborah had thought of Martinique as small, the atlas in the library showing that the whole island was smaller than St. Louis County, and she had imagined people walking from one side to the other. Now, as she looked up at the mountain that brooded over St. Pierre, she saw at once that whereas St. Louis was a smooth sheet of paper, this island was crumpled and folded, and in its deep green folds, whole worlds could be hidden.

Mr. Short had told her that St. Pierre was called the pearl of the West Indies, the little Paris of the Antilles, but she had never seen or thought much about the big Paris of Europe. Looking around, she supposed the phrase referred to the delicate, formal architecture of the public buildings overlooking the wide ocean, now less blue than on the voyage. To the north, the imposing peak and curving flanks of Mt. Pelée towered over the city. Deborah's eyes were drawn from the city monuments and buildings up the steep, narrow streets where the colored people of St. Pierre must live in the tiny brightly painted houses, two-storied with shutters and ironwork rails around balconies, or in smaller, one-story houses, all shades of pink and blue, mustard, yellow, and coral. At the top of the street, straggling up the slope, perched gray-brown shacks precariously balanced on the hillside. These might be homes for the poorest people, she thought. And from there, the street narrowed even further into a simple dark muddy track that curved and disappeared up the green slope. And there, somewhere, Sans Douleur must lie waiting for them, ready to provide solitude, recovery, and leisure after the rigors and demands of socializing in St. Pierre.

In the center of the city lay a large botanical garden, clearly a source of pride for fashionable people who strolled through it, admiring themselves, each other, and the cascades of European flowers that managed to survive in this climate. The native flowers, which drew less attention, were almost indecent in stark outlines and brash colors, undressed and loud, like birds rooted in the mud.

Deborah had drawn roses, peonies, and other sentimental favorites in St. Louis, so their fluffy textures were less novel. But the birds-of-paradise and the other angular, polished, fantastical flowers, with brilliant orange stamens, hairy centers, scarlet and gold wings—flowers whose names she never learned—these were all new. Her fingers itched for a sketchbook, but she would have to rely on her memory, draw them later, and look for them at Sans Douleur, where she could enjoy them in solitude, unhampered by social niceties.

But first, there was tomorrow evening's formal party for the visitors to enjoy or endure, with dining, dancing, and endless muted conversations Deborah would struggle to follow. She knew her pink dress would seem too bright for the pastel fashions of St. Pierre, designed to emphasize the paleness of the bodies enclosed, the icy whiteness of the rooms. She knew how to waltz and hoped she would be asked, knowing she could acquit herself well. But according to the de Rognac brothers, there would also be mazurkas, which she had never even seen.

"Perhaps you would also care to learn the *kalenda*?" Henri suggested with a smirk at his younger brother, who laughed and then smoothed the sparse little moustache that graced his baby-smooth upper lip. She knew this masculine trick of using her own desires and curiosity against her, these sideways looks, the pleasure some men seemed to take in her confusion, as though her ignorance increased their standing. She had seen this attitude before and always found it objectionable, ashamed the first few times, then puzzled, and now merely tired. She had not thought to encounter the same baffling pattern here in this new place. She thought she was brought here to avoid such things, insults from which Tante Charity intended to shield her. It was insufferable to receive the same treatment at the hands of these horrid boys. Deborah drew back her skirts as though from an encroaching flood of dirty water slopped by a careless servant, raking her eyes across Henri's face, evaluating and finding him negligible. In French, she hissed, "*C'est une bêtise,*" that's stupid, before she swept out of the room. She had learned that much from her great-aunt.

The grand party was set to begin about the time Deborah would ordinarily have been retiring, saying goodnight to Katy and climbing into her bed back in St. Louis. The guests flooded in, elegant, upright, and pale, murmuring in a quick, elusive accent, exchanging conventional words of meeting and greeting. Even if one of them had an original thought or genuine opinion to voice, Deborah would not have been able to understand it. She attempted to match their style of interaction, smiling more than usual, trying to gain a foothold in the crowd. She did not want to be the kind of American that drew Tante Charity's scorn by always preferring all things American, but here she saw nothing and no one to admire. Before the introductions finished, she was tired and sought a seat against the wall next to an elderly woman wearing an elaborate white evening hat with a great number of diamonds ornamenting her neck and hands. The *belle dame* smiled at her, murmured something that sounded polite, and then dozed off, giving Deborah respite from the chore of conversing in French.

In the midst of the great party, as the white linens began to show splotches of grease and wine, as the first dancers of the evening began to wilt and fan themselves, replaced with a second wave of partners circling the room in perfect time, Charity spotted Jean-Louis Monset. When she had visited St. Pierre as a girl, Charity had been quite a sensation, with more beaux even than Gussie. She had thought that Jean-Louis, the most desirable because the wealthiest of the lot, would propose, but the time slipped away, and she had returned home unmarried.

When the crisis of the Emancipation of slaves brought about the threat of financial ruin for many plantation owners, Charity was glad she had not staked her fortunes with Jean-Louis or one of the others. Sans Douleur had weathered the storm with an infusion of capital from American investments. In spite of disastrous predictions, disaster had been averted; most of the owners regrouped, adapted to the new conditions, and continued to own, if not people, then certainly everything else on the island.

From across the room, Jean-Louis, older by so many years, corpulent and moustached as a walrus, his eyes watery from years of rum punch, his fat wife on his arm, was a ruin of the young man she had once wanted. She moved in his direction from one cluster of guests to another, receiving homage, a ghastly gaiety in her manner designed to show him that she, Charity, was still erect and slender, still clear of eye, in spite of him. The challenge seemed to suit her, and she was distracted enough that Deborah was able to slip out of the room to the balcony, hoping to recover from the scents of flowers and wine and women's perfume and men's shaving lotion and smoke.

She was surprised to find no relief there, no cooler air, no quiet to be had in the dark, even under such brilliant stars set in the black velvet sky. The night pulsed with the roar of a not-too-distant surf as it crept in and out, sounding to Deborah like the beating of the island's heart. The insects of the night shrilled, not with the peaceful, homelike burr of the crickets she had heard all her life, but louder, like an aggressive army building up energy, waiting for the signal to attack. If they stopped, she feared her breath would stop as well. Then, from the unlit street below came a cry of anguish or desperation carried, as it seemed, on the last mortal breath of a lost soul. The sound planted in her being an impulse, a clarion call to rescue, to save, to find help, and she turned in a panic and ran straight into the starched white chest of her host, M. de Rognac.

"You must help!" she begged. "Someone cried out, *aidez!*" and in her panic, she could not find the French to say it all. "Someone screamed! You must help!"

"Compose yourself, *mon enfant*," he said calmly, his hands on her arms, gazing down into the shadows of her face. "A drunken woman, perhaps. They need no help. They are *comme les enfants*, like children who injure themselves. They need nothing."

Deborah fell silent, although she still trembled.

"Return to the company, the soirée, mademoiselle. All is well."

It was a measure of his mastery that she turned and left the balcony even though she knew something must be wrong to make someone scream so. She knew that children who hurt themselves were the very ones who needed help. In the big room where the dancers still wheeled, she saw brown women feeding the white people they had dressed and groomed for the party, waiting on the spoiled white people, people like herself, as though they were helpless babies.

She sat out the mazurkas, but then it was discovered that the American mademoiselle could waltz, and she was whirled around the room by a succession of handsome and not-so-handsome young men, an exciting experience for a sixteen-year-old at her first big dance. But when she tried to fall asleep in the early hours of the morning, head still spinning, she remembered the wild cry and wished to hear the lullaby again.

~~~~~~~

The following morning, somewhat later than planned, the two American visitors, both short-tempered from the dissipations of the previous evening, were bundled with their luggage into their host's second-best chaise and transported out of St. Pierre, not up the muddy roads Deborah had seen, but north over the Roxelaine River and then up a steep slope into the hot green darkness of the mountainside.

They stopped at midday for a hasty picnic and transferred to an oxcart with their luggage, sending the horse equipage back to St. Pierre to the de Rognac's stable. The oxen were stronger and could pull the grade better than the fine fashionable horses with which they had set out. The axles groaned as they traversed the deep ruts, and the oxen blew and groaned when the pitch increased. Deborah felt every jolt as though it must surely be the last, but each one was followed by another, equally bone-jarring. When the wagon stopped, Deborah realized she had unaccountably dozed and thought at first that perhaps a wheel was stuck or one of the oxen was refusing to go farther. Then she saw that Tante Charity gathered her netted bag and adjusted her hat to step down onto the track. And there, at last, was Sans Douleur.

The house itself was smaller than she had imagined, a brown, two-story structure without the balcony and grillwork she had seen in St. Pierre. Behind it were stables where the oxen would be penned up. In the curve of the garden that lay below the house, a white stone wall glowed with bougainvillea and flaming yellow blossoms. A table and chairs were arranged there on a block terrace, as though one might enjoy an afternoon tea, but it all looked deserted, the table showing streaks of rust down its thin legs. The smell of burning sugar hung in the air, a sweet, promising scent that soon palled and left a sour taste in the back of Deborah's throat. A rhythmic thrum of machinery came from somewhere on the plantation, and leaves rustled high up in the canopy. She felt curiously hemmed in.

Life stretched before her as a series of boxes in which she would find herself. But at least in this one, she could avoid the visiting, the parties, the predictable conversations that weighed on her spirit and made her long to escape. And there would be so much to paint here. A flock of blackbirds sped across the narrow stretch of sky and disappeared. A gray finch came to rest on the garden table and pecked about before retreating to the scarlet-flowered shrub, perching there and adjusting her wing feathers with a shake.

The oxcart driver unloaded their luggage and vanished with his cattle. The only human being in the scene was a pretty black youth of sixteen or so, dressed in a ragged, bright yellow shirt and blue striped pants held up by faded red suspenders, standing with his arms folded, a straw hat on his head, a scarlet hibiscus flower tucked into the hatband. He leaned back against the house and watched them curiously until a long brown woman emerged and ran him off by flapping her white apron at him as though he were a stray hen. He slouched away, looking back over his shoulder, and the woman approached, her apron still held out.

"Madame," she said, leaving Charity to make the introductions.

"This is Villette, our housekeeper. My *petite niece*, Deborah. Deborah, you must let Villette know if there is something you require." Tante Charity pushed past her toward the house to see that the linens had been properly aired, to arrange for the much-needed nap that would refresh her spirits and ready her to tackle the business of the plantation.

"Tea," she said as she moved away, leaving Deborah to study Villette, the person on whom she would depend for her comfort in this new household. She hoped Villette would be a friend, though her expression was not inviting and the interaction not promising so far.

"Who was that boy?" Deborah asked to prolong the conversation.

"Auguste. Or Ludger. Or maybe Sylberis."

"His name is Auguste? Or Ludger? What do I call him?"

"Sometimes the girls name him Sanson."

Villette said no more until Deborah pushed for more information.

"Why?"

"Maybe he is strong. My nephew," Villette said in careful, slow French, "the youngest son of my sister. He is a bad boy."

"Why is he bad?" Deborah hoped he would talk to her. She hoped he would let her draw him, the wide eyes, the insouciant tilt of his head, the loose-limbed ease with which he moved. She imagined a charcoal sketch that might convey all that, or perhaps a formal portrait that would reveal even more.

"I tell him go work in the city or fishing in the south, make some money, but he is a bad boy. He stay here like a bad cockroach."

"He doesn't look so very bad," Deborah said.

Villette drew back; her eyes turned away from this foolish white girl who must want trouble and not have enough sense to enjoy the peace that white people could have.

"I say he is a bad boy," Villette repeated as she sheared off toward the house and kitchen, where the old lady was probably making mischief with the two silly maids who were there to do Villette's bidding. "You don't trouble with him."

And Deborah had to be content with that. She felt certain she would find plenty to do in this new place, ways to while away the slow hours she would spend alone surrounded by the steamy air and the trees. She would unpack her things, find her sketchbook and her paints, and start to explore the colors of the place, variations of green and darker green in the shade of the trees. She wished passionately that Miss Singleton could be there to help her, to point out the things she couldn't manage on her own, but mostly to be amazed with her at this unimagined world and talk about it. The shimmer of leaves, swift birds that split the sky, flashing hummingbirds among the flowering bushes, Sanson's easy walk, all seemed to arise from a different rhythm than she had known. She felt as though she might explode or disappear if she couldn't put everything on paper. She would use the watercolors she had been allowed to bring with her.

~~~~~~~

The pattern of Deborah's days quickly became established. An early breakfast was brought to her room, and she had freedom to wander around the plantation until the noontime dinner was formally served in the dining room. Neither Deborah nor Charity had much appetite in the damp heat. All the long afternoon, Deborah painted the hummingbirds or the house or read and dozed in the garden.

Her only outings were occasional trips to St. Pierre with the old man Carlo who did the shopping in the market there. As Carlo moved from one stall to another, visiting with old friends, presumably looking for the freshest fish, the ripest fruit, and the best bargains, Deborah stayed by his side, silent and wide-eyed. When she returned after such an adventure, her mind was full of images of the bright dresses and turbans, glittering bangles, movements both languid and sharp, the dance of buying and selling set against the rhythm of the lapping sea. She found her watercolors sadly, hopelessly, inadequate to portray such scenes when using the techniques she had learned from Miss Singleton. She had to forgo the delicate use of white space and apply the color forcefully, the way oil paints should be used. Still, she was not pleased with the results.

Deborah had better luck capturing the menace of the strangler fig; it grew behind the house and reached out with long, exposed roots like tentacles to surround a small outbuilding where only a bit of weathered wood was still visible in the center of the fig's imprisoning cage. She painted the brilliant purple and red flowers tangling across the white flagstone walkway and the bright birds that flitted in and out of sight; sometimes, she left crumbs for them on the ground and induced them to remain still enough for a quick portrait. She occasionally caught glimpses of Sanson as he passed through on one errand or another, or possibly up to no good. He always turned his head toward her; he smiled or made a face, but he didn't stop. She wished he would sit down and talk. She wanted to draw him.

One hot afternoon, Deborah drifted to sleep in a hammock on the veranda that wrapped around the house, stunned by the heat but pleased at how breathing the heavily scented air was like pulling in a liquid, a soup of flowers and fruit and rum-scented smoke. When Sanson's face popped up next to her, his eyes opened wide, she knew he intended to startle her and then vanish. He seemed to expect her to gasp so that he could laugh at her and run away, but he laughed instead at her composure, opening his mouth wide, his fierce white teeth looking sharp enough to bite through anything. He was slender but full-muscled and bare-armed, unlike the suits and waistcoats that had pursued her back in St. Louis, then in St. Pierre. His body, unlike theirs, did not seem withheld from view but lived in and freely shared. His skin was just inches away from her hands. He smelled like toasted coconut. She stared.

"Is this where you sleep, little *béké*? Aren't you afraid the wild *marrons* will do you a harm? Aren't you afraid the *jumbees* will get you?" His French was lilting, so unlike Tante Charity's staccato delivery that it could have been an entirely different language.

"I'm not afraid of the marrons," she said. "And I don't believe in your jumbees."

"Oh, be careful, little béké. The jumbees steal a curl from your head while you sleep," Sanson said, running a curious finger along a shiny ringlet. "Then you have to do what the jumbee master say."

"I'm not afraid of the jumbees," she said again. She sat up and ran her hand over his rough head, and when he drew back, alarmed, she tightened her fingers in the tangle of his hair and held him still, so that he couldn't escape from what he had started. She laughed at his wild eyes, the shiny black centers surrounded by white, like the button eyes on her old stuffed dog Fido, who still sat on the shelf of her bedroom back in St. Louis, a universe away. She kept her hold on his head like an angry stepmother might do, knowing that she was hurting him a little. She held his head back and studied his face, ran her other hand over the thick velvet skin on his arm, his smooth chest, and felt that this was her opportunity.

The men in St. Louis, like the odious Henri de Rognac, had smirked and flirted and primped their moustaches in her direction, only a few venturing to touch her at all. Even when she liked the men, she hated their tentative hand squeezes, although they left her inwardly panting and bereft, wanting to reach out and touch, but restrained by their coyness, by her own good sense, and by Tante Charity's presence in the next room. But here in this hot garden, here was life, color, a place out of time, a chance to open herself and be opened. She could explore this body and herself, and so she smiled at him, rolled out of the hammock, and laid him down behind the jacaranda bush, this little béké girl he had hoped to scare.

She was surprised but unafraid of her own pleasure, unafraid of his force once he caught his breath, meeting him this first time almost violently, then exploring the unfamiliar maleness of him, feeling the textures of his body, mapping the variations in the colors of his skin, seeing how he gleamed red and purple and gold in a ray of sun that discovered them, examining the shape of his flat, peasant feet and the gray and pink of his soles and palms. He was not a flowery, effusive lover, not even bothering to be gentle with her. Deborah was not gentle with him either, except when she examined him as he lay back and dozed. This was meant to be the big mystery, this bundle of flesh that shrank back. It explained so little about her response to her own sensations and the smooth invitation of his back, the bunching ripples of his buttocks, the exploration of his hands, the taste of his mouth.

After that first time, Sanson came to her almost every day during sieste when the maids were drooping at their posts and Tante Charity was sleeping, her temples steeped in *eau de toilette*, drowsy with her afternoon dose of laudanum to soothe the headache brought on by tropical heat.

At her bedside was the volume of Montaigne she always traveled with, not because she enjoyed him but because he was a great French writer and his essays put her to sleep. Out in the garden, or in her pure white bed, her great-niece was debauching and being debauched. But only Villette knew. Sanson was her nephew, and besides, Villette knew everything.

3

~ *Sketches* ~

Deborah was both sorry and somewhat relieved when Sanson disappeared from Sans Douleur. His embraces had not become unwelcome, but she was increasingly worried that Tante Charity would discover them or someone would talk. She assumed he had gone into St. Pierre to work the docks or south to crew with a fisherman off Diamond Rock. No doubt he could take care of himself; he had taken the gold locket Gussie had given her, probably stealing it while she lay asleep after the rigors of their last encounter.

She missed him a little, but missed the locket more, grieving the loss of her parents' faces. She had been stupid to mistake caresses for affection, intimacy for friendship. She had foolishly expected loyalty, even though she had been warned. He was, after all, a bad boy.

~~~~~~~

Charity intended to remain in the humid green embrace of Sans Douleur only three months, but the business took longer to arrange than it would have stateside, with Americans instead of islanders running the errands, filing the papers, delivering the mail. The delays were irksome, and her temper, never merciful in any climate, was seriously tried by the heat, making her waspish with Villette and downright hateful to the maids, who stared at her from behind their hands and then giggled nervously once her back was turned. And then she had perforce to stay even longer until another unanticipated problem could be settled quietly.

Deborah had tried to ask Villette what it means when a girl's monthly doesn't come, but the answer was cryptic, like all of Villette's answers.

"Baby in the house soon," Villette said, her brown eyes sleepy and knowing. Then she turned back to chopping onions for the evening's *bouillabaisse*, absent-mindedly adding a handful of the hot creole spices she had been ordered to omit, scraping the now red onions into the soup pot. Deborah didn't know if what she said was true or just a superstition.

She tried to feel out Tante Charity on the subject. "You know how Villette says that if you kill a cockroach, money will find you. Is that true?"

"Of course not," the old lady sniffed, not bothering to raise her eyes from the altar cloth on which she was stitching a lily of mercy with short, vicious jabs. "Villette is a foolish half-savage pagan. They are all full of superstitions like that. You mustn't listen to the gossip of servants."

"Villette says," Deborah continued cautiously, "that if a girl misses her monthly, there will soon be a baby in the house. Is that true?" She fully expected Tante Charity to sniff again and wave her off. But the way Deborah's arms were wrapped around her waist, something in her voice, some departure from casual curiosity, betrayed her.

"Oh, my good God in Heaven!" Tante Charity rose from her seat on the sofa, her motion so abrupt that she overturned the slender-legged table with all the tea things and her headache medicine from the local doctor, her movement inundating the carpet with hot water and laudanum and scattering shards of china and glass. Her eyes were wild with disbelief, then rage. "What are you saying? What have you done, you stupid, stupid girl? What have you done?"

If she had not been so startled, Deborah could have defended herself better, but before she could raise her arms to ward off the blows, Tante Charity attacked, slapping and shaking her as if to reduce her to small pieces that could be swept up by the maids and thrown out with all the other broken things. She seized Deborah's hair, dragged her to her room, past the frightened faces of servants, and flung her on the bed. There Tante Charity left her and locked the door. She composed herself with a quick restorative brandy and then conferred with Villette, who seemed in this moment not like an ignorant savage at all, but her best, her only, ally and confidante.

"The girl is pregnant," she breathed hotly, her lips trembling slightly despite her attempt to press them together. "Who could have gotten to her? Who has been here?"

Villette regarded her with the same unreadable face with which she listened to complaints about the dinginess of the white linens, the dryness of an overdone fowl at the dinner table, or the disappearance of a hambone from the larder.

"Some young gentleman might come on horseback from St. Pierre," she offered. "Maybe some young gentleman on a fine brown horse."

"Who was it? Who came and got to the girl?"

Villette shrugged, conveying a regret, a mock-sadness, that she would never have the effrontery to look a young white gentleman, a béké boy, straight in his face. It would be improper.

"No one must ever know. I'm counting on you for that." Villette's look shifted just enough to make Charity go on. "I'll make it worth your while. You must help her with the baby and keep the maids quiet. Can you do that?"

"Oui, Madame," Villette said, as though she had been asked to get a letter for the post to an errand boy or arrange for fresh fish.

"Of course, we must take good care of her in this unfortunate condition." Charity had a fleeting hope that her impossible, disgraceful great-niece and the bastard she was carrying might both perish. Such things did happen to women. She had an uncomfortable feeling that Villette had read her thought. Then it occurred to her that Villette might serve as an accomplice, perhaps using some mysterious island remedy to rid Sans Douleur of this disgrace.

"I take good care of the young lady and the baby," Villette said. "Poor little things. I keep anything bad from them." Her ironic eyes put an end to Charity's uncharitable thought, which she promptly forgot she had ever had. She was a woman of upright virtue.

"The minute that baby is born, the very minute, you must take it away from her. We must treat this entire disgrace as though it never happened. Do you understand?" Charity glared, and Villette nodded.

"I take it soon as his eyes see the light of the sun," she promised.

~~~~~~~

Tante Charity's attack was less surprising than the idea of a baby, an idea Deborah hadn't really entertained, expecting it would to be dismissed out of hand. She lay back on the fluffy white bed and considered what a new life in her care would mean. It was clear that Tante Charity hated the baby, and Deborah felt a partisan loyalty to this strange creature who would be helpless, unwelcomed, detested from the very start, even before the first day of life began. That it would grow into a man, into a grown woman, was inconceivable, and Deborah held her softened belly in her arms, cradling the unknown and protecting the two of them.

She strained to remember everything she knew about this business of having babies, but at first could only bring to mind the clothes they wore, the little bonnets and gowns, the pale colors, the proud mamas and papas who strolled through the park with their perambulators on fine Sunday afternoons in St. Louis. Others would stop and peer under the blankets at the little prizes within, but Tante Charity had never paused for such foolishness.

Girls at school had proudly announced the arrival of baby brothers and sisters, but their accounts of the birth were contradictory. That there was pain, Deborah knew from Katy, who had often told the story of helping with her sister Rose's birth when she was just nine. Pain and blood. *And then joy,* she thought, *once the baby was out of her and swaddled up like Baby Jesus and adored.*

Her belly would swell up like her neighbor Mrs. Haskell's, and like Mrs. Haskell, she would have to hide away once that happened, but she was already well hidden in this steamy green world and, for a moment, she longed for the freshness of early winter days in St. Louis in the time before the people who loved her had died, first her mother and father, then Grandma Gussie. She couldn't remember why she had ever cried in those days.

A baby. She held the pillow in her arms, but it was bigger than any baby would be. A baby would fit into her joined hands, but no, she was thinking about a baby bunny she had once held. A baby would be bigger than that. Her old dolls were back in St. Louis, packed in a trunk in the attic; she wanted them now to help her prepare, to give her something real and present to hold on to, not this ephemeral not-yet baby who might turn out to be only a madness of Tante Charity's, a misunderstanding instead of a promise. It might blow over and be forgotten, but she didn't think so. She was pretty sure there would soon be a baby in the house.

How soon? It would take time, Deborah thought, for her stomach to grow, then even more time after the baby came for her to recover. She forced her mind back to Mrs. Haskell, but she had not cared at the time how long Mrs. Haskell was cloistered in her home. Weeks or even months, she thought. If it had been for just a few days, no one would have visited her.

The Haskell baby had slept for most of their visit, her tiny face impassive and so pale that the rise and fall of the blanket over her chest was the only sign of life. The baby's skin was a fascinating pearly white with all the colors of abalone, but the colors bloomed invisible under the texture-less skin. A beautiful scent hovered around her, and Deborah had leaned over the crib and breathed in that soft sweetness, not listening to the sibilant conversation of the reclining mother and the solicitous visitors. She wished now she had listened.

Then the baby's face had opened startlingly into a shrieking wet red mouth, eyes not gently closed but squeezed shut so that Deborah never saw their color. A nursemaid hurried in to take the baby away, and the visit had ended.

The air in the bedroom was hot and thick, like air everywhere in Martinique. Deborah could feel her thoughts shading into dream images as she lay back on the pillow and let herself float into sleep. She would think carefully later.

When she woke, the only light in the hot little room came from a candlestick illuminating Villette's face, a dark oval outlined by the turban she always wore. Her eyes shone white, reflecting the pointed flame from the wick back to the startled Deborah, who sat up staring. She could feel the heat from the little fire, too close.

"What do you want?" she asked, frightened because Villette never sought her out, never spoke to her unless to serve food or ask what she wanted.

"I have something for you, *doudou*. Something so good, something you want." Her velvet voice was softer than Deborah had ever heard it, with a wheedling tone that was unfamiliar, twisting the words as they came from her mouth. She dangled a long chain from her almost invisible fingers, a locket, Deborah's locket, swinging it back and forth through the circle of light, passing in front of the candle, an invitation to reach and be burned, teasing, tempting, snatching it back as soon as Deborah reached out.

"Listen, nice girl. My nephew, little black boy, not such a very bad boy, eh? Not so bad at all. Not *méchant*, not a devil, I believe, just a little careless? I give you the beautiful chain and picture of mama and picture of papa. You forget you know Sanson, forget his name, his maybe not so good face. Yes?"

"What will happen if I tell?"

"Oh, then I throw this little prize into the deepest ocean, and there it rests with the fish."

"No, Villette. What will happen to him, the one you want me to forget?"

"Something very big and bad. They beat him. They kill him. They throw him in the *carcel* to die. That old devil will punish us, everyone. You can't say, not at all."

Villette must have read acquiescence in Deborah's face. She laid the chain carefully on the sheet, and when Deborah looked up from her intent study of the portraits inside the recovered locket, Villette was gone, leaving the candle on the bedside table. Only creaking insects broke the silence of the hot dark night.

The next morning, hoping that a night with a guilty conscience and burgeoning fear of her great-aunt might have made Deborah more malleable, Tante Charity brought her a tray with coffee and a slice of melon. She found her niece pacing around the room, one eye slightly bruised and a red mark down the length of her left cheek where a long fingernail had scraped the skin. Tante Charity set the tray on the bed, and Deborah cautiously began her breakfast.

The fierce old lady sat in the straight chair and prepared to take care of business. "Who is the father?" she wanted to know. Further reflection had suggested that perhaps a marriage could be cobbled together soon enough that the story would die down and, after all, if Deborah married here, nothing or very little of the scandal would travel to the States to damage her reputation.

"My child," she said coldly, "you must confide in me. You must trust me completely. Who is responsible for this?"

Deborah didn't answer. Until Villette's night visit, she hadn't thought about the baby's father at all, which she realized now was stupid, a childish mistake of the kind she could no longer afford to make. She looked down, not out of shame, but to hide her defiance. If she told, Sanson would be destroyed. He would be beaten violently and thrown in jail, and if he didn't die there, he would die elsewhere very soon, crushed and broken by this woman and others like her, the laughing grotesques of St. Pierre's high society. Finally, like a child, like a prisoner, she murmured, "I don't know."

This would be her answer to every question in the long, grueling interview that followed, an interrogation intended to arrive at the truth so that coercion and pain and marriage could be meted out by the cold white hand of justice. Deborah was silent since the truth threatened her ownership of the remarkable private experiences that brought her this public exposure where Tante Charity stood as an agent of the world, prying, accusing, and then condemning. Deborah didn't know what would be done or who would help, and she longed for Katy as though longing could bring her across the rough and pitiless blue ocean.

At last, Tante Charity found she could not attack, badger, shame, threaten, trick, or bully Deborah into any useful disclosure about how she had come to be in this shameful condition; she decided to confer next with Father Mary, the priest at Morne Rouge, an out-of-the-way parish that would have little to do with the cosmopolitan society families of St. Pierre. He could use his clerical network to find a respectable couple, hopefully on another island, who would raise the child for a modest annual consideration. Then Deborah's unthinkable lapse could be forgotten, although never, never forgiven. It could not be allowed to stain the reputation of the Millais family at home in the States.

"You want to take the baby away, but you can't be allowed." Deborah interrupted Charity's train of thought. "It's my baby; it's not yours." She rose to her feet and braced her shoulders in an unconscious imitation of Tante Charity's formidable stance. No one could imprison or punish a baby as far as she knew.

"You cannot keep such a child," Tante Charity told her firmly, not bothering to rise or look at her. "If you attempt to do so, I will instruct Richards to cut off your allowance. I will throw you out of this house and leave you stranded on this hideous island with no friends to support you." Then leveling her reptilian gaze at Deborah, "Do you imagine Villette will take you in? Do you imagine that she's your friend? No, absolutely, without money, she would let you starve. Villette cares only about what you can give her, and you have nothing to give."

"People wouldn't let me starve if I went to St. Pierre, then. People there would help me and the baby."

"If you go to St. Pierre in your condition, or with your little bastard child, without a cent to your name, no one of good society will take you in unless it is to send the child away and make you a servant. Or you will be made to prostitute yourself. Do you know what that means? You would be used roughly by men, any man who wanted you and had a few pennies to pay for his pleasure. You would have no choice. Thirty men a night just to get enough money to keep you and your miserable child alive. No one would help you, Deborah, not even God." Tante Charity's face twitched as she described the corruption and vice she was picturing, rough dirty men with ugly hands, violating the soft body of her great-niece, men of every color. She shuddered. Then she rose and turned away, taking the tray and locking the door behind her. Let the little fool think it over.

Sitting at her desk, she attempted to regain sufficient composure to write to Father Mary. The poor girl had been raped, at least taken advantage of. Charity tried to believe this, but deep down, she knew that Deborah was one of those women of no dignity, no self-respect, one who would seek out the company and the caresses of men. There had never been such women among the Millais family, never, not even Gussie. The taint must have come through Deborah's father and his family, probably his Italian mother, whose father had been a violinist, really no better than an organ grinder.

As long as Deborah concealed her shame from the world, Charity would see her suitably settled back in the States. One must find the right marriage for her; then, it

would be up to the husband to control her and Charity Millais could wash her hands of the whole filthy business.
Deborah recognized that she had almost nothing to
bargain with. Tante Charity could take her baby away,
could cast her aside to be poor, poorer even than the poorest people she had ever seen, could remove all of the pro-
tections and care that stood between her baby and the cold
death of beggary. Even Deborah's youthful optimism
quailed before this vision. She would lose this battle; she
could see that. But she would have the final say when the
power finally passed into her hands. Time was on her side.
A victory lay hidden in the humiliating defeat in this con-
test with the hateful old woman.

And so Deborah and Tante Charity entered into a pact,
as carefully argued and laid out as any legal document.
Deborah would move to La Maison, the garden house farther up the mountain away from any possible contact with
visitors from St. Pierre. She could stay there with Villette
until she had recovered from the exertions of childbirth.
After the lying-in, they would return to St. Louis, where
Deborah agreed to marry the first respectable man who
made her an offer. She would have no right of refusal. She
would leave the arrangements to Tante Charity. She would
never tell anyone what had happened on this island. She
would erase the whole shameful affair from her mind. She
would not attempt to trace the child or contact the foster
parents. She would remain forever silent about the child,
especially to her husband. He would be informed before
the engagement only that she had been taken advantage of,
but only if Tante Charity deemed it advisable and then
only by Tante Charity herself.

"Keep the same stupid silence you have kept with me,"
Tante Charity said. "He will interpret it as innocence." Her
initial outrage hardened into a carapace of bitterness that

made her even more brittle and poisonous, as though a human hand that dared to touch her pallid skin would come away burned and bleeding.

In return, Tante Charity agreed to arrange a modest amount for the child's care to be sent to the foster parents through Father Mary. This payment could be disguised as a donation for the upkeep of the little church so that Richards would have no hint of anything untoward having occurred. Tante Charity would leave her will unchanged so that even after her demise, the family name would continue unsullied. To do anything else, to leave the money outside the bloodline, would be eccentric, would raise eyebrows and cause talk. Deborah had only to keep her own counsel and marry as soon as possible. Any indiscretion would invalidate the agreement, and the penalty would be Deborah's disinheritance. Money for the upkeep of the bastard child would cease and the child would vanish into the hot green island forever as if it had never been; she would be powerless to find it there. Tante Charity had devised the arrangement. It was all for the best.

~~~~~~~

Deborah had found life at Sans Douleur slow and monotonous compared to the clanging trolleys, the rattling of carriages and wagons, and the cries of peddlers in the streets of St. Louis, but once she and Villette relocated to La Maison, she realized how much movement and life there had been: workers passing through the courtyards, the distant thrum of the cane press, the occasional snatches of songs, the chatter of maids as they stood, their brown arms plunged into the white suds of laundry tubs. At La Maison, only the leaves moved, small green slivers of grass in the yard twitching in the breeze and the yellow-green flags of the banana leaves constantly in motion, stirring the air, the motion making Deborah seasick if she watched too long.

Her new solitude suited her in some ways since it removed the constrictions of ladylike behavior and let her think, still under Charity's control but unobserved except by the disinterested Villette, who fed her and remained at a distance, ignoring her attempts to make friends. Deborah filled her sketchbook with line drawings of the palm and banana trees, the little house, the garden rows where Carlo tended vegetables, the old man standing, bending, carrying a basket, the curve and bulk of Villette's back as she turned away from her to make the pineapple-sweetened tea Deborah craved.

She drew the impossible rise of Mt. Pelée as she had seen it from St. Pierre; here, there were no distances, just a wall of shifting leaves against the sky, the green roof of the canopy that surrounded and shaded and sometimes suffocated her. She had no paints now, no pastels or crayons, only her sketchbook and pencils delivered in the oxcart. She drew the shapes that made up her moss-green, wet-green, yellow-green, golden-green, flame-green world in black and white, presence and absence, texture and movement, light without reflection, heat without mercy.

When she tried to draw babies, she couldn't remember seeing more than their faces, so the proportions came out wrong, like the stiff baby Jesuses she had seen in medieval paintings. She vowed to look at her baby. She would remember. Until then, she contented herself with sketches.

Tante Charity dutifully visited once a month, bringing whatever was needed at La Maison and leaving the next day, her cart carrying fresh pineapples, bananas, green beans, and onions from the kitchen gardens to feed the house staff at Sans Douleur. She did not bring paints, although Deborah continued to request them at every visit. Such foolishness had caused the trouble and marked this wretched girl from the beginning. No need to encourage her now that her folly had found her out. Perhaps her husband would allow her to make pictures. Men were unaccountable.

As Deborah's belly grew big and round and her breasts swelled, she spent most of the hot days and sometimes nights on the veranda, napping and dreaming, always hungry, sticky, and uncomfortable, sometimes sad, sometimes focused on the elation that bubbled up unexpectedly. Villette said she was carrying a boy, carrying him high, and after that, Deborah found that all of her dreams, sleeping and waking, began to center on her son. His name might be Pietro after her father's grandfather, but perhaps something softer in the mouth. Gianni. Johnny. The soft vowel in the center seemed like a cry of longing. Ah, Gianni. My Gianni. My little John.

Then one day, she felt the first movement of the baby inside her, the quick brush of a butterfly wing, a darting fish in the round bowl of her body, swimming free in the ocean of that world. In time, the kicks grew stronger until she felt as though her little warrior was battling already, preparing for the hard life that would be his as he waited on some other island for her return to claim him. If Gianni never thought about her, she hoped he would be happy and carefree. If he longed for her, she hoped he would know that she would return for him when she could. All of her silent absence would be built around that moment of return. She began to really believe that her baby would come and began to knit a layette set until Villette took it away, saying, "That baby cook in such a thing. Baby don't need cover."

The Christmas holiday passed with only a baked pudding dotted with imported French currants to mark the occasion. In St. Louis, there might be snow, and every family would hang shiny ornaments on a tall tree and surround it with gifts and Christmas sweets for the ones they loved. Deborah had no one to love and nothing to give here, where the hot air hung like heavy vines, where the vines hung in sheets, and the trees blocked out the light, but she made a sketch of Villette, regal and proud, copying the pattern on her favorite shawl and rendering the turban headpiece with its points in careful detail. Villette pretended not to be pleased with this attention, but she stayed with Deborah to have a plate of the strange bland pudding, finished off with a cup of black tea.

"How long?" Deborah asked, now that she had Villette's attention. "How long, Villette, before the baby gets here? When is he coming out?"

"In good time," Villette said. "A few more weeks, maybe tomorrow. You good and big now. Soon."

"How do you know about babies? Did you ever have a baby?"

Villette leaned back in her chair, and at first, Deborah thought she wouldn't answer.

"I have seven babies in my life," she said. "Two daughters still alive. One live with a man in Morne Orange. One I don't know. Maybe she live somewhere, maybe go to my sister Emeline in Dominica."

"What happened to the others?"

"They died. One thing or some other. My oldest boy Platty, he lived to a man. He died from a fishing boat, drowned in the water around St. Luce."

"You have a sister, though. At least you have a sister."

Deborah felt again the sorrow of the song she had heard her first night in St. Pierre and the rising tide of

misery she had sensed in the woman's cry as she stood outside the de Rognac's party. She imagined a chorus of sorrow, like a distant murmur of rain, constant, each life
distinct, each trajectory downward, the constant faraway
roar of deaths and mourning and injury and hopelessness,
announcing a storm that had raged unheeded below the
polite clatter of silverware and fine china, the endless
"ooh" of murmured French. Now Villette's dead children
were swallowed into the dank maw of history with the rest.

"My mama come from the other days, the slave days,"
Villette continued. "She made eleven babies in her time,
but one child taken away and sent to France. The rest dead,
I think, except for me and Emeline."

Deborah looked around the little dining table, set for
the token Christmas feast celebrating the birth of a baby
who would die and then return from death, whose mother
would grieve for a while and then rejoice forever, and the
whole world would rejoice with her.

"Emeline's boy, my nephew, you know, I see that one,
I know him. Everyone else, I don't know. I think your baby
will resemble like his father." And with that, Villette rose
and gathered up the few dishes, tucked her portrait into
her apron pocket, and left Deborah with her thoughts
about mothers and children, Mother and Child.

Gianni started coming that evening, but he did not
come easy. As Deborah stood up from the table, she felt a
flood of water down her legs, warm and smelling of life,
splashing over her bare feet.

"Villette," she called out. "Help me! Villette!" but Villette had already gone out of the house into the dusk to
look for the stubborn white hen who refused to lay her
eggs in the coop and instead hid them away in the rank
bushes lining the muddy roadway. The first pain came like
a stinging whip, not in her belly where she expected it,

coming seemingly from outside, a deep vicious lashing. The shriek that tore through her brought Villette to her side.

"Now," Villette said. "Now, the baby."

Each pain left Deborah gasping for air, for a clean, fresh breath, but instead, drawing in the heavy, sodden exhalations of the endless green jungle. At first, she tried to prepare herself, to gather up courage and dignity to face the onslaught of the next contraction, but it always came too soon, before she was ready, and she cried out in spite of herself. Another. Another. Wave after wave, blow after blow, pain that took her breath away, then relief and the renewed attack. When the pain was there, it blotted out everything, even the knowledge that it would recede in time. It receded, leaving the clear knowledge that it would return, would return, and would return again. There seemed to be no end to this night and its tortures.

Villette was there, was not there, was back again, rubbing oil and harsh-smelling leaves against the tight skin of her belly and between her legs, shushing and murmuring in Creole. Villette pressed her to drink hot, bitter tea, made her sit up, didn't make the pain stop no matter how Deborah pleaded. Villette, tormentor and savior by turns, her only friend, her mother.

"Open your eyes," Villette said when a pain started, and Deborah stared but could only see the lamp and the wavy reflection of the lamp in the mirror, the image shimmering with pain.

All night Deborah writhed and thrashed in this desperate state, screaming, crying, begging for relief, begging to go home. When Villette said, "Think of your baby," Deborah could hardly make sense of it. There was no baby, only pain. It had all been a mistake, and suddenly she blamed Villette for it. Villette was the cause of all the horrors of this night.

Villette just nodded and said, "Soon time for pushing, doudou. When you feel pushing, you push. Soon."

Eleven times Deborah felt her body convulse, squeeze, and push down, and she gladly pushed with all her strength. Now the baby was coming. Now there was a baby, her baby, and the pain was less, meant nothing in the face of this undeniable fact. At the final push, she felt him slide through her, making her shudder and then shiver in spite of the warm room. Villette tied him off, wiped him with wet towels, and wrapped red thread around his wrists to protect him. Deborah saw him for the first time, visible in the pale green light of earliest morning, her soft, perfect boy, his light gray-brown hair in tiny whirlwind twists on his long head, his black eyes wide open. The baby, her baby, her own Gianni. She couldn't think of giving him up, not now, not after the night they had passed, the battle they had won, the breath-stopping beauty of him.

Villette washed the sweat from the new mother's body and covered her with a linen sheet. "You be his mother now," she said. "Carlo already gone down to Sans Douleur to tell Madame. She be here soon as soon. You love your baby now, enough for his life. She give him away, you know, but not to some béké family to raise. No, not this little mulatto child you make."

Deborah didn't raise her eyes from the curve of his cheek, the tiny button nose, his petal ears. "Don't let her hurt him. It's not his fault. He's just a baby." A baby, my baby, my Gianni. A wonder, a soft wrinkled little creature, a sweet miracle. She thought she would never recover from the sight of him, the love of him, the loss. She had agreed to part from this vision, but she had not known how horrible it would be to release him. She had thought of him as a child who would need food and shelter and care. She had not thought about the wrenching pain of giving him over to strangers, of losing him, and the enormity of it all made it impossible to think about.

She thought she saw a shadow of her mother's face in her child, and although it was comforting to think so, she couldn't say where the resemblance lay. He did, indeed, look like his father with his square face and blooming pink lips, his bold stare. There would be no way to pretend he resulted from an indiscretion with one of the rich béké boys from St. Pierre. She loved him all the more fiercely for the perils that lay in front of them. And she realized that the sense of her mother she felt so strongly was present in the curve of her own smiling lips and the light that warmed her eyes as she looked at him, her Gianni, her baby.

"Look at your toes," she said, touching each tiny nail. And she kissed his feet and his hands and his smooth neck, breathing in the smell of heaven, the clouds of glory she had read about in poems. The silken sliding of his cheek against her fingers, the curve, the tiny ears, the fuzzy twists of hair, his deep eyes which seemed to search her face for love. She thought she had never seen anything as wonderful and funny as his quick pink yawn. She smoothed the bare skin on his back and closed her eyes, just for a moment, just to rest a little from the night's hard work, and when she opened them, it was the hot middle of the day, and he was gone.

Villette would answer no questions, saying only "*L'enfant est bien,*" the child is well.

"I will come back," Deborah said, "when I can. Tell him I will." She held out the locket with her parents' portraits, the only token she could offer to soften the baby's fate, all she had to give.

"Of course, you will, doudou," Villette assured her,

tucking the locket into her apron. "Martinique is the *isle de revenant*, the island of returning. Everyone come back here, the living and the dead."

~~~~~~~

When Villette placed the new baby in the old lady's lap, the blood drained from Charity's face, and she almost toppled from her chair. Villette caught up the child again and offered her mistress a tot of rum, which she gulped down. For Charity, the baby's great-great aunt, there was only the horror of his color, the scandal, the sickening truth, the abomination. She would never forgive Deborah for this, never. If she could have destroyed it without staining her hands, perhaps leaving it where insects would devour it, she would gladly have done so, but Villette seemed always to hover nearby. After writing a quick note to Father Mary to inform him that the baby had died so no foster parents would be needed, she bribed Villette to send it away somewhere to be raised with its own kind; the last she saw, it was wrapped in a cloth in old Carlo's arms as he stumbled higher up the mountain track. She wanted it never to be spoken of again. She would return with her great-niece to St. Louis, marry her to whoever would have her, and never return to this godforsaken hell, never allow this disgraceful episode to be exposed.

4

~ *The Marriage Contract* ~

The voyage back to the States was dreadful for Deborah. There was no Mr. Short to enliven the journey and, even if he had served on this ship, she would not have been able to converse with him as she had before. She now had a secret that lay like a hot coal in her stomach, radiating a bitter heat that ran through her nerves, and she had to be silent and endure it. There would be no natural conversation again; there could be only silence or subterfuge.

Her suffering was not just the suffering of the heart and spirit, though that was intense. Her body was also in pain. She had not entirely recovered from the birth, but there was no safe doctor she could see who might advise against the abrupt return to St. Louis, a nineteen-day journey with stresses and challenges enough even for a less vulnerable traveler.

For most of the voyage, Deborah lay in the cabin she shared with her great-aunt and slept, dreamed, woke, and cried, at first with choking sobs, then silently but with tears that seemed endless, weeping until her eyes burned and salt scalded her cheeks. She felt the pressure of the water around the hull of the boat, the containment, the isolation of a ship alone on the ocean, and was conscious every waking or half-waking moment of the wretched bargain she had been forced to make, not sure she could bear it. She closed her eyes or turned her head to the wall to avoid the sight of her great-aunt, an unavoidable, uncaring party to the contract that took away everything that mattered and with whom she shared the narrow space.

She could think of nothing but the baby, Gianni, her baby, and she ached, womb, breasts, heart, arms shot through with pangs of longing to hold him, the baby, the baby, the living, please God, the living child that she had loved so briefly and so completely. The baby, Gianni, her child. She ate almost none of the crackers, porridge, or broth the captain sent down. Whatever she ate made her ill. Nothing in her life, not even the loss of her parents, had prepared her for such grief, a longing that drowned out everything else she might have thought or felt or wanted. She lay in a narrow bed in the belly of the ship and let the waves of sorrow wash over her, not even trying to swim to shore or find her footing in the shallows.

On the last day of the voyage, as Charity bustled about packing and fussing with the luggage, the captain made a formal call on them, apologetically intruding into the ladies' quarters but duty-bound to see for himself how the unfortunately ill girl was faring. Other passengers, lost in the nightmare of seasickness for the first few days, had all recovered and emerged from their rooms to enjoy the voyage. Only this one, this pale girl with the plum-colored bruises under her eyes, silent and suffering, remained on the sick list. Deborah sat passively in the chair where she had been ordered to make room on the bed for the portmanteau that held Charity's belongings. The captain took Deborah's hand and spoke kindly to her. She could hardly respond, exhausted by the assaults of emotion that diminished only slightly, echoing through every act and interaction, no matter how kindly meant.

Then, he turned and drew Tante Charity aside, concern writ large on his broad forehead.

"Your niece is suffering dreadfully," he said. "I fear that a train trip added to the rigors she has undergone may be more than her constitution can bear. I beg you to delay in New Orleans and consult a physician before going further. Otherwise, you are surely running the risk of losing her."

Charity thanked the captain for his concern, letting him know he had no business interfering in the matter, firmly closing off any further discussion. The girl would recover better at home. She had her physician there. The poor man, as all men who braved Charity's displeasure were poor, could only expostulate again and take his leave.

He stopped on the way out to take Deborah's limp hand again in his strong one.

"It seems your prolonged seasickness has left you weak," he said and wished her a quick return to health once she was on land again.

"But I'm a good sailor," Deborah said to his departing back.

She turned and saw a disturbing expression on Charity's face, the shadow of a passing thought no sooner formed than forgotten. The problem of her disgraceful niece might yet come to a graceful end. Left to his own devices, *le bon Dieu* might sort it out and save Charity the trouble.

Deborah's rally to health, her return to will and energy, began at that moment with her accurate reading of the old lady's usually guarded face. The bargain had been struck, there was no way around that, and she had been forced to give up her Gianni. But she had time. She would strive to see beyond this present sorrow to the happy reunion that lay ahead. When she regained her strength, she would make the most of it, would play the game with the optimism and daring of youth.

Deborah extended her weakened arm to a tray on the bedside table and lifted the cup of broth—now room temperature and rather horrid but nourishing. She could feel it all through her body, salty as her blood was salty, her tears. She stood, moved carefully to the door, and opened it to address a passing steward.

"I should like more broth if you please," she said. "And a plate of bread and butter."

When she turned back, she saw Charity at a loss for once and enjoyed the moment. "I'm feeling much better," Deborah announced, and the old lady was correct in hearing the challenge in her words.

~~~~~~~

Once they were home in St. Louis, the marriage must be contracted since Deborah had not conveniently died en route, though it took her almost two weeks to be declared fit by the German doctor Charity found, a doctor unlikely to be summoned to minister to the needs of those in the best social circles. He did not mention the signs of recent parturition but started to offer his opinion that his young patient would be unlikely to bear children. The old lady froze him in mid-statement and whisked Deborah out to the waiting carriage. If she were known to be barren, that would hardly facilitate the task of acquiring a husband, and a husband must be found. Whoever he might be, he was to take responsibility for any further misdeeds Deborah committed. He must be identified, ensnared, locked into an engagement, and brought to the altar.

Charity was torn. Of course, one wished that Sans Douleur would be well managed and kept intact in the family. For this, one would seek a marriage partner of prudence and enough wealth of his own. One required a man who would keep Deborah in bounds, and if she did bear him children, they would help erase the memory of the child she had so shockingly produced in Martinique. Of course, the man would need to possess a strong character, but not so strong that Charity could not manage him as needed. Not so strong that he would ally with his wife rather than the great-aunt. Perhaps a young man starting out, a younger son who was entering the world of business. Perhaps Richards would have some ideas.

On the other hand, she secretly wished to see Deborah buried in a marriage with a villain, a philanderer, a bad father to his children, a man who withheld his affections and his worldly goods, a man bad at heart. Deborah deserved to be punished and guarded as mercilessly in her new household as in the one she would be leaving. But such a man would hardly add to the respectability of the family. It was a bind.

A number of young men in their circle of society were of marriageable age and eligible circumstances. There were numerous parties and dinners at which young people could pair off under the eyes of their elders. Deborah was a pretty girl, pretty enough to collect admirers. Yet when any one of the young blades began to press too closely, to approach that moment from which a gentleman cannot retreat without dishonor, Deborah fended him off with the simple expedient of talking about her great-aunt. She declared herself unhappy unless she spent at least six hours every day in Tante Charity's company. She described Tante Charity as absolutely crucial to her in any situation, personal or domestic, in which she required guidance. She gave credit to her great-aunt for anything a potential suitor complimented: her complexion, her dress, her light step. All had been inherited or learned from the cold gray figure who looked on from the corner of the room. By invoking the threat of Miss Charity Millais, Deborah effectively quelled even the liveliest fire burning in the heart or loins of any young man who seemed to fancy her, thus avoiding open declarations and unwanted proposals.

Deborah had her eye on Judge Osmund Huntworth, a semi-retired widower, as the best matrimonial prospect for her purposes. He seemed kind enough, and she would find something to love in him, perhaps in his embraces once he had shed the starchy shirt front and stuffy men's suiting that disguised his body. She thought his gray lamb's-wool curls, his mutton-chop beard, and his distinguished profile might become endearing over time. He was not likely to outlive her, so she could look forward to a time of greater freedom. And at his age, he would be foolishly flattered to discern her preference for him if she could convey it forcefully enough to attract his attention.

She would have to seek out his company at every opportunity, and though she probably couldn't blush, not being at all abashed, she could try to seem shy and affected by his conversation and compliments. She could gaze at him too long, look down as though her gaze had betrayed her, then look up again, letting her eyes suggest to him that she was drawn irresistibly, despite her modesty, to his person. She had observed other girls engaged in this exercise, and she played it rather well. Even when his conventional compliments, his fatherly, then avuncular, increasingly lover-like utterances bored her, she could listen with grave fascination to the deep chocolate rumble of his voice and wonder at the thick tufts of hair on the backs of his hands. She wanted him as intensely as if she had fallen in love.

Charity had taken the earliest opportunity to approach Richards and intimate that a suitable match was sought. At first, he felt a stirring of hope in his prime position as her man of business. He knew the full extent of the Martinique income flowing into the family coffers but quickly realized he was asked to broker rather than participate in the union. He agreed to keep an eye out and listen to the gentlemen's conversations over port and cigars after the ladies withdrew. It should be easy for him to determine which men might be predisposed to take on the proposition and who was attracted to the girl.

Although Judge Huntworth did not speak unguardedly on the subject during these masculine exchanges, Richards noticed that he focused on conversations that concerned Deborah's prospects, her looks, her family, the sugar plantation, and sometimes drew the topic out by asking questions in his calm, judicial way.

When Richards informed Charity of the Judge's apparent interest, she directed him to be encouraging, to seek out a private opportunity to confide that the family would be open to a proposal from that quarter. Any objection to the age difference she dismissed summarily. Judge Huntworth was by no means young, but he was a vigorous man, just a bit younger than Charity herself. It would serve Deborah right to be attached to him, a man she would never choose for herself. It was a pleasure to look forward to broaching the subject with her, to witnessing her dismay as some younger, more attractive choice was pushed out of the picture. The Judge must be brought to the hurdle as soon as possible to forestall an offer from some suitor Deborah might have in mind. A very short engagement would be in order followed by a conventional wedding, and the problem could be solved in a matter of weeks. The troublesome task of controlling Deborah would be in his hands.

Richards arranged a meeting between the two elderly parties in his office. He hoped to be invaluable to them in working out the thornier issues that had the potential to ruffle feathers in an April-December union such as this. Provisions concerning the husband's death, hypothetical to a younger gentleman, were likely to be taken personally by a snowy bridegroom. Richards was the soul of tact.

After a brief nod at the proprieties, he helped the two of them hash out the details of the marriage, questions of religion and property. Deborah's preferences were not consulted.

Deborah had been raised in the family faith as a Catholic. The Judge was a pillar of the Lutheran church, serving as an elder of that august body. The two old people finally agreed that any male issue would be raised in his father's faith, any female offspring would be consigned to the care of the Catholic Church, whose nuns could be counted on to shape her character. Deborah herself would attend Protestant services with the Judge one Sunday and mass with her great-aunt the next, a day on which Charity could pry into her great-niece's marriage and detect any variance from the dictates of propriety.

That issue settled, they moved on to the question of property.

The Judge owned the grand house that he occupied along with his two daughters, Florence and Lily, and, in addition, several office buildings downtown. He had also invested in a block of low-rent, low-maintenance, high-profit apartment houses for poor laborers and their families. He held numerous railroad stocks and government bonds. His wealth was more than adequate to cover the minor expense of adding a wife to his household.

Before this meeting, the two men had agreed to begin negotiations for the wife's allowance at a paltry sum, anticipating that the shrewd old lady would drive a hard bargain on behalf of her niece. To their surprise, Charity merely nodded her acquiescence. It would be sufficient. And Deborah's inheritance as a widow would be equally small.

"And I believe the Millais family estate in Martinique . . . ?" Richards prompted, as he knew this was important to the Judge.

"Deborah will inherit this, of course, in the event of my death," Charity said. "And her husband will manage it on her behalf."

Having settled the business, they agreed that Judge Huntworth would propose to Deborah the next morning with the consent of her great-aunt. Charity was somewhat startled to hear the Judge flatter himself that his suit would be favored. It gave her a suspicion that Deborah was playing a deeper game than she had supposed possible. But surely not. The Judge's assurance must arise from the vanity so typical of established men of his age. Deborah would accept his offer because that was the bargain on which the support of her mongrel child relied. She had no power to refuse. Let him imagine otherwise if that gave him pleasure.

But first, Charity had to speak to the Judge alone. She dismissed Richards brusquely from his own office to stand about in the hall like an errand boy, speculating about the conversation that was going on without him, unable to fathom what either of them could discuss that wasn't already known. When the old lady swept out of his office, followed by the Judge, her bleak eye forestalled any questions that might have issued from his lips, and she bid him a firm good-day in a voice that brooked no impertinence.

That evening in his study, the Judge reviewed the agreement he had entered into as he enjoyed his brandy and smoked a fat cigar. Apparently, the girl had been taken advantage of in a strange land, forced perhaps (and the thought was not entirely unpleasant), which seemed to justify the ungenerous allowance he and Richards had offered. She was charming but was coming to him with her virtue in question, damaged goods, almost a charity case—an amusing addition to his life and comforts, but not really top-notch.

For her part, Deborah kept her counsel and waited for the proposal; she accepted with clear-eyed gravity, hoping to learn to love Judge Huntworth as well as to make use of him. His suit having been met with the expected complaisance on the lady's part, the wedding was scheduled for the following month.

The engagement dinner took place almost immediately, and the Judge's daughters, Florence and Lily, one older and one younger than the bride, made clear they did not intend to soften towards Deborah or cease to regard her as a dangerous interloper who could carry their ruin in her womb. Not a son, they prayed. Please, God, don't let her have a son. They treated Deborah with cold patience, never becoming outright rude but always looking away, keeping their distance, and refusing her little offers of friendship. The marriage was a foolish indulgence, but at least there would be money on both sides. If only the inheritance they had learned to expect could be preserved. If only the bright clink of wealth meeting wealth would attract the attention of suitors so they could form establishments of their own instead of living in the shadow of their father and his girlish new bride.

Not until Deborah asked to bring Katy with her did she realize how much power she had given up. She thought she had only to join the Judge in his bed and behave nicely in company, preserving the illusions as Charity's words had prepared her to do. She did not realize what was lost in this later bargain until it was too late to back out. Her headlong escape from the prison of Charity's scrutiny was to leave her stranded on an island of respectability where no one knew her, not even to hate her as Tante Charity did, and certainly not to love.

The Judge shook his head, amused.

"You are no longer a child," he said. "You can hardly

expect to bring your nurse. You will find that the servants in my house are more than adequate to meet your needs."

She pleaded with him, tears standing in her eyes like sheets of melted glass that twisted and blurred his gray face, but he merely shook his head again, pleased with his purchase but obdurate. Katy was not to come with her but to stay with Charity and train as a housekeeper. It was settled. He had ruled. Deborah was to have no one familiar, no one to love in his dark, over-stuffed house. She was meant to become like one of the cold naked women in Horace Norbuckle's private art collection, frozen in place as her heart stopped between one beat and the next, and, like them, she was required to serve blindly. The only concession she could win was to have Katy sit up with her the night before her wedding, the last night in her childhood home.

On that night, their last time together before parting ways, they moved slowly and silently through the familiar childhood ritual of bedtime: the bath, the nightgown and dressing robe, the little fire in the fireplace, a cup of cocoa, though Deborah insisted that Katy join her on this occasion. After Deborah's hair had been brushed and plaited, she set a surprised Katy down on the low stool. She removed Katy's hairpins, letting the red hair ripple down, indulging a childhood fantasy of playing with Katy's red, copper, and mahogany hair as it slipped through the brush, over her hands, like a silky river of flame and wood, gleaming in the firelight. After her initial protest—"It's not fitting"—Katy relaxed and allowed herself to be lulled by the hypnotic pull of the brush, the tugging and smoothing, the pleasant scratch of the bristles on her scalp.

"I'm going to tell you a story now," Deborah said, and she silenced Katy before she could argue with a tug on her hair, as she had been silenced many a time when their positions had been reversed. "I'm going to tell you a magic story. I can only tell it once, and then it can never be told again. Once it is told, it vanishes forever and is forgotten.

"Once upon a time, there was a beautiful princess with long flowing red hair, as red as the sunset over the ocean, as red as flowers. She was the pride and joy of her parents, the king and queen and lived happily every day in the castle. But then something very sad happened. The king and queen died and left her to the care of a very wicked witch. The witch saw that the princess was happy in the castle (though, of course, she was sad about her parents) and took her far, far away from everything and everybody she loved to an enchanted island and locked her up. There she met a prince . . ."

"A handsome, charming prince . . ." Katy prompted.

"Maybe," Deborah said, "but a bit weak. The princess and the weak prince met secretly for a while, but then the princess realized that she was with child and she could not conceal this from the witch. The mean old witch was furious and screamed at her until her voice was as hoarse and ugly as a crow's. And the witch waited until the child was born and then set it in a boat and sailed it away to another island where it was found by a queen and raised as her own."

"Like Moses?" Katy murmured, her body half-asleep but listening carefully.

"The witch used a magic spell to make the island where the child lived vanish as if it had never existed and whisked the princess back to the castle and locked her in. The only way the princess could break the spell and return to find her son . . ."

"And the prince?"

"Well," Deborah said, "not the prince, who wasn't really all that charming after all. He drops out of the story.

But her son. And, Katy, listen: the only way to break the spell was for the princess to remain silent for a hundred years and to marry the first fool who asked for her hand when they returned to the kingdom."

The fire crackled and sparks flew up the little chimney. Deborah began to braid the bright ropes of hair that slipped through her fingers like water, making one thick rope that flowed down Katy's back.

"And that's the end? Did she live happily ever after?"

"The hundred years isn't over yet," Deborah said. "I don't know how it ends."

Katy turned on the stool and looked up at the girl, now a woman, who had been hers to wash and dress and feed and cosset, who had just told her the forbidden story of the sadness that had been spilling from her eyes ever since she had returned from that heathen place with nothing to tell except that it was always hot. It seemed to explain why she had unaccountably agreed to marry Judge Huntworth despite his bushy white eyebrows and long hanging ears. Katy found it easy to think of him as the first fool.

"It's a most sad story, indeed," Katy said. "I've never heard the like, and I'll never repeat it to a living soul." She felt as though she had been enchanted and knew without knowing, which is how good stories work. "But you must promise to tell me the ending someday," she said, and Deborah kissed her and sent her to bed.

Deborah sat long into the night with the fire kept burning, drawing pictures of Gianni as she remembered him and as she imagined he might become. Then she fed them one by one to the fire, and when they were all turned to ash, she went to bed.

~~~~~~~

The wedding took place the next morning in a long, tedious ceremony conducted by an ancient minister whose thready voice squeaked and whistled, detracting from the solemnity of the occasion without adding any of the levity that enhances a joyful event. The old man's repertoire of vocal accidents merely interrupted Deborah's desire to enter a state of waking sleep. There she could retreat into her mind and block out the simmering anxiety that made her shiver in her wedding finery, her veil seeming to shimmer in front of her eyes. She would be reminded of the maddening series of pops and whistles that night as she lay awake and endured the snoring of her new husband.

The bride in her satin gown was given away by Richards, serving this role in the absence of any male relative to whom she could reasonably be said to belong. He was delighted to fill the gap, feeling for once like a friend of the family rather than a general factotum. Florence and Lily Huntworth, at the bride's side in matching rose-colored gowns, decorated with jewels inherited from their dead mother, stood as still as if they were nailed to the floor. They exchanged only one glance and then stared ahead, enduring.

The rather cheerless celebration following a final whispery prayer was replete with expensive champagne, frothy music from a string quartet, and heavy plates of heavy food. The bride and groom led the dancing with a waltz, the Judge holding Deborah at arm's length and surveying his new possession while Deborah looked over his shoulder at the pictures on the wall. Charity added the congratulations of her acquaintances to her self-congratulation on a successful end to the dangerous business of Deborah. The guests spoke either in subdued murmurs or just with their eyes. Florence and Lily moved together through the crowds, defiantly repeating that they were charmed by their father's new bride, that she was utterly charming, that they were pleased that their father had arranged to add to his comforts with this charming new bride, though everyone present knew they were lying and eyed them sympathetically, or maliciously, or with some maddening combination. But the decencies must be preserved to comply with their father's orders.

After the happy couple had been chased away with rice and flowers, the ordeal was over, and the guests began to trickle away, then flooded out into the open air where they could breathe and talk freely. Florence had a quick impulse to take a bottle of champagne upstairs to share with her partner in disappointment but dismissed it. They would certainly need to talk over the whole embarrassing event before retiring, but they would preserve the decencies, and drinking champagne in one's bedroom was not a ladylike activity, however tempting. They would send down for sherry instead.

~~~~~~~

On the short honeymoon that followed the wedding, a trip to Chicago where the groom had business to attend to, the hotel bridal suite was so highly decorated that Deborah was seized with vertigo and with a sudden longing for the shadowed, bare walls of La Maison. The Judge tipped the bellboy and kissed his young bride chastely on the forehead before going to take a brandy in the gentlemen's lounge. He was prepared to be gentle and patient. He expected shyness and perhaps even fear on her part. But his needs were modest and he looked forward to enjoying her smooth young body.

"Prepare for bed, Deborah," he said, turning to look at her meaningfully, hoping she would be charming and not cry too much.

When the Judge returned to the room, fortified and feeling young, he was careful not to wake her. He disrobed, slipped on his nightgown, turned out the light, and then slid between the sheets next to her. He was startled when his tentative hand found naked flesh rather than cloth under the covers. Waking, Deborah turned and reached out, taking his warm member in her strong, agile young hand, but he drew back, alarmed, and it fell softly from her grip.

"Deborah," he said, his voice stern and shaken. "You must never do that again!"

She saw that she had not escaped from Tante Charity, that the prison devised for her surrounded even this cozy space, which might have been a place where the rules could be relaxed. Left alone with the old man to whom a private oath and public vows bound her, she had thought to recapture the liberty she knew with Sanson, to play, to tease, to satisfy her own curiosity. But she was to be blocked here as well. There would be no respite until both of these elderly tyrants died. She could have cried out at the pity and the waste, the discipline she would have to exert, the great loss and the small deaths she would have to endure without the luxury of mourning.

The newlyweds lay side by side in the tall hotel bed, cool air flowing over them from the window that opened onto the park, bringing the scent of tired trees and grimy alleys and the sound of a cab horse clopping along, sneezing the city dust wetly from its muzzle. A motorcar chugged by.

"Unless I ask," the Judge added.

5

~ *The Ark of God* ~

Deborah's married life was dull once the honeymoon, which had included a few moments of excitement and pleasure, had been put firmly in the past, and the routines and practices of the Judge's conventional family life took over. She had thought of time as her ally—she could outlast the two old people who stood in her way—but she had not realized how hard it would be to wait, longing, and then wait more. The youth that gave her time and resilience also rendered her powerless and invisible. Hostility towards her great-aunt had given Deborah energy, but she felt no such anger at the Judge. After all, she had courted him, won him, and now had only to live with her success for as many years as he lived. She could not wish him dead, and yet she sometimes did.

Deborah was plagued by a shadowy feeling that she had not been clever enough, that she could have avoided exile from Gianni. In the cold, dark hours before dawn, she reviewed the bargain she had entered into. Would other schemes have united her sooner with her lost Gianni? Had she overlooked some source of power or leverage? Had she been outwitted? Perhaps Villette might have helped her, in spite of what Tante Charity said. The house in St. Louis belonged to her, so perhaps she could have arranged to sell it? Deborah felt a rising hope at this thought. But no, she was just seventeen. She would have to be twenty-one before having control of the property. And she had been required to marry almost immediately after their return from Sans Douleur.

Perhaps the Judge had not been her best choice, though she had felt quite pleased with her strategy in selecting him. Had she been blinded by the sense of power that strategy provided? What had she overlooked? Might there not have been a young husband who could have been persuaded to help her? But would any husband have sought to unite her with her illegitimate mulatto son? At times, Deborah thought that she had no one to blame but herself, but she recognized her aunt's voice in that conclusion. There was no peace to be found in her swirling thoughts or the painful feelings they evoked.

Deborah looked for someone in the Judge's household to make friends with, a substitute for Katy, but the servants resisted her tentative advances, choosing to go about their business instead of stopping to chat with this minor, entirely powerless, member of the family. Their loyalty lay with the first Mrs. Huntworth and they had no patience for her replacement, taking their cue from the temperamental cook, Mrs. Hogg. The late Mrs. Huntworth had been appreciative, complimenting Mrs. Hogg on her skills and conferring with her over special dishes the Judge might favor, arranging to meet his personal needs as befits a proper wife. This second Mrs. Huntworth dutifully met with her on Monday afternoons but had no interest in the family menu, agreeing to anything, eating whatever was placed in front of her, and making no demands at all.

The Judge's daughters treated their young stepmother with icy civility in their father's presence, with indifference when he was away, with much exchanging of meaningful looks communicating amazement at her apparent stupidity. Deborah felt it sharply at first, as their companionship might have provided a slight comfort in a most uncomfortable situation. But they would not forgive her for marrying their father and threatening to reduce their inheritance by producing a male heir.

Deborah took a sly revenge by teasing her new step-daughters with the pretense of a certain delicacy of physique, fluttering her hand at her bosom as though faint or overheated, accepting food from the servers with a grimace that spoke of suppressed nausea and distress. Given the German doctor's warning and the rarity of the occasions when the Judge did more than sleep in the big double bed, she supposed herself unlikely to conceive an heir. Still, it pleased her to feign pregnancy in front of Florence and Lily after the Judge had left the table, just to see them blanch. In time she relinquished the game as meanhearted. They didn't like her, and perhaps they never would. They had done nothing to harm her, though, and they were perfectly correct in thinking the marriage a shameful arrangement.

Deborah turned her mischief, which had grown close to malice, to her great-aunt. She took a dark pleasure in toying with Charity's suspicious nature by exaggerating the wide-eyed innocence and naïveté expected of a good American girl fortunate enough to marry such a respectable member of St. Louis's upper crust and to live in a beautiful home with every luxury at her command. Deborah's daily life was above reproach. She didn't gad about or seek the company of giddy young women who might put her in the company of scheming, amorous young men. She made no complaint about her lot. But on shipboard on the last day of their voyage home, Charity had seen the fire of battle in Deborah's eyes and could not afford to let down her guard.

At the cathedral every other week, Deborah and the rigidly corseted Charity shared a prayer book and sat together, attending religious ceremonies. Their skirts, sky blue and ashy gray, touched with a feminine sibilance, and

Charity observed that Deborah prayed with her disturbing eyes wide open as though God could be seen in the world instead of in the dark recess behind closed lids. It seemed indecent, though one could not say why. It was distracting.

Deborah let her great-aunt know that she frequently arrived thirty minutes before Mass to go to confession. She made sure Charity was there to see her heading for the confessional looking either resolute, as though she had determined to make a clean breast of it, or depressed, looking for sympathy and forgiveness of her sin from the priest who would hear—everything!

The possibility that Deborah would confess her actual sin, the abomination of her bastard child, to Father Michael. The possibility that Father Michael would find it too good a story to suppress and would let it slip some day when he had imbibed too much of the Irish whiskey he was so fond of. The possibility that the world would discover the chink in her otherwise impregnable respectability. And when Deborah emerged from the confessional with a look of calm relief, it nearly drove Charity mad, but even she couldn't bring herself to pry into the sacred privacy of the sacrament of confession. Charity found herself unable to sleep, spending restless nights marked with pointless tides of silent debate. Surely Deborah wouldn't. Surely Father Michael wouldn't. But then again.

In time, even this game palled, and Deborah was left to face the perpetual loneliness and grinding monotony of the life she had been forced to choose. The weeks dragged on with only slight variations on the same interminable theme of family life. Every weekday was the same—one was to arrive in the breakfast room at exactly 7:30, fully dressed, and to exchange the same words: Good morning, I trust you slept well. After a hearty repast, the Judge left his wife and daughters to chat over the remains of their breakfast. He retreated into the inviolable sanctity of his study to nap, take care of correspondence, or occasionally organize his collection of art photographs from Paris. Because he was looking forward to getting his hands on the sugar plantation and rum mill at the Martinique estate, he sometimes read pamphlets and made notes about improvements and scientific methods that would swell the tide of money rolling in after Deborah's great-aunt had passed away.

The income would be welcome to pay for some of his daughters' extravagances and would perhaps soften their resentment of this late marriage he had contracted and help them find husbands of their own. And if he should have another child, a son—not impossible, as he was a vigorous man for his age. But of course, he said nothing of this sensitive matter to Deborah or his daughters.

Every morning, the Judge's departure from the breakfast table left Florence and Lily free to share news about acquaintances in their circle, express disingenuous wonder at their shortcomings, and deplore their morals, manners, and especially their fashion choices: in short, to gossip. They giggled, cast their eyes about, and spoke in murmurs so that Deborah had to strain to hear about people she didn't know or care about. It seemed likely they took the same specious pleasure in disparaging their regrettable stepmother in her absence. Deborah ignored them and took refuge in her own melancholy thoughts; they considered her silence a sign of dim-wittedness.

After breakfast, Florence and Lily ascended to their rooms to change from morning dress into outfits for formal calls, extending a tepid invitation to Deborah to join them. They were visibly relieved whenever she politely declined. Her presence put a damper on their desire to gossip about her with their friends. Even so, the two sisters went together to complain to the Judge that she shunned company, and after he had a stern word with Deborah about the obligations of her social position, she went with them regularly on Mondays. She hoped they realized that she was aware of the dampening effect of her presence and was generously giving them one day a week to display her inappropriateness so that they could discuss it in subsequent visits.

In the afternoons, the Judge went down to the courthouse to preside over the messy lives of persons less august than himself or to study briefs and law reviews in his dark office. Deborah was left alone in the house most of the time. Had she been younger, had she not been grieving, she would have enjoyed exploring the large house on her own, seeking treasure in the dusty attic, playing at dress-ups, or imagining adventures. Now she merely drifted through the lonely space, looking for something to pass the sluggish time, anything that would speak to her sequestered heart and relieve her troubled mind. She had no one to talk to. She had nothing to say. Her only respite was retreat into tropical daydreams of Gianni and the life they might someday lead in Martinique.

Sometimes she took paper from the Judge's desk and drew tiny pictures of Gianni, of Villette, of hummingbirds, crowded onto the page to make the best use of this purloined resource. Villette at work, Gianni as a baby, as a little boy. One of these pages was found by a maid, who showed it to Florence, who was shocked at Deborah's subject matter and delighted to show it to her father.

"Really, sir, why is she drawing mammies and pickaninnies? What is she thinking? It unsettles the servants! It's unaccountable!"

Florence folded her hands at her waist and waited for her father's verdict. He took the sheet of paper in his hands and pretended to study it while he considered his best tactic. Although he outwardly maintained an air of judicial composure, he was well aware of the friction in his household, especially the resentment towards his wife. The Judge was not an unreasonable man. All he required from the females in his family were obedience, respect, consideration of his needs, silence, and behavior of the utmost propriety. He generally managed to have these requirements met by presenting a grave exterior and judiciously conceding at the first sign of trouble, meeting his daughters' demands, catering to their wishes, and, of course, financing their fashions.

"Very well, Florence," he said. "I will speak to your step-mama." And so he did, calling her to his study like a parolee who had left the city without permission to attend a family funeral and must now suffer the consequences.

"Deborah," he began, frowning at the offending paper he held up to her view, "these images are from your earlier life, I think. And that life is over. You are a married woman. You must put all this behind you. Do you understand? No more of these disgraceful Negro pictures. No more pictures."

Deborah was momentarily distracted, vividly reminded of Miss Thrash, who hadn't liked her pictures either, holding her Happy Autumn work up for judgment. Even though the memory was not a particularly happy one, it was still welcome as it reminded her of something that had mattered even before Gianni was born. Then she realized that this, too, the making of pictures, was being prohibited by her stern husband. She started to object, but he stopped her with an upheld hand. Had she burst into tears, he might have reversed his decision, but she stood stock-still, appalled. She had not supposed that even this comfort would be taken from her. She had lost Gianni, and the prohibition from drawing meant that she had lost herself as well. Her desolation was complete.

"That's all, Deborah," the Judge said and pretended to turn his attention to the papers on his desk, relieved that the matter had been so easily settled. Deborah was limited to viewing pictures that still inhabited her mind and occasionally tracing images in the tablecloth with her fork handle when no one was looking.

~~~~~~~

On most Saturday afternoons, Florence and Lily shopped in exclusive downtown shops for more fashionable gowns and ornaments to signal their wealth and style, set off their looks, and attract the envy of other women and the attention of men. Deborah was often unable to accompany them on these jaunts, begging off because of one of her "horrid headaches," which lasted until she heard them leave the house. And, of course, on Sunday, obligatory visits to the stuffy rectitude of the Lutherans or the ritual irrelevance of Mass. The comfortable family routine drove Deborah deeper and deeper into a shell of secrecy and silence.

From time to time, the Huntworths were invited to fancy dinner parties at the conventional homes of the Judge's conventional friends and colleagues, providing a break in the routine. At the Judge's request, Florence and Lily helped Deborah dress for these occasions, which she would otherwise have attended in drab day clothes, her hair knotted carelessly at the back of her head. It was a look entirely too childlike, and the daughters took special pleasure in dressing her hair in the latest style. Deborah sat silent and passive under their ministrations, enjoying the sensation of being touched. Even though their medium was trivial, she took note of the artistry—the vision, composition, skills, and techniques—they demonstrated. She took pleasure in the reflection of their faces in the dressing table mirror as they admired not Deborah, of course, but the results of their handiwork. Her feelings alarmed her, as though she might in time accept the Huntworths' vision of her and cease to be herself entirely.

~~~~~~~

Deborah had agreed to this marriage, but she had not realized how slowly time would pass, the days crawling by with nothing to do, the weeks dragging into months of sameness, and by the time she reached her third wedding anniversary, even the Judge noticed that she was not well. She had become thinner, had lost the energy of her first entry into this crucial game—no longer a game to her, but now revealed as an endless trek, companionless and desolate. She was denied even the support of drawing her thoughts on paper, making a map to avoid getting lost entirely. At first, the Judge supposed that perhaps his rare attentions were taxing her and took to sleeping in his dressing room. Deborah's isolation became more bitter with the loss of the physical comfort she had drawn from his warm, bear-like presence.

The Judge's fear of Deborah's incipient invalidism prompted him to visit his old friend, Dr. Oates, to see if he might recommend a tonic or regimen suitable for the situation. An appointment was arranged. Dr. Oates, though recently retired, still met with his old patients and had opened a part-time clinic at his residence. The Judge took Deborah there for a consultation. Deborah was deposited in the sitting room with a pot of tea for refreshment and the doctor's wife for company while the gentlemen had a frank initial conversation about her symptoms, a discussion that might be distressing for the patient to hear. In deep, rumbling voices, the two men considered possible diagnoses for what ailed Deborah: female anemia, uterine inadequacy, hysterical nerve disorder, melancholia.

Meanwhile, Mrs. Oates served tea and eyed the young wife. She knew that often these elderly gentlemen who chose to marry girls were not really up to the task. However, she knew numerous techniques to help heat up or tamp down marital relations as needed. It was such a shame to see young women suffering needlessly. Mrs. Oates prided herself on being a plain-spoken woman, so she spoke plainly.

"Perhaps you are finding your marriage unsatisfactory. Is your husband able to perform in the marriage bed? Are his advances shocking or painful to you?"

"He's fine," Deborah said, taken aback at this unaccustomed directness. "I like him in bed."

"Is there another, perhaps younger, man you are pining for?"

Deborah thought of Gianni, who would be starting to talk now. "No," she said. "There's no one else."

"Are you taking some powder or pill to avoid pregnancy?"

"No."

"Are you taking laudanum or alcohol to soothe your feelings? Are your menses regular? Do you experience cramping?"

No laudanum or alcohol. Regular menses with only occasional mild cramps.

"Do you need a larger dress allowance? Do your step-daughters plague you? No? Then what is depressing your spirits? Your husband is concerned about your health. Tell me what you need."

Deborah was silent, as she must be until death broke the bonds of marriage. Mrs. Oates leaned forward and laid her warm hand on Deborah's arm. "My dear Mrs. Huntworth. You have your husband's attention now, and you must make good use of that as it is unlikely to last. Perhaps he cannot give you your heart's desire, but what can he do for you to improve your situation? Think hard."

Deborah thought hard, forcing herself to put the vision of Martinique aside. She could not break her pact of secrecy with Charity or she would forfeit the pittance that supported Gianni and lose him forever. She had to consider what would help her endure the life she had chosen until the time came when she could live the life she longed for. She blurted out the first thing that came to mind.

"I want to draw, and I want to paint."

"Why can't you draw now? It seems an innocent enough activity."

"The Judge has forbidden it. He said I was to make no more pictures."

Mrs. Oates sat back in her chair and began a lecture she had given to other distressed wives while their husbands were safely sequestered with the doctor.

"My dear. I am an old wife, forty-five years married, and I tell you this from my experience. You must behave like a lawful wife, not like a stray child. Stand on your dignity, speak to your husband as his wife, and tell him what you want in no uncertain terms. He is unlikely to refuse you if you speak your mind."

And with that, Mrs. Oates went to see if the gentlemen required anything, and she slipped a hastily written note into her husband's hand. It read: "She needs a hobby." Dr. Oates would deliver this prognosis in more elaborate language as his professional opinion to the Judge, along with a bottle of nerve tonic just in case.

As they returned home in the carriage, the Judge was preoccupied, wondering if Deborah might like to play the harp like Florence or the piano like Lily. She would be unable to match their proficiency, yet he feared his daughters would resent a novice incursion into their territory. And there was the question of sharing the instrument. It would not do. Perhaps Deborah could do charity work with the Lutheran Ladies' Society, though the Judge was not really in favor of coddling the poor. And there was the risk that she might develop inconvenient religious notions. Or she could press flowers. Or engage in spiritualism, which he was told was popular among the ladies. He drew the line at women's suffrage—that he would not countenance.

On the other side of the carriage, Deborah reviewed her situation. She had been startled and stimulated by her conversation with Mrs. Oates, whose questions and advice had drawn aside the curtain of chronic longing that had been darkening Deborah's spirit and let in some light. She could hold her dreams of Gianni deep in her heart and turn her thoughts to the life she had to work with. She need not drown in the sea of grief; she could build a boat.

The Judge cleared his throat to draw her attention and asked with unaccustomed hesitancy if there were a hobby she might like to take up to occupy her free time. The doctor had suggested it might be salubrious.

Deborah summoned up her courage, taking the Judge's hand in both her hands and meeting his startled eyes with gravity.

"Osmund," she said. The name sounded strange to her, so she said it again with more conviction. "Osmund. I have not asked you for a great deal. And I am asking now. I want to draw and paint. I need a room somewhere that can be used for this purpose. I need to buy supplies and equipment to set up a studio and then a small monthly allowance to maintain it."

The Judge was touched and relieved by her relatively conventional request. Ladies did like to paint. He didn't see the harm in it; he didn't recall that he had forbidden this activity a few years earlier.

"Of course, my dear, if that will make you more cheerful. That all can be arranged." He patted her hands with his free hand, pulling his trapped hand free.

"The old nursery will be quite suitable," Deborah said. "There's running water there, and the light is good. I will have that room cleared out to make space for a worktable and an easel and make a list for the shops. Thank you, my dear."

And so it was done.

~~~~~~~

The return to her art was a great joy for Deborah. Simply moving a pencil against a paper surface, the sensation of slight pressure and contact and the sight of the track on the page awakened a part of her that had been languishing and threatening to vanish altogether. She sketched her surroundings: the new easel she hadn't used yet, the old nursery furniture pushed against the wall, the window curtains, her own foot.

Then her memories and dreams came to the forefront of her mind. She drew the wrecked carriage from her childhood dreams, Katy, and irises, the strangler fig tree at Sans Douleur, Mt. Pelée, and Villette, drawing less from memory than from memories of what she had drawn before. She produced a few conventional still life pictures to shield her real work from the view of annoying visitors like the Judge, who came to witness the effects of his benevolence. Florence and Lily visited to make certain Deborah had not received a benefit that should have been theirs. The household staff dropped in to see what she was doing and asked questions, collecting information to discuss around the kitchen table at the end of the day with the censorious Mrs. Hogg. Deborah had to persuade the upstairs maid to forego "tidying" the studio with a lengthy analogy to Mrs. Hogg's kitchen. What a mistake it would be to wash up flour-dusted cake pans or to throw away rising bread or cakes left out to cool.

Deborah was glad when the novelty faded and she was left alone to work. She began to draw Gianni over and over, in pencil, charcoal, crayon, and watercolor, each medium speaking in its own way, letting her touch his face, recreating him, feeling the love and grief in her waking heart, and recalling the deep seriousness of her commitment to redeem the child held hostage somewhere in Martinique.

Lily was the only one who continued to visit, attracted by the mysterious atmosphere of the workshop. She had a sorrow of her own to heal. It seemed Florence had taken up with a new, exciting acquaintance, Miss Eleanor Blimpton, and now Lily was reduced to being a little sister who tagged along, shut out of delicious secrets and jokes, who only mattered when no one else was around. Lily withdrew from the social engagements that had once bolstered her and now caused her distress, seeking restorative silence in the little studio, her old nursery, to soothe her hurt feelings. She first attempted to forge an alliance in the only way she knew, by finding fault with Florence; she felt sure that Deborah, who certainly had grounds for resentment, would enter in.

"Did you see Florence's dress this morning? Why does she think maroon is her color? And she really doesn't have the right shape to sport a peplum. You'd think her dear friend Eleanor Blimpton would give her a hint." Deborah merely looked up and said, "You love your sister," and returned to the work in front of her.

Lily was nonplussed and mortified by the rejection. But she stayed, relieved somewhere deep in her heart that her worst impulse had been so gently corrected. She sat silent then and in subsequent visits, sometimes reading, sometimes with a book lying unread in her lap, listening to her own thoughts. Deborah ignored her at first, then used her as a subject like the window curtains and discarded toys—her hands, her ringleted head, the melancholy droop of her pretty mouth when she drifted off into daydreams.

Although Deborah had included oil paints, solvents, canvas, and hog bristle brushes in her initial purchase of art supplies, it was more than a year before she found herself ready to explore oil paint, the exalted medium of the great masters. She prepared by poring over books from art shops, bookshops, and the library, books of famous paintings, and, more usefully, treatments of color, texture, and brush techniques. After long months of study, exercises, and experiments, she was ready to try and fail and try again.

Her first mildly successful work was a large portrait of Florence and Lily in the classical style, seated side-by-side on a plum-colored love seat, their looks slightly improved but easily recognizable. Of course, they were portrayed in elegant gowns with careful delineation of each flounce, frill, and ornament. The frame was heavy, ornate gilt, emphasizing the constrained, traditional composition. This was a Christmas gift for the Judge who chose to hang it in the sitting room across from his own somewhat larger likeness over the outsized fireplace.

For each of the daughters, Deborah painted much smaller, more satisfying pictures, which she privately preferred, thinking of them as spiritual portraits. For Florence, a lively garden scene almost overwhelmed with a profusion of red and peachy roses, yellow and purple pansies, blue larkspur, pink foxglove, bold daisies, and deep purple bougainvillea, like no garden ever grown in St. Louis or anywhere else in the world. Lily's painting was a single, gleaming lily, pearlescent white, delicately furled, yearning, vulnerable and exquisite. These gifts were quietly received and hung in each young woman's bedroom, where they were much studied and wondered over.

Florence and Lily, Lily and Florence, each felt that her painting was best and that she had been seen to the core, appreciated rather than judged. They had not felt this kind of love since their mother died, leaving them in the care of their dutiful but unimaginative father. Florence sat on her bed and wept, holding the picture in her lap. Across the hall in her room, Lily smiled and placed her treasure where she would see it every morning when she woke.

~~~~~~~

During his years of marriage to Deborah, the Judge became increasingly stout, red-faced, slow, and sometimes alarmingly short of breath. The doctor recommended that he forego spirits and rich foods and add an evening walk to his daily regimen. A walk was simply not in the cards, though his wife and daughters offered to accompany him. Though prepared by Mrs. Hogg in strict accordance with the doctor's orders and followed by the entire family, the spartan diet brought out a new irritability and almost childish peevishness. His former mild benevolence, it seemed, had been the result of his life of control, comfort, and pride. Now he would not be pleased. It was not long until his heart began to fail, and he was confined to bed, with daily visits from the same grim-faced physician whose warnings had not been heeded.

Deborah patiently attended the Judge in the final weeks of his illness, anticipating his needs and easing his struggles and pains when she could, disregarding his petty complaints and bitter invective. She hushed his fears and held his hand. When he died and his horrid breathing stilled at last, she dressed in mourning black, wept at his funeral, and comforted his daughters in their grief. The Judge had been kind enough in his heavy-handed way. She painted a triptych of his face: a child, a man, and in death. The piece was small, almost small enough to fit into a locket. Although he never really knew her, he had provided her space to work in, and that had made all the difference.

The funeral was solemn and prolonged. It seemed every leading light of St. Louis society wished to pay tribute to the Judge's civic-mindedness and long, distinguished career. Deborah sat between her stiff, unfeeling great-aunt and her weeping stepdaughters and was sad, triumphant, and weary by turns. At the front of the church, their expressions pious, the Blimpton sisters sang harmony to the approval of the black-robed minister, their heads tilted towards each other as though the lines of melody would be more likely to meet that way.

"Like Noah's weary dove," they intoned in family harmony, their long Blimpton faces drawn even longer by the sustained vowels of the song. Deborah felt a tide of weariness from the sustained effort of nerve that kept her faithful to the bargain she had made, but she pushed it away, waiting for the Blimptons to sing the line about "every longing satisfied." That was the promised balm at the end when she could forget about the Judge, Charity, and St. Louis with its tedious demands and return to herself and to her son, every longing satisfied.

When the Blimptons reached the apocalyptic final verse, when only those who have entered the ark of God are saved from the sea of fire sent to destroy the earth, Deborah pictured the breathtaking blue of the Antillean sea turned flaming red and an ark to keep her and Gianni safe. She imagined leaning on the rail of that ark in perfect safety in the company of a man like Mr. Short. Her long plan, entered into as a girl with very little notion of what it would entail, might yet bring her success. Once Tante Charity was gone, Deborah would board her own ark to freedom and return to the dock at St. Pierre, see Mt. Pelée's face again, return to Sans Douleur, which would be her own "dear abode." She would take her little Gianni into her arms and live again.

~~~~~~~

At first, the death of Judge Huntworth changed very little in Deborah's life. She was so accustomed to the household's daily routine that she continued to rise at 6:30 for the same breakfast at 7:30. She found it steadied her and settled the anxiety of the servants. She was still in thrall to Tante Charity, so she kept the Sunday rotation in place, Catholic one week and Protestant the next.

After giving her situation some thought, Deborah abandoned the nursery studio and rented a dingy little apartment where she could paint whatever she wanted without regard to the sensibilities of the household staff. She had not realized how constrained she had been until she painted, at last, in privacy. Her first work was a series of nudes, self-portraits in pencil, then in oils, exploring the bold, tender, lush, and sometimes awkward shapes of her lived-in body. This process involved finding a pose in the mirror and studying it, memorizing as much as possible to transfer to the page or canvas. Then she wrapped herself in the Judge's old dressing gown that she had brought for rags but didn't have the heart to cut up. If the day was warm, she simply worked naked, sitting at the worktable or standing at the easel.

She pleased herself with a few encounters with Brently Mallard. He had made a condolence call at the Judge's house and admired her painting of Florence and Lily on the wall. She liked him and invited him to visit her at her studio, where his pathetic gratitude betrayed his wife's unwillingness to carry out her wifely duties. Deborah was certain that he would never cause trouble for her or disturb the placid life she led to keep her contract with Charity. He had his own pressing reasons for concealing the infidelity.

Florence and Lily turned to each other for solace in their shared bereavement, weeping together, sitting silently, or playing melancholy, slow-paced piano and harp duets, always in a minor key. Deborah's feeling about the Judge's death was primarily a swell of renewed hope with just a pinch of sadness. She would not have been able to mourn with her stepdaughters without playacting, and the notion was distasteful. The sisterly bond now superseded Lily's former attachment to Deborah and mended the rift between the two grieving daughters. They were once again Florence and Lily. And yet.

Deborah could feel something in the air, at first supposing it was her own rising hope of release, but there was something bigger than that. It was everywhere—excitement, a new sense of possibility, invention, risk, and discovery, a brisk wind that swept away the trappings of the past and made room for the dangerous and exciting new. The changes began slowly in the Judge's household, and then it seemed that everything changed.

The staff began to take longer and longer half days, extending them to full days to attend workshops and evening classes for general self-improvement or to learn a trade. Several left to take retail employment or to open small businesses of their own. Mrs. Hogg went to Deborah demanding authority to hire a new kitchen maid, as it was too much on her own. Deborah suggested simplifying the workload—breakfast might be laid out on the sideboard, for example, and a cold collation would be sufficient for the midday meal. Soon dinner shrank from a formal production served in courses to just a few simple dishes set on the table, family style. Mrs. Hogg grumbled, complained, and went to the library in her spare time to read up on ancient Egypt and the pyramids.

The Judge's daughters began arriving late for breakfast, sometimes not arriving at all if their activities had kept them out late the night before. Lily brought piano music to the table to look over as she finished her coffee, preparing to play for the Wednesday night youth choir practice led by the recently hired assistant minister, Reverend Stephen Schaeffer, a gangly young bachelor from Wisconsin. Meanwhile, Florence might be sipping coffee while studying a circular on the benefits of bicycling for women or a tract on the educational needs of immigrants. The Judge would never have countenanced such activities at his breakfast table.

Lily spent more and more time at the Lutheran church, participating in the Women's Institute, the missionary society, and the flower committee. Whenever possible, she took on the role of secretary to increase the necessity of consulting with Reverend Schaeffer. She initiated a women's Bible study group in close collaboration with Reverend Schaeffer. She made it her pursuit to make

Reverend Schaeffer feel welcome in his new church home. Deborah found it amusing to follow the progress of Lily's determined campaign to win the hand of Reverend Schaeffer. He seemed like an interesting fellow. And there was a glint in his eye that suggested Lily's vigorous courtship entertained him and that he had already decided to make the match.

Florence was reserved about her own interests and spent more and more time with her friend Eleanor. She was taken on a trip to Chicago as a guest of the Blimpton family because of her special friendship with Eleanor and a hope in Mrs. Blimpton's bosom that Florence would be a good influence. Mrs. Blimpton hoped such a close friend could steer Eleanor in a conventional direction, removing the danger that her headstrong daughter would pursue a dream that did not include marriage and family. When the two girls requested an afternoon to go downtown shopping, just the two of them, it seemed a hopeful sign, and Mrs. Blimpton's permission was readily granted. Their secret agenda was a pilgrimage to Jane Addams' Hull House to see for themselves what measures could be taken by energetic, progressive women like themselves to improve the lot of the poor; Eleanor had written ahead and they were expected.

When Florence returned from the Chicago trip, Lily and Deborah could see that she had changed: she was unsettled; she was galvanized. She alternately brooded and sizzled. She was setting her plans into motion and biding her time until she could present a *fait accompli*. One fine morning, she broke into the casual atmosphere of the family breakfast table, turning away from the sideboard with a sausage suspended over her plate, still clenched in the serving tongs.

"I might as well tell you now," she said. "I'm moving

to Chicago to become a social worker. And Eleanor is going to train for a practical nurse. We plan to study together, and when we know enough to be useful, we're going to work in a settlement house. We leave in three weeks." She plopped the sausage down and turned her attention to the muffins swaddled in a cosy to stay warm. She took one, and after some thought, another. And a generous pat of butter. She set her plate down and seated herself across from Lily, who stared, wide-eyed, with the piano score she had been annotating clutched against her chest.

The long silence that fell between the two sisters was deep, layered, and rich, like an old river, like imagined music that rises and falls, modulates, risks dissonance and resolves: old assumptions melting away and new ones forming, memories re-remembered, new thoughts replacing old worn-out ones, habits of a lifetime set aside, values tested and revised, the bonds of family re-evaluated and reaffirmed. Florence nodded and began her breakfast.

Lily set her papers back on the table and lined the pages up carefully.

"How will you find a husband?" she asked mildly.

"I don't intend to marry. Neither does Eleanor. We reject the bondage of matrimony."

"You'll be an old maid," Lily pointed out.

Florence bit into her sausage and chewed thoughtfully. "I'm already an old maid, my dear. So is Eleanor. And so are you."

Lily reached out across the expanse of white tablecloth as though to lay a gentle hand on her sister's arm. "Be happy for me," she said. "Stephen proposed yesterday, and I accepted."

Florence took the offered hand briefly, and then they both turned to look at Deborah, as though they had forgotten she was there but were now hoping to gauge her acceptance of the very different paths they had chosen. She realized they were expecting her to judge.

"I'm not your parent, of course," she was quick to say, "but I am greatly pleased with your news and happy for you both. I look forward to hearing more about your plans as they develop."

Deborah drank the last of her coffee and stood. "I'm thinking a celebratory family dinner is in order, perhaps Friday evening. Invite your chosen companions, of course. And now I'd best go consult with Mrs. Hogg."

As she left to perform this happy errand, Lily asked, "What do you suppose Father would think?" Deborah didn't hear Florence's reply, but she heard the two of them laughing, trying not to laugh, and laughing all the same.

~~~~~~~

One evening, two years after the old century had passed and the new one was underway, Charity Millais returned from a social gathering rather earlier than expected, took to her bed, and by morning was clearly very ill indeed. She shivered with fever and coughed, stirring up the contents of her lungs like a shaken snow globe and, when all had settled, she coughed again. She drank tea but could eat very little of what was brought to her. The doctor was concerned and did everything in his power to keep her alive. She chose to receive no visits from her acquaintances; only Deborah was admitted to the sickroom and only Katy was allowed to wash her and change her linens. Charity slept long hours in the daylight and fitfully in the night. Surely the death must come soon.

Deborah sat at Tante Charity's bedside watching the rise and fall of her rackety breath, listening to the rasping jerks of inhalation, the strange puffs that exploded outward from her drawn mouth, creviced and cracked like dried mud after the rainy season. She held the cold claw in her own warm hand, but with the same amount of interest and compassion she would have felt for a dying crab, perhaps less. She dutifully kissed her great-aunt goodbye in front of the doctor and the nurse who mixed the medicines and knitted a long sulfur-yellow scarf between administering doses to the choking patient. But gleaming hideously from between reddened eyelids, Charity's cold gray eyes still glared behind the paper-thin lids, judging, disapproving, disposing.

Surely no one, not even the fearsome Charity Millais, could hold off the dreaded visitor forever. Even her grinding, metallic eye would be dulled in the end; her whiplash voice heard for the last time, a hoarse whisper, then stilled forever; her will an official document now, not to be altered, a question of paper rather than the ruthless force and determination with which she imprisoned those around her.

While Deborah waited for news of the death that would finally set her free, she painted and dreamed. Once at Sans Douleur, she would see Gianni and favor him, teach him, look after him and live with him. If she got that far, other difficulties could surely be surmounted. He would grow to love her. If a white mother with a brown son couldn't be accepted in Martinique, they could go together to some country where the color of his skin was not a scandal, a living emblem of her shocking union. But, of course, somewhere in her mind, pushed away from awareness, too painful to bear, she knew that there was no such place on earth.

She supposed that she would stay indefinitely in Martinique. She could never bring Gianni back to St. Louis, where the colored people were penned up in poor neighborhoods like Ville, on dusty streets with no side-walks, in little ramshackle houses, crowded and dark. As a child, she had accepted this arrangement. Now she wondered if they found a measure of relief, shielded from the eyes of the white people who had owned their parents, some comfort in the company of others who had suffered like them. She seemed to hear the same song that had haunted her in St. Pierre, the sound of a people trapped in a time that beat them down, sung here with a different rhythm.

~~~~~~~

The day Katy brought the news that Charity Millais had finally died was typical for Deborah. She painted with the few supplies not already packed for Martinique. She entertained Brently Mallard and sent him on his way. Setting aside her Mt. Pelée picture, she stood at her easel, brush in hand, palette scraped and ready, running her hand over the blank canvas. She thought about painting Brently. She would need to start with a sketch drawn from memory, and then she could choose whether to portray him as a lover, a respectable man, an anguished husband, or some more fanciful depiction. She let the images take form in her mind but was distracted by unusual noises from the flat downstairs.

The people who lived below her little hideaway seemed to be moving furniture, perhaps moving out, moving on. Their baby wailed, a man shouted, and the baby was quiet again. Thump and thud, heavy boxes and the firm bang of the hammer closing up crates. She wished them well, whoever they were, hoping with a warm fellow feeling that they were sailing away to a better place, and their leaving seemed like another sign of good things to come.

She moved lightly across the room, the Judge's warm robe gathered around her, and peered down at a drayer's cart, where working men struggled to force the heavy crates up and into the half-filled space. A woman in a light blue shirtwaist and black skirt, a black bonnet tied firmly under her chin, held the baby; she watched the handling of her family's belongings with an air of satisfaction. So that was all right—a happy day rather than a descent into worse circumstances.

Look down at your baby, Deborah thought. *Glory in the sweet smooth curve of his cheek, his bright eyes. Touch him for me. Breathe him in.* Instead, the mother raised her eyes to the window and stared at what she saw there— Deborah's face framed by loose, tousled hair evidently enough of a scandal in broad daylight. The mother below clutched the baby close to her ruffled chest in a gesture of protection and hoarding, then climbed up with her husband's help to ride away. Deborah watched the cart reach the second corner, where it turned right and disappeared.

The onion man in the street below sang out and jangled his bell to bring the housewives out to haggle with him over the few limp vegetables left in his barrow after a day of selling. The sound of his cry reminded Deborah that it had been all day since she had been fed. It was time to make her way to Russell Street and catch a hansom to deliver her to the Judge's house on Lafayette Square, where Mrs. Hogg waited to confer about today's problems and tomorrow's menu and to disapprove and complain about Deborah's general lack of interest to anyone who would listen. To be content with a pauper's meal in the evening! Breakfast at all hours! Not to notice whether the dessert was a chiffon cake or a lemon curd tart!

Deborah had been informed by Katy, who gathered her gossip from some mysterious servants' network, that the excuse of being in mourning for her husband and then the great-aunt cut no ice with Mrs. Hogg. She knew for a fact that many widows spent the mourning period consoling themselves with rich cakes and puddings, emerging from tight black gowns when the year was up into a new wardrobe in a larger size. Mrs. Hogg had no patience with this little widow who wore the black, as was proper, but seemed indifferent to its solemnity, as though it were just another color of the rainbow rather than color itself sacrificed out of respect for the deceased.

Deborah had also been informed that Mrs. Hogg suspected she was up to no good, although the suspicious old lady was too busy, too housebound, and too unimaginative to form more than a hazy notion of what she might be up to. Deborah considered buying a handful of leeks from the onion man on her way home and requesting Onion Soup à la Chinoise just to keep Mrs. Hogg occupied for a few more days or weeks at most until the prize was firmly in hand. Deborah could keep the faith this close to freedom, this close to her heart's deepest desire. Then came the knocking on the door and Katy's breathless announcement.

Deborah left the studio with Katy at her side, eager to take care of the business of ending this seemingly endless phase of her life. She summarily ran Richards out of the house where Charity had breathed her last breath, a house which would now belong solely to Deborah along with the estate and all of Charity's fortune. Richards was very much in evidence there, as Katy had said.

"There is too much to do here," Deborah told him. "I will expect to see you after the funeral, not before." She made an unconscious gesture, flapping one end of her shawl like Villette shooing chickens, combining this movement with the straight backbone she had learned from Tante Charity, and sent him on his way.

~~~~~~~

Tante Charity's funeral was a cold black event held on an unusually dark, cheerless spring day. The gloom hovering over the heads of those gathered had nothing to do with grief over their loss. Instead, it was a generalized regret that life ends, even the life of such a stubborn old witch. If even she had succumbed, so would they all. For Deborah, the only punctuation of the dreariness was the beautiful hat on Katy's head, an outmoded bonnet of the style of fifteen years earlier, well preserved as though never worn. Its elegant bow, chiffon rose, shiny red cherries, and fluffy feather all bore testimony to the endurance of beauty, which waits patiently through dark times and reappears in the spring when it is safe to bloom.

Deborah felt deep satisfaction. Charity Millais, now removed, washed away, called Home, the priest was saying—devoured by Father Time, surely a gristly morsel, in Deborah's view. She pictured a tall, bony figure in a black gown slicing Charity into pieces with his scythe, cramming her into his ravenous mouth, cracking her hard eyes between his teeth like sour balls, and next to the broken old body a trail of clothing shed like a snake's skin. Tante Charity was gone at last, her predatory claws no longer poised to restrain, her harsh cries to reprimand, her hateful eye to threaten.

The ceremony was conducted as directed in the will, stifling in its insistence on the proprieties. Her corpse was consigned to the grave to be ornamented, once the sod had settled, with a headstone, the inscription carefully chosen by Deborah, reading:

Charity Danelle Henriette Millais
March 30, 1820 - April 10, 1902

"Here Safe Thou Shalt Abide"

Her ornate coffin was buried in the Millais family plot next to her younger sister's resting place.

> *Augusta Charlotte Marie Millais Baird*
> *Beloved Wife, Mother, and Grandmother*
> *March 15, 1822 - October 3, 1887*
> *"Gone To Be With God"*

6

~ *Martinique* ~

The morning after Tante Charity's funeral, Deborah was visited in the bright breakfast room of the Judge's house by Richards in his capacity as her great-aunt's attorney. The will was perfectly in order, as, of course, it would be. Aside from a few personal bequests to old friends and servants, Deborah was to receive the bulk of the considerable Millais fortune, some old-fashioned family jewels, and the sugar plantation and estate, the main source of the river of money.

The practicalities of Deborah's departure were taken care of. The keys to Tante Charity's house, which had been Deborah's parents' house, were entrusted to Richards with instructions to find posts for the servants and tip them generously. The last details would be sent to his office: what was to go, what was to stay, what was to be sent later, what should be given away, and what could be discarded.

Richards professed himself more than willing to act as her man of business in the Indies. In his opinion, a lady shouldn't have to concern herself with such things. After all, sugar was no longer being exported, the market being what it was, and the business had changed. A respectable young lady should not have direct contact with the manufacture of rum, even if it was the largest source of her income.

"I will be traveling to the estate myself," Deborah said, brushing aside his offer. "I went once as a young girl, as you know, and I should like to see it again. I expect to remain there for at least six months. I will count on you to see to my business here until I return."

She turned her mild eye on Richards and gave him a look as implacable in its way as her great aunt's had ever been. "I confide this to you as my attorney. I do not wish it to be shared. Is that very clear? You may say that I have gone abroad if you are asked." He felt as though he were hearing her great-aunt's deep voice in concert with Deborah's sweet one, an unholy but wholly imposing duet. "Thank you," she said and stood, causing Richards to stand as well and, without ever having delivered the expostulation that had been on his lips, he found himself in the hall with a sense of déjà vu, eager for a stiff drink and the company of men.

Deborah had expected to depart from New Orleans but found she could arrive a few days earlier if she traveled to New York to board the *S.S. Roraima* there. Her exhilarated heart could not brook delay. She cabled the consulate in St. Pierre, requesting that Villette be instructed to expect her on Ascension Thursday, a special feast day on the island. She hoped the holiday would not make any difficulties. The ship was sometimes a day earlier or later, depending on conditions at sea, but the harbor master would be informed of any changes. The reply was cabled back from the island, evidently composed by someone more literate than Villette. It said in precise French that Villette would have a cart and driver there waiting for her and would bring the child along, as she requested.

The only disappointment for Deborah was that Katy would not choose to accompany her to the island. Katy's head had been filled with visions of the 1904 Louisiana Purchase Exposition to be held in St. Louis, an earthshaking event that had already engendered endless conversation in the newspapers, the gentlemen's clubs, and among servant girls like Katy on their half-days off.

"I couldn't miss it, not for anything," she said. "Already the buildings are going up, and it will be the grandest thing that ever was, right here in St. Louis. I'm sorry, miss, but I can't leave now, not for anything."

"I need you," Deborah said. "I need your company. The exposition isn't for ages. You can come with me and see the real world, see the blue ocean and the place where bananas grow on trees. Wouldn't you like that? Isn't that better than just seeing plaster models and pretend places?"

But Katy wouldn't budge, motivated as much by fear of going as by desire to stay. She agreed that she might come later, after the excitement of the Exposition was over, but neither of them really believed it. She had already been offered a position with Lily Schaeffer, née Huntworth, who was expecting the arrival of her first child before the end of the year. Deborah could see that she would still have to do without Katy.

~~~~~~~

Because all had been arranged and there was nothing left to organize, Deborah allowed herself to fly into a state of agitation, her heart fluttering in her chest. She hardly recognized the unguarded satisfaction and joy she felt, tempered only by a sense that she could have been broken, could have been reduced to incessant weeping, could have forgotten herself and become the empty, blind, compliant doll she pretended to be. It had been her art that kept her whole, allowed her to repair the damages of social constriction and live freely in color, shape, texture, perspective, and discovery—the miraculous flow of painting.

The nearness of her journey stirred up longing she had worked hard to contain, making it difficult for her to sleep, making her dreams so intense they shoved her back into wakefulness, dream changing to imagination, then to thought, then to awareness of the dark room. She lay awake the night before she was to depart, picturing the end of her journey, amazed that this time had arrived, that she had played her hand against such formidable adversaries with only time and art as her allies. She breathed in the heady scent of victory and tried to calm the buzzing of anticipation that kept her sleepless.

Deborah knew she would see Gianni first at a distance from the deck, would struggle to pick him out from among the many, would see him grow larger as the ship approached the harbor and, at last, would have him there where she could drink him in, approach and speak to him. She would touch his face with her fingertips, then draw him into a long, long-awaited embrace. Although she knew it was irrational, she was certain that she would recognize him even in the mosaic of colorful clothing and brown, yellow, dusky, and black faces constantly moving in the dockside crowd. Her Gianni, whose face she had studied in the lamplight, sketched and painted so many times, a face grave or laughing, always full of love in her pictures, full of fun like his father, but not a bad boy. She would become at last one of those who return, the *revenants*, living or dead, drawn back to seek the dreams they have left behind on the island, to awake from the nightmares that kept them away.

Two weeks after the funeral, Deborah's boxes and bags were loaded onto a train bound for New York, and she departed from St. Louis, she hoped, forever. Not until she boarded the train did she wonder what Katy would have made of Villette and how Villette would have coped with Katy. Perhaps it was just as well she traveled alone.

The physical hardships of a train ride of more than a day meant nothing to Deborah. She was strong and determined, and she hardly noticed the discomforts and minor inconveniences, plagued as she was by her increasingly frantic desire to arrive. After all, she had waited patiently for weeks, really for years, to push forward to her heart's desire. The train was nearly full, and although she was indifferent to the noise and swaying of the train compartment, the conversations and conventional pleasantries of her fellow passengers nearly drove her mad, especially as they seemed to expect her attention and response in kind.

I have a son who is holding my heart for me in St. Pierre, she wanted to say, the only fact that seemed to matter, but they would think her mad for telling that truth.

A Mrs. Washington, round and smiling, introduced herself to Deborah after settling next to her. She retrieved an embroidery hoop from a portmanteau at her feet, a copy of *Ladies' Companion*, and a small sack that smelled of onions and cheese.

"No relation to George," Mrs. Washington assured her fellow passengers with a roguish smile, as though they shared some naughty secret about the nation's first president. She was traveling just as far as Richmond to assist her third of seven daughters, Della, with the birth of her third, a coincidence that seemed to strike her as bordering on the miraculous. With seven daughters, all of them prolific breeders, and all of their offspring remarkable for one thing or another—second place in a spelling bee, curly hair, a strong tendency to develop warts—Mrs. Washington seemed as though she would never run out of material for the entertainment of the car.

As she started in on the family of daughter number five, wife to a dairy farmer, mother of five outstanding children, the flow dwindled to a mumble, and she began to nod off. Deborah held her breath, and she could see the other passengers doing the same. In time, the rocking and the rhythm of the tracks had their usual effect, and almost everyone dozed.

Deborah could not imagine an existence that would lend itself to such a luxury of openness, a story that could be told to all and sundry, to strangers in a railway car. The closest she had come to disclosure was the night she had almost told Katy, but that was a fairy story, concealing even as it revealed. Her life of enforced subterfuge and secrecy had rendered her incapable of normal human interaction. She could only lie or say nothing, and either way, she remained isolated. *I am a desperate woman*, she thought, though she wasn't sure precisely what she meant. But it seemed to explain the stew of impatience, apprehension, tension, giddiness, and desire that stirred her heart and drove her forward even as she sat very still in the company of others, still well behaved, still unaccountably incandescent.

She relieved the agitation that made each minute painfully long by watching the stiff gentleman seated across from her. Once he had politely removed his hat and placed it on the overhead rack, his hair was revealed as white and fuzzy around an oval of shiny baldness. When sunlight came from behind, the play of light highlighted the areole of curls, almost opalescent at times. When a shadow fell across the window, it brought out the few dark hairs sprinkled throughout. As dusk drew near, the hairs became almost invisible. She watched the shifts and sparkles, aware that she wanted to feel the texture against her hand and through her fingers, surely not as soft as it appeared, not as complex to touch as to sight. She tried not to stare, but when the object of her scrutiny got off the train in Baltimore, he bowed to her ceremoniously, saying, "Good day, madam," looking up at her through his thick eyebrows with bright dark eyes before he straightened up and donned his hat. So perhaps she had stared. For just a moment, she missed the Judge.

Deborah traveled from the train station by cab directly to New York harbor to board the Indies-bound steamer scheduled to leave early the next morning. The *Roraima* seemed smaller than the ship she had been on for her first voyage, though perhaps she had seen it with the eyes of first experience. It was a melancholy thought, how young she had been, how open-hearted and unguarded.

Up on deck to watch the city as the steamship pulled away, Deborah stood among the others as they admired the great statue, Lady Liberty, implacable rather than welcoming to Deborah's eye, though more beautiful than she had supposed. She felt relief and a loosening of tension in her chest, a tension that she had not realized was there. This lady would not kill her, and unlike her parents, she would return to her child.

When she first entered the small cabin she was to occupy, she felt a moment of cold panic, as though the close white walls formed a prison or a grave. But after that first *frisson*, it was a delight to be alone to dream and feel and stretch body and spirit, to revel in freedom, not merely freedom from the invisible bondage of her old life, but more: the freedom to be herself, to see and express what she could see, seek to see more, to feel more. Gianni was at the heart of the reverie, the child of her newly emancipated body, her son. She laughed there alone in amazement that she had managed to arrive at this moment, and when the laughter was spent, she smiled.

The company of travelers with whom she would share the voyage was made up of women and children, two older gentlemen, a small company of eleven all told. She hoped to find a temporary companion to pass the time, to marvel

at the sea, to gaze in silence at its mysterious, shifting surface. She looked for Mr. Short or someone like him, but the
chief mate was a Mr. Scott, not inclined to engage in
extended conversation, and the other crew members,
though courteous enough, offered only occasional reminders of Mr. Short's friendship on her first voyage: a nod, a
kindly smile, a keen blue glance, a muscular thigh. She responded to these, but these busy men were not Mr. Short,
and Deborah was no longer an innocent young girl.

Among the passengers was little Rita Stokes, seven
years old, almost the same age as Gianni, and Deborah
quickly made friends with her, telling her stories and listening to her artless prattle about what Mama said, and
what her rich aunt in Barbados owned, and what her nurse
Miss King promised her if she would be a good girl. Deborah made a sketch for Rita of her favorite doll Amanda,
amusing herself by making the portrait both accurate and
deceptive, giving Amanda the life and personality of a real
child, tilting the head slightly in the way a wax doll can't,
giving her cheek the texture of skin, putting a sparkle of
mischief in her eyes. Rita was utterly satisfied. Then Deborah unpacked her watercolors and painted Rita wearing
her pink Sunday bonnet, a privilege negotiated with both
Mama and Miss King, hedged about with provisions for the
care and return of this important hat unharmed. It made
Deborah think of Katy.

Mrs. Stokes accepted the charming portrait of her
daughter with delight and seemed to warm up to Deborah,
seeking to sit with her at meals and in the saloon; her attention became somewhat unwelcome as she prattled
sweetly about what she had told Rita, the clever things
little Eric had done, her concerns about baby Olga's snif-
fles, how Mr. Stokes had died, and how difficult it was to
manage the nurse, who was always spoiling the children

with promises and bribes. The only real cloud in her mind was worry about what her sister might think of her. This was an issue that drew worried lines in her otherwise smooth, open brow, but she would soon dismiss it only to re-open it, like a thief trying to count, while also concealing, his booty.

Whenever possible, Deborah avoided these attentions by spending her time leaning on the ship's railing, the bright wind full in her face, gazing at the return of the astounding blue sea as they drew closer to the heart of the tropics. She watched as the sea became impossibly darker, bluer, brighter. Hours passed for her in a trance, carried by the infinite tide of time, lost in imagining what would be found, sometimes unthinking, sometimes wondering how Gianni would like her, if he would be uncomfortable with this new white mother, wondering if he knew and how she would tell him, what he would be losing and gaining as his life was so completely changed. She wanted him to have been loved, but not too well. She wanted him to have felt her absence, to have felt a void she could fill. She counted the days at first, then the hours, in company with the glint of sunlight on the shifting crystalline facets of the waves.

She failed to hear, then failed to credit, the rumors that Mt. Pelée was acting up, spewing smoke and ashes, filling the rivers with steaming mud. A sugar factory had been lost to the flood, they said, washed away into the sea. The inhabitants of the village of Prêcheur had flocked to their church and, in what was said to be almost a miracle, had been saved. An earthquake was feared. The gentlemen on board conferred among themselves with stupidly solemn faces about the cables coming to the ship from the authorities in St. Pierre. They pestered the captain and reassured the ladies in hearty tones. Then the passengers' alarm turned to the unaccountable rise and fall of the ship's barometric readings. On the night before they were to arrive, a sudden storm blew up out of nowhere to batter the ship with screaming winds and towering waves that seemed to arrive from all sides at once to pitch the ship in every direction, so that the usual tactics for surviving heavy seas were rendered useless. The passengers were all sent below to wait it out.

I have not come this far to die at sea, Deborah thought. *These men will take us safe to harbor.* And she found herself humming the song the Blimpton sisters had sung in church, "Like Noah's weary dove"—and then the part about the safety of the ark in the sea of fire, and every longing satisfied, but she couldn't remember quite how it went, so she gave up and lapsed into the litany beating in her heart, almost drowning out the scream of the storm. *Tomorrow, I will see him tomorrow, tomorrow, tomorrow* until she lost any sense of what the word meant and dozed intermittently, one foot jammed between mattress and bed frame to anchor her as the ship writhed in the boiling sea.

The morning of May 8th found the *Roraima* already in St. Pierre harbor, having anchored just before dawn in the company of other ships, all there to deliver goods and passengers, taking care of the business of Martinique, bringing in supplies and carrying away its riches of rum and fruit to the rest of the world. Little fishing boats bobbed between the larger vessels while the fishermen coiled their ropes and checked their nets.

Deborah woke early and made her way to the railing, her step light as though she were dancing. She felt life rising within her heart and limbs and soul. Every detail, every human face and petty concern that had populated her vision, every intermediate moment could be disregarded and dismissed. She would be reunited with her child at last and redeem everything that had been wrested from her by

Great-Aunt Charity's extortion and her own calculated compliance.

She leaned on the ship's railing and held her face out to catch the scent of home. *Like Noah's weary dove*, she thought. But the scent was not of fruit and frangipani and rum, as she expected. The air from the island had a sharp, ashy smell that burned in the back of her throat. St. Pierre was not as bright and brave a city as she remembered. Its colors were faded, muted, as though a smear of gray had been added to temper its brilliant palette. At first, she thought it a trick of memory, the vividness of her childhood vision now darkened by the drab mind of experience, but she had always trusted her eyes, and the city was different, as though coated with an early morning frost, its spirit depressed.

A plume of white steam rose from the fog that veiled Mt. Pelée, and then a second cloud formed above the peak, boiling up and forming a dirty brown cloud shaped like a cauliflower, growing to giant proportions that defied reality, that ripped apart the sky. The air shivered as though stirred by an invisible hand, and a groaning roar bellowed out, unbearably loud and threatening. Ash began to fall on deck, then hot stones pelting down added to the din.

She heard the captain's bell ring, a light clang over the deep thunder, and the steward urged Deborah down to the saloon for a farewell breakfast, suggesting that a cup of tea would be soothing and relieve the unpleasantness of the harsh air and the unaccountable debris from the mountain. Disembarking would be delayed some hours in any event, while the shipments for Santa Lucia, stowed inconveniently in the way of St. Pierre's, could be sorted out. Of course, the gritty air was deplorable, but the port authorities were reassuring; the volcano had quieted down for several days. One could rest assured that the worst was over; there was no cause for the ladies to be alarmed despite the curling white smoke that rose from Pelée like a lamb's fleece or the brown billowing cloud that rose from the mountaintop, taller than the mountain itself, improbably dwarfing the sky and blocking the sun. They would all be more comfortable below.

Deborah descended reluctantly to the saloon, fear making her steps unsteady, unable to feel her feet, her heart rattling as she stumbled downward. She tried to know what was happening, why the world had gone wrong, why the air had turned to powdery ash, to falling stones. She turned back for one last desperate glance at St. Pierre, hoping to make sense of the jerky movement of people on the crowded quay, to have that moment of relief when a seeming threat resolves into the safe and familiar. Just a shadow, after all. Just the wind. Villette would have brought Gianni along in the cart. If she looked hard enough, she would discern which one was the child she had come over the ocean, through the years, to claim. But the rest of the passengers, eager for their breakfast and exclaiming over the unforeseen excitement, were on her heels, urging her forward down the steps.

She was about to turn away when the mountain exploded.

With the sound of a hundred shrieking freight trains, a monstrous cloud of black fire filled with hundreds of lightning bolts erupted from the side of Mt. Pelée and rolled down its ravines, swallowing the island as Deborah stared, not stopping at the harbor, but threatening to overcome the ship. It was unthinkable, not of this world. The ship was bombarded with burning stones that struck her face, and the passengers behind her screamed and pushed at her so that she lost her balance and tumbled the rest of the way down the stairs. The weight of the scrambling bodies that fell on top of her pressed her down, burying her in a welter of clothing and burning human flesh.

Deborah couldn't move. She couldn't catch her breath. The air was unbearably hot, and the smell of burning rock choked her. She was horrified by the roaring black fire cloud and the incessant hail of rocks. She heard the screams and groans of the other passengers and smelled them burning, the smell of a hot death surrounding, entering, and destroying them, making the air a fiery poison that could not be breathed, could not be avoided. She was drowning in blackness. She was blinded by the pitch-black air all around her as she struggled to escape the fierce atmosphere.

She found a small pocket of air in folds of clothing, hot but not deadly, and she sheltered there as long as she could bear the weight of the other passengers. When the air had cleared a little and she had caught her breath, she struggled out from under the human haystack that entombed her. She could see where the ceiling of the lounge had disappeared, and a fire raged on the stairs where she had lately stood. Among the bodies that had fallen, some were still, others moving feebly, trying to crawl to some non-existent relief, but there was nowhere to go. They cried out for water, but when an unrecognizable man with a charred face brought them some, most could not drink it, choking when it trickled into the ruined throats that had swallowed the fire.

Rita Stokes lay whimpering with her face buried in the skirts of her moaning nurse. Mrs. Stokes lay next to them with her other two children in her arms, both dead, the mother silent and soon to die. Deborah struggled to her feet. White ash fell and covered them all, the dead, the injured, and the dying, so the only color came from the burning world. The ocean itself was on fire, flickering with blue and yellow flames in the black cloud that surrounded everything, adding the smell of burning rum to the brutal stench. The smaller boats were gone; the other ships were burning as they foundered amid orange flames rising above the hellish sea.

Deborah realized then that she was burning inside her clothes and screamed as the pain overcame her and she fell. She felt herself being lifted by another pair of arms, one of the crewmen, who laid her gently on the less damaged foredeck, next to an ash-coated man, ghostly white. She realized that there were more bodies laid out beyond him in a row, and then another was placed next to her, like pastel pencils in a box, but all the same dusty white except where a few had bled, injured by something other than the fire-cloud or the fire that still burned. She heard Rita's voice but couldn't call to her. She was able to drink some water when it was offered.

"I'm not dead," she said to the gray goblin face above her. "Please don't bury me at sea because I am not dead."

"Rest easy, lady," he said in a voice savaged by the smoke. "They'll be sending a rescue boat soon enough."

She closed her burning eyes at this assurance and let the crying and choking of the survivors, the shouts of the crewmen, the crackle of the fire that burned around them merge into a frenzied song, passing into the dark unconsciousness of trauma and exhaustion.

She opened her eyes again briefly to find herself swaying on a stretcher carried by shocked men with blackened, bleeding faces, eyes bloodshot and awash with horror. As they tilted her up to carry her onto the rescue ship, she saw patches of desolation through the black smoke, stretching out where St. Pierre had been. Black stubs of tree trunks obtruded through the rubble; fires raged across the hellish plain where the city had stood, flaming up across the black hills. The unrecognizable streets were buried in ash, veiled in a black vapor that drifted through the ruins. In the heaving ocean, patches of rum were burning blue.

The smell of burning rock and flesh and rum filled the air. Bodies and groups of bodies and parts of bodies floated derelict on the burning water, their shapes gray and black and ghastly amid the stew of wreckage. She saw the ship itself was burned and still burning, saw the lines of corpses laid out on the foredeck, and then saw nothing. The blackness was complete.

7

~ *La Catastrophe* ~

Coming alive was a slow process for Deborah, slow, painful, confusing, full of turns and reverses, elusive thoughts, laudanum dreams, surprising bouts of fury, despondence, and denial, lost memories, memory regained and memory refused, returning energies of the body, pain, pain, sorrow, and fog. The unease in her mind swelled to a stinging fear, a panic that dissipated as quickly as it developed but left a compelling message. Something was wrong. Something was horribly wrong. The world had ended, she had lost everything, and she was still alive, and that was horribly wrong.

The whitewashed walls promised cool relief to her eyes, but the damp heat was unrelenting, and the air hung in place despite the fan that turned slowly overhead, failing to stir the soup of hot air. She thought she must still be in the islands by the steamy heat and the smell of green things that hovered beneath the odor of carbolic and human rot, which would have told her only that she was in a hospital somewhere. She recognized the Martiniquean rhythm of the noise coming in through the open, uncurtained window, the wheels on cobblestone, the birds, the sea. Inside her head was a tense, uncomfortable silence, like a coming storm, a black cloud blotting out the sky. Faces had blurred above her from time to time, and she thought once that Katy was there, then her mother, though, even in her delirium, she knew it wasn't so. Voices chattered meaninglessly like parakeets gathered in the dusk, or they knifed through her silence to command her to drink. She understood almost nothing at first except the water held to her lips, a smooth hand on her brow, and the sense of loss and horror.

She was afraid they would quit giving her water if they knew she was dead. *French. I must say "merci" so they will know I'm still alive.* She couldn't tell if she had said it aloud or only intended to, and then she slept again, but with a stronger spirit, believing that she would solve the problem of what was wrong, why she was weeping, what burned across her left cheek and cut into her arm, the bitter ashes in her throat, at the back of her nose.

She woke again, turning her face away from the spoon held to her lips. "English," she said, meaning to say that she could not understand French, could not think of the right words to ask the unformed questions that made her head ache, could not tell what she had to tell in any language other than her native tongue. Again, "English," she said.

"Not at all," came a harsh voice. "Both mother and father hailed from Dundee. I'm a Scot born and bred. Are we waking up then?"

Deborah struggled weakly to sit up, aided by a strong arm at her back and a simultaneous brisk pillow fluffing. The woman's breath smelt of onions, whiskey, and peppermints, her green eye gauging the patient's condition, seeing first her returning confidence, and then the returning memory, as Deborah's eyes sprang open, stretched with fear. The black cloud, the disappearance of St. Pierre, the black plains flickering with fire that replaced the city, the buildings in flame, the ship.

"The city, all the city," she asked. "Did it happen? Is it all gone?"

"My name is Nurse Fyffe. You are in the military hospital in Fort-de-France. Doctor will be here later to talk with you. And I believe he has a cable from the States to

deliver as well. Till then, just rest and have some porridge.
We'll be needing our strength."

"Are they all dead?"

Nurse Fyffe hesitated, but the patient seemed strong
enough to bear it, and there was no gentle way to break the
news. Let the poor creature cry her heart out. Best to get
over the worst so the healing could begin. "Yes, Mrs. Huntworth," she said. "Every soul of them, the whole city of St.
Pierre and half the countryside around."

The darkness that closed in on Deborah at hearing
these words was not the coming of blessed unconsciousness, but the return of memory, of the blackness, the falling stones, the smoke, the fire on the water, the burning
ship, the shrieks of the merciless mountain, the shrieks of
the burning humans who breathed its exhalation, who
swallowed its fire. In that moment when she had looked
back over her shoulder, standing on the stairs of the
Roraima, that last moment before the world ended, she had
seen the death of everything, a city, a dream, all those people, and that child, her Gianni, all ruined and burned,
erased and gone forever. There could be no coming back
from such a complete, black death.

For just a hopeful moment, she wondered if that horrible vision were true or if perhaps she had gone mad and
was confined in this hospital until her wits returned so that
she could continue to St. Pierre and claim her son. Then
the truth again threatened to crush her, weighing down on
her, making her small, drawing her down into a burning
point of pain. All gone. All gone. All gone. And though she
repeated it, she couldn't make the phrase dissolve into
nonsense. Everything was gone. She drew the sheet over
her head and wept, curled into that first posture of life, before comfort is needed, before consciousness brings its
penalties, before knowledge of good and evil has granted

its ambiguous gifts of experience, responsibility, and help-lessness. She wept. Even as her body expelled cries and groans, tears and incoherent words, she was reminded of the first time she had wept for Gianni after the endless pains of his birth night, but this time there was no Tante Charity to hate, no defiance that could finally take her back to her child. It was not human malice that had taken him away this time, but a greater cruelty. And there was no bar-gaining, no waiting for time to pass, no miracle that would end in reunion. Time had betrayed her. As she buried her face in her hands, even in her grief she felt the bandage on one side of her face, from chin to brow, and the pain be-neath the bandage began to bloom, watered by the vio-lence of her grief.

She slept briefly, then awakened to a regular throb-bing in her face and left arm, also wrapped in gauze, stained an unpleasant yellow. At least she knew the worst now and could begin to understand, to color in the blankness, per-haps in some wretched way to heal—scarred, broken, ruined, and lost, but still perversely alive, still carving her path through time. There would be nothing to live for, she thought, and she wanted to make that thought take form in the world. She wanted to say, describe, and commemorate the loss and pain and horror of what had happened. She wanted to bear witness.

"We haven't touched our porridge. Eat it up, or Doctor will be displeased with us."

Deborah obediently lifted the spoon of slimy gray por-ridge and put it in her mouth. It was wonderful. She had worked her way through the bowl when Nurse Fyffe re-turned with the small French doctor, well dressed, his dark beard flowing into a bifurcated goatee that reached his tie.

"You have the very fortune," he said in strangled Eng-lish. "The blessings, *blessés*, the hurts of Madame are not grand, not serious. All goes well."

When Deborah laughed, he looked concerned and took her wrist in his elegant little fingers, timing the beating of her pulse.

"You have lost family?" he asked.

Deborah nodded.

"My condolences," he said, as though the matter could be closed with that phrase. One was told that it was the English way, and presumably, Americans were even less emotional. "Your visage and arm burn at the catastrophe, without doubt." He looked inquiringly at her over his glasses frames. "But all will be well in the time of the good God, yes? You comprehend?"

"Yes," she said.

"You have a great fortunate woman," he repeated, nodding to himself. "Your child also will be in health."

Deborah knew it wasn't true. She knew that one small child, however loved, could not survive the destruction she had seen. Surely all the children of St. Pierre, loved and unloved, were dead. But the doctor had said, had said what he said. Deborah's heart froze and then beat wildly. "My child? My Gianni?" She clutched the doctor's lapels and almost shook him. "What are you saying?"

"Please, Madame Stokes, I beg you!" He freed himself from her hands and smoothed his rumpled front. "Young Rita rests with her *bonne*, Mademoiselle King. They sleep in the next compartment. You soon see your infant."

He was astonished when she unleashed a stream of curses in mixed English and French, cursing him for the naked dog of an idiot, a shit-covered pig with a head of cheese, the despicable son of a diseased *putain*. He withdrew hastily to confer with Nurse Fyffe, who had hurried in to settle the patient. Soon, he approached again, this time with her chart held like a shield in front of his chest.

"My pardon," he said stiffly, studying the file as though it were the offending party. "Madame...Untvort, I believe."

Deborah turned her face away and closed her eyes, the dissipation of the adrenaline that had inflamed her blood sending her down into spiraling unconsciousness again. Pain disturbed her sleep, beating a staccato rhythm that suggested words, a chant, and she couldn't understand, even though it might have been a message, could have been instructions to replace the dream that had ended. She moved restlessly in her sleep, turning onto her injured side and gasping at the sudden pain. She woke to find that a little ward attendant had brought her tea and toast on a tray and stood staring at her with scared eyes, at this wild white woman who didn't die like everyone else and who cursed the doctor.

"*Merci*," Deborah said and sat up to take stock of her surroundings; the silent figures stretched out on the six other beds in the long room, unmoving. She realized that she and the attendant would be the only creatures there to see the sun rise the next morning. All of the bodies were either dying or already dead. It was only the latest insult to her sanity, and she turned away. The whole thing struck her at that moment as a farce, the hateful trick of a hateful God. She decided that she would not be destroyed. She would live, and God could deal with it.

Someone had left a cable addressed to her on the bedside table, and she took it up, seeing that it came from St. Louis, from Richards, who, she thought, must have relished sending it, whether he knew it or not. It read, with typical telegraphic terseness:

Regret Act of God. Plantation destroyed. Bank destroyed. Inheritance gone. House price disappointing. Awaiting instructions. Richards.

But first, Deborah must take stock of her situation,

beginning with her physical state. She pushed aside the thin sheet, seeing that her lower limbs were still there, evidently unharmed; she wiggled her toes and stretched a little, then more. Her left arm and her face had been burned and both throbbed, but the rest of her seemed as though it would work. She drew up her legs and swiveled, planting her feet on the floor. She waited until the swimming sensation lessened and then stood, holding firmly to the bedside table. Then she sat, unsure if her watery muscles could be trusted, flexing and stretching, making a closer connection between body and will. When she stood the second time, she felt secure in her power to go, do, move, support her intentions.

Deborah walked to the window and leaned on the windowsill. In the street below, a crowd of islanders jostled and surged, looking out towards the seafront, waiting for news, for sight of relatives who would not appear, for assistance in this disaster. The faces in the crowd were strained, eyes darting in an effort to see, to understand *la catastrophe*. Women cried, and the children were silent and hid among their mothers' skirts. The street itself was smeared with ash where the bare feet of the people had passed, and in the distance, the beautiful, horrible mountain Deborah had longed to see was hidden in gray clouds, the mountain that had exploded and killed a city. The air held only the slightest taste of the volcano's black, pitiless breath. Fort-de-France had been spared. It seemed only St. Pierre had been destroyed. Only.

"Back to bed with you. It's time for medicine." Nurse Fyffe again, briskly giving orders.

"Why aren't there more people here in the hospital?" Deborah asked. "Is Rita Stokes really in the next room? Are all these people dying?"

"After you are feeling better in a few days, you can

visit her yourself if you wish." Nurse Fyffe hustled her back to bed as though medicine could only be efficacious if administered to a patient lying down or at least sitting in her proper place. "Goodness knows that nanny is useless with her, poor thing."

"So the passengers of the *Roraima* are all dead? Mrs. Stokes and her little ones?" How could it be otherwise? Deborah remembered the bodies lined up on the foredeck, the cries for water, the choking, and the cessation of choking.

"It's not to be mentioned in front of the child."

"Did they die? Yes or no?"

Nurse Fyffe was reminded flickeringly of her first month of nursing school when the instructors had been uniformly unforgiving and stern. One of the benefits of her profession had been the power to assume the same kind of authority over her patients, but Mrs. Huntworth's demeanor recognized no such hierarchy. She had seemed such a soft lady, but Regina Fyffe had learned to obey authority and had been secretly impressed with Deborah's fracas with the doctor, one of a breed nurses are trained to treat with reverence, especially to their faces.

"Yes, Mrs. Huntworth. Only a few of the crew are in the next ward, poor fellows, and not likely to survive, most of them. And the blacks on the ground floor, still coming in on foot. And they're all half-hysterical; it's more than we can do to handle them, so don't expect to be treated like a queen. We're doing the best we can."

"Not from St. Pierre?" Deborah felt a familiar lift of spirits, a rising hope that ended each time in bitter disappointment, like a wild animal leaping to freedom, only to be jerked back by cruel chains, falling back bruised and beaten, trying again.

"No one from St. Pierre. How could there be? It was

completely leveled by the volcano. No one from the hills, either. Morne Orange was spared, but the rest of the north is gone. All those lovely homes as well."

Deborah sipped from the spoon, only half of the dose offered, enough to soften the pain and still allow her to act, then dismissed a temporarily chastened Nurse Fyffe with a brief thanks. She wanted to see Rita, a living child who had lost her mother and who must be very much in need of a friend. Deborah could feel her energies returning, a humming current that made her want to move away from this white room with black bed frames, the only color the sickening yellow bandage and the slice of gray-blue sky at the top of the window.

She would be scarred, she knew, perhaps disfigured, but she found that idea less distressing than she would have anticipated. Both of her eyes seemed to work. She could walk and would get stronger. Her grief would be a constant companion for the rest of her days, agitating, stupefying, disabling, and constricting, coloring her life, she thought, with an ashy film. She would mourn later, again and again, all of her days, but now she would find the child, any child, who still lived.

Two rows of empty beds stretched to both blank walls of the hospital room next to Deborah's, appearing as though some sinister force had extracted the patients, or dissolved, or eradicated them. Perhaps the dead had been removed. But in the nearest bed, Rita Stokes sat with a crumpled pillow clasped tightly in her arms, her eyes ringed with dark bruises. Her torso, neck, and arms were wrapped in white bandages seeping yellow, like Deborah's. Her long, fine hair, which had been so pleasurable to paint where it had ringleted down from under her Sunday bonnet only days earlier, was now burnt to black stubble. Deborah reached up reflexively and felt the scratch and prickle and grease on her own scalp where the fire had burned and some unguent had been applied. Rita reached out desperately when she saw Deborah, and Deborah flew to her, collecting and claiming her, her fellow sufferer, her mirror image, her companion, her living child. They held each other as a drowning sailor clings to a lifeline thrown to save him, like the dazed children of disaster they were, and wept together.

"Oh, Mrs. Huntworth," Rita said when she had stopped sobbing. "Where is my mama? Where did they all go?"

After a long moment to find the words, Deborah answered her as gently as she could, remembering her own childhood loss and Katy's calm manner. "They have all died, my dear. Most of the people on our ship, and also in the city we saw from the ship remember? You said it looked like a toy city. Those people are also dead, killed by the volcano."

Rita wept again, but now Deborah was the adult who comforted her, who was wiser and would know what to do.

"Are they all in heaven now?"

"Some are, I imagine."

"Is my mama and my brother and my baby sister and my Amanda doll in heaven?"

"Absolutely," Deborah promised.

"Miss King isn't in heaven, though," Rita said, and at first Deborah supposed that she had consigned her nurse to hell, then realized that a form lying in the next bed, so small and still as to be unnoticeable, was Miss King, bandaged much like the two of them, but with most of her scalp covered as well. "She almost wakes up if I touch her, but she only cries, so I'm letting her sleep. And now that you're here, I have someone to talk to, so that's good."

"I'm just going to get my few things," Deborah said.

"I'm all alone in my room, too, with no company. So just wait, and I'll be right back. I'll be back in just a minute, so pick out a bed for me while I'm gone."

Back in her own room, Deborah found Nurse Fyffe facing her empty bed, hands on hips, on the verge of expostulation on the foolishness of patients who will not stay where they are put, but her runaway charge interrupted before the words could be spoken.

"I'm moving to the next room to stay with Rita. Her nurse is too injured to be of any use to her, and she shouldn't be alone. I need you to arrange a few matters for me, clothing for Rita and Miss King and me, nothing fancy but include a change of linen and some kind of hats for our poor heads. And a doll for Rita—she must have a doll. And paper and paints, pastels, colored pencils, whatever you can find."

"Mrs. Huntworth! You can't simply change beds willy-nilly. It's against hospital rules! It's highly irregular!"

"My dear Nurse Fyffe," Deborah said, as gently as she had spoken to Rita. "The circumstances are anything but regular, so I imagine the rules can bend. Oh, and I need you to arrange a cable for me to my man of business in the States. He will forward me funds, and I can reimburse you for your expenses and your trouble."

She took up the message she had set aside earlier when it seemed too much to cope with, and with a hand only a little shaky, wrote a crisp sentence or two on the back, requesting that Richards send her funds that she supposed would be more than adequate for her needs while she recuperated and decided where to go and what to do there. She would send for the remainder when she had settled, or stopped, or run out of money, or found the other edge of the world.

"My injuries are starting to hurt again. Perhaps you

could bring fresh bandages and more of that lovely medicine and tea and lunch to my new room. Rita looks as though she could use some nourishment as well."

Rita had picked out the very best of the beds on offer, the one across the aisle from hers, best because they would see each other when they first woke up in the morning and sat up in bed. She was glad to have the diversion of a shared meal, almost a picnic, with Mrs. Huntworth. But first Nurse Fyffe must change their bandages, a process that revealed to Deborah the grotesque wound on Rita's little face, as though her cheek had been scooped out by hot talons, a still oozing expanse, mottled red and purple, striated, almost impossible to believe even when revealed.

"It hurts. It hurts very bad," Rita whimpered.

Nurse Fyffe's impulse to offer brisk advice was stopped by Deborah's quick response.

"Yes, it does. It hurts."

The sight of Rita's marked face and, even more, Rita's distress when she saw Deborah's, told her enough. She would figure out what her ruined face meant in the time to come. For now, they worked their way through the tepid, bland soup and the soft bread brought up from the kitchen while Nurse Fyffe roused poor Miss King enough to treat her wounds. Her face was perhaps less affected than theirs, and her arm had the same ripples in the burnt flesh as theirs had, but the skin seemed blacker and the flesh ashy dead. As soon as the pain of the handling grew less, Miss King fell back into a sounder sleep. She had not spoken. She had not seemed to know where she was or what had happened.

After lunch, Deborah and Rita, newly dosed and with their hands and the uninjured parts of their faces washed, napped curled together in Deborah's bed, where they would sleep for the next two nights to Nurse Fyffe's indignation. She had sent the cable and brought them fresh clothing, as requested, ready when they were able to get about a little better, possibly in a week. The other, more frivolous errands had been placed in the hands of Élodie, the little ward maid, who regarded these naughty patients with fascination and respect. First the doctor, then the formidable Nurse Fyffe. Americans, Élodie thought, were a brave and reckless people.

Her shopping for the Americans was less successful than Nurse Fyffe's. Neither a fine white béké doll nor artists' supplies would be easy to come by, most likely could only be obtained by special order from France, a task Élodie could not possibly perform any more than she could live at the bottom of the blue sea. She did her best, though, hoping that her efforts would guard against that remarkable American wrath.

She combed the marketplace, where the usually strident sellers, now subdued with sorrow, fear, and exhaustion, were offering their goods: fruits, fish, rolls, spices, nets, and a few shell trinkets to give as love tokens. She resisted the calls of the market women and continued her search until at last she found a doll for the little girl at the back of the market where cloth goods were sold. She cautiously entered the grand store where the white people sent their foremen and servants for house repair supplies, and there she found paint and brushes, paper, a box of charcoal sticks, and a watercolor set for the little girl. She hurried back to the hospital with her bundles to catch the Americans before they had supper.

Deborah was concerned when she saw the doll: black cloth face, yellow turban, its eyes buttons and its mouth embroidered with red thread, nothing like the pale charms and pastel dress of the lost Amanda, but Rita was immediately enchanted and retreated with her new acquisition into the childhood world of play, so real at the beginning of life and so hard to re-enter once the work of the world has imposed itself. Deborah spread out Élodie's purchases on her behalf, so ready to begin that she was sure she could work with whatever was there: black enamel, probably used for fretwork and fancy iron gates, red enamel, small cans of white, sea-blue, and yellow-peach paint for the houses of the black Martiniqueans, who appreciated color. The charcoal sticks would be handy for a different project than the one she could feel approaching. A child's paint set completed the inventory of media. One large brush, such as might be used to paint a wall, two smaller brushes appropriate for woodwork or cabinetry, and the tiny child's brush were the available tools. No canvas, no drawing paper, but a roll of newsprint, adequate for sketching. With its horror and suffering, this disaster was far too big for paper. She would start with a black background to cover the blank white wall at the end of the room. This wall, so hygienically empty, called to her.

Deborah studied the space. She wanted a big picture, wider than her arms could stretch. There was the risk of running out of paint, but she could work from the center out. Then if there was black paint left, she could feather out the edges. The wall was rectangular, but her sense of the painting was not. She would see how it developed.

Rita had to tug at her gown several times to pull her attention away.

"Did you see my doll, Mrs. Huntworth? Did you see how Élodie gave me my doll?"

"Of course, my dear. She is perfect, and her dress so bright! What will you name her?"

"She already has a name! It's Amanda, it's Amanda, and she didn't die. It's Amanda; only she's burned. I'm going to put medicine on her every day to make her better.

Of course, she will look different now because of the fire. So she wasn't in heaven after all."

Deborah was scarcely listening. She could get the shiny black background laid down in broad strokes, starting in the middle, so it would be dry enough when she was ready to start the white outline of the dead ship. And if the white and black bled together, that could be interesting, too. She could work with it. She pried open the lid of the black paint and began sloshing paint on the wall, first in the center, pushing the paint out to the edges, letting the stucco add airy texture where the brush ran out of paint, creating an impenetrable smoke cloud dissipating into white air. The screaming blackness that had seemed boundless and endless would now be seen as monstrous but mercifully finite.

She outlined the dying ship plunging at a slight angle through the blackness, bound toward the bottom left corner of the black sea, as though seen from above by a cormorant, though no real sea bird could have possibly hovered there. Now for the burning. Deborah took the red paint and added red spray springing flamelike from the furrow plowed by the ship in the burning sea. Next, waves outlined in white, lit with red and peach and purple flecks floating on the uneasy surface like sparks. Red and peach tongues of fire curled up and around three corners of the engine house. On the black deck, the dead were to lie side by side. Perhaps on white shapes like cots or like coffins rather than just on black, where they would disappear from the eye. White shapes would make them central to the composition, stark white in the middle of the lurid sea.

Deborah laid down the white shapes, which seemed to float upward from the surface, an effect she hadn't anticipated, but that seemed right.

"Amanda and I made a picture for you, Mrs.

Huntworth," Rita said, tugging at her, sheets of paper bunched in her hand. She had painted princesses and flowers and rabbits and houses with smoking chimneys and angels.

"Those are lovely, my dear," Deborah said, though she could hardly, at that moment, tear herself away from the picture of ruin she had begun. "Here," she said, moving the medicine cabinet closer to the wall and lifting Rita onto it. "Stand here and make pictures on the white bits—of the people who died on that boat. Can you do that?"

"Nurse Fyffe is going to be very cross with us," Rita pointed out.

"Doesn't matter," Deborah said. "I need this."

They painted together, Rita making first Mama in her blue hat, then Eric with a frowning mouth because it wasn't fair, and then baby Olga, all the same size, all with blue dots for eyes. As she painted each one, she chattered, telling them not to cry, that Miss King would get better, and singing "Oh, the baby" over and over as she painted Olga. She added her dead papa smoking his pipe, its tiny bowl filled with glowing embers that seemed to be in league with the killing fire of the ship, an unexpected effect.

Deborah used three of the white shapes, one for Villette of the yellow turban, one for Sanson, who seemed to be sleeping, and the last one for an unknown brown boy, turned away on his side, unseeable even to the artist's eye. The mother, the son, the invisible ghost. The crone, the absent father, the dead son. She had intended to include herself, but she found no place in this picture for her image. The habit of longing that had kept her tied to the dream of return would not serve her any longer, though it would die slowly. She finished with her signature: DH.

Deborah lifted Rita down, and together they backed away from the mural, almost to the far wall to see what had happened there, to drink in the whole breath-taking effect. Deborah was deeply pleased, and she felt for an instant like dashing herself into the wall, attacking the blackness and pulling it into her body, embracing and swallowing, containing and owning. Rita was dazzled by the bigness of it, and the unrestrained messiness, and the fact that an adult had been the ringleader. But she was afraid again as she had been on that burning deck, afraid of the unleashed fire and now, afraid of the sadness. She burst into tears, and Deborah hugged her with one arm, but she didn't take her eyes from the picture. *La Catastrophe.* She was exhausted, trembling, and marked with paint; her hospital gown, her bandages, her hands where she had pushed at the paint and raked fine lines into the fire with her fingernails. Rita was no more presentable. The air was heavy with fumes. The mural loomed into the room.

This scene met Nurse Fyffe's horrified eyes as she bustled in, leading a group of gentlemen, spectacled, whiskered, tweedy, a delegation newly arrived in Martinique on a mission of fact-finding and scientific investigation into the volcanic eruption. They goggled at the sight of the wild-eyed, panting madwoman, the weeping child held close to her side, and above all, the violent mural, which had the effect of rushing towards one, merciless and inescapable. Except for Nurse Fyffe's short bark of shock, everything was frozen into silence, motionless, caught for an instant in the net of the unthinkable.

It was at this moment that Miss King sat up, opened her eyes, and screamed.

8

~ *The Grave* ~

It took Nurse Fyffe several minutes to silence her screaming patient. It took a few minutes more to usher the distinguished gentlemen down the stairs to speak with the little doctor while she sorted out the rest. She had to promise George Kennan, the journalist among them, an opportunity to interview these survivors, assuming that he would give them time to recover, would not excite them or tire them out. Then she hastened to move the bedaubed and dazed Deborah back to her original room, though she was alone there, no dead or dying victims to keep her company.

Back in her bed, Deborah cried in long, choking sobs whose meaning she couldn't understand, whether relief or joy or unbearable longing, perhaps the first turn into the plummeting spiral of madness. She felt as though great clouds of black smoke were billowing out of her mouth, and she tried to stifle the eruption with her hands, to hide her inner darkness that threatened to fill the room. The long wound on her cheek had started burning as though the gauze had burst into dancing flame.

"Stop it! Stop it this instant, you damned bletherin' besom. Stop it, or I'll slap you silly!" The nurse's furious voice was loud enough to be heard over Deborah's cries. Both women were shocked into silence. Nurse Fyffe struggled to regain her professional tone. "You have terrified that child and made quite a mess for others to clean up. I expect you to be more responsible in the future, a grown woman like yourself. Now you quit your hysterics and take your medicine. I'll have no more trouble out of you!" The bandages were replaced with clean ones, properly daubed with picric acid, then laudanum was administered, and a pot of tea was ordered.

"You are to stay away from that child. Miss King has settled down now and can care for Rita best without your interference." The vein that snaked down Nurse Fyffe's forehead gave her a dangerous look. Deborah merely nodded. She would leave Rita to Miss King for now. She had never meant to hurt the child.

Élodie arrived with the tea and helped Deborah into a clean gown after removing the paint stains from her hands and face, even from her feet where the blackness had dripped. Her timid dabbing proved ineffectual, so Deborah, who had always been a messy painter, took the rag and turpentine from her hands and finished the job herself. At the same time, Élodie looked on in admiring terror, glad to be so close to this strange woman, to be at her side. The story of the painting, whether explained as an exorcism, the drawing up of power into the American woman, or her possession by the spirits of the newly dead, had flown through the ranks of the maids and orderlies. No one, not even the worst of the syphilitic or mad patients, had ever caused so much uproar and excitement.

Rita and Miss King were moved to a new room to escape the horrible picture and the paint fumes that made even Nurse Fyffe's level head swim a little. There Rita clung to her black Amanda doll and her nurse's side and refused to let go of either one. Her painty nightgown had to be changed one arm at a time so that she could keep her hold on Miss King's hand. Her bed was moved up against Miss King's so that she could rest peacefully in contact as they both dozed and woke and dozed again. Rita's pain increased, and she required more medication and care than she had needed before the disgraceful, unthinkable incident with Mrs. Huntworth had drawn her out of her safe bed, creating such a shock to her already weakened health.

In future years, Rita Stokes would not remember the mural at all, would remember instead that a disaster-maddened woman had set fire to the hospital, and she and Miss King had to be rescued. She would remember Mrs. Huntworth only as a nice lady on the ship, one who had perished with the rest.

~~~~~~~

George Kennan, dispatched by *The Outlook* to report on the Martinique disaster, stood in the room now emptied of nurse and patients and surveyed the remarkable mural, considering the scene he had happened upon so unexpectedly. He remained there, lost in study of Deborah's creation, the intrusion of the burning ship into the room, the deep fiery gashes in the ocean, the dead placed in such orderly rows on the black deck. He wanted to know whether this depiction was the product of genius, a vision driven by madness, or an act of desperation. After a while, it seemed to him that it was all three and still a mystery.

When workmen came in with ladders and buckets of white paint to undo what had been so remarkably done, he wanted to stop them. But it seemed impossible that such a picture could be covered up with mere paint, or, more practically, that the hospital would be willing to apply as many coats as it would take. Kennan supposed that even if they succeeded, any patient assigned to this room in the future would be unlikely to rest easy, would be unconsciously troubled by the danger bursting invisibly from that wall. Kennan's business, though, was with spoken accounts of the disaster survivors.

The poor fellows who had manned the *Roraima* were laid out in a long ward at the end of the hall, where those least injured told Kennan everything they could recall of their experiences, of trying to save Captain Muggah, who was giving orders to save the passengers even with his face burned off and only his voice, though smoke-roughened, still recognizable. One crewman said he had seen the captain leap into the burning sea and lost there, though another thought perhaps he had been picked up by a raft.

"The sure thing is that the captain's not alive today, not as badly burned as he was."

The seamen related their early efforts to quench the burning decks with bucketsful drawn from the sea, only to have the rum-laced water flare up in tall blue flames, increasing the danger to all aboard. They had offered fresh water to the dying who begged for it so piteously, but their fire-sealed throats could not allow even a trickle or a drop to pass through. They had lost many a good fellow, the second mate's young son on his first voyage as a cabin boy, a fine captain, a fine ship, to the ravages of the firestorm. They asked anxiously after the passengers they had loaded onto the rescue ship and brought to Fort-de-France. Kennan was only able to tell them that, although most of those who had been removed from the *Roraima* had died on the way, he had seen the little girl and her nurse and another lady, all injured, suffering from shock and grief, but likely to live.

"The mother perhaps, Mrs. Stokes? Was it the child's mother?"

"No," Kennan said, "I am certain she is not the child's mother. Another lady."

By mid-afternoon, Deborah had napped and recovered her balance. She was thinking about her picture, the fierce intimacy of it. She felt as though in all of her work before that mural, she had been a girl playing at art, holding life at arm's length, as though a picture were a static thing contained on canvas. Now she felt her art to be a living, consequential entity unframed and bent on intrusion. She had previously created entertainment for the eyes, an ornament to experience rather than an extension of life's beating heart. "Please look at this," her earlier paintings had politely requested. "See what I see." With *La Catastrophe*, she had entered new territory, a place where she would challenge and implicate, grasp by the throat, and demand that her viewer not just look but feel, know, believe, experience, and respond. This, then, is what she had gained with the loss of everything.

Mr. George Kennan was ushered into Deborah's room by Nurse Fyffe. She had been hard to persuade but finally yielded to his request to interview this survivor, to record her version of the event so that he could write it up for his magazine. She was won over by his respectful manner, his long, drooping white moustache, and his interest in everything she had to say about managing a hospital under these difficult circumstances, with the Negro Ward crammed to bursting with the injured from outlying villages, and some who were just looking for a free bed and food. He wouldn't believe the trickery they could get up to and the foolishness of their heathen ways. The white survivors, those from the districts around St. Pierre, were mostly treated in the homes of Fort-de-France relatives or taken by boat to Dominica or St. Lucia. And the few who were housed in what was meant to be a military hospital, not a madhouse, were addled and unpredictable, as he had certainly seen for himself. Mr. Kennan sympathized.

After examining Mrs. Huntworth with a critical eye and determining that she was in her right mind again, Nurse Fyffe left them to it with a meaningful nod at

Kennan, though he realized as she bustled out of the room that he did not know the meaning she intended to convey. Kennan was not aware of any shared understanding of the now subdued lady who lay in bed, half-supported by pillows thrust under her shoulders. She appeared much tamer than the crazed painter he had first seen. Her arm was tightly wrapped to the elbow with the yellow stain of the medicine seeping through the weave in patches. From brow to chin, the side of her face was shrouded in gauze, with the eye half-covered but focused. Kennan felt a pang of compassion. A woman's face was her fortune, or so they said. What must be this young woman's suffering with the scars she would have to bear? Her looks would be ruined.

He knew, and his wife Lena sometimes reminded him, that his life, passed for the most part in the company of other men, often among strange people in foreign countries, had not prepared him to understand American womankind. But he was sorry for this young lady's great misfortune. He realized he needed to speak, so in a gentle voice, he introduced himself and requested a brief interview, offering to provide any assistance in his power.

Deborah recognized him as one of the gentlemen who had been treated to the spectacle of her mural and Miss King's shrill awakening.

"I suppose they have painted it over by now," she said. She saw from the look on his face that they had done so, and he seemed apprehensive as to how she would react, perhaps fearing a fit of hysterics.

"Art is fleeting," she said, with a slight shrug. "Didn't someone say that?"

"Longfellow," Kennan said. "Maybe Virgil before that." He drew closer to the side of her bed and continued. "Time is fleeting, though, not art. Art is long, according to the poets."

Deborah smiled. "It was not my wall to paint. I'm afraid I behaved badly, but I'm not at all sorry."

"As you know, Mrs. Huntworth," Kennan said, carefully setting his hat on the table next to the bed, taking a seat in the bedside chair, so their eyes were level, "I am here to report on the explosion of Mt. Pelée and the destruction of St. Pierre. And I must say that I learned a great deal about it from that picture of yours as if I had been a victim of the actual event. I wish the picture could have been preserved."

"It was not my wall," she repeated. "I just wanted to make the picture."

"Mrs. Huntworth," Kennan said again, "can you answer a few questions for me? To begin, tell me how you happened to be on that ship. What brought you to that fatal harbor at that very hour?"

"Oh, my story," Deborah said. "I hardly know myself." She had been grimly schooled for years by her great-aunt and by her own will to keep silent about the real story of her life, though she had longed many times to tell it. This gentleman was asking, but her exertions and stratagems and final victory had been blotted out. All that remained was sorrow and something too new for words.

"Perhaps you are not well enough as yet," Kennan suggested gently, but she waved her hand at him as though to clear his and her own confusion.

"I was on that ship," she said, "because I inherited a sugar plantation at the base of the mountain, of Mt. Pelée. I was going to be reunited with my son and live there, at least for a year or two. They were bringing him to St. Pierre harbor to meet me. I must have seen him in the crowd, but I couldn't pick him out. They were all moving about. He died there, and I saw the black cloud that killed him, that killed everyone. That tried to kill me."

The story of her disgrace, her delivery, the price she had paid, her ridiculous marriage, all of that meant nothing now. It seemed to have happened to a different woman, one who thought power could be achieved through strategy, that she could outsmart and outlast trouble and prevail in the end. She was no longer that woman. Yes, she was chastened, and grieving what seemed to have been a mirage. She was uprooted and alone in a foreign place. She was injured and in pain. She had been robbed and impoverished by this Act of God. And she had been enriched with an unsought gift—a new understanding of her art—though she would not tell him that. She would never tell anyone. "Was it worth it?" they might ask. And she would say, "It was not a bargain I made."

Instead, she told him about the voyage in simple terms, the various passengers, the blue sea, the rumors that flew around the *Roraima*. She remembered the horrible storm the night before their arrival and the wildly fluctuating barometer. The frosty look of ash-coated St. Pierre, the brightly dressed figures bobbing and dancing on the pier, the shiver, the unbelievably loud crack, and a black cloud full of lightning that blotted out the sun when the mountain blew up. Then the ship on fire and the dying, the falling rocks and horrid air, the shrieks of the victims and the roar all around, and the heroism of the seamen.

"The eruption happened in an instant, but the fire and destruction seemed to go on for hours. All the people in that bright city were killed, they say. Almost all of the people in the bay, on the ships and in the little boats."

Kennan asked her a few more questions about what she had seen of the explosion and its immediate aftermath, but she had been buried under a pile of people in the ship's lounge and had little to add. He could see that she was tiring.

"What will you do now, once you have recovered?"

"I suppose I will return to the States," Deborah said. "There is no one alive in Martinique for me. I know my estate was destroyed, though I keep thinking it may have somehow been spared."

"My colleagues and I are setting out to explore the outlying districts east of St. Pierre to assess the extent of the damage. I will certainly inform you if I hear anything about your estate."

"That is very kind," she said. "I would welcome any news."

"After we return, several of the gentlemen and I plan to charter a boat to take us to the site of St. Pierre to study the effects of the blast. I can give you a report on that trip as well if that will be helpful."

"No," Deborah said, sitting upright in the bed with a new energy. "Take me with you. I'll be much stronger then, and I have to see where he died, where they all died. I need to be there myself. I need to draw it."

Kennan drew back, alarmed. "This is not a sight for a young woman like yourself. You have already been through a dreadful experience. There is no need to suffer more. Besides, it's not an expedition for the general public. The party is made up of world-renowned scientists, experienced reporters, and intrepid explorers. I will describe it to you as best I can when we return, but I cannot in good conscience take a woman on a trip so dangerous."

"I'm intrepid," Deborah said, willing him to believe her. "I need to go. Promise me you will take me on the boat to St. Pierre when you get back."

"Think of those to whom your safety is of utmost importance," he cried.

"I have no family now. I have just this loss, this emptiness. I need to see where my son died."

He stared at her for a long while and saw in her eyes a steeliness, a strong will, and a firm command of herself, and he saw that he would end by relenting.

"Promise me that you will take me with you. I'm counting on you."

"Very well then," Kennan said, "against my better judgment; if the nurse says you are well enough and you still want to go when I return, I will allow you to come, as long as you bring an attendant."

"Promise me," Deborah said.

"On my word as a gentleman."

"Promise me on your word as a human being."

"I promise, then, on my word as a human being." When they shook hands, he felt her strength and was reassured that she would be up to the challenge.

That night she woke with Gianni's name soft in her mouth, Gianni, her baby. She wept quietly, this time not for the destruction of a city or the shock of the volcano's violence or the obliteration of the dream that had dominated her life. Instead, she mourned for a single child.

~~~~~~~

Deborah obtained clearance for the trip to St. Pierre from Nurse Fyffe through the simple expedient of informing her that she had been invited by Mr. Kennan to be one of the party and produce sketches of the ruins to supplement photographs he would take and the stereoscopes of his companion, Mr. Leadbetter. This was not true. She dressed for the first time in the clothes Nurse Fyffe had provided: a roomy shirtwaist and skirt, a wide-brimmed straw bonnet, and a black veil found in the nurses' station, part of an old-fashioned uniform left behind. Deborah accepted it without argument, knowing she would drape it back over the hat when she really needed to see.

Élodie had been chosen to accompany her, a duty she took very seriously. She armed herself with four flasks of water, four sandwiches, fruit, handkerchiefs, a thermos of tea, napkins, extra bandages and limewater, a shawl in case of chills, an umbrella, and a walking stick. She carried these along with the basket of art supplies she had wrested from Deborah as they left. She was the attendant. The American lady had only to walk carefully to the harbor, not tiring herself unduly, not being jostled by the thick crowd gathered at the seafront. Élodie led her gently through a throng of hungry, frightened people whose lives were disrupted, whose relatives were dead, who had heard that the refugees in Fort-de-France were being fed like kings and had congregated here in hopes of getting a share of the largesse.

Deborah could tell from the stiffness and distance between the figures of the men on the *Rubis* that her inclusion in the expedition had raised controversy. They had argued with Mr. Kennan, no doubt, that it was no place for a grieving, injured woman given to manic fits. It would only cause trouble and impair the ability of the scientific gentlemen to study the situation, making inferences and drawing conclusions. She would distract the journalists, who would be too concerned about her fragile state to do their jobs. Deborah determined that she would make no demands, not even to speak to Mr. Kennan beyond the requirements of courtesy. He had given her what she wanted and kept his word. That was all she asked. She would see where Gianni had died and been buried in the rubble and then make images of the dead city. She would cause no problems by weeping, fainting, throwing herself into the sea, or whatever other unaccountable behavior they might be anticipating.

Deborah and Élodie boarded the boat quietly, nodding to Mr. Kennan; they seated themselves on a bench on the foredeck, watching the lusterless blue sea stir about tamely under the overcast sky. The two women remained there, still as statues, until the tugboat rounded the steep point of Le Carbet and they saw the remains of St. Pierre stretch out like carrion at the foot of the still smoking Mt. Pelée. Then Deborah had to stand and move towards the rail, lean over and drink in the full panorama of devastation like a draught of poison. Not a tree stood; only a few partial walls broke the horizontal spread of broken gray rubble. No tree, no bird, no life at all. The slight movement of the sea waves seemed frenetic compared to this total stillness. The air as they approached smelled of dead flesh and burned rock.

"Good God!" one of the gentlemen cried out. "It's a vision of the inferno!" But Deborah had always pictured Hell as a dynamic place, horrid but full of movement and sound, flames leaping, demons cackling, lost souls writhing and lamenting their doom. Here was stasis, the ashes of Hell after the world ended, when even God had died. Everything was blackened or coated with gray ash except for the gloating green of the mountain. Nothing, nothing, nothing, and yet everything jumbled and torn and burned into a confusion of twisted, unidentifiable shapes as far as the eye could see. No streets could be discerned; all was rubble and ruin. Élodie burst into tears; she had never been to St. Pierre before and was not prepared for what an enormous corpse it would make. Deborah gave her a drink from the tea thermos and then took one herself. Mr. Kennan appeared for a moment at her side, ascertained with a glance that she was not ill, and then was off in the first group of men to be rowed ashore to explore and photograph and take copious notes.

Deborah and Élodie waited to make up the last

boatload to be transported towards what had once been a harbor, the extra room in the boat taken up by two chairs provided by the French captain, who was shocked at the cavalier brusqueness of the American gentlemen towards a lady injured and bereaved. He would attend to her comforts first. Whatever they wanted, *les sauvages*, they could procure for themselves.

Deborah saw, as they grew closer, that what had seemed almost uniformly gray was actually a *bricolage* of the city, plaster chunks from walls blown off their foundations and smashed, charred planks, blackened bricks, and twisted ironwork wrenched from pulverized windows. There was no movement except the eye's incessant darting over the rough surface from one unrecognizable object to the next, and the frantic efforts of the mind to assemble something—an idea, a picture, a response—from the chaos. No mourners except Deborah had come to search for the graves of loved ones. Only looters would have sifted through the wreckage, finding more death than treasure.

The broken ground underfoot shifted and slid. It was only with great care and mutual assistance that the two women could approach the dry land out of reach of the bobbing waves that bathed the shore. Élodie showed a distressing tendency to cling to Deborah, impeding her efforts to lay out her art supplies on a flat rock, set up her small easel, rid herself of the annoying veil, and do the work she had come to do. So Deborah removed Élodie's straw hat and posed her, back turned to the ruins, her face lit by the shine of the ocean. In her quick charcoal portrait, Élodie's round face could have been pouting had it not been for the tension in her shoulders and the drawn look in her eyes. Then Deborah did a version with color from the children's paint set. She found welcome relief in painting Élodie's red plaid dress, her blue skirt draped across it in the Martiniquean fashion, her coffee-brown face, rounded pink lips, and the elaborate red and yellow turban she had worn to show respect to the American lady. Behind this appealing figure, Deborah smeared the charcoal thin so that the gray background was a vague shape, almost unnoticeable. She wanted Élodie to remember this scene, not her appalling first impression. Élodie was flattered and pleased with her picture, especially with the fine detail Deborah had put into the folds of her turban and the drape of her skirts.

While Élodie was caught up in admiring her picture, Deborah considered the challenge in front of her: to compose a picture of this destruction, this scene that defied composition. She would look and look, sinking into the detail, choosing the square yard closest to her: an iron rail twisted into a half-circle, here a blackened stone, the base of a lamp, a strip of gray cloth, something metal, a shard of crockery, a charred tree limb, an exploded cassava. The bottom of a shoe, cracked and creased with either wear or heat or both, protruded from an ugly hillock of dried mud and ash. She realized she could not be certain that there was no foot inside the shoe, with a limb attached, a corpse buried in the pile of mud and debris along with the other meaningless bits and pieces. The shoe gave her a place to start with her sketch, a center to the chaos.

She found the black of her charcoal too bright, too full of sparkle to convey the matte gray and gray-brown of ash and stone and burned earth.

"Élodie! Fetch me some of the ash in this little cup! And some seawater to make it into a paste. *Pour faire un pâté.*"

The resultant gray smear across the paper was too thin, too much white shining through, so she started with a black background, an intricate pattern of household goods intertwined with skeletons and single bones over-laid in white. While the first layer dried, the two women ate their sandwiches as they looked out to sea, and then Deborah covered the whole paper in gray, wondering if the shapes would emerge after the mud dried and she brushed it away. Perhaps all of her work now would have this ele-ment of concealment, the visible unimportant, the real life buried, and she wondered if the marrons, the wild silent people of the mountain, had survived.

The constant, unrelenting heat of the island enclosed Deborah and caused the burn on her arm to catch fire again. She wet the gauze with the remains of her tea, though she supposed it might be exactly the wrong thing to do. But it was a relief and would allow her to do her work without distraction. She had painted the destroyed; now, she turned her eyes to Mt. Pelée, the indifferent destroyer, and studied the notch where it had burst open, spilling into the city and the sea beyond, indifferent but not unchanged. She traced the mountain's remembered curves and folds and found them the same, but it was no longer her lode-stone or her ally. She saw no spirit in it.

She began with the line where rock was divided from sky, up to the top where mist or fumes or death concealed the very peak from her view. She resorted to the gray paste, charcoal, and the pretty little green watercolor from the paint set to capture the sides and the muddy river val-leys, furrowed and desolate. On the eastern side, trees still stood, rivers ran, the grass and wild vines ran rampant. On the north where Deborah sat, nothing grew. The ruins of St. Pierre swirled past it like a river. It took several tries before she was half-satisfied with the colors of life and the color of death in her work.

When she had finished her painting of Pelée, she stood back to look at it. She thought about her son, her

Gianni, and what his short life might have been like. Surely he had laughed sometimes, had laughed with his friends, at puppies, in surprise, for the joy of laughing, at the splashing of water, the impossibility of catching birds on the sand. Surely the woman who had raised him up had loved him and told him stories, called him pet names, played with him sometimes. Had kissed him good-night and sung to him.

Deborah was suddenly afraid her son had been dis-liked, outcast, and treated harshly, the half-breed, the fos-ter-child, but the woman, whoever she had been, was dead now, and all her children alike. The thick white blanket of death was now pulled up to their chins, and whatever loves, hates, or sorrows they had felt were over.

Deborah had to look away from her picture and from St. Pierre towards the ocean's horizon. There in the offing lay the *Rubis,* waiting patiently for the return of the landing party. The captain stood on deck with his binoculars trained on the spot where she sat. She waved. The captain waved back. So she painted him a quick watercolor of his boat, making it a much cleaner, trimmer little boat with a taller, handsome captain; it was a child's picture with bright primary colors unshaded with gray, a white smoke-stack and white smoke curling up into the clouds that half-covered the sun. He would be repaid for his consideration and concern with the only currency she had in abundance. With that in mind, she did a few more pictures of St. Pierre, one for Mr. Kennan, and then a sweet imaginary garden to take to Rita as a peace offering.

By mid-afternoon, the heat and the exertion took their toll. A wave of fatigue overtook Deborah, darkened her vi-sion, and threatened to force her into a slump from which she might never rise again, as though she were pounded into the earth. The red-hot brand on her cheek, where the black cloud had kissed her with venomous lips, was on fire, her arm burning again, and she was helpless before the onslaught.

"Signal the boat, Élodie. J'suis pas bien." *Come get me. Rescue me. Make me feel safe. Save me. Protect me from this horror and this death.* She felt it as a cry to her mother, to Grandma Gussie, to Villette. To Katy, the only one still living.

The captain responded as soon as he saw Élodie's beckoning wave, sending two strong fellows to lift Deborah into the boat, Élodie following with the basket of provisions, the satchel of art supplies, and a portfolio of the pictures Deborah had wrested from the disaster.

When the captain saw how distressed and weak Deborah was, he wished more than anything that he could up anchor and return her to the hospital in Fort-de-France without delay. But of course, he could not strand his other passengers, the ones who had chartered the *Rubis*. After Élodie had carefully bathed the wounds with limewater, replaced the bandages, and given Deborah a dose of laudanum from the little vial Nurse Fyffe had sent along, the crisis seemed to be over. Deborah dozed in the captain's berth until the gentlemen returned, tired and shocked at what they had seen, but full of conversation and argument, striving in their own way to understand what had taken place in this city of death.

At the hospital, Deborah put off the task of looking for Rita Stokes to offer her the garden picture as a kind of reparation for any harm she had caused, doing for Rita what she had done for Élodie. The expedition had been a success, but it had exhausted her beyond expectation. She found herself glad to be bullied into bed by Nurse Fyffe, where she sank into sleep like a rock sinking into the ocean.

The next morning, Mr. Kennan dropped by the hospital to assure himself that Deborah had recovered fully from her exertions of the previous day and to offer his assistance before his departure the next day. He found her back in bed, pale but steady, evidently feeling the positive effects of a good night's sleep and morphia. She handed him the picture she had painted for him, and explained the medium she had employed to obtain the matte gray and the colorless jumble of the ruins. He studied it carefully and was for a moment back in that graveyard of a city, reminded of the pathos of the small household items—keys, birdcages, bowls, melted glassware, the bones of home life that peppered the wreckage.

"I am honored," he said. "I will treasure your work. I only wish I could have preserved your mural of the death of the *Roraima*. I hope you will paint it again someday."

Deborah smiled, knowing the catastrophe would always be present in her work, no matter what her subject.

"Mrs. Huntworth, I am aware that you have no family connections to act for you in your present situation. Please make me of use to you. Can I undertake some commission that will ease your return to the States? It would be my pleasure."

"You are most kind, Mr. Kennan. And yes, I have three errands I will ask you to do, as you have been so very considerate. I want you to book me a voyage to New York in two or three weeks' time. New York will be the best place to work, at least for now. That's the first.

"The second is that I don't know New York at all, and yet I will need to find a place to live rather quickly. I believe my funds will last me at least a year, but not if I'm staying at a hotel. A cheap apartment or boarding house would be excellent if you could inquire among your numerous friends and acquaintances."

Mr. Kennan nodded.

"And, third, I would like you to write to Richards, my man of business, and ask for the whereabouts of Miss Katy Kelly, Kathleen, I should think. Richards' address is on this cable. I would appreciate you not using my name in your inquiry. My plans have nothing to do with him."

"I can certainly do these things," Kennan assured her. "The first two I can undertake today. The third may take a deal longer. You must write to me at this address in Washington DC. Let me know where I can send any information about Miss Kelly and tell me how you fare. If I can ever be of further assistance to you, it will be small recompense for the pictures you have given me, in memory and now on paper. I thank you." And so he took his leave.

The only other bit of unfinished business was to send Élodie to find out where Rita and Miss King had been sequestered. But perhaps it would be better to simply send the picture. It would please Nurse Fyffe more, who surely could not take exception to a simple, happy garden. Élodie left with the picture in hand but returned with it a few moments later.

"Madame," she said, breathless. "Madame, the uncle of the little girl came this morning and carried the little girl and Miss King back to Barbados with him, both of them. He wanted to leave Miss King, but the little one cried so hard. Nurse Fyffe says Mr. Crownley was rude, but the others say he was handsome like a prince, with fine black hair and a cane. But certainly, the little girl is gone."

Deborah was disappointed. When she first heard that Rita had survived the disaster, she had thought of Rita as a motherless child, as her own child had been made motherless, as she had been. When she saw the bandages on Rita's little face, she conceived of her as a fellow sufferer. And then, when she had felt the need to explain the disaster to herself, which for Deborah meant making a picture, Rita had been her collaborator and companion in the great adventure of stealing a wall. She feared that Nurse Fyffe was right and that Rita had been harmed by the experience. And now she was gone, out of reach. Deborah let Rita's garden picture fall to the floor. It was not one she would need to keep. She had no more use for it.

Mr. Kennan was as good as his word. Élodie brought Deborah an envelope two days later containing a ticket for the Quebec ship *Fontabelle* leaving on the 22 of June for ports in the Antilles, then New York City and a slip of paper that read: Mrs. Elsie Hollenback, 124 Sullivan Street, Manhattan, NY. Having this information lifted Deborah's spirits. There might yet be a place for her.

~~~~~~~

A few weeks later, after Deborah had embarked for New York, Nurse Fyffe came in to make sure the room was clear of the disturbing American lady and ready to house new patients. She found Rita's garden picture where Deborah had discarded it and thought it quite charming. First, she pinned it on the wall in her quarters to enjoy and, in time, she framed it. She later took it with her to a well-earned retirement to live with her sister in Stobswell, no longer remembering exactly where it had come from or who the artist DH might have been.

9

~ *Maps* ~

Deborah's accommodations aboard the *Fontabelle* proved to be unnervingly luxurious, suggesting that Mr. Kennan had spent some of his own cash to supplement the money she had given him along with the commission to book her voyage. Deborah could have done with many fewer plump cushions meant to signal opulence, fewer velvet hangings in maroon and forest green and sickly blue. She was still occasionally turning to the comforts of laudanum, and the combination of satin stripes, paisleys, braided fringe, and fleur-de-lis flocking made her head swim and increased her appreciation of the plain white challenge of an empty canvas. Because she wanted to be left alone to think and work, she let the head steward know that she would be served in her room; she only went on deck when she could be certain most first-class passengers were sitting down to the rich, seven-course meals of first-class passage. She was not ready to face the reactions of others until she could face herself.

One solution for the social discomfort of Deborah's disfigurement was the black veil Nurse Fyffe had offered. It was intended to protect her from unkind looks or comments and to protect others from the shock and pity of unexpectedly catching sight of her face, whether bandaged or bared and, being stopped short, reminded of the vulnerability of all flesh. Deborah's solution lay in hastening the process of becoming familiar with herself, seeing intimately and owning the brands Mt. Pelée had burned into her body.

While still in the hospital in Fort-de-France, Deborah had allowed Nurse Fyffe to forbid her a mirror. She needed privacy to become acquainted with the grim companion that was to be with her for life. She had seen Rita's wounded face and the expression in Rita's eyes when her own face was uncovered. Deborah knew it would be ugly; she had taken the measure of the wound on her arm, from shoulder to elbow. The bleeding had finally stopped, but the flesh was still red, pitted, furrowed with yellow and blue streaks as though the heat had ripped down her arm, melting and cooking and digging deep. Not the brown of dried blood, but bright red as though newly cut. The damaged flesh would change, no doubt, as it dried and healed and scarred but, for now, her concern was the injury on her face still to be confronted, observed, and understood.

Until she was brave enough to do that important work, she would suit herself by staring at the sky or the horizon or the sea, as women have done from time immemorial, from hilltops, from widows' walks, through doorways and windows, waiting to see what new thing might arrive. What she saw now as she looked out into the distance was the same sea she had crossed before, as a girl, as a forlorn captive, and then returning in triumph like a goddess of Victory. She had seen the brightening of the ocean as the ship approached the tropics and the corresponding fade as she was borne away.

Now Deborah's overriding impression was of saltiness, tasted in the spray, smelled in the winds that parted at the ship's prow. She was less conscious of the color than of the water's rankness. Below the surface, whether glittering, foaming, or dull, lay a graveyard of fish, people, ships, whole civilizations buried in the muck on the ocean floor, or so she imagined. The pretty blue was merely the surface reflection of what was above, covering the death that lay at the bottom of the ocean, just as on land.

Her spirits were lifted by the occasional display of flying fish that flashed between sea and sky for one breathtaking moment, like shining souls newly risen, free at last from a briny graveyard. She wanted to look away before they plummeted back into the darkness, but she didn't. Deborah was coming back to life, a different life than any she had ever featured. Her thoughts were melancholy but tough.

Deborah would never return to Martinique, that much she knew, although the rest of her future was blank, to be filled in as she went. She might never travel again, given her reduced funds. Sans Douleur was gone, and the bank that had held the Millais fortune was lost in the blackened rubble of St. Pierre. All that was left was the money in a St. Louis bank from the sale of the house and the pittance she would receive each year from Judge Huntworth's estate. She had told Mr. Kennan that her funds would support her for a year, but that was purely a guess. She didn't care where she lived beyond a certain level of safety, hygiene, and decency. She would have to buy a few personal items, another change of clothing, perhaps a warm coat, but what she needed most urgently was a place to paint.

She hoped that she would find her way, could become an art teacher like Miss Singleton, or could find Miss Singleton somehow and ask her advice. Perhaps she would be able to sell a painting, though she knew nothing about the business side of things. But presumably, she could learn; Deborah's heart sank at the prospect. It would require fortitude, perseverance, and social skill—time and energy she wanted to pour onto canvas. But she would try. She would do what she had to. She imagined brusque, moustached men dismissing her with a wave of the hand, not even looking at her work. It was harder to imagine a deferential gallery owner, hanging onto her words, eager to sell her work. She might starve to death. She might fall into the life of prostitution Tante Charity had threatened, though she expected that her face would disqualify her there, a bitter joke. At least she could find out what was possible once she arrived. Her work now was the dreadful but necessary project of exploring and mapping her damaged face.

At first, she avoided this challenge by trying to sketch the shape of the waves, the reflective facets and striations, and the curling tangles of foam. Their shifting architecture gave her a challenge, to see quickly, to let repetition take the place of stillness in forming a permanent impression, creating a permanent image. Then she started her exploration by painting a triptych as she had done for her late husband. But now she painted her own face to mark the death of the dream of reunion that had powered her life—first as a sweet bright-eyed child, then as a strained and resolute young woman, and finally as the unscarred, peaceful old woman she would never become. She didn't weep. She finished the work and slept.

Deborah rose in the morning and went up to the deck as she did every morning to breathe the fresh air and greet the sun, which rose through peach and purple and gold stripes across the horizon. Back in her cabin, she drank tea and breakfasted from a tray, the privilege of infirmity. She opened the porthole to let the sun in, seated herself before the mirror of the dressing table with her children's paint set and a glass of water in front of her, and carefully removed the bandage from her face. For an hour, she stared at her reflection, turning her head, studying the colors and uneven shape, the rough edges of the wound. She realized that her left eye, which she had thought undamaged, was pulled down at the outer corner. She pulled down the right eye to match and stuck out her tongue at her reflection, like a bad little girl making faces.

The challenge would be to represent the texture, almost the topography; simple watercolors would want to flatten the surface like a map. So, to start, she agreed with her medium and painted just the shape and colors, a few shreds of pale-yellow skin still hanging like antique fringe where her jawline began, under her reddened ear. Purple mixed with gray and blue for the line running through the center, breaking up into finer lines at the bottom of this dry, bloody lake. A red the color of plums, sometimes shiny, appeared where the fire had eaten farthest into the healthy flesh. A darker reddish-brown lined with bright crimson for the islands of scabs that dotted the wound. A film like melted strawberry ice cream in the center, perhaps where the flesh was attempting to heal without a sound place to anchor itself. A thin, jagged, deep rose line around the perimeter of the wound, like dead seaweed left by a bloody tide that had gone out. She wanted oils.

She realized later, after lunch, a nap, another turn around the deck, and a staring session at the railing, that she had painted only the wound, not the face that had sustained it and would carry it out into the world. She had originally expected to paint a simple, realistic portrait of a wounded woman, not the portrait of a wound. She saw that she would need a series of pictures. Evidently, the exploration had just begun.

Colored pencils gave her more control than watercolors, but she missed the black, which was almost used up anyway, and resorted to the careful application of charcoal where darkness was needed. The result was pale and pretty, so what was pictured was a tropical flower instead of a wound, disorganized, wildly irregular but, still, a flower seen reflected in a stream or through shattered glass, its complex structure distorted but in no way sinister or horrid. An orchid perhaps, like ones she had seen as a girl in the Botanical Garden of a now dead city, in the company of people now dead.

That night and for many nights thereafter, the dreams that appeared as soon as she closed her eyes were of maps and masks, scars and islands; and in her dream-life, a map was a scar, an island a mask, and she was marooned on a map or concealed behind an island. Her heart beat so fast that it woke her. She would find herself sitting upright, and even the moonlight that shone through the open porthole seemed too bright, seemed to throb with her heartbeat and her raging wounds. She wanted laudanum to ease the pain, but she feared more laudanum would mean a return to the dreams that had haunted her at the hospital, of chasing Gianni through the black ruined streets of St. Pierre, hearing his laugh somewhere ahead of her and at last, finding him buried in rubble, only his foot protruding from an ugly bulge of mud. And that dream was harder to awaken from.

To move away from the unsatisfying flatness of her previous work, Deborah acquired newspaper and flour from the cabin attendant for making paste; she combined it with a half-empty jar of mucilage purloined from the passenger lounge where some girls had been making a scrapbook of their Caribbean souvenirs. She wanted to try for a papier-mâché model, though she was not experienced with the medium. It proved difficult to achieve the right consistency for molding the shapes with enough tensile strength for the hills and peaks, the *mornes* and *pitons*, as they were called in Martinique, to stand and not slump. She used her hands to shape the squashy material but also resorted to any tool that came to hand: comb, room key, a fragment of the black veil for texture, scissors, pens, and the little brush from the paint set, the bristles cut short for stippling the surfaces that were too smooth once the paste had congealed enough to be worked.

In the end, after much struggle, the model of her papier-mâché wound was close to what she had intended, ready to be painted later if she chose. Papier-mâché itself, however, proved not to be a medium she would use again. Blobs of paste threatened to gum the porthole shut and made smears on her sleeves and skirts. She found dried papier-mâché pellets in her hair for days, and her comb was almost unusable because of its missing, bent, and clogged teeth. The floor seemed to have a thin veneer of gummy wheat paste that clung to the soles of her shoes, letting go with a crackle. The crackling followed her as she walked around the deck. It was not long before the deck itself developed gummy patches, and as Deborah leaned on the railing to look at the sea, she could hear the crackling footsteps of other passengers as they passed behind her on their promenades.

She had used up most of her watercolors and ruined the brush. All she had left were the colored pencils and charcoal. The rest of her self-portraits called to her, but they would have to wait until she could get properly set up with an easel and oils and turpentine and canvas and brushes and rags and a palette and space to work. To while away the intervening few days, she drew little portraits of Villette and old Carlo and Mr. Kennan, but she was bored and restless. She was lonely. She wanted conversation, the sound of voices, of her own voice. She wanted to touch and be touched, to have the shape of her physical form outlined with the hand of another, skin smoothed. She craved the weight of another body on her own, the feel of a man's skin under her hand. Her face might drive men away and would certainly make things awkward, but the sunlight that shone on her face each day, once the bandage was removed, seemed to reveal changes to the wound, drying the surface, lightening the bright red, creating a matte finish like the dusty bloom on a plum. She could test the waters here on the ship before she was cast out into the larger world of New York.

Her first step into society might be to obtain a deck chair the next morning, and doze there while the passengers trooped by, so that they could see her bandaged face without having to meet her eyes. She thought they would look more freely and could talk about her over breakfast. Then, when they next encountered her, she would be a known quantity and they would accept her, as someone badly broken. But then some kind lady would want to chat, would press her hand to emphasize a point, probably to punctuate her own Christian charity in giving time to such a pariah, poor thing. But conventional contact wouldn't assuage Deborah's longing for intimacy, not even for a moment. It would be a step backward into a social life for which she had no value.

More than once, a gentleman had approached Deborah, hoping to strike up a conversation with her as she stood in her preferred place, leaning on the railing and looking at the sea. She startled each man away by turning abruptly to face him, to allow him to see the white bandage and imagine hidden horrors running down her face from brow to jawline. They rightly interpreted the rebuff and excused themselves courteously, moving away to seek more congenial company. She was sorry now that she had been so rude and resolved to handle the next man quite differently if another should come along.

She started that evening, thinking that dim starlight would favor her adventure and at least partially hide her face, giving her the courage she was annoyed to realize would be required. Her approach or acceptance of a man's approach in the past had been casual, a small matter that would or would not result in a tryst. She couldn't seem to regain that composure now. This foray would predict the future, whether she was doomed to a life of isolation and loneliness or if she still had the power to kindle the warmth of desire and could warm herself again in a man's arms. She had told Mr. Kennan that she was intrepid; she summoned up that spirit of exploration to meet this new challenge.

The gentleman who stopped next to her on the deck, seen peripherally, seemed young and sturdy, courteous and quite acceptable. He smelled slightly of shaving lotion and wool and soap. He remarked that he had not seen her before and hoped she had not been below decks with *mal de mer,* as many ladies had been. Ah, then she must be a good sailor and had found the voyage enjoyable as he had. His pleasantries were conventional enough and delivered with enthusiasm, as though he was delighted with the occasion for delivering them. He seemed like a man who enjoyed himself. She ventured that she was recovering from an injury and, for that reason, had spent little time in the public spaces of the ship.

"It appears that you are on the mend," he said. "But allow me to introduce myself. My name is Frederick Schilling."

"How do you do," Deborah replied without turning her head toward him or giving him her hand. "My name is Deborah Huntworth." And so the conversation continued, about the state of the evening, the calm of the ocean, whether the view before them was melancholy or uplifting, the pleasantness of the salt breeze, but surely she was growing chilled. He removed his coat and placed it around her shoulders. She thanked him for the attention, remarking on how warm and comforting, how kind. He asked about her injury, and she explained why she kept her head turned.

"It is not a small disfigurement. But as long as my head is turned away, you can imagine me as you see me, and that gives me pleasure."

"Believe me, madam, the pleasure is entirely mine." Frederick Schilling had heard of shipboard romances, though his heart was entirely pledged to Sarah Peabody of Brookline, Massachusetts, whom he planned to marry as soon as possible. But Sarah Peabody was in Massachusetts, and he had not seen her for more than a year. He could not honorably form a new attachment, of course. But he thought perhaps his honor could stretch as far as a flirtation with a stranger. The moonlight was so flattering to Deborah's skin, the movement of her bosom as it rose and fell with each breath was so disturbing to him, and her unusual conversation so inviting that further intimacy was not out of the question. He was prepared for such an eventuality, but he wished he were more experienced.

"Freddy," Deborah said, deliberately increasing the intimacy of their conversation by skipping directly to a pet name. "Freddy, I rather like you. Come with me to my room, if you want. We will keep the lights off, and I will keep my face and injured arm covered and out of the way. There will be nothing to distress you, I promise."

She thought him young enough to accept out of curiosity, if nothing else. He was willing but flustered by the unexpectedness of her invitation and the mysterious terms of the affair. He tried to come up with exactly the right thing to say, but Deborah placed her fingers over his lips and took his hand, leading him down the stairs to her room. She closed the door behind them and held him close for a long moment, rocking, as though he were a long-lost lover instead of one only recently found. Their clothing fell to the floor, with a great deal of fumbling at buttons and catches. When she laughed at their difficulties, he revealed a playfulness she had not suspected.

"If only I had a few more thumbs," he said, "I think this would be going better."

Once they were both at least half undressed, they stumbled to find the bed in the dark, laughing and shushing each other as though they were tipsy, as though they were old friends or playmates. His efforts first to find the German envelope he always carried in the inner pocket of his waistcoat on the advice of older men, and then the struggle to get it on in the dark room only compounded the laughter. In the end, with Deborah's help, he was wonderfully ready, and she drew him in with a soft cry.

At first, Deborah's wounds throbbed with the rhythm of their movements, with the increased beating of her heart. Then pleasure overtook the pain, became indistinguishable, and Freddy found ways to please her and she him. His skin was a joy under her fingertips, a smooth velvety texture that reminded her of Sanson. She kept her arm held to the side and her face with the unmarred side toward him, accepting his kisses as best she could. When they had finished, they lay in each other's arms and slept briefly. Deborah woke him, quite certain that she did not want the boy who brought her morning tea to find Freddy there.

"Up, Freddy. You have to go now."

Freddy stirred and sat up. "I want you to show me your face." He rose and started making hard work of the confusing business of dressing in the half-dark of an unfamiliar room where one has undressed in particular haste. Deborah was silent, the only sounds in the room the sloshing of waves, the constant distant roar of the ship's boiler room, and Freddy fishing around under the bed for his other shoe. She felt strangely shy now for having been so bold, so intimate.

"Please," Freddy said. "I'm a physician. Well, almost. But I'm coming from finishing up my residency at the Military Hospital in Barbados. So I am actually going to be a physician next Monday when I put up my shingle."

"Come back then, if you still want to, after breakfast. You can see my face in full sunlight; see what you have slept with." She wished she hadn't said the last part. She was not used to feeling diffident, and it irritated her. "Come back later," she said and pushed him out the door. She found one of his socks under her pillow when she tucked her hand there to shore up the rather thin feather pillow to support her head as she dozed just a few moments longer.

She supposed Freddy would not return, but he tapped on her door shortly after the morning tray had been cleared and she opened to get her first real look at him, older than she had thought, dark-eyed, dark-haired, doctor bag in hand. He smiled at her first, then drew her to the light, removed the bandage from her face with gentle fingers and studied her wound as closely as she had done herself. She found that she was not at all self-conscious.

"A burn?"

"Yes."

"Steam? It's oddly localized for steam, but it's very deep. One can almost see bone in places. It must be quite painful. Do you have morphia?"

"Of course," Deborah said. "Drops."

"Where did you board the ship?" he asked, and when she told him Martinique, he looked at her sharply but remained silent.

He removed a silver instrument from his neatly organized case and came back to her. "I'll just trim the dead skin that's sloughing. And it would be best to abrade the tissue just at the edges if you can bear it. It will heal better that way."

When that ordeal was over, he removed her shirtwaist and looked at her arm.

"I don't like this puffy bit here. Let's use some ichthyol ointment on it to draw out the fluid." His fingers, which had eagerly explored her body the previous night, now touched her wound almost imperceptibly. "I'll give you enough to use in the deep parts to prevent infection, which is the greatest danger now. It smells wretched, but it's quite effective. Apply it everywhere, actually, for a few weeks."

After digging about in his bag, Freddy produced a few little pots of black grease and some clean bandages. "How did your physician treat you in the hospital?" He kept his face impassive, but she could tell he was not impressed by her previous medical care.

"Let's see. The physician spoke no English. He mistook me for someone else who was dead. He gave me good news that wasn't true." She was feeling the effects of the stinky unguent already, easing the raw sting, and it was comforting as well to be looked after and to have a witness instead of being so alone with herself. "I yelled at him, and then I didn't see him again. There was just a nurse. She put some kind of yellow stuff on it."

"Hmmph," Freddy said, and it seemed to Deborah that this muttered comment might be something he had picked up unconsciously from an older physician he had studied with and admired.

"Let me tell you," he said, "what you can expect. You will always have scars on your face and arm, likely a mixture of pale shiny strips and puckered flesh. You should massage that skin flap at the corner of your eye. It's still healing, so you may be able to affect the shape. The colors will fade, and the area will diminish, but that will take months or even years. And it may still hurt from time to time. Sunlight is probably not going to help, so wear a wide-brim hat when you go out."

Deborah felt as though her feet were back under her, and she knew where she stood. Her grief would fade like her scars, her dreams would change, and it would take a long, long time to mourn. It would still hurt from time to time. But her life was not over. From her night with Freddy, she had learned that she had not lost the capacity to feel joy. She had not been robbed of the prospect of pleasures to come.

"Thank you, Freddy," Deborah said. And then, "Thank you, Dr. Schilling. You are going to be a wonderful doctor. Best of luck."

"Goodbye, Mrs. Huntworth. It has been a great pleasure. You are a remarkable woman. Best of luck to you, as well." They stood and beamed at each other in mutual approbation. Then Dr. Frederick Schilling turned and retreated to his own quarters, where he wrote a particularly good, though not at all comprehensive, letter to his darling Sarah Peabody of Brookline, Massachusetts, whom he planned to marry as soon as possible.

~~~~~~~

The final day of the cruise, as the *Fontabelle* sailed towards New York Harbor, brought out a wild excitement in the passengers, who exchanged addresses, offered invitations that would soon be forgotten by both parties, and shook hands or embraced as though they were being reunited rather than parting company. Deborah avoided looking for Freddy in the melee. They had said their goodbyes and anything further, performed in public, would ruin things between them. She was watching from deck as the island shimmered into view, and though she was again solitary, she was as glad as any traveler to arrive safely.

Deborah thought she had made peace with the giant, unfeeling figure who stood watch over the harbor; she felt only a slight pang of childish resentment. Then suddenly she was overcome by a bewildering paroxysm of panic so piercing she could barely restrain herself from shrieking. It seemed to her that an inimical foe had followed her from Martinique to complete her destruction. At any moment this island, too, would burst into flame, and a black cloud roaring with lightning would sweep across the scene, blow the tall buildings into the streets, topple the statue, and then flow across the intervening waterway to set the ship and its passengers to burning. Everyone, all those people, would perish again in the merciless, fiery black storm. All that would remain was destruction, desolation, and horror.

Her knees buckled and she collapsed onto the hard deck, gasping for air, her heart pounding, skin clammy. She shivered and wept, awash in fear, until the purser found her, assisted her into a deck chair, and enlisted the help of a lady passing by. This stranger pressed a cold wet cloth against her forehead and her uninjured cheek and plied her with hot tea and comforting talk. It was exactly what she had avoided the whole voyage—the assistance, the pity of conventional women such as this. But she clung to her now as to a mother, and the mother patted her back and rubbed her arm.

"You poor thing," she said. "There, there, my dear. You are still recovering from your injury, but you will be fine. There, there."

"You are most kind," Deborah said as these attentions took effect and her balance was restored. "I truly appreciate your kindness." She found she was able to release her hold and sit back. The offered tea was bracing.

She firmly dismissed her Samaritan with the lie that a

carriage would be waiting at the end of the passengers' ramp to whisk her away to a welcoming family and a family doctor's attentions. She needed nothing further, she insisted.

10

~ *A Bad Man* ~

Deborah stood in line with the other passengers disembarking from the *Fontabelle* and gripped her bag firmly. The panic that had overcome her had dissipated, leaving her exhausted and merely anxious. She had lost the grand sense of purpose her commitment to Gianni had given her for most of her life. Arriving in New York marked the first step she had taken without a plan. With a sense of desperation and inevitability and hope, she flowed down the gangplank with the rest, stepping into the human stream to join the immensity.

She thought she had seen crowds, varieties of people milling around in public spaces, but the energy in New York City was overwhelming. Each individual person seemed to radiate a desperate intention, a plan for success, or its poor relation: survival. The drops in this ocean of humanity demanded her attention one by one, even as they flowed together in tides and waves and currents. This face, this face, the basket, the shawl, the face, the hat, the story, the life, and always, this face and the next face. The muted colors, the bobbing heads and the roar of individual voices and wheels, and the ships' clanking, flapping, hooting in the harbor could not be understood, yet could not be ignored. She felt as though the invisible ash clouds she sometimes imagined trailing from her body were being absorbed into the general dirt, noise, stink, and smoke of life on the harbor in this unfamiliar city, the clouds dissipating into the larger chaos that lay in front of her and threatened to, and then did, swallow her up.

She walked through the crowds and carts and trolleys, on sidewalks, sometimes pushed into the filthy gutters, hearing through the racket of traffic and the confusion of the street market, speech so much quicker and more strident than the markets on that other island, where the vendors had laughed together and joked in the tuneful patois of Martinique. There were few black faces in this crowd, and it passed through her mind that the black people had perished, but she knew, of course, that this was a thought born of strain and anxiety, of fatigue. She felt for the first time that she might not be of much consequence, that in some way she had been made smaller and unsafe.

She was drowning in a sea of bodies and voices speaking in harsh accents or in languages she had never heard before. The vendors, the only stationary features in the moving collage of people, answered her inquiries, if they heard her at all, with instructions and advice she couldn't understand. She followed the general directions pointed out by waving arms that reeked of blood and iodine, hands with cleavers, greens, entrails, held high over mountains of fly-flecked red meat, fish, onions, and potatoes, over the heads of shoppers and passersby.

She had not entirely recovered from her vision on board the ship when it had seemed as though burning black horror would stream across the water to destroy this island and cover her in a blanket of pain and death. She felt unsteady and occasionally stumbled on the uneven ground. The walk through the loud streets of Manhattan was almost as unreal as the vision had been; she was still driven by the need to escape.

At last, she found the address shown on the letter from Mr. Kennan: Mrs. Elsie Hollenback's boarding house, 124 Sullivan Street, with a discreet hand-lettered notice reading "Room for Lady" in the window. The building looked like all the others on the street—soot-dusted brick, curtained windows, a few steps up leading to the front door, a few steps down leading somewhere else. This house might offer her a place to rest, respite for her exhausted senses and disorderly imagination.

Deborah knocked on the solid door, trying to think of alternatives if this wouldn't suit, perhaps a hotel, but she couldn't think of the name of a hotel or how to get there. The door was opened by a short, round-bodied woman, her dress a series of circles swathed in overlapping drapes of black and gray, a gleaming white collar in lace encircling her neck. Her round face was creased like Grandma Gussie's but with a plaintive expression of mingled grief, anxiety, apology, and suspicion. She blocked the doorway with her body and peered up at Deborah.

"Jah?" she asked sharply.

But it was not Mrs. Elsie Hollenback's shape or wardrobe or face that bowled Deborah over and made her certain that this was the place for her. It was the mix of heavenly smells curling down the hallway, trailing Mrs. Hollenback, a rich, tart, meaty, spicy brown scent over the welcoming breath of fresh-baked bread.

"I understand you have a room for rent. My name is Deborah Huntworth. I have a letter of reference."

Mrs. Hollenback took the letter and rummaged around in the labyrinthine folds of her shawl for a pair of pince-nez. She read the letter slowly, several times.

"We have no male visitors in the rooms," she remarked, looking out at the street instead of at Deborah. "This is a respectable house. Only the parlor, not at night. We have rules." She drew a wrinkled sheet of paper from somewhere in the depths of her swaddling and poked it at her prospective boarder.

Deborah took a deep breath of what would surely be served at dinner and read the boarding house rules, looking for potential hazards. The dinner hours, she was relieved to see, began at 5:30, which must be soon. She could live that long on the culinary fumes. The rest of the rules seemed easy enough to follow.

For safe home for the young ladies with cleaning, laundry, and good meals morning and night.

~ Breakfast 7:30-9:00
~ Dinner 5:30-7:00
~ Not to be late for these meals without agreement.
~ No food no cooking in rooms.
~ Entrance door at end of the day locked at 9:00. Any exception must be agreed before noon.
~ No visitors before 9:00 morning or after 5:30 afternoon.
~ No male visitors in rooms. The parlor is to use for visitors.
~ Cleaning rooms in two week. Cleaner knocks on the Door and has key. Keep tidy, please.
~ Rent pay first day of the month. Late or not paying means $5 extra or to go from premise.
~ No storage or shipping of personal goods left behind.
~ Quiet must after 10 night be kept.
~ One hot bath a week only on 2nd floor. No Towels provided.
~ Family is on 1st floor and private. No boarders in Kitchen or family rooms.
~ Laundry in hall will pick up Sunday afternoon. Return Tuesday morning. Name things on each item. If paint stains, scrub first.
~ No Animals.

"Your face," Mrs. Hollenback said. "What is this?" pulling her fingers down her own face to mirror Deborah's. "We have no doctor here."

"A scar," Deborah said, though she knew that it was much more like a wound. "I don't want a doctor. I want the room if it is acceptable. I will gladly pay the rent for this month and next."

"But your pack? Is that all?" The old woman narrowed her eyes at her prospective boarder's suspicious lack of substance.

"My trunk will be delivered," Deborah reassured her, though, in fact, the trunk contained only a few changes of clothing, most of its contents consisting of the work she had done on the voyage and what remained of her art supplies. "I would like to see the room as soon as possible."

The room at the top of the stairs and the end of the hall was good enough; afternoon light came through the one high window, a neatly made quilt-covered bed; a tiny table and chair were wedged between the wall and the highboy provided for her clothing. She would not be able to work in this space, but she felt confident, mostly borne up by the strong smell of dinner that seemed to have followed them up the stairs, that she would find a place to paint somewhere in this boundless, crowded city.

After Mrs. Hollenback collected her rent, Deborah lay down on the bed, her new bed, to rest up for just a few minutes from the exertions of her arrival and the strain of looking for this house, always propelled by the urgency of having nowhere else to go. She dozed until a bell downstairs woke her, and she realized she had heard the sound several times and ignored it in her sleep, mistaking it for one of the many bells that had marked time on the *Fontabelle*. She hurried down to find the dining room, where her fellow boarders, a bright bouquet of young women along with several young men and two little girls, or two versions of the same little girl, were seated around a long table.

Only a few turned their heads while the rest kept up a buzz of conversation. A shout of laughter from one of the men was quickly hushed, but the husher dissolved into giggles. The hubbub was interrupted by Mrs. Hollenback rising from her seat to introduce "Mrs. Huntworth," a new guest, indicating an empty chair at her right. She hoped they would make Mrs. Huntworth feel welcome. Smiles, a smattering of applause, a few cries of encouragement, and then they turned back to their beautiful food and conversation, leaving Deborah to concentrate on the generous plate that had been placed before her.

It was a deep dish of carrots, potatoes, and chunks of meat swimming in a reddish-brown broth that was velvet to the tongue, as nourishing as its scent had promised. She had not considered the consequences of subsisting on tea and toast, a regimen the steward on board had supposed an invalid would require. She was weaker and more exhausted, even after her unplanned nap, than she had realized.

Work, she thought. She was here to work. She would need to recover her strength and connection to her work. Everything was lost but this. She needed to complete her series of self-portraits and let herself be touched with the next impulse and then the next. There would be people and places and . . . her head felt light, as though it would float to the ceiling, and she couldn't think what else there would be, or what she meant by that. The full spoon had grown uncomfortably heavy and unwieldy in her hand. More would be too much. A kind face swam into her view, a version of Mrs. Hollenback grown younger and prettier, though still anxious and shaded with sorrow, and a warm hand was placed on her shoulder.

"Mrs. Huntworth," the angel said. "You seem tired. Let me help you to your room for a rest. If you wake up hungry in the night, come find me, and I'll heat something up for you. My room is behind the kitchen. The door is always open and a light on for my little girls. I am Liesl, Mrs. Hollenback's daughter."

As Deborah was led stumbling up the stairs to her room, she could hear behind her the plinking of a ukulele in the parlor, a mournful tenor launching into "Barbry Allen," and a flood of chatter like birds gathering on dew-soaked grass. Once her head was on the pillow, she heard nothing, not the ukulele nor the voices. Not Gianni's teasing whispers as he slipped into a dream cage of rubble, not the moans of the dying or the shouts of those who would save them. Whatever she dreamed that night was mercifully disguised or forgotten in the morning. Perhaps she dreamed of Freddy.

~~~~~~~

In the morning, the young women woke her with laughter and banging of doors as they hurried down for a breakfast Deborah hoped would be as divine as the dinner the night before had been. When the banging reached her door, she opened it to find a breathless, laughing, brown-eyed girl with a face like a flower, a bold pansy. This charming girl had come to be sure she wouldn't miss out on the "little pancakes," especially because one of the boys who took meals with them had come by early with a few baskets of strawberries.

"I'm your neighbor across the hall, Martha Holland at your service. I've been deputized to show you the ropes, probably because I would have done it anyway. Why not make it official! And next door to you is Frances Gold.

Don't let her frighten you. She's not as serious as she looks."

"Has my trunk arrived yet?" Deborah was hoping not to have to wear her crushed and soiled dress, the one she had struggled through the city in, the one which seemed crawly and unappetizing in the morning light. The trunk, it seemed, had not arrived, but Martha rummaged around in her own room and managed to put together an ensemble that was clean, though wrinkled, and much more colorful than any Deborah owned.

Deborah regarded herself askance in the mirror. Red shirtwaist, green skirt, brilliant yellow sash.

"You look like a gypsy queen in that outfit," Martha offered encouragingly. "Or a tropical flower."

"Or like I borrowed something to wear from three different friends."

"Or like one of those parrots, the ones that talk."

"Like a parrot then," Deborah said. "I am a clean and grateful parrot."

Martha laughed. "I borrowed the shirt from Emily last week. She can wait a little longer for its return, don't you think so, Mrs. Huntworth?"

Deborah wondered if she would ever be called Deborah by the rest of the boarders, who seemed so young and fresh the evening before when she herself had been spent and dulled by fatigue. She shied away from the thought. It's not as though they would ever really know her. She would be Mrs. Huntworth, the older lady with the ruined face, and all but the most forthcoming like Martha would keep their distance. She felt what age might offer: a chance to step back and enter the stream of life judiciously instead of diving in and being swept away. For a moment, she was weary with the burden of time, though she was only twenty-seven.

"Do you need to ... do something ... with the ... "
Martha made a flapping wave with her hand at the side of
her own face in a mirroring gesture Deborah realized she
would be seeing for the rest of her life.

"Yes, I have some ointment. I should have applied it to
my arm as well last night. Nasty stuff, but it seems to help.
I'm just afraid I will miss breakfast."

"Don't worry," Martha said. "There's always lots, and
I'll save you some strawberries."

"I'll be late," Deborah said.

"Really," Martha said. "Don't worry. Frau H. always
feeds us. Come down whenever you're ready."

With that assurance, Deborah washed up a little and
spread the salve Freddy had given her over the burns,
which woke from her touch and throbbed anew. By the
time she had finished and taken a judicious dose of laudanum to calm the pain, she was quite late. She went cautiously down the stairs, dreading an empty dining room
that would force her to go out, but instead, she found Liesl
and the little girls sitting at the table, the cloth littered with
crumbs and stray silverware and stained with a few strawberry blotches.

"Ah, Mrs. Huntworth! I hope you are rested and ready
for your *eierkuchen*. MarianneHelen—bring Mrs. Huntworth's plate from the kitchen. And the strawberries from
the cooler." The girls slid off of their chairs simultaneously
and scurried away.

"Which one is Marianne Helen?" Deborah asked, and
Liesl laughed.

"They are my twins, Marianne," she said, pausing.
"And Helen. The young ladies call them MarianneHelen,
like one name, and since they do everything together, it
seems to work. I have picked up the bad habit, I fear."

"And their father?" Deborah asked, thinking about the

awkward task of maneuvering her still undelivered trunk up the narrow stairway. "Does he help with lifting and such?"

"Oh dear," Liesl said. "No, my Karl died three years ago. My mother's dear friend, Ernst Kanda, had passed away, so she was all alone." She paused as though Deborah would recognize the name. "I came here to live then, just my mother and I and the girls. We have been a sad household. But then we opened the boarding house, and we enjoy our guests, you know; all the commotion is good for us."

"Ernst Kanda?" Deborah asked. "Why does that name sound familiar?"

"The artist," Liesl explained. "The great artist from Bonn, in Germany. My mother says he studied in Paris with Corot. He painted for royalty in Europe. He worked right here in this house, and we all admired him so much. He had the artistic temperament, you know. Now we have all our little art students in the house, but no one enters his studio. My mother keeps it preserved to his memory under lock and key. But I think maybe you are an artist as well? My mother seemed to think so from the letter you brought."

Deborah assented with a smile. Knowing that there was a place to work in such close proximity teased her with the prospective pleasures of working with real canvas and a full range of paints and knives and brushes. To have a real easel! She quelled the impulse to kick down the door and take possession and instead focused on the warm cakes and fragrant berries on her plate. The little girls, Marianne-Helen, sat across from her and watched her with big eyes, identical wondering expressions on their identical faces.

~~~~~~~

The first months of Deborah's new life were spent resting and making tentative forays into the art world of New York. Martha and others took her on guided tours to see museums and galleries, once to see their own student exhibit at Cooper Union. Many of them took classes there in the evening after long days in tea shops, cafés, dry goods stores, wherever they could work to support themselves as they pursued the elusive Muse. Martha urged Deborah to take a class, but she put it off. Once she had regained her health and her vigor, she planned to use her days studying and sketching from the works of Rembrandt or Vermeer, or bright smears of the recent Impressionists, as the fancy took her. In those first months of her residence at Frau Hollenback's boardinghouse, even looking at the work in galleries or window shopping for supplies left her exhausted by day's end, eager to be fed and retire to her room.

She did not forget about Herr Kanda's sequestered studio, so close, only a few feet to her left as she stood at the bottom of the stairs, behind a few inches of board and plaster. She spoke to Frau H. and asked the great favor of seeing where the late artist had worked, and after much demurring and much urging and reassurance, many caveats, Frau H. produced the key and opened the magic door. Once inside, Deborah prowled about, not touching but inspecting the paintings leaned against the wall, the paintings set on easels, paintings framed in elaborate gilt, the workbench, the dried-up palettes and jars of turpentine with brushes assembled in them. He had not been tidy, or perhaps had merely not expected to die and leave all this behind to be tidied by someone else or to stand as an untidy legacy of his art.

On the main easel was a painting of a dark man with a sparse moustache and wet eyes, staring into a middle distance as though watching something treasured move away, never to return. Deborah supposed, and Frau H. confirmed, that it was Herr Kanda's self-portrait. To Deborah's eye, it was a face of suffering and bitterness, the guilty expression of a man who has lost his center, his moral bearings, yet still retains the courage to open himself in painting in the service of truth or self-punishment. Not a bad face, but complex, isolated, hopeless, and unapproachable.

"He was a good man," Frau H. blurted out. "He was unhappy and often sick, but not so bad as he painted himself. He always meant to be good to me."

"I'm sure he was a good man," Deborah said. "I wonder if you would like a copy of this painting to hang in the house where you can see it."

Frau H. was uncertain, wringing her hands in her skirt, not sure perhaps what the household would be like under this desperate countenance.

"Of course, it would only be a copy," Deborah assured her. "I could not hope to capture all of the expression."

"Yes," Frau H. whispered, her eyes filling with tears. "Yes, I would like this."

And so it was agreed: Deborah would copy the portrait using the studio for her work. It might take as long as a month, perhaps longer. Deborah intended to work slowly, accumulate the materials, and enjoy the process. She planned to replicate the brash tones, the dark shadows, and the measured brush strokes in which the artist had recorded his self-disgust. She wanted to revise his self-assessment, reclaim the good in him, and replace the contempt in Herr Kanda's eyes with the love a woman needs to see when her man looks at her.

The finished portrait was a great success, applauded by all the household and accepted with thanks by Frau H., who had it hung in her bedroom where she could enjoy it in private. Deborah kept the key to the studio under the pretext of cleaning up the workspace. Over time, it came to be understood that she used the studio for her own work. She added a bit to her rent, which Frau H. accepted but did not acknowledge, and went out of her way to help Liesl and to buy occasional treats and trinkets for MarianneHelen, who reminded her of little Rita Stokes when they had first met on the voyage to Martinique, in that other life before the catastrophe. At first, the little girls were shy, afraid of the angry red scar that ran down her face. But as she was kind and didn't tease them like some of the younger boarders did, they soon adopted Deborah as their special friend.

Once her tenancy in the studio was established, Deborah went back to the art supply shops, buying everything she needed to resume her painting, adding some sketching materials and a small paint box. She had seen other painters set up in front of paintings in the museums, copying the masterworks, learning from the great artists of the past. A stiff interview with the secretary of the assistant to the assistant director of the Metropolitan Museum resulted in permission to join them, to study the works of the masters and explore with her own brush strokes, following them intimately, as though holding hands with a dead or dying spirit, inhabiting their intention, matching her own rhythm to the pulse and breath of another being, stretching to achieve their vision, accepting the exacting discipline of the other's art.

She painted in the studio a few days a week, tentatively, still finding her way. When she needed to step away from her own work, she labored at the Metropolitan, moving from one painting to another, approaching each as a puzzle to be solved. Deborah grew to be a familiar figure there among the others who slaved away, eye, hand, and soul.

She sometimes painted the subject matter and composition of one painting in the style of another, changed the palette, or added a goddess or nymph to a religious painting in a way that was harmonious, though clearly wrong. These experiments seemed especially pleasing to a stocky Frenchman who haunted the museum, sometimes watching her work and increasingly eager to make her acquaintance. Not a beau, she thought. Not that she would have risked scandalizing Frau H. by trying to sneak him up the stairs. And she found herself less interested in such things now that her work was in progress.

"Don't you know who that is?" one of the other copyists asked her in hushed tones, apparently astonished by her cavalier dismissal of the little man when she was particularly intent on the painting in front of her. "That's Remy, Remy Martin, the agent! He has connections with all the big galleries. He's the one who handles Samuel Waterman's work!"

"I didn't like the way he was hovering," Deborah said, though she was glad to be told. She thought it might be a pleasure to go look at some Watermans, maybe at Kleinmann's gallery, where several American impressionists were showing. There was a kind of light-heartedness to the curls and streaks of Waterman's brushstrokes that would be refreshing after the ponderous business of copying Dutch interiors and the dark, heavy faces of the aristocrats who could afford the most skillful portraitists of their time.

~~~~~~~

Deborah's first contribution to the life of the Frauhaus, as her fellow boarders called it, was to organize an outing to the Barnum & Bailey circus opening at Madison Square Garden. She intended to give the children a treat and give Frau H. a quiet evening. Her method of putting the party together was to convey her intention to Martha, who enthusiastically did the rest. At first, the response was lukewarm and Martha, Liesl, and MarianneHelen were the only members of the party.

Then the Parsons gallery opened a new show with Tellas' arresting series of paintings of clowns and acrobats, drooping rather like the dancers of Degas but imbued with a fascinating aura of tragedy, menace, and corruption. The exhibit set the critics on fire, and the boarding house party swelled to include almost all the art students and a few others tagging along for the fun.

Deborah's motives were several. She wanted to play a part in the tight community that had welcomed her and felt she had some fences to mend with the other boarders. A few months after her arrival, someone organized an outing to visit Coney Island, with special intent to see the St. Pierre volcano diorama, which was said to be spectacular. Her refusal had been felt as a rebuff, and though she regretted that slight, she could not filter out her aversion to seeing the tragedy that had obliterated her future re-enacted so that silly girls could shriek and seek comfort in the arms of the gentlemen who escorted them. If the exhibit was inaccurate, it would be a deep insult. If accurate, it could only re-injure.

She would never be one of the crowd. Her status as older and more advanced in her art had been established by the portrait of Ernst Kanda and her appropriation of his hitherto sacrosanct studio. She hoped that the circus party might repair her reputation of being cold and odd and restore her to "jolly" and "all right," as both descriptors seemed to guarantee good feelings all round.

She also had a secret reason to attend the circus performance, one that made her heart race and her injured
arm throb with a stinging rhythm. Barnum & Bailey had
pasted their garish posters all over town, and it was one
such advertisement that caught her eye and brought her to
a standstill, transfixed as she studied it.

"The Lone Survivor of the Tragedy of Martinique," she
read, surprised to see that some poor fellow had survived.
"The Most Marvelous Man on Earth," said the circus letter-
ing in another box with a picture of a dark man, his back
turned to reveal wide welts and scars, looking back over
his shoulder so that she could see his strangely familiar
face. His name was given as Ludger Sylbaris.

She had known him as Sanson, now back from the
dead past, it seemed, a connection to that city where her
dream had perished in black flashing fire, perhaps a connection to her lost son—their son—her unknown and un-
knowable Gianni. She had to find out, to collect any scrap
of information about Gianni: what he had been like, how
he had fared, who had raised him. She was reluctant to
plow up the settled wasteland of grief. But she had to ask,
and Sanson was the only one who had survived to speak.

The circus tent was hot and crowded, and from her
seat in the bleachers, Deborah waited impatiently for the
ringmaster to get through the acts, to bring on acrobats,
clowns, jugglers, trapeze artists, girls on horseback, trick
dogs, strongmen, and wild animals, put them through their
paces, and send them on their way. Finally, the ring
cleared, the spotlight dimmed, and the sonorous baritone
dropped to a theatrically confidential whisper. The ladies
must prepare themselves. Mothers should cover their children's eyes, for here, brought to the public view for the
first time, was a series of unnatural freaks of nature and
chance, marvels and wonders to educate the scientific

community and entertain the public.

"Ladies and gentlemen, the Crab Lady!"

The spotlight made a circle around her shelled body and claws, which clicked and rattled as she turned one way and another. The crowd oohed, but Deborah looked away to the rest of the darkened ring, where she discerned movement as upcoming marvels found their marks and waited for their spotlights to reveal them. The Ape-Girl from Borneo. The Fattest Man Alive. The Irish Fairy, decked in green sequins. The Walking Dictionary, whose tattoos were said to include every word in the English language. And finally, finally, The Luckiest Man in the World.

The spotlight found him in the center of the ring, his back turned to the audience as shown on the poster that had drawn her here. He was modestly dressed in the Sunday clothes of the islander, a loose white blouse and brown trousers. There was nothing remarkable, yet the crowd held its breath, knowing that this simplicity was the precursor to some thrilling moment to come. The ringmaster intoned the tragic story of the lost city of St. Pierre and how this one man had survived in an underground dungeon, unjustly confined until Fate had turned the tables. The luckiest man unbuttoned his shirt and lowered it to reveal the wounds that covered his back, the runnels and ropes that crawled there, the dark red and white and yellow and purple scars against his brown skin, beginning at his shoulders and extending beyond his waistband. The crowd gasped. Then he slowly turned to let the crowd feast on the sight of his burned chest, rippled and puckered with wounds and scar tissue, with patches of gray skin that seemed about to slough. His face was sullen but unharmed. He bared his teeth in a sly grin, and the light went out.

Next, more clowns and a sword swallower, but Deborah had no awareness of them. She swept out and went to find the burned man, the man said to be so lucky. The worker who directed her to Sylbaris' tent leered knowingly, but it didn't matter. She had to know everything Sanson knew.

What she would remember most vividly of this reunion was the sphere of yellow light cast by the little oil lamp on a table next to the cane chair where the damaged man sat unmoving, and the smell of old canvas and straw and animals, the smell of burning oil and Sanson and rum. The air swam with dust motes. He didn't move or look at her until she had seated herself on a chair just outside the circle of light in the velvet brown darkness. Then he spoke with a bored insolence.

"You come see the lucky man, yes? Many fine white ladies come. You see from close, maybe even touch the black skin? You pay, and I show you everything."

Any doubts she had harbored vanished. She felt his voice in her bones, the voice that had teased her in the garden at Sans Douleur and played with her and pleased her during those hot afternoons while her great-aunt napped. She studied his face silently, unable at first to find her voice. He took a swig from his bottle and spoke again.

"I can tell you how all that happened. I have said this story to many fine gentlemen and ladies. What you wish."

Deborah leaned forward momentarily into his circle of yellow light to lay a few coins on the table. She spoke to him, wondering if he would recognize her.

"I know your story; I know about Mt. Pelée and St. Pierre. But I wonder what your life, your family was like before. Who did you lose in the catastrophe?"

"Very, very sad. My dear father, my mother, my brothers, everyone," he said. "My beautiful wife and my six strong sons and six beautiful girls," he said. "All dead from the fire. Very sad. You must pity me."

His eyes were on her handbag rather than on her face. It occurred to her that he might attempt to rob her as he had robbed her before.

"And Villette?" she asked. He became even more still, frozen in that moment.

"What you know of Villette?" he asked sharply. "What of Villette?" His face was no longer a mask of indifference. Now he seemed furious, perhaps afraid.

"Is she dead?"

"What you know of Villette?" he asked again, his voice raised, scowling into the shadow where Deborah sat.

"Sanson," she said.

He sprang to his feet like a wild thing, and Deborah stepped forward into the light and raised her veil. He gazed at her stupidly, and she bore his gaze.

"Sanson. I am Deborah. We were together at Sans Douleur. You remember me. Not so long, *pas longtemps*." She instinctively used the Martiniquean French in hopes of making contact. "I was also burned, as you see."

"You some white whore, no? The little béké girl? The whore who open her legs to a black boy. Now you come to me for more." He let his open shirt slip from his shoulders. "Or maybe you have a secret; now maybe you have a rich husband, white man husband who can't know. A secret can be told or not told," he said.

She brushed aside the threat of blackmail. Her rich white husband was dead what seemed a lifetime ago. "You know I had a child, yes? Villette must have told you. What do you know about that child? What can you tell me?"

He stood silent, mouth gaping, and Deborah wondered for the first time if the torture he had endured had addled his brain. And for the first time, she was afraid.

"Oh yes, I know where she live," Sanson said. "I can find her. But not without the . . . " He broke off and made the island hand gesture requesting money. "You want this pretty little *jeune fille*, yes?"

Deborah saw it all then, contained in the ugly light of that space, the cupidity in his eyes, the pain; she saw that he was untethered, unreachable across the vast gulf that connected them, his abject suffering, his malice, his indifference, his drunkenness and lies, his awful history so like and so unlike her own. She saw the death of Gianni and all the children of that sparkling white city that had died in the burning darkness. She saw that there was no hope of learning anything from Sanson, and with the death of that hope came relief like a cool stream of sanity that restored her, followed inevitably by another wave of the gnawing grief that had become a familiar companion.

Villette had said that Sanson was a bad boy. Grown into a bad man, Deborah thought. A truly bad man. He would no doubt find a place in her pantheon of dreaming images along with the others that haunted her sleeping world. She pitied him for what he had endured there in his prison cell, the pain and terror and the long torture and hopelessness before rescuers found him and nursed him back to life. But she had no business to transact with Sanson, nothing unfinished, everything unfinished, but nothing that could come to any conclusion other than this goodbye.

That night, and in the years to come, Deborah would try to paint him—in the spotlight, in the lamplight—but she wasn't satisfied. She always scraped down the canvas and started over, Sanson full-length with scars, without scars, just his wicked face, or as a lithe young man. Sanson's portrait became her in-between project when she had finished something big and was waiting to start on whatever came next, a way to break her obsession and cleanse the palate. It was not until the day she picked up a stick of charcoal and idly sketched what she intended later to paint that she saw what she was trying to say—Sanson's face with Gianni's imagined face superimposed on it, or perhaps the other way around, Gianni looking out through Sanson's spiteful eyes with innocence and mystery.

There, she thought. That's done.

11

~ *Innocents Lost* ~

As Freddy had predicted, the wound on Deborah's face, though still inescapable, shrank and became less lurid as time passed, some days returning to prominence, then fading again and never as ghastly as it had first seemed. The pain came and went on its own schedule. The greasy black ointment was used up, and she rarely resorted to laudanum. Her arm, though the flesh was scarred, recovered much more quickly with its lesser exposure to the re-burning rays of the sun.

Grief seemed to follow a similar erratic course. Sometimes unexpectedly, it exploded to the size of the sky when she heard a child's laugh or caught sight of cherub faces decorating a building façade, or for no reason at all. But the sting of loss, the cruelty of it, the shock became less vivid to her as her physical wounds healed. When the sorrow of her incalculable loss assailed her in the streets, she fled back to her silent room to get her crying done before the rest of the boarders arrived home from their work.

She often sat on a park bench or wandered through the rackety streets, enjoying the frantic energy of so many people intent on their individual pursuits. The faces, the moustaches, and ladies' hats and kerchiefs, the smells of exotic food and exotic people, the outrageous fashions and costumes, the colors, sometimes brilliant, more often blending in blacks, grays, and white, all fueled her inspiration and her drive. Then she would return to the Frauhaus and her appropriated studio, full of images and impressions, to sketch and dream and outline, inwardly tasting the possibilities. The overwhelming fervor of her first paintings after the catastrophe had left her light and empty but she had faith that the energy that had fueled her explosive painting on the hospital wall would return. She mostly painted at the museums, at the will of the masters.

The loss of Sans Douleur and the consequent reduction in her income were hardships she could readily accept; her expenses were few and the Judge's allowance supplemented by unexpectedly modest revenue from the sale of the St. Louis house sufficed for the time being, though she knew the house money would run out in a few more years. She considered finding pupils, following in Miss Jean Singleton's footsteps, but kept putting it off, not wanting to step away from her own work and spend her precious time on the work of others. She had neither the patience nor the desperation of Miss Singleton. Besides, before the money dwindled away, she hoped to be selling paintings, though her earliest attempts left her discouraged and a little shaken.

She decided to test the water to see if there was a place for her work in the hot, mysterious, competitive, inhospitable, unpredictable art world of New York. The first difficulty was selecting which of her paintings to take with her. Perhaps she should guess which kind of painting would succeed. Would variety be seen as a sign of dilettantism? In the end, she settled on a still life, *Ginger Jar with Iris*, a sentimental dual portrait of MarianneHelen in their Sunday best, and her favorite, a menacing dreamscape of Mt. Pelée before the explosion, in which it seemed to be holding its breath, its valleys like dark wounds in green flesh, soon to run with blood and smoke. They were small canvases by necessity so that she could lug them through the city. She chose to try her luck at the Biltmore-Marcuse gallery because it was closest, and she usually enjoyed the paintings displayed in their windows.

The satin-haired gentleman at the gallery, Mr. Marcuse-Smith, was brusque in his refusal.

"We do not accept unrepresented work," he said. "Not from unknowns such as yourself. Perhaps if you had an agent. I'm sure your friends think you're talented. But I'm in business, and I only handle work I can sell. My sincerest regrets, madam." He turned away as though the interaction were completed, but Deborah was not inclined to accept this rejection as final, her work unseen.

"Look at them," Deborah said. "At least have a look."

"Madam, I assure you . . . "

"Just look."

Mr. Marcuse-Smith sighed and smoothed his already smooth hair. He took the three paintings into a back room and set them up on easels there. Deborah followed him.

She could sense that something was not quite right. Perhaps her pictures were not conventional enough, or perhaps they lacked a certain originality or whatever it was that she had gained when she had painted like a madwoman in Martinique. She hated feeling these misgivings and doubts, here in front of this unpleasing man who seemed to be studying her face rather than the canvases.

"So, if I may ask, what happened here? What happened to your face?"

Deborah stiffened. "I fail to see the relevance," she said.

"Well, look at it this way, madam. If we have a story to tell—hotel fire, burned trying to save a poor child, or maybe an old person—I can see how that could really work. Slashed by a jealous wife, maybe, or a spiteful rival. Acid. We use that story, or whatever story is most intriguing, sell it to the press, big sensation—The Wounded Lady or maybe The Lady with the Scar—I don't know—

something the public will eat up. We have a big opening—
and you're there for the reception, maybe a veil that goes
up—so what do you say? It's a way to see what the public
will buy."

"No." Deborah would not stay to endure further mor-
tification. She could sort out her feelings later in privacy.
She returned the paintings to her portfolio and secured the
fastening.

Mr. Marcuse-Smith called to her as she walked away.
"Wait, wait just a moment, please, madam, wait—"

But she didn't stop, and she didn't turn around. She
was not the Crab Woman. She was an artist. She began to
think that Waterman's art agent might not be such a pest.
She would look for a chance to talk with him.

But now that she was receptive, it seemed that the
man had vanished entirely, though she kept an eye out for
his distinctive, rolling walk and the tilt of his head. She
could feel the tug of vision pulling her to engage again with
paint and canvas and the big visible world and the even
bigger invisible ocean. Yet she had to haunt the museums
where she now was impatient with the masters, the careful
colors and conventional forms, things already painted.

She had almost given up when she spotted him standing in front of Rivaldi's *Crucifixion,* painted at the bidding
of his patron, the Count di Strazio, to hang in his family
chapel, intended, Deborah supposed, to demoralize his
servants into abject virtue. The Christ in the painting appeared to be newly crucified, his erect head turned and his
white eyes cast upward as lurid blood ran freely from his
thorny crown, streaming down his lean cheeks to merge
with the bright river gushing from his broken side, outlin-
ing the contours of his pale, muscular thighs.

Deborah approached the absorbed agent and stood
next to him. When he sensed her presence, he shook his

head slightly and said, "Ah, the poor, poor fellow. So very painful." He turned and started when he saw her, then suggested they take tea together in a nearby tea shop. She was surprised at this turn of events but agreed.

It wasn't lust; that much was clear. He introduced himself with the single name, Remy, and then inquired about her training, her work in general. Had she sold? Did she presently take classes? What were her connections in the New York art world? It threatened to unnerve her that her answers were no training, no sales, and no connections. Yet. She expected him to make polite excuses to end the interview. Instead, he complimented her effusively on her talent as a copyist, quite remarkable.

He related his own story. As a young man in France, he wanted to paint but didn't have the talent that he saw in the work of his fellow art students. His family had been delighted when, after a brief flirtation with the theatre, he turned to the business side of art, the part they understood. He had come to New York when he felt the tide turn from the simultaneously formal and quasi-pornographic art of the Paris salons to the brittle, imaginative, daring work being produced in the new world.

"And you handle Samuel Waterman's work, I understand," Deborah said.

Remy flushed and looked away.

"I am seeking an agent myself."

"Tell me, Miss Huntworth," he said. "Can you keep secrets?"

"I have done little else," she replied after a pause. "Yes, I can keep secrets."

"You are undoubtedly a woman of conventions, I believe? You have led a spotless and orderly life? Is this your intention?"

"I fail to understand you, sir, or how my morals

concern you at all. I do not believe you are proposing to seduce me, at least not for yourself. And I would refuse such a proposition, not from conventional morality, as you assume, but l would refuse."

He kept his worried brown eyes on her face and waited in a way that almost forced her to continue.

"But no, I have not always been constrained by social conventions."

"Ah," he said. "I want to commission a painting and the copy of another painting. For me—not for sale, not as a forger, of course, but as a brilliant copyist. Will you do that? The remuneration will be commensurate with the task, as one says. But you must keep our business entirely *entre nous*, in confidence, with no mention of me or the work, not even a suspicion. As if it had not happened. Do I interest you?"

She could put the payment to good use. She had started envisioning larger canvases, and they would cost. So let him have his private little Botticelli nude or whatever he wished. Thus the deal was struck. To her surprise, the paintings he commissioned were Watermans: the first a smaller version of *The Spring Park*, a Waterman canvas she remembered from an earlier visit to the Macbeth Gallery.

"Can you make arrangements with the manager there?" Deborah asked.

"No, no. I want you to look at it in the gallery but paint it in your little studio, in secret."

"That's not how it works," Deborah protested. "I need to check and recheck; I need to compare."

"I want you to make it winter, to paint the same scene in winter. For that, you will not need to paint in the gallery, no? Can you do this?"

"Yes, I can do that," Deborah said. "I'll have it in two

or three weeks, with any luck, a small canvas. What of the second one?"

"An interior in the Waterman style, exactly. Any interior you wish." Deborah noticed that his hands were shaking through fear or excitement or simple palsy; she didn't know.

"We will meet again," he said. "You shall be good to send me word when the work is ready." He handed her his card, bowed stiffly, and was gone.

Although she had not retained him as an agent, she had made a prestigious professional contact that boded well.

Deborah spent a morning in the gallery studying the Waterman, how the painter had conceived the piece, composed it, balanced and then unbalanced it so that the eye was continually surprised to find itself trying to look past the edge, under the frame where the scene surely continued. It was a charming effect, gently playful, a trick of placement and color. She let herself picture this park covered in white, the purple and red and yellow of the flowers gone, the piquant green of the leaves in the foreground covered in crisp snow. How to make the scene sparkle even in stasis, how to imply spring. She paid special attention to Waterman's signature, the jagged orange W that asserted the authenticity she intended to counterfeit. She took her impressions back to Ernst Kanda's studio to wrestle with.

Deborah's preoccupation with Remy Martin's project made her almost a ghost in the life of the Frauhaus. She feared she would be interrupted, cajoled, and urged to reveal her work to them, but she had never had her working life treated with such respect. The other boarders understood, protected, and even envied the fever that drove her, accepting the secrecy of her work, and clearly Frau H. and Liesl had experience dealing with the artistic temperament they had met with in Ernst Kanda—providing food, drink, and silence, giving the artist uninterrupted time for the sacred pursuit of art.

After experimenting with the color and brushstroke that would create a hard crust of snow while implying the green spring just under the surface, Deborah was reminded of the marrons in her paintings of Mt. Pelée and the technique she had used there: an unevenness in the surface of the dark paint where darkness had seemed to hide. In the winter scene, the new growth below would be implied by sparkle on the white surface.

Satisfied with her work, she turned to the Frauhaus dining room for the required interior in the Waterman style. The composition came easily, the bowed walls and the white-paned doors at the end of the room, but the colors refused to create the movement implied by the detritus of an everyday dining table. She had not found the key, the smiling nudge that typically unlocked the subtle whimsy of a Waterman. And the yellow of a half-emptied bread plate that occupied a central position—it was . . . something. Too yellow, not yellow enough. Too bright and forward. Too simply happy. She would have to scrape it down, much as she hated the process, and patch in some other yellow.

This felt like a good time to step away from the work, take a walk in the fresh air, see what the world was doing, and come back with a fresh eye and a rested hand. When she opened her studio door, she found MarianneHelen standing there, hand in hand, gazing up at her, four blue eyes blazing with excitement.

"Oh, Mrs. Huntworth!" one of them said, echoed by the other saying, "Oh!" They put their hands to their pink cheeks and waited for her reaction.

"My goodness, girls, what is it? What is your news?"

"Oh, Mrs. Huntworth! Oh, we are to go on the ship for

a picnic! Not next week. Or the next. The week after that one. The *General*, it's called. It's bigger than anything! We wanted to go last year, but we had chickenpox. But this year, we have not even a spot!" They held their arms out for her inspection.

"All the *Kinder* from the neighborhood and the church are going, and we are all to dress up in our very best dresses. And Mama is taking us!"

"And we are to have new hats! Mama is making them now."

"And her hat is so beautiful! It has pink roses!"

"So," Deborah interposed, "is Mama going too? And what about the Frau?"

"*Oma* won't come. She is afraid of the water. She has bad dreams, she says."

"But we aren't afraid! We shall be on the big ship, waving flags!"

"Mama said you wouldn't want to come with us, but she said we could ask you. But not to disturb you."

"So we waited all day."

"My dears, how sweet of you! But no, your wise mama is right. I will rather finish my work here." Deborah gently touched the two shining blonde heads, planting a soft kiss on each one. "Thank you for thinking of me," she said, thinking how dear they had become to her, while inwardly she could not keep herself from evaluating the color of their silky yellow heads, thinking no, not at all the right yellow. Too silver. Too heavenly.

Her walk took her to Washington Square and a satisfying rest on one of the many park benches, eyes closed, breathing in the smell of spring, the perfumes of the fashionable ladies, the mix of horse droppings and fumes from the factories and occasional motorcars. The sounds of the city, which had once seemed overwhelming, now almost lulled her to sleep.

On her way back to the Frauhaus, happier for the break and refreshed in spirit, she stopped to purchase a tin of turpentine and a variety of yellows, though she was resigned to being defeated by the challenge, at least for today. On the next corner was a little shoe shop, and in the window was a pair of children's boots, shiny, soft chocolate brown, lovely things. On an impulse, she stopped in. They were just as pleasing to touch and to close inspection. They smelled rich and wonderful. Deborah took the risk, paying for two pairs with money she could ill afford until the secret paintings were paid for. It felt to her like a gesture of good faith, of belief in the possibility of good fortune.

Back at the house, she left the boots on the dining room table and returned to her studio for another two hours of work before she would be fed and would take herself to rest, her head full of color and mystery. Through the visionary world she was living in, she heard the squeals of pleasure from MarianneHelen when they spotted their beautiful new boots, the murmur of Liesl hushing them, and was satisfied. But now, the plate was almost orange, not right at all, especially when she appended Waterman's quavering jag of a signature. At the far end of the table in her painting, she added two little boots, one standing upright, the other fallen on its side. But that damn yellow!

She decided to let it go, let the paint cure for a week or two, pack the pieces carefully, deliver them to the address Remy had given her, and collect her fee. He could have them varnished in a few months when the paint had completely cured. She wrote him a note to set a time for delivery at his flat. If the work was good enough and he wanted her to undertake more, he would have to make a clean breast of the prodigious secret she didn't know but was already pledged to keep.

~~~~~~~

On the morning of the mysterious appointment, Deborah was aware of a heightened atmosphere in the house even before she set foot on the top stair. Liesl and MarianneHelen stood on display in the dining room, decked out in their holiday outfits for the admiration of the breakfasting boarders. Liesl looked like a rose in a deep pink hat and shawl, her children like pastel rosebuds at her side. The twins held out their feet to show Deborah the boots, which apparently fit and added to the sense of celebration and adventure that bubbled up. The little girls were so mad with excitement that their mother wisely sent them out into the hall to go up and down the stairs, where they could be heard singing as quietly as they could, in deference to any still sleeping boarder. They sang a rhythmic chant of their own devising: "Slow-come, Fast-come, General Slocum, good-bye my lady, good-bye." Even the usually imperturbable Liesl had a pink wash to her cheeks in anticipation of the outing. At last, the three were off. The house felt hollow in the silence that followed their exuberant departure for the pier to board the steamship for its annual expedition up the East River to a picnic ground on Long Island.

~~~~~~~

Deborah stepped lightly on her way to meet with Remy again, buoyed up by the charming Frauhaus scene she left behind her, glad she had contributed to their pleasure. She was, however, thinking more and more of the agent's strange manner and preparing herself to retreat if the situation required it. His flat was the second floor of a long yellow building where the first floor had been converted from stables to automobile garages or small studios for artists lucky enough to afford them.

Remy himself answered her knock and hurried her into his sitting room, taking the portfolio from her and leaning her paintings against the back cushions of a loveseat.

"Perhaps I might have a cup of tea?" Deborah did not wish to be treated like a peddler. These were commissioned works, after all.

"But yes, of course, *mamselle*," Remy said, but he made no move, staring fixedly at the two paintings, his eyes narrowed. She realized he was holding his breath. She walked past him and found the kitchen where she filled the teakettle and set it on the ring. When she came back, having managed a tray with two cups and sliced lemon, he took his cup absently, his eyes still on her work.

"These are most excellent," he said, smoothing his moustache. "These are indeed Watermans, as I requested. Most remarkable."

Deborah waited. She felt a surge of panic that she was being manipulated in some devilish way, set up to take a fall, or possibly for blackmail. She felt in that instant as though the floor was floating beneath her, as though she had come unmoored. With the greatest effort, she clutched the arms of the chair and prevented herself from crying out or dashing out the door. She needed the money, and the work was good.

"Yes, very admirable!" Remy said. "And could you produce more, larger pieces?"

Deborah gathered her dignity and glared at Remy, asking in a frosty voice, "Does Mr. Waterman know you intend to forge his work?"

Remy smiled. "Shall we go upstairs to his flat and ask the good gentleman?" He seized the paintings and bounded out of the room, followed more slowly by Deborah, who was still chilled and stiff with confusion and trepidation.

An unpleasant old woman in black opened the third-floor apartment door just a crack and peered out at them.

"What'll you want?" she asked.

"Clara, open the door." Remy moved her gently aside and strode across the hall into a long dark sitting room, lit only at the far end where a remarkable older man was seated as though on a throne. His brush of silver hair shone, and he was dressed in day clothes but with night slippers on his feet and a nubby blue afghan over his knees. He wore incongruous riding gloves, giving him an air of eccentricity. When he spoke with a slight brogue, his voice was cool and musical with a little pleasant roughness that revealed age and a predilection for spirits. Deborah had seen his self-portrait in the gallery. It was Samuel Waterman himself.

"You'll need to forgive Clara," he said. "I just dismissed her for general uselessness and larceny, the silly old biddy, and being fired seems to have soured her outlook. She's just leaving."

Sure enough, the front door closed rather loudly. Samuel Waterman shrugged her away and turned his bright eyes and attention to Deborah.

"What are you bringing to me, Remy? Will this be the little ventriloquist you've been on about? Let's have a gander at the work, then."

"Samuel Waterman, I introduce Mademoiselle Huntworth, the copyist of whom I have spoken. Wait till you see," Remy said, setting the two pieces on an easel and standing back next to Sam.

"Bring it a bit closer into the light," Sam said.

Deborah took a seat and waited for events to unfold. The sturdy Frenchman and the tall Irishman stood in front of her Watermans and murmured, speaking in an aesthetic code she was oddly reassured to understand.

"First, the winterscape."

"So many green shoots under the snow. Is that right, Sam?"

"They fade against the little snow prisms. It's one way. Late winter, I should think, so we're getting two views, a palimpsest."

"The lateral balance? What do you think?"

"Look, Remy, the whole scene is sliding, falling down through the center, isn't it. It's about to melt away, which is clever. You know I like to paint a little clever when it doesn't interfere. She's got that. Surprising."

Sam Waterman turned to Deborah. "You must have a mind as well as an eye, Miss Huntworth. Not just a ventriloquist then—a clairvoyant."

Next, the Frauhaus breakfast room was set up for view.

"That courtyard at the back, through the open door perhaps, is too bright," Remy said, though everything he offered sounded more like a question than a statement.

"Maybe," Sam said. Then, "No, I might do that, like the millinery store. Makes the interior harder to decipher, deeper. Gives them something to look for."

Deborah moved to enter this arcane discussion and stood at Waterman's other side, tilting her head to match the angle of his own. "You like to trick the eye," she said, "just a little. Just enough to engage, not enough to be tiring or hostile."

"What's the trouble here? Something. It's not the shoes. They're intriguing, at least to me."

"It's the color of the bread plate," Deborah suggested.

"I couldn't figure it out, so I left it wrong. What do you think?"

"It's not so bad," Remy said, but the two painters studied it intently, until almost in unison, they said, "Mustard!" exchanging a look of satisfaction and agreement.

"That's done it!" Waterman said. "Mustard."

The men seated themselves, and Deborah took a seat in the remaining chair flanking Waterman's, all equals now.

"Mr. Waterman," she said. "What is this all about? Why do you want me to forge your paintings?"

A heavy silence followed her question. Sam Waterman held out his hands to Remy, who gently peeled off the black gloves, revealing gnarled fingers, twisted knobs, and swollen joints, painful to look at, like sea creatures washed up and motionless. He turned them palms up, though his hands remained curled instead of open.

"What can I do?" he asked. "I can only paint a dab or two, and the pain stops me. I can hardly manage a sketch from time to time. I used to drink the whiskey or take laudanum and work through, but it's not enough now." He set his hands down gingerly in his lap, and Remy laid the lap robe over his painful secret.

"What can I do, Miss Huntworth?" he asked again. "I realize that my painting days are over, and there's nothing to be done about that. I've made my peace. But I still need the money, you see? When I was young, I was too young to save money, and now I'm too old to economize. I need to sell, produce and sell."

"The market is very eager for Watermans right now," Remy added. "There's quite a vogue, especially with the west coast collectors. I could sell them if we had them to sell."

"And that's where I come in," Deborah suggested.

"And you do realize, being adults and not naughty children, how very dangerous this is? Let's be clear. If we are ever exposed, I will be sent to prison for forgery, fraud, and conspiracy, possibly for the rest of my life. And they will not allow me to paint in prison. Mr. Waterman stands to lose not only his freedom and his income but also his reputation and his legacy. None of his paintings will be above suspicion."

She turned on Remy. "And you, you would lose your freedom, your reputation, yes, and the reputations of any painting you ever touched. Your other artists will be tainted by their association with you, and their careers will be blighted. The three of us may be willing to risk ruin for ourselves, but will we risk it for them as well?"

"We must be extremely cautious," Remy said. "Mr. Waterman and I have been discussing this plan for a while now. We can't have you carrying canvases around in public, so we think you must work here exclusively in this flat. If you wish, there is a separate room where you can live. We will say, and people will assume, that you are Mr. Waterman's new housekeeper. Does that offend you?"

"Or his fancy woman," Sam suggested, "now that Clara has left me?"

It seemed to Deborah that he was probing to see how easily she might be offended. She chose to ignore him.

"I would guess that I will end up doing some housekeeping, but it shan't cut into my painting time much. I should warn you, however. I am a most indifferent housekeeper."

Sam Waterman laughed. "We'll get along, I'm certain."

"We must remain united, my friends," Remy said, "even if we get caught. Mr. Waterman and I have done business for twenty years now. We have a long-established relationship, and we have discussed this arrangement, as you see, for quite a long time. I like you, Miss Huntworth, but . . . "

"But you don't trust me yet. That's understandable. But you have already revealed the crime to me. All that remains is to commit it. And, by the way, we cannot stand together if we get caught.

"If I am caught, I will say I had no idea the paintings were sold as genuine. And I will have my own paintings and my housekeeper's income, yes? On the other hand, if Mr. Waterman is somehow brought into question, he can claim ignorance of the plot between his agent and his housekeeper. If Remy is caught, he can claim ignorance about the paintings, which he accepted in good faith as always. That way, we can each clear ourselves and muddle the situation."

"Ventriloquist, clairvoyant, and now I believe we have found our ringleader." Sam beamed at her. "Let's have a drink on the strength of it! May the luck of the Irish follow us like a shadow!"

"I'm not Irish," Remy and Deborah said in one voice.

~~~~~~~

It was with a determined gait that Deborah set out for home, her mind full of details, thoughts and questions about the shady conspiracy she had just agreed to. What seemed most important to her was the question of what she would paint for them. It would be good to find out from Remy what Waterman's last pieces had been and what was likely to sell. Not portraits, she thought, which was good. She had learned a lot from copying Ernst Kanda's self-portrait, but her picture of MarianneHelen had only been for herself, really. Portraiture generally required subjects to sit for them. And in any case, it would be too great a challenge, especially at first. The city was a more likely subject. As she walked, she felt as though she were seeing the city around her through Waterman's eyes, trying on his quirks and mischief, but also his deep appreciation of the world and the beauty of it.

She was so absorbed by the look of things that it took her a while to notice a faint scent of salt in the air. Then she was struck by the unfamiliar look of the city around her: people simply standing, sometimes singly, more often in clusters, sometimes silent, more often buzzing, gesticulating, crying and comforting one another. The city was always full of sound, but it seemed now to include a new sound, shouts of pain, loud cries, as though its usual industry and purposeful rush had been replaced by agony, which has no purpose and no structure. It wasn't panic, she realized. It wasn't anger that stirred the air. She was hearing more and more the sound of a community taxed with grief, a sound heard before in Martinique, marked there with an island French accent. She broke into a run. At the little shoe shop, a woman sat on the stoop, wailing into her shawl while her husband hovered behind her, helpless and white with shock.

The front door to the Frauhaus stood wide open, revealing a dark rectangle like a mouth drawing in breath to release as a cry. Inside, boarders bunched at the foot of the stairway and strung down the hall, some weeping, some arguing in hushed voices, some just standing like gravestones.

"Good God!" Deborah shouted. "What has happened?"

She grabbed the nearest one by the elbow and turned her. "Martha! Tell me!"

The girl's eyes were puffy and reddened, her voice, usually so jolly and bright, now ragged and shaking.

"Oh, thank the Lord you are here, Mrs. Huntworth. We just heard the news."

"Tell me, Martha! Just say it!"

"The ship caught fire," Martha said. "And it seems they all died. That's what we've been told. That's what everyone is saying."

"Liesl?" Deborah asked. "And the little girls?"

"That's what we were told. Two of the boys have gone to the island, where the authorities are pulling bodies out of the river. They're going to check."

"When did they go?"

"As soon as we heard."

"And Frau? Where is she? Who is with her?"

Martha shook her head. "I can't think what to do."

Deborah flew down the hallway and into Frau Hollenback's bedroom to find the old woman alone, huddled in an armchair too big for her shrunken form, staring blankly at the wall. Her hands were icy cold.

"Martha," Deborah shouted. "Come quick."

Martha's frightened face peered in.

"Make her some tea and find something warm to eat—toast, maybe soup. She is about to perish here from the shock."

"Is it true?" Frau H. asked, clinging with surprising strength to Deborah's arm. "Are they truly gone and gone without me? All my angels *zuzammen*? *Alle*?"

"I don't know," Deborah said, wrapping her arms around the old woman, sliding down next to her in the soft chair. "It seems likely."

She held Frau Hollenback and rocked her. "I am so sorry, my dear Frau. We should have further word when the boys come back."

Frau Elsie Hollenback wept then until she was empty of everything but grief. Deborah saw that her desolation was complete.

"The little girls," Frau said. "The little ones. All those little girls, all those beautiful young women like my Liesl, my sunlight, all my hope and comfort. I was so unhappy when Ernst died, and then Liesl came home and my little angels, I always worried that she would marry a new man and leave me. Wicked thoughts to grudge her what she herself must wish."

This was followed by a long string of muttered German words. Frau Hollenback was praying. When she had finished her prayer, she looked up again at Deborah, asking the same question she had started with, as though she might be given a different answer.

"Is it true?"

"I know almost nothing, my dear Frau, only what I've been told. We will be strong and wait for the news together."

When the two shocked young men returned, they gathered everyone into the parlor.

"I can't tell this over and over," one of them said with a shaking voice. "I can't keep telling it. Let's get it over with." His audience fastened their horror-stricken eyes on him as he stood in front of them and began. He addressed his remarks to Frau H., who had been guided into the drawing room by Martha, seemingly resolved to redeem her earlier failure to act.

"We were directed to go to North Brother Island, and this reporter fellow offered us a ride up in his automobile. They had the bodies on the shore, in rows, but they were still pulling them out of the water. They showed us the latest survivor list, and our people weren't listed. So we walked along the shore looking for them, and we found Liesl there, with one of the twins."

"Only one?" someone asked. And the answer was,

"Only one."

It seemed like grief overtopping itself that Marianne-Helen were separated in this catastrophic death. They should have been together. They should have.

Deborah knew about bodies in rows. She had been one of them, had taken her place between one dying soul and another, waiting for death or rescue or both. She could feel memories of her ordeal aboard the *Roraima* rising up in her, her pain and grief surprisingly fresh. And she realized that what she had lost, a dearly loved but unknown child, a long hoped-for reunion, was a different anguish than this. Frau's grief would be renewed daily by memories, but not of a face seen only for a short night like the lost Gianni's. Frau's mourning would be defined by a history of years and a long-established habit of loving, susceptible to ceaseless reminders of faces, voices, ways, words, and living.

Frau H. appeared to Deborah on the verge of collapse, so she led her back to the bedroom, helped her into night things, and arranged for a hot water bottle to be placed at her icy feet.

"What more can I do for you?" Deborah asked.

"Schnapps. A little schnapps. Behind the flour in the pantry."

Schnapps was duly found, poured, and sipped with trembling lips. It seemed to give momentary relief to the exhausted old woman.

"Rest now," Deborah said. "We'll take care of ourselves. We'll take care of you."

The shaken boarders gathered around the table that had seen so much conviviality when Liesl had been there to steer, encourage, and enjoy their arguments and conversations. They were white-faced and subdued, some with set, grim faces, others weeping openly. The meal Martha and several of the others had cobbled together was hot but peculiar—odd chunks of potato and beets stirred together, topped with a handful of chopped celery, ham slices glazed with a film of peach jam, beef broth with circles of carrots. Sour lemonade and raisin bread. The stoics ate doggedly, the more openly emotional picked at their plates and occasionally sniffed. Frau's chair at the head of the table sat empty. Even when Deborah looked away, the three empty chairs at the foot seemed to throb with light. One of the young men sprang to his feet and moved the vacant seats to the kitchen.

"Thank you," Deborah said. "And thank you, friends, for cooking our dinner. I think we should all meet back in the parlor to consider what we can do when Frau decides what she needs. And how we can take care of her and each other. And ourselves. I expect this is the end of the Frauhaus, much as we have loved being here."

"And loved them," came a soft voice. "Love them."

The meeting in the parlor generated a number of impractical schemes for keeping the house together: taking turns doing the chores, trying to raise enough money to buy it, looking for a woman to take over Liesl's function. Then the talk turned to loss and death, each speaker having lost someone: a beloved cousin fallen through ice on a Wisconsin pond; a younger sister lost to tuberculosis; a handsome brother trampled by a panicking horse; mothers taken from their grieving children after birth struggles—all the mourning that accompanies, sometimes seems to occupy, life, marking the ratcheting progress of time. Deborah said nothing. She slipped out to look in on the sleeping Frau, pulled the coverlet closer about her, and softly closed the door. Tomorrow would be a day to think. It was not until she lay exhausted in her own bed that she remembered the conspiracy she had entered into earlier that same day. It seemed years ago. She would send Remy a note to let him know she would be delayed.

In the morning, Deborah woke late and dressed quickly, heavy-hearted. She found Frau H. seated at her usual station, and there was hot chocolate and bread and the rest of the ham if she could find the appetite for it.

"Mrs. Huntworth," Frau said. "I have sent to my brother Peter who farms in the north from here. He will send a cart for me and my things. I will ask the girls to help me choose. And someone to pack. I think the cart may come Saturday or maybe Sunday."

"Is this your best wish?"

The old woman waved the question away. What was there to wish for in this sad life?

It was eerie to stand in the increasingly dismantled household, listening for the stilled beating of its lost heart, and Deborah wept as she packed up her art supplies and a few paintings to take with her. An art dealer came and took away the Kanda paintings, leaving a somewhat larger payment than Deborah expected. An auctioneer's assistant came to evaluate, insult, and take away the heavy furniture. He was followed by an estate agent come to value the house. The agent was brusque in giving the boarders just a few days to find new accommodations. Deborah was kept busy most of the day caring for the grief-stricken old woman and making the best decisions she could in the face of Frau Hollenback's exhausted indifference.

On Sunday, the young men loaded the farm cart while Martha and a few other girls stood by and shouted mingled encouragement and cautions. Frau Hollenback opened her door, and the handful of boarders fell silent and parted as before royalty to give her a path to the cart, the farm, and the rest of her life. Deborah stood with the others in the street to say goodbye. They watched the cart roll away, Frau H. a small mound on the seat, bouncing with every jolt. The corner of a framed painting, paper-wrapped, stuck up in the very back of the cart.

It was quick work for Deborah to gather her own belongings and contract with a carter to haul it all to Remy's building. She felt a nagging anxiety that this future she had chosen would have disappeared, and her steps to begin this new life quickened to a run. She knocked briskly on Samuel Waterman's door, and when it opened, she said, "I'm going to live here. I'll paint for you."

With a nod and a wink and that peculiar mouth-clicking that often accompanies a wink, Sam opened the door wide. "That's the ticket," he said.

12

~ *The Waterman Years* ~

After a few months of indecision, hesitation, and false
starts, the Waterman conspirators found that their
enterprise was succeeding; they could produce and sell
works painted by Deborah and signed by Waterman. After
the second forged Waterman sold without raising any
questions of authenticity, they relaxed and fell into a comfortable routine they would follow for the eight years they
were in operation. Sam had grown reclusive so as to conceal his twisted hands from public view and Deborah preferred paint to people, so they had little contact with
society. Remy, however, continued to circulate, keeping
abreast of the market, trends, emerging artists, and, of
course, gossip of the art world, which it amused Sam to
hear.

This time was to become known in art history books
as the most productive period in the distinguished career
of the great Samuel Waterman.

Sales went well, some paintings finding places in the
great houses on the California coast, often in the collection
of the Bobinette sisters, Rachel and Eula, who celebrated
the rewards of outliving their male relatives by spending
the family money on charitable causes and a large collection of American art, especially the works of Theodore
Robinson and Samuel Waterman. Some of Deborah's
Watermans ended up hanging in board rooms and
corporate offices, where discerning decorators sought
paintings that would interest and ornament without tempting the minds of the captains of industry to wander off into

erotic fantasies.

True to her word, Deborah was not a good house-keeper. When Remy could no longer bear conditions in Sam's flat, he would hire temporary help to restore things to some order. They developed a routine as forgers. Deborah would go out and identify possible scenes, trying to look with Sam's vision and sensibility, guessing what would interest him. He might go out later for a solitary stroll to see it for himself. She would make a few pencil sketches, always adding an element that one would never see in a Waterman, a snowman or fashionable lady or a sea-gull, to throw any acute observer off the scent though it was unlikely that such an observer existed. Then a meeting would take place over the sketches she had produced, Remy to consider what might sell and to mediate between the two, Sam to choose a few and comment on their possibilities, color palette, composition, while Deborah argued with him about how a Waterman would best be realized.

At first, the arguments caused Remy some concern for the feasibility of their project. Then he realized that the friction between the two painters was a source of enjoyment to both, a flirtation or seduction, teasing, but also exploring the mysterious and fascinating other.

"So, Mr. Waterman, you are asking for another garden scene, but you never want to use pink. Why is that?"

"You've not used your eyes, then, have you, Miss Huntworth, or you haven't seen many of my bits."

"You use pink for elements in the composition that aren't pink, like highlights and underlit shadows and reflections of red. But you don't just paint pink things."

"Are you saying, then, that highlights and reflections aren't things? Now that's not very painterly of you."

"What is it, Sam? Are you afraid of being accused of Irish sentimentality? Of having a soft heart?"

"I don't paint hair ribbons, missy; they don't interest me. So the lilies are yellow, like I said, brilliant yellow. Not mustard, as you're no doubt thinking. And don't go playing tricks on me either."

"Then you'll want me to leave out the bunnies?"

Sam just laughed. Deborah would paint as accurately as possible in the Waterman style. And her work had been impressive so far. The empty park bench drenched in rain was particularly fine to his eye. He wasn't sure he could have achieved that effect of horizontal depth, the texture of falling water as a screen and a lens, a clarifying blur. But he was willing to take credit for it.

When Remy reported that Eula Bobinette had expressed interest in seeing and possibly purchasing a Waterman with human figures, Sam refused outright.

"I don't paint people. I never have. I only paint things I like, and I don't like people. Tell her no, it can't be done."

"Maybe someone in the distance, maybe a skater in a winterscape? An old person at the fireplace in an interior? Come on, Mr. Waterman, maybe we should branch out."

"Watermans don't portray people, as you know. Or bunnies. Or snowmen. So just tell her no."

"But think what a challenge!"

"You, missy. You're the only challenge here. And I won't sign it, and that's that."

But in the event, when confronted with a winter sunset—the sky wild with orange, scarlet, and vermilion, in the darkened foreground, a frozen lake with one lone skater curving towards a fringe of gray weeds, the colors of the sky's reflection lighting his silhouette—Sam signed.

"It just shows that even at this stage in your career, you are still developing and growing! That's a good thing, right?"

"No more," Sam said. Eula Bobinette got her painting,

and that was the last of it.

Since the conspirators did not want to flood the market with Watermans, Deborah was encouraged to work at a moderate pace in the silent studio, Sam having been banished for making occasional, unwelcome suggestions—irreverent, intrusive, or bawdy, always distracting. He would have his opportunity to guide her when the painting was almost ready. He would have the final say, but his presence as she worked was an irritant that interfered with the process. The resulting solitude also gave her the privacy she needed to paint her own work in secret, with only herself as audience.

Deborah's paintings were kept covered when a rare visitor came calling, perhaps an old friend of Sam's, more often a younger painter wishing to pay his respects who, shyly or with bravado, revealed work from the shabby portfolio he had brought. Deborah would take the visitor's coat and leave them to chat, taking the opportunity to gather up cups and plates that had accumulated on tables, bookshelves, sometimes the floor, and wash them. She didn't linger, as she wished to remain unremarked, but she looked forward to hearing Sam's scurrilous summary of the conversation after the guest had departed.

"He wanted to talk about the artistic temperament, the woolly-brained goatherd! He thinks he has it, he says, and that's why he's misunderstood. What a ballyhoo! He's misunderstood because his work is an embarrassing, criminal hodgepodge of the worst flaws in the visions of better men!"

"Perhaps you won't allow him entry another time," Deborah offered helpfully.

"It'll be a cold hell when I do, that I promise you. Pretentious little windbag!" Sam took his restorative tot of whiskey between twisted hands and guided it carefully to his lips.

"And what will I tell him if he calls?"

"Tell him I'm indisposed with vapors. Tell him I'm running an artistic temperature. What a useless lot of wasters these new fellas are, to be sure."

"You look tired," Deborah said, but Sam was already resting his head against the tufted chairback, and his eyes were closed. She resisted the sudden impulse to smooth the back of her hand from the sharp cheekbones down the long jaw of this face that was becoming so familiar, to trace the smile lines in his cheeks and follow the bow of his lips with her fingertip. She stood entranced, lost, absorbed in imagining, rehearsing the gesture, until Sam moved his head slightly and broke the spell. Deborah shoved her hands into her skirt pockets and abruptly took herself out of the room.

Sam Waterman's spirit was strong, but Deborah and Remy worried about his health. He seemed to tire easily, and there was a shadow on his face when he thought himself unobserved. The doctor he had reluctantly consulted warned against over-exertion, fearing the onset of a debilitating or fatal apoplexy. In spite of medical advice, Sam continued to enjoy his drink in the evenings, claiming he'd rather die tipsy than live sober.

"I'm not so old as you think," he told Remy. "I've still some vinegar in my veins."

Remy just shook his head at this.

"You're old enough to know better," Deborah told him, but both knew he would keep living as he wished, being Samuel Waterman.

Deborah worried most when Remy was out of town, as he frequently was, "peddlin' me pictures," as Sam liked to say. On one such night, Deborah awoke from her dream of smoke and loss, in a panic that Sam had called out, that he needed her help. She ran to his bedroom and flung open the door to find him sitting up in bed, reading by lamplight, surprised by her precipitous intrusion but clearly not in distress.

"I thought you were ill," Deborah blurted out. "I thought you needed me."

"Not ill," Sam said. "Just a wee bit old. Come sit with me for a moment and let's gather up our wits, shall we?"

She pulled a chair to the side of his bed, and so they sat and considered each other, undisguised, no longer masked by the veil of seduction and the chitchat of flirtation. For a long moment, they simply gazed, seeing the beloved other with loving eyes. It was Sam who spoke first.

"You've a kind heart, Miss Huntworth. You've a kind and a caring heart." Sam cocked his head to one side and spoke in his best brogue. "Surely you wouldn't let an old man die a vairgin?"

Deborah laughed and slipped into the bed next to him, sharing his pillow, feeling the warmth of his long body.

"I've all me manly parts in working order," Sam said, "but sadly, I've no hands to love you with as you deserve."

"I have hands," Deborah said.

~~~~~~~

In the second year of the conspiracy, a letter from George Kennan arrived bearing good news: Miss Kathleen Kelly was said to be living with a sister, Rose Kelly, on Manhattan Island on Mulberry Street. He hoped that this would be enough to enable her to contact her friend. The note was short and apologetic. He was working on a monograph about his travels in the Caucasus, and the business end was troublesome beyond belief. He would write more later. He wished her luck in her search.

Deborah was thrilled by the very notion that Katy was here, almost under her hand, which she stretched out unconsciously as though to tug at Katy's sleeve as she used to do. Katy here! Katy so close! Here, in New York! It was possible she had passed Katy in the crowded streets, had missed her in the passing stream of strangers. Her heart seemed to find a new rhythm, a hope that she could reunite with the much-loved companion of her childhood. And now she had a street name to work with.

But further reflection brought misgivings. Mulberry Street was not in a well-to-do neighborhood. Katy couldn't be in service in a good house, then, where she would be safe. And the idea of Katy in penury or privation or danger prodded Deborah into action. She left the flat and found her way to Mulberry Street, through streets that grew narrower and dirtier. The buildings loomed over the rough crowds, who jostled and sometimes stared at Deborah. She kept a firm grip on her handbag and pushed her way through. Each block she traversed was more disheartening, the streets narrower, the colors drab, the smells thicker and more unpleasant, the faces more drawn, more frightening.

In the first building she approached, she was met by the stench of cooked cabbage and human filth and smoke. She accosted a ragged woman who leaned listlessly in the doorway like an abandoned broom.

"Excuse me, is this where Miss Kathleen Kelly lives? With her sister, Rose?"

The woman glanced at her with clouded eyes but gave no answer.

"Who lives here? Are the Kelly sisters inside, Katy and Rose? Please help me find them. I can pay you for the information. It's most important."

The woman held out her dirt-lined palm and waited.

When the few coins arrived, she closed her hand into a fist and shook her head. "No," was all she said, disappearing back into the dark hall. A rush of dirty children stampeded past Deborah, their faces pinched, and then men who pushed her to one side, laughed, and insulted her in tones she didn't think she had ever heard before when she appealed to them to answer her question.

"Ye'd best clear out," said a voice at her elbow, the woman reappearing. "There's not many Irish here. There's rats under them stairs that'll bite you if you stand still. And the menfolk will go to drinkin' and havin' second thoughts most likely. Ye'd best be gone."

Deborah didn't look at her mentor but turned and walked briskly, more than briskly, toward the safety of Sam's building, away from this horrible place where Katy might be. As she fled, she was already working on a new plan since the action she had impulsively taken appeared to offer a great deal of danger and not much possibility of success.

Remy was aghast when he heard what she had done. "Oh no, my *chère* Miss Huntworth, no, no, no. Oh no. This is not to be done. Please, Miss Huntworth, promise me that you will not continue in this fashion. This is madness!" His pale face was even paler as he pleaded with her.

"I can see it won't work," Deborah said. "What do you recommend?"

"With so much misery comes the despair, you know, and the humanity is all lost. Anything, everything could happen! A lady alone, oh no, no. Not to be done."

"I know," Deborah said patiently. "But I can't leave Katy there in that hell; you must see that. So, Remy, as a man of the world, what do you recommend?"

After more remonstrance and scolding from Remy and more assurances and promises from Deborah, they decided, in consultation with Sam, to hire a detective agency to find Katy in the dark maze of the New York tenements. As the most knowledgeable and mobile of them, Remy would arrange it.

"But not the Pinkertons. I won't be party to that," Sam warned. "They're a rascally lot."

But even after the best operative of the second most highly acclaimed detective agency in New York had searched the area, interviewed its denizens and paid informants, Katy remained lost, and Deborah could hardly bear it. Her mother, her father, her baby, a dream, a life, Liesl and her beautiful little girls. The recollection of her lost loves, with the longing, grief, and guilt that accompanied each loss, threatened to give her Waterman paintings a bitter humor that was not Waterman at all. She struggled to recapture Sam's light touch and playfulness.

"I seem to be having a dark period," Sam remarked. "You'd do well to take some time to paint the hell that's preying on your mind and ruining my pretty pieces. When you're ready, then come back to me."

Deborah let her walks take her back into the narrow streets where she would examine every woman's face in passing, thinking that surely if Katy lived in this slum, she would venture out from time to time, if only to breathe. She studied so many faces she began to doubt that she could really remember Katy's at all, as if her memory had faded away, lost by the scouring of time, or permanently blurred by the effort to make the features of so many strangers fit the increasingly uncertain image in her mind.

One winter day, she spotted a head of brilliant hair where the woman's shawl had slipped down. She plunged through the crowd to follow, heart pounding, calling out her name, but the cry was swallowed by the roar of the city street. As her quarry turned down a side alley, Deborah caught up with her and tugged on her shawl, saying, "Katy, is that you? Katy Kelly?"

The woman turned, and unlike the glimpses of strangers that dissolved into disappointment, this face, though older and worn, flooded Deborah with absolute certainty.

Katy pulled away and snarled at her. "Leave off, ye daft bugger! Leave off botherin' me, or I'll bother ye for sure, I will, and you won't be soon unbothered neither!" She raised her fist to threaten or to strike.

"Katy," Deborah said. "Stop, Katy, it's me, Deborah. It's Deborah. I found you!"

Katy shrieked and turned to run, but she slipped in the turgid mixture that ran down the center of the alley and fell, still screaming. She was rigid with panic when Deborah lifted her up and drew her further into the alley, out of the incessant stream of humanity, keeping a strong grip on her heaving shoulders and patiently waiting for the panicked babbling to cease and for Katy to come back to her rational self and her common sense.

"You've no claim to me," Katy said, crossing herself repeatedly. "You'd best not touch me! I'll not keep company with the dead. Leave me be! Clear off! Oh, dear Mother of God, don't let her take me away."

"Katy," Deborah said. "I'm not dead; really, I'm not. See, I'm as alive as anyone." She pinched the back of her own hand as though to wake herself from Katy's bad dream. "I've been looking for you. Who told you I was dead? Why aren't you still in St. Louis? Where is Rose?"

"You're not dead, then. That's what you would say, though, isn't it?"

"I'm really not."

"You were blown up, weren't you now, in that far-off heathen island you're so fond of? You would go, and then you were blown to smithereens. That's what I heard."

"I was badly injured, but not killed. Not killed, Katy. I'm as alive as you, and I've been looking for you."

Deborah guided the still shaken Katy to a pile of packing cases against the gray wall and sat her down, keeping a firm grip on her arm in case she tried to bolt. They stared at one another in silence as Katy let her mind get used to this unexpected turn.

"It was that *divvil* Richards then," she said. "He's the one told me you were gone forever, and then himself had the firing of me, lying about me to Miss Lily and getting me sent off without a name. There's no one would hire me after that, would they, so I came here to find Rose.

"Oh, Miss Deborah, she is so bad; she's likely to be one among the angels sooner than not. Oh, Deborah, if it is you and alive, I . . . " and the grief and misery welled out of her. They wept together as women do, holding each other in the damp alleyway. The sorrow of loss and the joy of reunion tumbled out in a flood, and whether anyone passed them or paid them any mind at all, they didn't know.

Katy pulled herself together first. "There's no need for such caterwauling. What's lost is lost, and what's found is found. But it does my heart such good to see your poor ruined face, my dear. Not that it's so very bad, you know."

Deborah laughed. "Let's go fetch Rose," she said.

"Ah, but she's that feeble, she can hardly put her foot down to walk. And I've no place to take her where it's better."

"Leave it to me," Deborah said. "I have a place." The important thing was to fetch Rose without being stopped or hindered or molested by the frightening inhabitants of the building. "We must be intrepid," Deborah said. "And fast."

Luckily, the dinner-hour commotion was over, and

the building was quiet except for the rattle of voices behind closed doors. Katy grasped Deborah's hand and they swept up the stairs, gaping faces staring out at them from the landings, a shout or two following them up to the dark room that had been Katy's home in New York. The occupants of the room, three women hunched over a plate and four crying babies, were steeped in dirt and misery. The smell was overwhelmingly of dirty babies and cabbage and onion. Rose lay trembling on a pallet of rags on the floor, a jug and cup next to her. Her skin was gray and blotchy, her mouth slack, and she whimpered like a small kitten when she saw Katy return.

"They've took my blanket," she said. "I'm near froze, and they've took it while I was asleep, the damned villains."

Katy snatched a gray blanket from the shoulders of one woman and wrapped it around Rose just as she had wrapped and held and cosseted her on the day of her birth. "Hush then. Hush then, my little darling."

Deborah made herself as imposing as possible, facing the astonished women with a forbidding demeanor, the only useful skill she had learned from Tante Charity. Between the two of them, they half-carried Rose's limp body down the four flights of stairs and into the street, where Deborah bribed a fish deliveryman to leave his post and convey them to the brighter side of town, to safety, which to Deborah meant Sam and Remy. Rose lay back against Katy's shoulder, so thin, her fluttering eyelids the only sign that she was still alive. Deborah felt a deep satisfaction at having rescued her Katy and Katy's Rose, having brought them out of the dark suffering, returning them to her fierce care. There were many she had lost, but these she had saved.

Remy was just stepping out of his flat when he

encountered them mounting the stairs and after a moment of confusion, took Rose from Deborah and the woman with brilliant red hair, carried her up the next flight, past a startled Sam, and laid her carefully on the bed that had been Deborah's. He fetched hot water and towels so they could clean her and clothe her wasted body in a clean nightgown from Deborah's wardrobe. He fetched hot broth from his own kitchen along with an assortment of liqueurs that might prove restorative to either the patient or her attendants. He disposed of the filthy rags that had swaddled the little body and stood by, waiting to see what was needed next. His reward was a bright look from Katy.

"You're quite a right fellow," she said, and Remy wondered if he could be falling in love. All this time, Sam hovered uncertainly in the hallway, struck silent for once. When Rose was clean and had swallowed a spoonful or two, they left her there to rest from the exhausting move. When they returned to the main room, they found Sam had seated himself in his customary chair, his throne. Deborah and Remy stood before him like supplicants while Katy made herself scarce.

Remy started to speak, but Sam raised his hand for silence, making it clear that the real Samuel Waterman still wielded power and would not be manipulated or taken advantage of. He indicated with a gesture that they should seat themselves, and so they did. Remy watched Sam anxiously, hoping he would go easy and let the visitors stay at least the night until something could be arranged. In the prolonged silence that Sam held, Remy internally prepared a long speech about the importance of extending charity to one's friends and the friends of one's friends. Deborah just waited.

"I never realized life could be so exciting," Sam said. "Presumably this is your misplaced Irishwoman and her ailing sister, dragged in like the laundry. You're quite the ringmaster, Miss Huntworth. What on earth do you suppose you're about?"

"I found us a housekeeper," Deborah said. As if on cue, Katy entered with a tray of little hot griddle cakes, topped with a dab of butter and a shiny coat of honey, all she could make out of the sadly ill-stocked pantry. Hot coffee with Remy's liqueurs. Somewhere she had unearthed a set of damask napkins and a sugar bowl. Remy pulled another chair forward into the circle and tenderly seated her.

"Do you intend, then, for Miss Kelly here and her sister to be part of the household?"

Deborah nodded.

"There is," Sam pointed out, "the question of discretion. This is a new wrinkle I hadn't foreseen. Can Miss Kelly be trusted with secrets?"

"I can be silent as the grave," Katy said. "I've no one to talk to, but I can surely keep secrets that need to be kept. I'm that trusty."

"Even, mademoiselle," Remy asked, "if the secret involves something . . . not quite on the up, as you say? Something in the shade?"

"It doesn't hurt anyone," Deborah assured her. "But we could come under the law."

"I'll not even ask," Katy said. "You've saved my life and taken my darling little sister in. And if whatever you're up to is good for Miss Deborah, then you carry on with your shady tricks, and I'll try to put the house to rights. I'll not betray you, and I've never been one to favor the police anyway."

The three conspirators nodded, Deborah out of trust, Sam out of curiosity, and Remy because he wanted Katy to stay. She heard a soft cry from the room where Rose lay and went to see to her, leaving the three to talk over whatever it was. But a few minutes later, the door flew open, and Katy stuck her head in the doorway, causing Deborah and Sam to draw back; Remy leaned forward.

"Not a bordello," she said looking directly at Remy. "I won't be party to such a thing. I'm a good Catholic girl." She blushed under his fascinated gaze, a tide of brilliant pink that combined with her glowing red hair in a startling sunrise of a picture he would never forget. Remy smiled at the vision, feeling his heart leave his chest entirely.

"You are a magnificent Catholic girl," he said. "Let nothing worry you. Not a bordello."

Little Rose, as they called her, rallied under Katy's devoted care, with regular food and the warmth, light, and safety of Sam's flat. The new situation the two sisters found themselves in, however irregular, immoral, or illegal it might be, was heaven after the life they had endured in the tenements. Any time Katy had stepped out to earn a few pennies scrubbing down wards in the lung hospital, or to spend a few pennies on bread or boiled potatoes for their supper, she would return to find Rose lying on the bare floor, cold as the grave. Katie would look around to identify the thief and do battle for the dirty blanket that might keep her sister warm and alive another day. She was known to be a fierce fighter, but still, the depredations had continued. She now poured that energy into caring for Rose and for the whole household, knowing that her place was secure and there was no danger of being thrown out.

All three of the conspirators concerned themselves with little Rose. Sam sat with her and told whimsical stories to divert her or send her to sleep. Remy cooked tasty French things to tempt her appetite. And Deborah comforted both sisters as best she could, brushing Rose's hair as it spread on the pillow, giving Katy respite to recover her energy. Katy made herself a pallet on the floor so she could care for Rose in the night. She cooked and kept house for Sam and Deborah, improving the domestic scene considerably and feeding the artists well enough to keep the creative fires stoked and burning bright, even as the pale flame of life flickered in the bed that had been Deborah's.

Little Rose, ashen-faced, coughing, panting for breath, seemed to shrink under the coverlet as the days passed but still she held on. With Katy safely ensconced, Deborah could bring the lively spirit back to her Watermans with a strong, whole heart. Even as she loved and battled, was absorbed and transported by the power of her medium, the challenge of balance, the sensuality of form, the magic of color, she was celebrating Katy's presence in the flat and grieving for little Rose. In the very back of her thoughts, she worried about Sam. He rarely went out now, even for a walk, and had added a morning nap to his day. His hands were increasingly painful in spite of the warm poultice Katy insisted on applying every morning over his gruff objections.

"It's no good for what ails me," Sam would say. "You're a foolish, gaggling girl to think it."

"There's nothing can be done about your wicked ways, old man, that's for certain sure," Katy would reply. "Not even the whiskey can help you there. So stop your blethering and let me get on with it. I've more to do than listen to you carry on." With sure, gentle hands, she finished the job and left him sitting in front of the fireplace, his swaddled hands resting in his lap.

"I'll be back in a bit to unwrap your paws, mean old bear that you are. Just you leave off your fidgeting. You're not too old to learn a bit of patience." And there he would sit, sometimes nodding off, something defeated in the slump of his shoulders.

Deborah woke one night to an empty bed and found Sam leaning heavily against a bookcase in the hall outside the room where Katy tended to little Rose. He was listening to Katy's lullaby, a keening, sorrowful song of loss and comfort, full of mother love and yet empty of hope. Deborah stood next to him and let the tune wash over her, reminded vividly of her first night in Martinique when the servant woman had sung her to sleep and then seemingly vanished into the liminal space between waking and dreams. Katy's song ended, and Sam wiped his eyes against the sleeve of his dressing gown and laughed a little shakily.

"My father was a no-nonsense Englishman," he said. "It was my mother was Irish."

~~~~~~~~

On the first truly temperate day, Katy opened the window for an hour or so to let in the spring air, keeping a sharp eye on Rose, who sat up against the pillows, a transparent pink flush on her hollow cheeks.

"Can you hear the birds, Rosie dear? Silly happy things, getting ready to build nests for their young ones to come. Can you smell those lilacs from across the way?" Katy pulled a chair to the bedside to share the spring with her dear one.

"The doctor said I wouldn't last the winter, Katy. I heard him," Rose said in a faint breathless sigh. "But here I am in springtime and all."

"So you are, my dear, and looking like spring yourself."

The two sisters, the oldest and youngest of their many siblings, sat with hands intertwined, content for the moment with the presence of the other, unspeaking until Rose whispered, "You mustn't let my going grieve you, dear.

Think of the others that love you and know that I'm happy and safe where I'm bound."

Katy laid her head down on the bed where she knew her little sister was dying and cried in spite of herself, with Rose's weak fingers touching her still bright hair but without the power to do more. Rose grew worse as evening arrived, with chills and fever and the hopeless, racking cough of the consumptive. Then came that intense sleep presaging death, with breath as slight as the wind from a butterfly's wings, shattered from time to time with a desperate gasp. Remy was sent to bring first the doctor and then the priest. Sam stood by, hardly able to bear his powerlessness to help. Deborah sat in silence with the two sisters, and as midnight passed and then as early morning began to dim the candlelight, she sat with the sister who still lived and grieved.

Several days later, after a funeral mass and then a sad, sweet burial service at the cemetery, the four returned home, acutely aware of the empty room where Rose had been. Katy went with Remy to his flat, and it was only after their cold supper, set out earlier in the day, that Deborah and Sam realized Katy had not returned from Remy's, and that would be the way of it. She had sought out and found the warmth and human comfort she so sadly needed in Remy's arms. She would be back to keep house for them, of course. She and Remy would bake in his flat and cook in Sam's, where the four of them began to share their evening meals. Remy's most casual cooking far surpassed anything the others produced, so it was to the satisfaction of all that he seduced Katy away from a standard fare of meat and "taties" and taught her the fine points of French household cuisine.

~~~~~~~

In spite of the risks they were taking, Deborah would always look back on the Waterman years as a time of safety and would treasure the kind of companionship she had not enjoyed since Miss Singleton had come into her life and the luxury of conversation with someone who could talk about art. The addition of Katy, someone who knew her story, added to her contentment. Even Deborah's dreams eventually shifted away from the nightmares of black, shrieking fire and of lost children buried alive in ashes, nightmares that had marked her time in the Frauhaus. She dreamed instead of colors and angles and the light within the hearts of things, and increasingly about a dream exhibit of her work, wall after wall of blank canvases and empty frames, the paintings she had lost when she had lost everything in the catastrophe that still marked her, and paintings yet to be realized.

The harrowing rage and grief that had prompted her wild painting on the Fort-de-France hospital wall had played out, but the deep promise remained. She needed to step away occasionally from the profound whimsy of Sam's vision and connect with her own. She painted, not for the last time, a pink, glittering self-portrait she had envisioned on her voyage home, with the wound on her face transformed into a playful ornament. She didn't share her work with either of her co-conspirators. She was not concerned that they would belittle her. If Sam were flippant or Remy disparaging, it would not cause her to doubt herself or her work; she knew it was important, commanding, and original. She knew her worth. She would reveal her work to them in time, once she was sure of the growing love she felt for the two of them, her unexpected family.

13

~ Showing ~

Deborah had been quick to inform George Kennan of the successful rescue of Katy Kelly and to thank him again for his troubles. Kennan wrote back to congratulate her and express his satisfaction at the outcome. Except for a brief notice of Rose's passing and his return note of condolence, the correspondence flagged. Deborah's days were spent on the business of producing Watermans, conferring with her accomplices, and working on her own pieces. She rarely visited the galleries, not wanting to become known to that world and endanger the Waterman conspiracy, finding it possible to follow the swirling news of the New York art community through newspaper columns, *American Art News*, and Remy. Still, she was a bit restless in this peaceful harbor she had reached; she felt a perverse desire to rock the boat.

So she was pleased to receive Kennan's letter saying that he and his wife Lena would be in the city for a few weeks towards the end of the year and would like to meet with her if that should be convenient. He hoped to see more of her paintings if she would afford them this privilege. And he had a concern he would much rather broach in person than entrust to writing.

After a moment's consideration, she realized that, yes, she would indeed enjoy seeing Mr. Kennan again to thank him in person for Katy, and she was curious to meet Lena. So she replied by inviting the Kennans to a private showing in mid-December. That gave her three months to prepare. She would take this opportunity to unveil her work to Sam and Remy as well, counting on their good company manners to keep them civil. She would cover the false Waterman she was working on for Sam, a dim alleyway lit up with red leaves of Boston ivy clinging to dark brick walls. It would wait until she finished the latest piece she had been working on for herself, black crumbled earth against a sea-washed sunset. She would serve tea and have Katy make lemon cookies, offering a nice sherry but also a respectable whiskey to underline the seriousness of the occasion and to avoid appearing too ladylike.

On the appointed day, the Kennans arrived punctually, George with his bowler in hand, and, by his side, a clear-eyed little woman in gray. After introductions all around, they were seated, George and Lena Kennan, Samuel Waterman, Remy, and Deborah, with Katy bringing the refreshments. The cookies were lovely. As usual, Remy made sure that Katy joined them, as he absolutely rejected the notion of Katy as servant. At first, the conversation was general and tentative: weather, travel, accommodations, but Remy's conviviality and George's natural curiosity served to move things along.

"Mrs. Huntworth," Kennan ventured, "how glad I am to see you so well, so fully recovered. I hope your health continues good."

"Thank you, yes," Deborah returned. And turning, "Mrs. Kennan, I must tell you how very helpful your husband proved when I was in greatest need of help."

"In the islands," Lena said. "How you must have suffered. I found myself so moved by George's account. The devastation, the loss of life, all the suffering."

"Which islands were these?" Sam asked innocently, adding, "Miss, uh, Mrs. Huntworth?"

"Martinique." She avoided Sam's eyes and moved to a more comfortable subject. "I believe there was something you wished to discuss with me, Mr. Kennan. Please feel free to share it in this company. These are my very close friends."

"You could say we have no secrets among us," Sam said.

"Mrs. Huntworth, when I was in St. Louis last year to find out what I could about Miss Kelly here, I called in at the residence of your man of business."

"Richards," Deborah said.

"Exactly. He did not strike me as a trustworthy fellow, to be quite candid. In fact, he struck me as a bit dodgy, if you will forgive my saying so."

"There is nothing bad you could say about Richards that would offend me. He has never been a great favorite of mine," Deborah said.

"At first, this Richards denied that he had ever heard of Miss Kelly. When pressed, he informed me that she had worked briefly for your late husband Judge Huntworth's daughter, your stepdaughter Lily."

"Yes," Deborah said. "When Lily was confined with her first child."

"And a lovely boy he was, for all he had his grandfather's ears," Katy offered.

"She had been dismissed, he said, for impertinence and theft, and he seemed to remember hearing that she had gone to the dogs and was now deceased, though obviously, that is not the case.

"Richards particularly wanted to know the origin of my interest in Miss Kelly and seemed more inclined to seek information than to provide it. At length, I took my leave of him, sorry to have such sad news to bring to you. However, at the foot of the stairs, the little maid whispered to me as she brought my hat. She told me that your Miss Kelly had been let go from her position and had gone to live in New York City with her sister. I feel certain this was information that Richards had withheld from me deliberately."

"Sure, he's a true son of the Father of Lies," Katy said and sniffed. "That Richards was never up to any good."

"If I may, Mrs. Huntworth," Kennan said, "I strongly urge you to find a new man of business, as there is something unsavory about Richards. I suspect he has not dealt fairly with you."

"If I may venture," Remy offered, "I act as you know for Mr. Waterman. I would be pleased to assist you, Mrs. Huntworth, while you seek to replace this Richards person. It would be a great pleasure to act on your behalf. It is a role for which I have some qualification."

"I assume you are already the agent for Mrs. Huntworth's paintings?"

"I would assume this as well," Remy said. "And as her agent, let me invite you to step into the studio and let us view her work, shall we?"

He led the way down the hall, and they followed, each energized by a different spark: Mr. Kennan, expecting to be moved again as he had been when they first met and Lena to get a glimpse into this woman who had so remarkably gained her husband's respect. Katy was curious and ready to admire. Sam wanted to see what else would be revealed about Deborah, and Deborah wanted to look through their eyes and invite them into her world, to show them what she had created out of the horrors and pains of her life.

Deborah had decided to show a recent version of her hospital mural, *La Catastrophe*, which she knew Mr. Kennan would recognize. It was flanked by two self-portraits sketched on the voyage and realized several years later once she had achieved working space.

La Péri Rose (The Pink Fairy) portrayed Deborah as a black woman. She wasn't certain why she had done that, but she felt it was necessary to express something, a chain of somethings, an alchemical circle of meanings: the singer of beautiful sorrows on her first night in Martinique, Villette's lost children, her Gianni, Rita Stokes' black Amanda doll.

The expression on the figure's face is Villette's—knowing, withholding, indifferent. She stands before a luminescent mother-of-pearl background composed of clouds or feathers, draped in a ragged gray robe like a beggar. Her hair is wrapped in a pale pink scarf, a turban with no points. Over one side of her face, she holds a half-mask covered with pink sequins, its surface pebbled with points of light, gleaming like scales on a fish, like the shine of a rich woman's choker in candlelight. Faint purple-black hands reach toward her from the lower margin of the canvas, to touch her, to grab her, to pull her down, to steal her power—the marrons come to demand their share of her invisible, painful magic.

In the second self-portrait, *La Reine* (The Queen) sits on a throne of shiny black, behind her, rich draperies and golden tassels. She is robed in gold, trimmed with geometric ruby and emerald patterns at the neck and the flowing sleeves. Her white hands with long, curving fingers are adorned with golden rings crafted in tight Celtic ropes, bright stones of opal, coral, and moonstone bezel-set in the knots where gold and silver cross, recross, and disappear. Her wrists are clasped with broad gold bands, enameled with purple stars, and engraved with runes. Around her neck and spilling to her waist, a river of gold beads, seed pearls, diamonds, and topaz cascades down the cloth-of-gold panel of her robe. A simple, golden band circles her brow. The left side of her face is made entirely of worked gold with ornamental jewels set in a paisley from temple to jawline, rubies, seed pearls, emeralds, and garnet cabochons creating, not a pattern, but an ornate island. Her face is serene. In her cupped hands, she cradles a burning heart.

At first, unmoving silence—then an incoherent exclamation from Remy. Kennan stepped forward and back, Lena keeping step with him, making use of the pince-nez that hung from a ribbon around her neck.

"Oh, my dear," she said. "Oh George, this is even more desolate than I understood from the slides or the little picture you brought back. So much destruction, so much death." And when they approached *The Pink Fairy* self-portrait, she glanced at Deborah's scarred face and away, seeing what the artist had intended and greatly moved by the courage that could make beauty resonate even through disaster.

"Most remarkable! Most original! It is indeed a privilege to see these works. I'm not an art critic, just a reporter. But these paintings draw one's attention to look deeper. So beautiful!" Kennan went back and looked at each piece again.

Remy tried to seem as though he were familiar with these works since he had claimed to be Deborah's agent, but he wanted nothing more than to be left alone to look at the paintings simply as an art lover. Sam leaned against the far wall and stared at Deborah, who avoided his gaze. After the Kennans seemed to have looked their fill, the party retreated to the sitting room briefly, with compliments to the artist and preliminary leave-taking. As the guests departed, there was a whispered colloquy between Lena and George, and then an appeal to Remy, another round of farewells and thanks, and the conspirators sat down again in what felt to Deborah like a new arrangement, in which she was vulnerable to loss. The silence seemed to last forever until Deborah simply had to end it.

"Well," she said. "What do you think?"

"I am your agent; is this correct?"

Deborah nodded, so Remy went on. "Yes, of course, I will place your work at once. I have one or two galleries in mind to whom I may owe a favor. And any place would be most content, no, excited with your pieces, especially as one of them has already been sold! Yes, the little Madame Kennan would have it!"

"You know, I would have given them anything they wanted, Remy. I can just send it along."

"No, no, no, no, my dear lady. No, you must be launched!" Remy rose and paced around the room, dancing on his toes, gesturing with raised arms, his voice cracking with excitement. "You, my dear Deborah, our magnificent artist, our darling, you must make this debut, and I, Remy, I who discovered you, I will provide the good champagne! You must shake up this city of poseurs and amateurs!"

His head was still spinning from the revelation of Deborah's work, and he dearly loved the bustle of producing a show. Then he clutched at his heart theatrically and turned to Sam. "But of course not you, Sam," he said and would have gone on, but Sam dismissed the disclaimer with an awkward wave of his knotted hand.

"Don't be a fool, man. I have eyes of my own."

Remy continued to bubble with energy, pacing and exclaiming until he stopped in mid-caper and shook himself like a dog stepping out of a river.

"You will excuse me this fit of enthusiasm if you please. I am over-bowled, I am flabbergast, I am on the side of myself. But I remind myself that I am also your interim man of business, yes?"

"Yes," Deborah said. "You are indeed my man of

business as well as my agent."

"Ah, then. I will draft a letter to this Richards requesting the transfer of all documents he holds for you. I will need to have details, you know, of what business there has been. Then we will find a more dependable man here."

"That sounds fine. It's very good of you," Deborah said.

"I must go out now. I thank you a thousand times for this honor, for this miracle, this revelation! I must look around for the best venue for such a brilliant moment. We will talk business later, yes?" he said and frisked out the door, past Katy, who shook her head and said, "Well, there's one off with the fairies for certain. I'll just go and make sure the man wears his overcoat, as he's likely to forget in such a state."

Her departure left the other two in an unexpected, uncomfortable tête-à-tête. Deborah crunched her way through the one lemon cookie that remained on the plate, sorting through the events of the afternoon. She had not realized how tense she was until now. And now she had an agent, a very reputable one at that. She had sold a painting. The doors that had been closed to her seemed about to open. And Katy!

"I just have the one small question, Deborah."

She gave Sam her attention. He had always called her Miss Huntworth except in their most intimate exchanges, but evidently, the showing had introduced a new informality into the situation.

"Your late husband, this judge Mr. Kennan mentioned," Sam said, his voice teasing but also a bit wistful. "He'd have been a rather elderly sort of fella, wouldn't he?"

"He was centuries older than you, Sam. You are my evergreen."

~~~~~~~

Remy took his new responsibilities as Deborah's agent and man of business with great seriousness. Her painting impressed him to a degree that required major adjustment to his internal world. And he wanted to handle her work, her fresh, original visions, to help her find a place in the world of art from which she had been compelled to keep a safe distance. He herded her like a solicitous collie with a new lamb. Over coffee the next morning, he sat down to interview her. Sam offered to give them the room, but Deborah assured him he was welcome to stay, that she wished he would.

"I'm tired of my secrets," she said. "I don't know who I will be without secrets, but I'm tired of them all the same."

"Tell me all: your father's name, your date of birth, address in St. Louis, the judge's, but also your childhood home." He wanted dates and details of her life, writing them down in his notebook to use later. Sam sat by, thoughtfully learning who this Deborah, his lover, his partner in crime, truly was. Deborah answered all Remy's questions directly and simply, hiding nothing. She opened the story of her life with the death of her parents, then her life with Grandma Gussie and Katy, and the coming of Tante Charity. The trip to Martinique and Sanson and the birth and loss of her Gianni. Then the bargain with Charity, her marriage to Judge Huntworth, his death, her secret studio, finally, the death of the dragon, and her release to return to Martinique and Gianni.

"I was on a ship in the St. Pierre harbor when Mt. Pelée exploded. I didn't die, but I lost . . . everything."

She related her manic painting in the Fort-de-France hospital, her acquaintance with George Kennan, and her return to the destroyed St. Pierre. And then her New York life at the Frauhaus and the deaths of Liesl and the twins, her gradual recovery from the nightmares. The only detail she omitted was her one night with Freddy.

The telling of her secrets to these two seemed to be happening outside her control, outside her body, the result of something stronger than her own decision, something like a butterfly pushing its way out into the light after a long sleep of becoming. When Deborah stopped, having arrived at the present moment in her story, it was Sam who broke the silence, speaking to them both.

"It's over, my dears, my very dears," he said. "We had a good run. But no more Watermans. That's over."

~~~~~~~

The big Huntworth show opened after almost half a year of work: Remy busy in the intricate doings of the art world of Manhattan, Deborah in the studio where it took her many hours to shake the sense of being scrutinized as she painted, knowing that her work would be open to the public gaze. The invisible watcher who hovered behind her was often critical in unhelpful ways. *They're not going to like all that black. That's not it at all.* At other times, the inaudible voice breathed a kind of vain flattery that was even more demoralizing, suggesting that the show's reception might be boosted by a few coy references to her sad history. In time, Deborah was able to dismiss this plaguing presence by plunging deeper into the canvas and imagining the pleasant voice of Miss Jean Singleton, her first colleague in the art of painting the world.

Deborah had expected to feel excitement and triumph—victory at last—but her mood was somber. She felt responsible—to herself? to Remy? to the art gallery that would host her exhibit? Perhaps to the work itself, to the muse. It was a troublesome, irritating time for her, and she avoided Sam's company during the day as he was almost certain to make a remark that would annoy. But she nestled closer to him in the silence of sleep, craving his warmth and the reassurance of his measured breath.

Remy approached her in a gingerly fashion to consult about the details of her debut, the text for the program, a slight change of title from *The Pink Fairy* to a more modern sounding *Pink Fairy*. He also insisted that she buy a new costume, and for this purpose escorted her to the shop of a compatriot of his, a Madame Auberge, who undertook the task of finding the correct dress and accessories as well as managing the querulous customer, who at first was pleased with anything and then with nothing at all. At last, they arrived at a dark purple silk dress with sheer, lace-trimmed black sleeves to the wrist and military braid at the shoulder of the short plum-colored bolero. The skirt draped gracefully from a high waist and made the most of her figure. A small black hat with a white plume topped off the ensemble.

"Good God," Deborah said, confronting her reflection in the looking glass while Mme. Auberge stood by, ready to adjust the folds of the gown or cajole the customer as needed. "I'm not looking for a husband, Remy. Why all this fuss?"

"My angel," he said. "You look marvelous. Be happy!"

Remy was relieved to have the chore accomplished successfully and ready to turn Deborah back to her work. He anticipated another struggle on the evening of the show when he approached her with a case of makeup, tactfully hoping to tone down the scar on her face to be less noticeable. She submitted calmly to his attentions. He added just a touch of rouge on her cheekbones and declared that she was perfection.

"What a pretty frock!" was Sam's comment. "It suits you." He was decked out in a green satin weskit under his good dark suit, black gloves, his long white hair brushed back, tamed from its usual wild Bohemian look. Deborah admired the way it curled on the back of his neck in perfect little circles against his dark collar. Remy was elegance itself, his wine-colored satin cravat a reference to Deborah's colors. Katy wore a dark emerald skirt and tunic that Remy had chosen to spotlight her bright hair, now streaked with silver. She added a white silk rose to Deborah's hat, and they were on their way.

Deborah was grateful to have Sam as her champion and Remy to arrange it all, but the throng of furs and the miasma of perfume and cigarette smoke made the air stifling. She disliked the sharp cries and barks of reaction, whether they signaled approval or disdain. Sam was watchful to fend off the most obnoxious admirers, and no one had the temerity to ask about her scarred face, though she overheard some solemn speculation that she might have been present when the Shirtwaist Factory went up in flames and perhaps had rescued someone at the cost of her beauty.

"Don't be bothered. They'll say almost anything," Sam assured her, "as long as it's an interesting lie."

Remy circulated through the crowd, in his element, full of bonhomie, answering questions, clapping backs, shaking hands with the gentlemen, and kissing the proffered hands of the ladies. Deborah had been concerned that Katy might feel out of place at the show, but she saw that the colorful Bohemian tribe of artists there knew Katy well as they hailed her arrival and drew her into their conversation.

Sam was soon commandeered by Remy to meet a

distinguished patron of the arts who wanted to know what he thought about the show in general and what he could say about the style. Sam had many fine things to say, but Deborah was left on her own to survey the scene. She hoped someone there, at least one person, might be touched or moved by her work, but she couldn't tell.

A voice at her elbow drew her attention.

"Mrs. Huntworth, this is so wonderful. We always knew you were bound to make your mark. But perhaps you won't remember me. From the Frauhaus." The lady stared intently at Deborah as though that would make it easier to recognize her.

"Martha," Deborah said, finding the name on her lips before she was conscious of it. "Martha Holland! I am so happy to see you again! This makes my event complete. You are really here!"

"Martha Wilson, Martha Holland as was, at your service! I looked for you after the Frauhaus closed, but it was as if you had vanished! And then I went home to Michigan and married—husband, five kids, and a farm to manage. But when I got notice of your exhibit, I took a leave of absence. Kissed them all good-bye, even the cows, hopped on the train, and here we are!"

"My heavens, this is marvelous! Let me have a look at you!"

"I just had to say hello for old times' sake. I mustn't monopolize your time, I know."

"Please, please, do monopolize my time, like an angel. Let's just slip back into the office where we can talk. It sounds like you have been very busy!"

She drew Martha around a corner and into a dark, messy little business office smelling of paper and dust, away from the color and din of the exhibit. Martha perched on a low filing cabinet while Deborah sat on the desk on top of the papers strewn there.

"Now, my dear! It looks like family life is suiting you very well. Tell me everything!"

Martha hesitated. "You know, I had a wonderful time taking classes and painting my pieces, really wonderful. But it wasn't the same after the disaster, and I never meant to stay in New York forever. And then there was Henry pestering me to get married and my folks missing me. It was just time for me to go home."

She searched Deborah's face for signs of understanding and went on. "I'm not an artist like you, and your work is so exciting and challenging and wild, you really will end up successful and famous, you know. But not me. I hope you don't disapprove too much."

"Not even a little. As long as Henry is a kind-hearted man."

"Oh, he is the kindest fellow ever."

"And he makes you laugh sometimes."

Martha's face lit up. "Like a hyena," she said.

"And he is absolutely wild about you."

"He must be, mustn't he," Martha said. "He could easily have found another girl to court. But not him. So evidently, he is truly wild about me."

"Then I do wish you all the blessings in the world," Deborah said. "And you're right; yours is not a choice I could make for myself. We must all follow the dictates of our own hearts. I am so happy for you. I can see in your face that you chose a life that suits you. Did you expect me to scold you?"

"I did, rather," Martha admitted. "I thought you would say it was somehow my duty to be an artist, though it sounds silly when I say it aloud."

"It sounds deadly stuffy!"

Their conversation was interrupted by Remy, worried

that his artist might have decamped. Martha promised to write her when she got back home, and Deborah returned to the fray with a lighter heart for knowing that someone at the showing did, in fact, like her work.

She had agreed to give an interview to the protégé of one of Remy's cronies who covered the art scene for the *Tribune*, but after her open, easy conversation with Martha, she found the fellow's questions tedious and yet vaguely threatening, as though her words would inevitably become false even as they were printed, even as they were spoken.

"Mrs. Huntworth, what is the message of your work?" The earnest young man prepared to write down her inspired message.

"I don't know yet."

He waited hopefully for her to expand.

"Sorry," she said. "I really don't know. Ask me something else."

"Who are your greatest influences?"

"There are many painters I admire."

"What do you think of the Impressionists? Would you call yourself an Impressionist?"

"I . . . I don't call myself anything. And of course, any artist worth her salt owes a debt to all of the artists who have come before, what they have seen, the rules they followed, the rules they broke. Is that what you mean?"

Deborah was relieved when Sam extricated her from the reporter's questions at last, and she could go home. In the photograph snapped by the journalist's companion as she left the show, published to accompany the story, she looked like she was under arrest and probably guilty.

The four of them read the reviews aloud to each other over a breakfast of cafe au lait and croissants. The remarks they read were mixed: glowing, confused, condescending,

positive, and positively mystifying. More than one reviewer compared her unfavorably to Mary Cassatt, suggesting that a woman who abandoned the tender, domestic
realm for a grander vision was unpleasant, not to be
trusted, and most certainly out of her depth. Sam argued
with the reviewers on every point; Remy criticized their
characters and revealed their peccadillos with the
knowledge of an insider. Katy let out occasional huffs of
indignation and nodded in approval when a reviewer was
complimentary.

Deborah was content to let it wash over her. She had
a foothold in the art world. She had witnesses. She had
Katy. Katy had Remy. And they all had Sam to take care of,
his aging increasingly evident, as if he had been diminished
by stepping down, even as he was delighted by her successful entry into what had been his kingdom. She knew that
in time they would lose him. She would have that grief to
fold into her heart along with the others.

Even in the exhilarating flurry of setting up the Huntworth show, Remy had not lost sight of the financial concerns of his *chère* Deborah. Richards had not responded to
a formal request for documents, so Remy contacted his fellow agents and art dealers in the St. Louis area and hired
an investigator to visit the St. Louis Courthouse whose
mass of records contained bits of information that combined to build a case against her former man of business.
He found that Richards had purchased Deborah's family
home for a surprisingly low price. Records of the transac-
tion showed that Richards had resold the property at a remarkable profit a short time later. Since he was listed as
the agent for both sales, Richards had also collected a hefty
commission for each.

None of this was outright illegal, and the investigator
had found that Richards had a number of connections with

the district attorney's office and local judicial powers that might make prosecution challenging and conviction unlikely should charges be brought. Even a lawsuit for damages would be difficult and expensive given the time that had passed and the distance between St. Louis and New York. Straightforward remedies seemed out of reach. So Remy hatched a plan.

Using all his linguistic ingenuity, he crafted a second letter, a masterpiece of innuendo, feigned naivete, threat, and invitation, portraying himself as a less than honest agent who had taken on Mrs. Huntworth's business affairs though somewhat unfamiliar with American property laws. The letter suggested that there might be other pools of money to be drained and that he might be bribed to overlook any irregularities, might even be willing to play a part in further depredations into resources still remaining.

Mrs. Huntworth, he wrote, was a broken, feeble invalid with no family or connections, one who relied on him entirely. He requested that Richards come to New York to explore the possibilities face to face, as some matters are best not recorded in writing. He used his most florid courtesies and old-fashioned French expressions to sweeten the proposition and bait the hook.

Word came back that Richards would indeed be agreeable to such a meeting and would be in New York on a separate matter in two months. Remy had plenty of time to work his magic. He rehearsed the household and coached them until Deborah began to wonder if the outcome would be worth it. She was called to stand in the kitchen with Katy and wait for the bell. Then Katy was to take a tray to the sitting room where Remy sat in Sam's chair, a small table in front of him. Then Katy was to return to the kitchen, and when the bell rang again, they would both enter carrying kitchen chairs and sit on either side of Remy.

They were to remain silent, impassive if possible.

"Can I at least glare at him?" Deborah asked.

Sam suggested neither woman could look at Richards without at least that much reaction.

"Be reasonable, Remy," he said. "They're not actors—they're humans."

Deborah promised not to strike Richards across his despicable face. Katy added that she personally would not scratch the lying eyes out of his head or beat him to death with the fire poker. Deborah topped this by suggesting that she would refrain from slitting him open from crotch to gullet with a kitchen knife. As much enjoyment as this exchange afforded them, they had to stop when Remy objected.

"Please, my dear ladies, my friends," he said. "You alarm me with such talk, such ferocity! No more of this, I beg of you. Let us behave like civilized beings and take our revenge in the way that will hurt him most. We attack his filthy purse."

14

~ *Prophecy* ~

When the day arrived for the great conference, Richards mounted the stairs to the flat where he had been directed. He was ten minutes late when he rang the bell, having spent twenty minutes pacing up and down the block, as Remy had observed from a bedroom window. Apparently, Richards believed that tardiness would present him as not too eager and thus improve his position in any negotiation that might take place. It was a calculated rudeness.

The door was opened by Remy in a maroon smoking jacket and a peacock blue beret, the conspirators assuming this a likely costume for a pretentious continental business agent of questionable ethics. He invited Richards into the sitting room of Sam's flat, where Sam, who had insisted on being present at the event and had promised not to speak, was sitting at the fire, only the top of his head showing above the wingback chair. A small desk and two chairs were arranged in the middle of the room, evidently to transact the business at hand. A stack of documents and file ledgers suggested as much. Remy gestured broadly for Richards to take his seat.

"You will make yourself of the utmost comfort, my dear colleague. Please, to sit, and I shall arrange for a small *apéritif*, perhaps?"

Remy went out of the room, waving his hand airily at Richards, leaving him alone with the unexplained old man. Richards stood with his hat in hand and his overcoat half off and no servant to take them, no place to put them down. It was awkward, but he settled on placing the hat on the table and draping his coat across the back of the chair. When Remy returned, full of effusive chat, Richards sat heavily in the chair, made lumpy by the presence of his coat.

He had approached this meeting with high confidence, expecting to have the advantage by virtue of his superior American cunning, but somehow it had already slipped out of his hands. His discomfiture was augmented when he glanced up at the red-haired servant who responded to Remy's bell with a tray of the requested refreshments. He thought he recognized her, but since she gave no sign of recognition, he couldn't be totally certain she was the same Katy, that he wasn't merely mistaking one Irishwoman for another. When she was dismissed, Richards became aware that he was goggling at her back and that his mouth was open. He snapped it shut, took out a silk handkerchief, and wiped his brow.

Remy beamed at him unnervingly.

"And now, my most excellent colleague, tell me how you came to have the charge of the affairs of our Mrs. Huntworth."

Richards was happy to relate that he had handled her family's business and Judge Huntworth's as well even before the marriage took place, so it was natural that he would continue when her husband passed away.

"Now that marriage, if I do say so, would not have come off at all without my taking a hand. Deborah was a very difficult girl, much too warm and forward, if you know what I mean." All this delivered with a wink and a nod. "I was almost caught out myself at one point when the little chit took aim at me, but I was too wise to be snared, however tantalizing the bait!"

The old man at the fire stirred slightly. The

Frenchman listened politely. Richards wondered why, being French, he was not eager to hear the salacious details. This was meant to be men's talk, to establish a temporary bond that would enable him to manipulate the strange little man who had called this meeting.

Richards warmed to his topic, however, reassured as he often was by the male rumbling of his own voice. "Quite a fresh dish, to my way of thinking, though you might not think so now if she's so broken up and ruined. A shame such a stuck-up little piece has fallen so low. But it serves her right, really. Poetic justice and all that. She now has to depend on men of business such as ourselves and pay handsomely for the privilege, eh?"

Remy said nothing.

"Perhaps she has tried her little tricks with you as well. Be warned, my friend. She was a vicious little minx as a girl, and I don't doubt her troubles haven't sweetened her disposition any." Richards could hear that he was talking too much, that he was trying too hard. Could that have been the same Katy? What was she in a position to reveal?

"And her lying Irish harpy," he began, but his words trailed off as Remy rang the bell and Katy and Deborah entered the room with their chairs and took their seats on each side of Remy as they had rehearsed. The three of them stared at Richards, Remy with merciless indifference, Deborah with disgust, and Katy with pure Irish rage.

Remy finally spoke. "You are mistaking yourself, Richards—I may call you Richards, I trust—you are mistaking the purpose of this meeting. Let me provide the clarity."

He removed documents one by one from the files, arranging them courteously with the print towards his guest, reaching over to point out pertinent details as he spoke further.

"It is a matter of record that you have been defrauding

our mutual client, Mrs. Deborah Huntworth, for the entire time during which she entrusted to you her affairs, capitalizing on her tragic losses and impaired health. It has been relatively simple for you to perform this fraud as Mrs. Huntworth did not intend to return to St. Louis and so relied entirely on your expertise and integrity to help her meet the expenses of what would be, of necessity, a reduced household. You have taken full advantage of her vulnerable circumstances and pocketed whatever you could."

Remy had rehearsed this speech and delivered it with a suave neutral tone. A strangled cry arose from the now trembling Richards. He sputtered but couldn't arrange the words to protest this outrage.

"Did you say something, Richards? No? Let me continue then. The details of the house sales are shown here, both the absurdly low price for which you purchased the house and the much higher price for which you then sold it, only three weeks later. That was a most pretty penny! Here are listed the commissions you collected as the agent for both transactions. The numbers in this column show your exorbitant charges to Mrs. Huntworth for the handling of disbursements from Judge Huntworth's estate, and this column shows smaller fees paid by his heirs for the same exact services, just as a reference. But perhaps you will say that I misunderstand American methods of bookkeeping?"

Richards said nothing, feeling hot, with sweat trickling down his full neck onto his expensive cravat and, at the core, frozen with shock and fear. He searched his mind, scrambling to find an angle of approach, to bluster, argue, bribe, threaten, anything to keep from being exposed. His mind was as empty as a newly dug grave.

"I can't . . . I'm not . . . " Richards croaked. "I . . . " and he trailed off in horror.

"I understand you," Remy assured him. "You can't . . . deny your crimes. And you are not . . . willing to go to prison for them. Is that your position?"

Richards nodded dumbly.

"Then it is time to discuss reparations, is it not? Here is a plan I have drawn up by which you will repay the whole amount within twenty-six months. I think you will find the terms more than fair under the circumstances. Take your time to review it. We shall wait."

Richards took the sheet of paper in his hands where it fluttered so wildly he couldn't read it. He set it on the table, then just handed it back to Remy and nodded.

"Your signature, of course, is required. And the payments are to be made to Mrs. Huntworth on the dates shown. Any default or deviation will incur the actions listed, including public proceedings, both criminal and civil. The second copy is for your files."

Richards signed with a shaky hand. "This is an outrage!" he said, finding his voice at last, a voice that had both his usual baritone bravado and a hint of childish whine. "This is outrageous!"

Richards rose to his feet, and to his horror, the old man who had been settled at the fireplace rose up and towered over him. The fire backlit his corona of white hair into a hellish halo and cast his long shadow across the room to darken Richard's face. He spoke like an Old Testament prophet with the thunderous voice of the Almighty.

"You don't deserve the name of man, for you're no man at all. You're nothing but a puppet show for bad children, and there's nothing in you but lies and playacting. Your black, shriveled heart is buried so deep in your chest it's shrunk down to the size and semblance of a raisin. May your God-forsaken soul be lost from your body to wail and gibber in the dark and the cold! May Satan claim his own. Begone!"

Richards staggered, knocking over his chair, grabbed his coat and hat, and fled. He could be heard stumbling on the staircase.

Deborah and the others stared at the unearthly being who had risen up with his unholy incantation. The ferocious energy that brought him to that pitch slowly ebbed, returning the old man, returning them all to their senses.

Sam folded his arms across his chest.

"Close your mouths, you three," he said. "I meant to keep silent. I didn't beat him with the fire poker like the women were saying; I just lost my temper, that's all."

Deborah, Remy, and Katy still stared at him, and then Deborah began to laugh, and the others were caught up in the laughter.

"Good God, Sam! You cursed him! You actually cursed him! I've never heard anything like it!"

"Outside of the melodrama, anyway," Remy said. "That monster will not soon recover himself, no?"

"I couldn't stand the way he was talking about the ladies. Got my dander up."

"It was marvelous," Deborah said. "It was perfect!"

"This will be a right time for the drink if ever there was one." Katy brought out the whiskey decanter. They stood silent, each formulating a toast appropriate to the moment.

Remy led off. "To the success of our little dramatic! Well played, all! To our success!"

Next Deborah. "To Samuel Waterman! Take a bow!"

Sam bowed and delivered his toast. "To Remy, manager and stage manager extraordinaire! Well done, my friend!"

"I can't well say 'to absent friends,' can I now," Katy said, "as that was no friend to any but himself and the *divvil*.

So I'll make it, 'To Richards—Begone!'"

They raised their glasses, caught up in the excitement and triumph of the moment, energized by the release of tension. More drink, as they took turns intoning the bits of Sam's curse they remembered, adding their own variations, but always ending with the resounding "Begone!" that had blown Richards out the door and brought the curtain down on their scene.

Remy brought up some champagne and set up his gramophone. Surely this event called for music! Then he undertook to teach them the Turkey Trot, a new dance he had learned on his last trip to the West Coast. Sam soon tired and sat down to watch the others, cheering them on, calling out occasional commentary and advice. "More tail feathers, Deborah!"

Had they been younger, the hilarity and wild release in the room might have gone too far, too much drink leading to carelessness, misunderstandings, harsh words, hurt feelings, perhaps a scuffle or a lover's quarrel. Being older, they knew when they were tired, and the spontaneous celebration came to a natural end. Remy whipped up a simple omelet *aux herbes* for them, and the warm food reminded them of warm beds that awaited. Deborah saw Katy and Remy down the stairs, each calling one last "Begone!" as a good-night benediction. She roused Sam from the chair where he was dozing and tucked him in, kissing his forehead, taking a moment to marvel at the astonishing role he had played. She couldn't stop smiling.

It was not yet midnight; the fire that had so dramatically outlined Sam's looming figure had burned down to a few pulsing embers. Deborah sat in Sam's chair and stirred the coals with the unbloodied fire poker. The casual gaiety of the evening was a new experience for her, so unlike the awkward parties of her youth and the dreadful, dispirited

Huntworth family celebrations. There had been moments of fun at Frauhaus, but there she had always been on the margin, her secret grief and pain keeping her isolated and alone. Always outside, she thought.

She had not realized how lonely her life had been; loneliness was the price of safety for her Gianni, now ripped away from her twice. She had lost the habit of counting Gianni's age and felt a pang of guilt when she realized he would now be a young man if he were alive. She blamed herself intensely for just a moment, for not having picked her way through time more carefully.

But she had painted, and that was her salvation. Every loss had ended up on canvas; she had never given up, not after the debacle at St. Agnes School for Girls, not under the pressures of Tante Charity, the Judge, the catastrophe. She had been driven in a straight line by the demands of her art, even as her lifeline had veered, wavered, and threatened to derail. And she had been loved and was loved now. She shook herself and laughed a little. These were melancholy thoughts for someone who had just prevailed over an enemy with the assistance of her boon companions. Her only real worry now centered on Sam, and that worry could be held at bay by stretching out next to his long body, feeling his warmth, and seeking her much-needed rest.

~~~~~~~

A few months later, Deborah rose uncharacteristically early one morning and went for a quick walk around the park, just to clear her head and then let it fill with impressions, ideas, little moments. She was beginning a new series, or what she thought would be a series, of something red, Chinese red perhaps, and coral—something spirited, hopeful, disobedient, insistent. Saucy, even. Angles, incongruities, juxtapositions all danced and arranged themselves on her mind's canvas

All of it vanished when Deborah arrived home and found Sam on the floor, slumped against the bed, his head at an uncomfortable angle, not moving. He made no response to her when she called his name, patted his face, called him again. She pulled him down to lie flat on the floor, thinking he had been stunned in falling and would return to awareness soon. But in this new position, his jaw fell slack, and she heard his breath whistle in his throat. His body twitched in her arms, and she drew back; his eyes opened, and she saw fear there.

"Oh, my dear," she crooned, "don't be troubled. Sam, my Sam. My darling Sam. Don't be troubled." She couldn't tell if he heard or understood her. She shouted for help.

Deborah's cries brought Remy up, then Katy, and together they moved Sam to the bed where Rose had lain, where there would be more room to attend to him. Remy called for a doctor, and Katy fetched a basin of water and a cloth to bathe his forehead. Deborah sat with him, one hand holding his cool, twisted, unmoving hand, her other hand pressed on his heart. His breath was shallow and uneven, but he breathed. The doctor sent them all out of the room to perform his examination; they sat numbly and waited. At last, he emerged from the sick room and gave them the news they were dreading. Samuel Waterman had been felled by a massive stroke. They must prepare themselves for the worst, as there was no chance he would recover.

Prepare ourselves, Deborah thought. *What does that mean? Prepare to suffer this loss for the rest of my life? To lose Sam? Sam gone? What will this mean? How will I bear it?*

She laid her head on the pillow next to his head and

tried to catch his thought, to dream his dream, but there was only the rasp of his dying breath and the silence of her living desolation. When she lost all hope for even one more moment of Sam, she sat up in the chair and felt nothing except pain as she pressed her hands together in her lap. She wanted to pull the walls down and bury them both, bury the world.

"My dear Deborah, may we speak for a moment?" Remy's voice was beautifully soothing, like a trickle of cool water on a feverish cheek, a reminder that the world still existed and required attention. "I have sent for the priest to come for the last rites. He will be here soon."

"But Sam wasn't Catholic. I don't know what his belief was." She wanted to shake his still body, to make him say something. *Wake up and tell me, Sam*, she thought. *Tell me what you were. Tell me everything I will never know. I'm not through with you, Sam Waterman. Wake up!*

"Indeed, he was raised Catholic by his mother, though he did not follow the faith after her death. But a bad Catholic, you know, like Sam or like me, is still a Catholic. I am very certain he would appreciate this last attention."

So the priest was brought in.

As the sacrament was performed, Deborah wandered out to the sitting room and sat heavily on the divan. She felt that Sam was being dismantled, taken away from her by all the emerging details of his life. She didn't want some Catholic Sam; she wanted the Sam that belonged to her: his heart, his mind, his eyes, his long limbs. She had inhabited his artistry with great faithfulness, and she had supposed that to be the totality of his spirit. He had been immense, and time had shrunk him down to this. When death came, his immensity, everything, would vanish, and the world would have to close around the emptiness and somehow heal the rupture.

Deborah woke hours later, covered with a blanket. She could hear Katy and Remy talking quietly in the room where Sam lay dying. She stood and slowly folded the blanket, not wanting to startle herself out of the state of numbness protecting her. She walked down the hall on unfeeling feet, and she saw from their faces that Sam was still living. Katy embraced her and led her to the low chair at the bedside to watch and wait.

"He'll not be with us much longer, my dear. A peace come over him after the priest was in, bless his darling soul. I'm thinking he'll be gone before morning's light. He has the look."

Deborah tried to see peace on the pale face before her, but all she saw was the mouth that would never speak to her again, would never kiss her, the eyes that remained obdurately closed and would never gaze at her again. *I am selfish*, she thought, and took his poor hand in hers, gently tracing the contours of the swollen joints that had given him such pain. She sat there all that night, dozing and waking, and in the morning, he was gone, just as Katy had said. Then the grief broke out anew in waves that crashed against her heart. She wept wildly, and the doctor was called in to give her a sedative, something to calm her and let her sleep.

~~~~~~~

The funeral displayed none of Sam's whimsy; it was proper and well attended. The graveside service was lavish in the number of floral tributes that arrived there from admirers and fellow artists. Remy arranged everything to give Deborah as little trouble as possible, as he knew Sam would want. Deborah stood in the drizzle in her black dress under a black umbrella and tried to breathe without letting escape the sobs and screams that were lodged in her throat. Katy accompanied her home and tucked her in bed with a cup of whiskey-laced tea on the bedside table and a hot water bottle at her feet. There Deborah dreamed of Gianni as a young man, bright and gentle, and she was comforted. Then she awoke, and Sam was still dead.

The last will and testament of Samuel Elam Waterman was brief and impersonal. He bequeathed small sums to each of his two living cousins, both in Montreal. The remainder of his estate was to be divided equally between Deborah Huntworth, Remy Martin, and Kathleen Kelly.

Katy was thunderstruck. "Is he daft? What is he playing at?"

"Perhaps your friend Sam means to let you bloom!" Remy offered.

"Me? Bloom? And what is that French for, if you'll not mind my asking?" Katy's bewilderment made her cross. She wanted to give the old man a telling off, to continue their rough, affectionate wrangling, but it seemed Sam had managed to have the last word.

"Whatever am I meant to do with it all?"

Remy smiled. "I am eager to see what you will do, my dear Katy. Perhaps you will wish to travel? Or begin a business? Perhaps a teashop or millinery? Not a bordello, I know."

Katy slapped at his arm. "Go on with you," she said. "You know full well I'm a good Catholic girl."

"Yes, you are a magnificent Catholic girl, without a doubt." Remy hesitated. "You agreed some time ago to become my wife, and that is a great honor you do to me. If you wish to delay or withdraw under these new conditions, I will understand. I will pursue you still, always, my Katy, but I will understand."

"Oh no you don't," Katy said. "You'd best scoop me up

now, my boy, before some other Frenchman decides to marry me for my money."

~~~~~~~

Deborah was unable to find a place of calm and composure or even sanity in the days and nights that followed Sam's death. The days saw her wandering from room to room, her mind wrapped in cotton wool, her apathy at times giving way to bouts of weeping that exhausted her. She ransacked bureaus and drawers of Sam's sad, inconsequential belongings, letters, books, leaving it all in a heap on the floor. There was nothing that spoke to her, nothing to heal or comfort or make him live again.

She stood in the studio, with its paintings in different states of completion, and wept helplessly, unable to touch a brush or even smooth a canvas with her hand. She was waiting for that possession, the creative fury that had overcome her in the Fort-de-France hospital, but she remained unvisited and powerless. At night, she sank onto the bed she had shared with Sam and slept heavily or not at all, or slept and awakened with a startled cry, shaken to consciousness by a dream of black fire burning up the world, or a half-waking vision of Sam rising up to shriek and shake his fist at her.

She rebuffed Katy, who left trays of tea and delicacies created by Remy outside the door of the flat, which Katy found sometimes picked over, sometimes untouched, when she returned to retrieve them. To Katy's knocking, Deborah said, "Go away. I need to be alone. I don't want you."

By the fourth night, Katy took a firm hand, first with Remy, who was inclined to take Deborah at her word.

"I'm worried she'll do herself a harm. It's no matter

what she says, she's that unhinged in her grief. She's in no state to judge what she needs. And if she doesn't need us, so much the more do we need her. Come along with me then, and bring your key."

The two of them assembled a tray with hot tea, a bottle of whiskey, and a big plate of jam butties and went up the stairs to minister to Deborah, willing or no. They found her in the midst of the chaos she had created, sitting on the floor in her nightclothes, candles burning on the low table in front of her.

"I can't find myself," she said, looking up at them. "I can't find Sam. I don't know what to do."

Her face in the candlelight was pale, framed by wild, tangled locks of hair. Remy set the tray down and poured her a cup of tea which she absently sipped.

"I can't paint," she told him. "I'm sorry, Remy, but I can't even try to paint."

"You are not to trouble yourself, my dear friend. Only drink your tea and let us take care of you."

Katy found a hairbrush, and just as she had when Deborah was a little girl, she brushed her unruly hair, scolding the tangles under her breath, teasing them out and smoothing Deborah's hair at last into a single, loose braid down her back. The familiar pull of the brush and warmth of Katy's closeness, the rhythm of her breath as she worked, all this brought Deborah a measure of peace. The jam butties completed the pattern from her memories of the days when Katy had first cared for her.

For his part, Remy was reminded vividly of his youth, when he and his friends would often gather, sitting on sofas or on the floor, lounging around such a table in warm, honey-scented candlelight, drinking wine, arguing amicably about art, about politics, about the theater, about old ideas newly discovered. It was an intimacy but impersonal in a way so that one was free to speak without inhibition. It had been a time of free companionship, and the memory made the present scene familiar to him as well.

He was moved to speak. "I first met Samuel Waterman, it would be since twenty-some years ago at a showing of work by a group of artists from the Paris salons, disciples of disciples, as one could say, men who could paint as, alas, I had found I could not. I was without doubt envious. These lucky fellows remained content with following the manner of others, a matter of technique only, no spirit. It seemed to me a great tragedy to see this talent creating nothing— such irrelevance, such an emptiness. For me as an agent, I would not have represented such art, even though they were successful, as I sadly was not at that time. Consider, I had just lost my first and only client to a vile fellow, a mountebank, but that is another story.

"Samuel Waterman had achieved some public notice by this time, though not so grand as today. I greatly admired his work, and I was certainly aware that he was in attendance.

"Evidently, my distaste and disappointment with the display were written plain across my face, and Sam had note of this. He introduced himself, to my surprise, and asked me if I liked what I saw, and I had to say that no, most unhappily, I did not like it at all.

"'Come see me,' he said and held out his card to me. He had such beautiful hands then, smooth and strong. I always remember the beauty of his hands, especially when they became painful later. But at this time, ah, they were like the hands of a saint, I thought. I did visit him soon, and soon after that, to my delight and good fortune, I became his agent, and we were friends for all these years.

"And his painting—so light and so full of life. It was the greatest honor to manage his works. I have never known a man more generous. I have lost my oldest, my dearest friend in the world." Remy sighed and fell silent.

Katy sighed as well and picked up the thread.

"You'll both know when I first met Himself, as the both of you were there. I was that afraid, him being master of the house and all, he would send me on my way and my poor little sister with me. I was in a desperate state for sure, and I didn't want to cause any trouble for you, Miss Deborah, so you can be sure I was holding my breath and praying. He wasn't a bit troubled, just said he was finding life interesting, which seemed a bit of a daft thing to say, and me in no position to argue. I took what was offered in both my hands and vowed then and there to be faithful and patient, though in time he did try my temper, as you know, that he surely did.

"In spite of us being strangers, something dragged in by the cat, meaning you, Deborah, he had a fondness for my Rose, and there I had to love him. He would tell her stories to amuse her, just gentle little stories about animals and such. And, you won't know this, Deborah, but after she passed on and I was grieving, it was that same Samuel Waterman arranged a mass every month for a year in her memory. Even though a bad Catholic himself, he knew it would bring me some comfort and ease, and so it did."

"I knew Sam," Deborah said, "almost from the inside out. I knew his saint's hands, Remy, because I wore them like gloves when I painted his art for him. I wore his eyes and breathed his spirit. He spoke to me, and I spoke for him. I can't explain it any better. It was a rare closeness we had. Hard to believe it was a crime at all. And when he ended it, the painting, and sent me off on my own, I was so grateful, but also a little sad. I missed him then. I'll never have that again.

"He taught me to play, to see the playfulness in the

world, the play of vision and sharing the vision. I don't know how to explain it. It was just Sam. He taught me how to play."

Remy shifted uneasily, finding that he had become a little stiff, and transferred himself from the floor to the divan. He was no longer the ardent young student he had been.

"Deborah," he said, "did you not find his sketchbook? It would give me great pleasure to see it if you would permit."

"I don't know about it. I didn't know he was still sketching anything. Where would it be?"

The three of them rose and began to hunt in his bureau, under the bed, and finally, Remy found the treasure in the heap of books and letters Deborah had tossed on the floor in her grief-driven frenzy to find something of Sam. It was a small notebook, nondescript but full. They gathered around the kitchen table, turned on the light, and examined their find. The sketches were pencil drawings, sometimes shaded and complete little pictures, more often just a few lines, the curve of a woman standing in a doorway, a figure who floated off the page, recognizably Remy, though one could not say why. Katy's arms and her hands, which seemed to cup something, insects or sticks or ginger roots. Scenes from their lives, the outline of Deborah's body, Deborah in her art show finery.

They pored over Sam's sketchbook together, identifying and remembering, laughing even, though Deborah would not have supposed she could ever laugh again. When they came to the end of the sketches, they agreed to look for more sketchbooks in the morning. Deborah slept that night, a natural sleep that signaled the first steps towards healing, body, mind, and heart.

Though the worst of her grief passed and Katy helped

restore the flat to order, uncovering several more of Sam's books, Deborah was restless. She felt confined by the walls, and when she went out to walk, hoping to find relief, she felt the pressure of the city all around her, buildings, people, machines, commerce; she couldn't break free and rise to the surface of this roiling pool of lives, buffeted by the noise and the kaleidoscope of abrupt colors and shapes.

"I have to go," she told Katy. They agreed that St. Louis was unlikely to suit her. And she assured Katy that she would not return again to Martinique. "I would never sleep there; I have no reason to return."

"I can't paint," she told Remy, "not here. I can't even begin. What will I do if I can't paint? Who will I be?"

As an agent, Remy was familiar with the demands and peculiarities of the lives of artists, the "artist temperature," as Sam had called it. He suggested a change of scene—a new flat elsewhere in the city or a cottage in a charming French village. An apartment in Paris? Or even a villa in the Italian countryside? Remy would without doubt make all arrangements

"You will most certainly paint, Deborah, beautiful, wonderful work. Many of my artists have found themselves, temporarily only, in this desert of inspiration."

They mulled over the possibilities, but in the end, it was a letter from George Kennan that settled the matter.

2 March 1913
Medina, New York
Dear Mrs. Huntworth,

I read with regret about the sad passing of your friend, the great American painter, Samuel Waterman. Mrs. Kennan and I want to offer our deepest sympathy for your loss and our sincere condolences. We have often spoken of the remarkably convivial atmosphere we experienced when you kindly invited us to view your work and to meet your friends. Mr. Waterman made a great impression, even in that brief meeting, as a kindly, charming man in addition to his reputation as one of America's premier artists. It is commonly said, "I am sorry for your loss," and so I am. Both Lena and I are deeply, sincerely sorry.

Please forgive my forwardness in adding a note to offer you my unsolicited advice. Perhaps the extraordinary circumstances of our first meeting gives me this temerity. You and I stood on the grave of a murdered city, and your informal sketch of that deathscape is one of my prized possessions, prized for the awful sensations it conveys and for the skill with which it is executed. Its value is only exceeded by your oil painting *The Grave*, which Lena was entranced by and which we took the liberty of purchasing. *The Grave* does something I did not suppose possible. It makes of the scene something as beautiful as it is haunting.

I cannot think of what you suffered without pangs of horror and accompanying respect for your courage under the burden of your losses. I admire the strength that brought you out of that tragedy, a strength which I hope will see you through your present bereavement.

I have been barred for political reasons from further exploration in the Caucasus but have agreed to undertake several other journeys and several other projects that will keep me away from home for another stretch. Lena is undertaking her own journey of exploration to the new state of New Mexico. She has already taken a house in the capital city of Santa Fe and writes me to urge you strongly to join her there if you should be free, able to travel, and ready for a change of scene. She is a great admirer of your work and hopes you will fall in love with the Southwest, as she has evidently done. Her own warmest invitation will no doubt reach you shortly. I urge you to accept it.

Respectfully yours,
George Kennan

P.S. Lena says the light in the canyons and mountains is like nothing she has ever seen, the colors clear and vivid, the shapes of the various landforms truly remarkable. The sky, she says, is an intense, transparent blue, huge beyond description. You must paint there.

~ *Epilogue* ~

The sun shines on a woman sitting silently on a flat dun rock at the edge of the canyon, her sketch pad beside her, a dusty black dog lying at her feet. The thin air of the high desert delivers only the sun's sharp light, not its warmth. The heat dissipates, flying up to return the last drops of moisture from the almost waterless snow still sheltered in the shadows of tufts of chamisa and deer grass and in the vertical slashes that run sheer from the canyon's rim to the canyon floor below.

At this moment, she is looking at a shallow recess halfway down the opposite wall, a blue horizontal shadow in the polished, sandy rock, imagining for a moment reaching across with a giant hand and probing the cool cave floor, finding powdery dust, bones, perhaps a colony of sleepy bats farther in. The smooth rock, striated in shades of brownish red, white, bone-white, pink, and charcoal, stands in contrast to the tumbled rock and sand of the canyon floor. What she sees around her, and returns to see again and again, is the gentle starkness she will always love and never become used to, the unexpected softness of shapes where wind, water, and time have carved their record, the sharpness where a stronger rock is revealed, its edge honed. High overhead in the endless cerulean, a single hawk rides the wind.

The woman is still but alert, her body unmoving, her eyes surveying the close, grainy texture of her rock and the sandy dirt beneath her feet, then the bushes clinging to the canyon rim, the far wall, the stretch of ragged desert, a faraway plume of dust marking the progress of an invisible truck on an invisible road, the joy of blue mountains, and hovering over them, flat-bottomed clouds in shades of silver to white to gray blue. Behind her runs the rutted, weedy track on which she will return home and then the dun hillside, gullies cut by water from occasional high mountain rains, scree and rock and brush, the stand of mesquite and the scrub pine where she left her little wagon and tethered her donkey.

Deborah is no longer young. She has cast aside the trappings of feminine display and is nondescript in an unadorned white shirtwaist and coarse brown skirt, with thick workman's boots in case of rattlesnakes and a man's crumpled straw hat to protect her from the sun. Her face has lost its rosiness; the scar she carries from her early life has filled in and faded, now a series of pinkish-gray lines as though an artist had run painty fingers playfully down her cheek. Her hair, untidily swept away under her hat, has faded but not yet grayed except around her face, where eccentric crinkled white strands have escaped and move erratically in the slightest breeze.

She has not painted, only looked. All she has sketched today is a portrait of Bruno as he lies with his big head resting on folded paws, giving special attention to his long muzzle dotted with rows of whiskers, the crackled leather of his black nose. She gives him a friendly nudge with her foot, and they both rise, stretch, and walk to where Jenny waits patiently like a good donkey. Deborah harnesses her up and turns her nose towards home.

~~~~~~~

When she first came to this land, she painted every day in a frenzy, as though it might vanish, driving paint onto canvas, trying to master the landscape, garish and muted, flat and infinitely textured, coarse, deep, dangerous, startling, irresistible. "Look, look, look! Just look!" her pictures had shouted in strident hot umbers and olive and gold.

After that first six months, once the fever had passed, when her paint box was nearly depleted and she waited for delivery of replacements from New York, she had perforce to stop, breathe, think, and take stock. She saw that the shapes and colors, light and shade, would not disappear but would change with every day, and the truth of it would not change. She spent her workdays then walking through the desert, listening to her own receding panic, weeping at times, breathing the cold, thin air, letting herself be unprotected and true. There was no one here. There was no one to lie to. There was no camouflage, just the present moment, the ever-changing face of eternity.

The shipment arrived from New York with its treasure of colors so gorgeous she could understand for a moment the spiritual custom of painting oneself, face, arms, bathing in the look of the world. She turned her earlier frenetic paintings to the wall and began again, working with new-found patience to find her perilous relationship to this art and this place, its rhythms, seasons and contradictions, its awfulness and its beauty. Deborah had opened her heart, and it was not broken.

~~~~~~~

Now she gives herself time to see, to feel, to record, to celebrate the people who truly belong here; the sunsets; the rain clouds in the distance emptying gauzy veils of moisture, always on some other mesa, never here; the mountains that define the horizon yet leave an enormous expanse of turquoise sky to invite and defy her gaze. She feels sometimes she might lose her soul if she looks too long, that it would rise up and up.

When Deborah arrives home, she unhitches Jenny

and gives her food and water in the little pen behind the house, where the goats come out to greet them. She leaves her hat and boots on the porch, slips her feet into sheepskin moccasins waiting just outside the doorway, and stands looking out. Teresa emerges from the house, smelling of corn and soap, ready to head home for the evening. They wait together, as they do most evenings, studying the cloud bank on the horizon, piled-up clouds that are just beginning to glow, edged in brilliant gold, promising another glorious sunset. Soon a peach strip of cloud breaks through the purple-gray mass and then shifts into fiery orange, watermelon, and brilliant crimson spread wide across the darkening sky as the red sun sinks. *Beauty*, Deborah thinks. *I am surrounded by beauty.*

She pulls herself away, turns, and enters the house, exchanging a brief glance with Teresa as they go their separate ways. The evening meal has been set on an oilcloth-covered table in the kitchen: beans, corn tortillas, green chile stew with chunks of mutton, fresh tomatoes, and onions raised in the garden behind the house.

Deborah feeds Bruno and then sits at the table and eats what has been given, savoring the bite of chiles and onions, the mild warmth of the tortillas. It's the last day of the month, a day to pay her bills and put her accounts in order. When she has done, she promises herself the reward of a long look at the starry dark sky. She pulls a bundle of paper and her bankbook from a drawer in the wooden kitchen table, sighs, and begins to write checks. Invoices for painting supplies, the rent for this six-room house, wages for Teresa and Jorge, and for Teresa's sister, Magdalena, for helping clean up after last week's party. Oh, that party!

~~~~~~~

The visitors from New York had descended on Deborah around eight o'clock in a flurry of exclamations, furs, smoke, and beards, the smell of perfume and mineral spirits. They crowded in, congratulating her on the perfect place she had found to paint, being reminded of Greece and the Aegean light, being reminded of Florence, asking questions without the patience to listen for answers, full of excitement and ego and life. Some of them had been to see Acoma, the seemingly inaccessible pueblo village on top of a mesa and only a dirt path grooved like a gully to struggle up. Evidently, the New Yorkers had been disconcerted to be refused entrance, and no amount of money or charm or social connection changed that. Deborah laughed when she overheard one painter refer to it as "The Lost City," as though it needed to be discovered like an out-of-the-way nightclub to truly exist. Deborah herself had been to Acoma one cold February day to watch the corn dance, invited to go along with Teresa's family. It seemed that Jorge had a second cousin married to an Acoma man.

The New Yorkers had brought liquor, and they mixed cocktails on the rarely used formal dining room table while shouts of laughter and argument made it difficult to pick out what had been funny or what an argument was about, especially for someone like Deborah, so far removed from the controversies and the history of their scene, the galleries, the shows, the personalities, the scandals.

"The cat!" one young woman exclaimed, twisting sinuously in her shiny green tube of a dress and impressing her audience with her kohl-lined cat-green eyes. "Once you have painted, really painted, the cat, the essence, the spiritual truth of the cat, there is nothing left. The Egyptians knew this. That is the secret of the pyramids . . . "

Deborah hoped that one-eyed Emma, the ancient tabby who had come with the house, was somewhere listening. No doubt she would agree.

She left the cat-girl's following and edged closer to the center of another group to find a very young red-faced man claiming vociferously that painting was a dead art, that photography was the modern medium that had killed it, and that only modern photographers like himself could be considered artists at this point.

"Brushes and pigment!" he sneered. "Gobbing colored mud onto canvas! Why? The image can speak for itself! The image is everything! Painting is dead and buried!"

The older men laughed and winked at each other knowingly. Quite a claim for someone who was drunk in the house of a painter on the gin provided by painters, surrounded by painters like themselves, for whom paint was a living medium, the most important thing in life.

"Hobby, Eliot!" one of them shouted back at him. "It's just a hobby!" using a catchphrase in this argument that would be sure to inflame him further.

Deborah forestalled Eliot's hot response by laying a firm hand on his arm and drawing him behind her through the crowd, through the kitchen where several couples had chosen to neck, and out into the cold night and the cold moonlight, where she intended to sober him up. He broke away from her and threw up against one of the automobiles standing in front of the house.

"I'm sorry," he said, wiping his face with his sleeve. "I don't mean to be rude. I don't usually drink this much. But it's been all day with the same bunch, and they keep at me. It's just that photography . . . "

"No," Deborah said. "It's a boring argument on either side. Just sit over here and talk to me about your work."

She led him to the wooden bench against the animal corral, where Ambrose, the meanest of the donkeys, was scratching his side, startling Eliot and making him jump.

"He won't bother you," Deborah said. "He's grumpy, but he rarely bites. Now, I have been so curious about the latest photographic pieces, what happens when you form an intention, what you are looking for. And there's no one here to ask, usually. So do me a favor. Sit down and tell me two things: first, how you became interested in photography, and second, what you love about it. Oh, and third, what you are seeing as its future."

Under this tender attention, Eliot was able to slow down, not anticipating opposition, and feel his way through the answers to her questions in tones that vibrated with love and hope and wonder. His doubts, his early experiments, surprising breakthroughs, failures, all that made up his young life, his artist's life. He became so lost in his own thoughts and words, that when at last he drew to a conclusion, he could hardly remember who his audience had been and what she looked like. He could only be certain that he had been heard.

Deborah thanked him and asked to visit his studio when next she was in New York.

It was really just a bed-sitter, he warned her, not a proper studio. The bathroom doubled as a darkroom, and one of his roommates was working in cast stone, so the kitchen was not used very often as a kitchen. Deborah said it all sounded quite jolly, and she would be sure to look him up, to take a look at his work if he would allow.

"Just one favor, though, please, for now. I want you to find Gerald, the fellow with the green spectacles and the long black beard, and I want you to say the word "cantina" to him loud enough to be heard. Will you do that?"

Of course, he would, and she had the satisfaction of hearing the word picked up in shouts and shrieks, and then the party flowed in broken groups out her front door onto the porch, down the steps, into the automobiles, chugging down Canyon Road to the plaza at the center of Santa Fe, where the sleepy little cafe that sold beer smuggled in from Mexico was about to receive an invasion of already intoxicated gringos.

Her house stood, still bellowing jazz, empty of people but full of their leavings. She turned off the gramophone, opened the windows to let the clean wind blow out the smell of cigarettes, wine, and dancing. She left the glasses and napkins, but she emptied a beautiful little Acoma bowl of cigarette stubs, carefully washed it out, and set it back on the shelf where it belonged.

~~~~~~~

Deborah shakes her head and lets the memory of the party go. Her invoices paid and business done, she sits quietly in lamplight and then sees that there are several sheets of stationery covered with her handwriting at the bottom of the drawer. She pulls them out and reads:

Santa Fe, New Mexico, March 14, 1926
My dear Katy,
Thank you for your latest letter. You will notice that I am answering right away, trying to avoid being scolded for my careless habits as a correspondent. It is good to hear that you are doing well.

Things here are much as usual. The two nanny goats have produced seven kids between them, and you know from your visit last year what fun it is to have the little ones bouncing around. I am working, of course, and feel that I am still finding my way, that the best is yet to come. The latest pieces have a deeper feel, not so demonstrative, if you can see what I mean. Less incredulous, more in love. Which, since you asked, I am not and have no interest in being. The luxury of being a single woman, especially one who makes enough on her work to cover expenses and then some, is not one I would forego easily. What I have seen here of the drama and fireworks of love and marriage is not tempting. Perhaps if Valentino moved in next door, I would give the question another think.

I am still planning to move farther out of town—there is just too much coming and going here. I cannot seem to keep out of the various schemes and social events—I played the role of the wicked witch in a homemade musical of Hansel and Gretel, for example. I am told my performance was "understated," which I take to mean that I came across as wooden as I felt. My singing did not elicit comment from anyone, so I suppose I shan't be asked again. Most of this is cooked up by Gerald and several other neighbors up the road, the ones you met plus some newcomers, more dazed refugees from the big city who have tried the cure at the sanitarium here and are afraid to go back to the air where they come from.

My friend Olive is the one who eggs me on to do such foolish things when what I really want to do is paint. And paint more. I think when she gets back from her trip to Chicago, I will talk her into an expedition south to see the "badlands" where ancient volcanoes left extensive deposits of black rock. Sometimes I just need to see things for myself. And I might like to paint there, having a history with volcanoes.

Thank you very much for enclosing the *St. Louis Dispatch* in your packet. I am glad to see that Richards was defeated again in his race for mayor. Evidently, the voters see it my way. I will read the rest when I get a chance. And I will write to Remy under separate cover about the invitation from the Corcoran Gallery. I am thrilled, of course, to be chosen for an exhibition of 20th-century women

artists. Three pieces, I think. Of course, I am always in love
with my most recent work, but I leave it to the curators to
work out with Remy which ones they want. I will keep his
letter short, as I send all of my news to you, assuming that
you know which parts he will want to hear.

Teresa and her family continue to flourish. Teresa
sends her best wishes. I think she still feels guilty about the
chili pepper when you were here.

All my best love to you and the lucky Frenchman,

Your loving friend,

Deborah

She sighs and considers whether to add more, including an apology, or to seal it in an envelope with Katy's
address and a stamp or two if she can find them, to leave it
where Teresa will see it, and assume Katy will understand.

She sighs again and picks up the pen. She has made
friends in Santa Fe, but there is no one in her life like Katy,
who was her witness and companion for much of her life,
her lifelong friend. Katy may disapprove at times, but at
least she knows the whole story.

Santa Fe, New Mexico, April 20, 1926

Dear Katy,

As you see, I wrote you a wonderfully detailed letter
and didn't manage to mail it. Perhaps I have done this
before? The news in it is rather stale, though, so I will bring
it up to date and leave it out where Teresa will see it and
take it to the post office for me.

Let's see what else I can tell you. I have purchased a
small house farther up the canyon and will be moving in a
month or two, depending on how long it takes the various
officials to do whatever they do to make certain that it is
truly mine. The windowsills are two feet deep, painted a

particular blue that I am told keeps evil spirits out. So that should be okay, don't you think? Good space for flower vases, sleeping cats, or me sitting and daydreaming. The walls are thick, so the house will stay warm or cool. I am in love with everything, even the critters that inhabit those walls. There are two bedrooms and an outbuilding I will use as studio workspace when weather permits.

Teresa will still be looking after me, thank God. I have given Jorge the flocks of chickens and goats since he might as well look after them at his house rather than mine. I will receive eggs, occasional plucked chickens (dead), and invitations to view the newborn kids whenever I need a lift. And Jorge will continue to provide vegetables from his garden. Porch swing, Katy, for talking into the nights. You must come visit again soon.

And speaking of flocks, I was descended on by a crowd of easterners last week, brought over by Gerald, I think to clear them out of his house. The talk was amusing but exhausting, as always. I think they have headed out for Taos by now, where they will be met with plenty of drama and gossip, as well as the good, serious conversations I always appreciate. No one remembers me from my short career in New York; I think they are too young to have visited Waterman's studio. You might hear about it from their perspective at one of those horrid cocktail parties you and Remy attend.

I must remember to tell you that in my second look at the *St. Louis Dispatch* you sent, I spotted the obituary of my old acquaintance, Brently Mallard. Do you remember him? It seems he has now passed away, leaving seven children, thirteen grandchildren, and a widow by the name of Josephine. I suspect this is the same Josephine who lived with them to take care of the invalid wife, her sister. I'll never know, of course, but I cling to my story like a true believer. He was such a sweet and desperate man—he deserved some happiness.

I assume Remy has seen the reviews of the little show he set up in San Francisco. Both Simmonds and Hardeman were quite positive in their reviews, though Simmonds professed himself slightly disappointed by some feature of my technique which he described in terms so abstract and sentences so far-flung that I couldn't make any sense of it at all. He will have to live with his disappointment, I say, since I can hardly address a shortcoming I can't identify. Of course, you know I wouldn't change it even if I knew what it was. I received my little bit of the take and popped it in the bank, where my nest egg is growing quite plump indeed.

Lena and George Kennan are still living in upstate New York at her family home. Her latest letter says that George's energy is flagging, which is hard for me to imagine. He was always so vigorous and active, but I suppose at seventy-nine he is entitled to slow down a bit. My heart is perpetually full of gratitude for all the kindness they've shown me. I think of the Kennans as fairy godparents, though I would never distress them by saying so.

You ask, dear Katy, if I'm not lonesome out here with the cactus and the wild Indians and the outlaws, and the answer is no, I am not lonesome. You will read above about all my socializing. If I sound lonesome, it must be because of how much I miss you. I hope you will plan to accompany Remy on one of his San Francisco trips and stop here. And stay here with me while he does that magic thing he does with our canvases, turning them into money for more canvas and more paint. Then, if he insists, he can pick you up on his way back. What do you think?

I am always at home here, more than I ever felt in St. Louis or Martinique or New York. And there is so much beyond what I've seen remaining to explore, especially once I get my little automobile. (I thought I would just slip that in!)

I wonder how I was directed here, or drawn here, or at least ended up here. Sam would have said the luck of the Irish, which, as you know, I am not. You would probably attribute it to Providence. Remy might credit *le bon Dieu*. Lena would point out in her matter-of-fact way that she invited me. Whatever it was, however it happened, I am so grateful to be where I belong.

Write me again soon. I'm going out now to breathe some evening air and soak up the starlight, then bed.

My best love, as always,
Deborah

THE END

AUTHOR NOTES

This novel arose from my curiosity about Kate Chopin's short story, "Story of an Hour," describing a single hour in the life of Louise Mallard, unhappy wife. I responded by writing a simultaneous arc showing how that time might have been spent by Brently Mallard, Louise's absent husband. I suggested that he was in the arms of another woman. It seemed natural to wonder who that woman was, so I continued with a sequel about Deborah Huntworth, now the protagonist in *Deborah's Gift*, a sequel that turned inexorably into a novel.

I am indebted to Kate Chopin for Brently Mallard and his sister-in-law, Josephine. In addition, I used family friend Richards, since I had taken an irrational dislike to him and wanted to explore him as a character. I have been true to my admittedly idiosyncratic reading of Chopin's classic work. Any slippage is due to human error and/or poetic license.

There are many sources of information on the eruption of Mt. Pelée, the most destructive natural disaster of the twentieth century. Here are a selected few:

- *Mont Pelée and the tragedy of Martinique; a study of the great catastrophes of 1902, with observations and experiences in the field* by Angelo Heilprin, 1903.
- *The Day The World Ended* by Gordon Thomas and Max Morgan Witts, 1969.
- *La Catastrophe: Mount Pelée and the Destruction of Saint-Pierre* by Alwin Scarth, 2002.

The names of ships are historically accurate: the *Roraima*, the *Fontabelle* and the tugboat *Rubis*, often spelled *Ruby* in English-language reports. Characters aboard the ill-fated *Roraima* come from contemporary accounts of the disaster:

- Captain Muggah
- Mrs. Stokes and her children Eric, Rita, and baby Olga
- Miss King, the Stokes family nurse, and
- Mr. Crownley, Rita's uncle

In addition, I drew from the writings of contemporary explorer and journalist, George Kennan. *The Tragedy of Pelée,* 1902, was fascinating, and I also read "St. Pierre and Mont Pelée: Through the Stereoscope," though sadly I was unable to locate the stereoscopic slides that the booklet is meant to accompany. I was so taken with George Kennan's energetic writing that I brought him into my novel where he plays a significant role. I also included his wife, Lena, and their family home in Medina, New York.

My character Sanson is based on Auguste "Sanson" Ludger Sylbaris, or Cyparis, who, in fact, survived the Mt. Pelée disaster while incarcerated, was nursed back to health by Father Mary of Morne Rouge parish, and toured with Barnum & Bailey as "The Most Marvelous Man in the World." My major source of information on Sanson was Peter Morgan's *Fire Mountain*, 2003. Although this does not appear in my novel, in fact George Kennan played a crucial part in providing aid to Sanson and validating his account, which other journalists at the time found questionable.

The *General Slocum* disaster of 1903 is well documented. The source I found most helpful was Wikipedia, which I support wholeheartedly.

Historical figures whose names I borrowed in passing are Horace Norbuckle, a pillar of St. Louis society, and George Robinson, American impressionist.

As on-the-ground research, I travelled to beautiful Martinique, where I visited the Musée Heritage in St. Pierre and stood in the prison cell where Sanson survived the blast. I later spent time in Manhattan looking for a location for the Frauhaus and a site of Sam Waterman's flat.

The New Mexico section of the book relies largely on memories of my varied experiences growing up there rather than on research. Another person's New Mexico may differ somewhat.

In reading what I have written in this book, I find debts owed to "The Story of an Hour," of course, but also to Jean Rhys' *Wide Sargasso Sea*, Shakespeare's *Othello*, Stevie Smith's poem "Not Waving, but Drowning," the sonnets of Edna St. Vincent Millay, Dorothy Bryant's fearless approach to fiction, and the brilliant novels of Margery Sharp.

READING GUIDE

Deborah's Gift
A novel by Lois Ann Abraham

1. How did you interpret the title? What possible meanings does the word "gift" have in this novel? What is given and received throughout the plot?

2. The first section of *Deborah's Gift* is titled "Prologue." Yet the time frame of this section doesn't narrate events that take place *before* the events in the first chapter, as you might expect. Instead, the prologue jumps ahead to the middle of Deborah's life, like a preview of the pivotal moment when she is free to return to Martinique. What effect did this preview have on your reading experience? What was your response to finding the same events later in Chapter 5?

3. Conventional wisdom of novel-writing holds that the protagonist must have a goal, an intention. What does Deborah want to achieve? What does she need or long for? What does she learn to value?

4. Formal French phrases and syntax are used in the beginning of the novel by Tante Charity, a native English speaker who admires everything French. In the final chapters, Remy is a Frenchman with English as his second language. The Creole French of Martinique is spoken by Villette and Sanson. How do these various speech patterns influence your reading?

5. The loss of a child is a devastating, life-altering disaster. How does Deborah cope with the loss of Gianni? What makes her loss different from Frau Hollenback's losses of her daughter and grandchildren?

6. Choose a scene or two that was meaningful or moving to you. Why do you think these scenes came to mind?

7. Discuss the relationships between Florence, Lily, and Deborah. How do their relationships change as these girls go from adolescence to adulthood?

8. Among the minor characters, who is your favorite? What do you like about them? What makes one of these characters memorable?

9. Discuss Deborah's choice of lovers. How are these men similar and how are they different? Sanson, Judge Huntworth, Dr. Frederick Schilling, or Sam Waterman. Remember Brently Mallard?

10. How does Deborah "make beauty resonate even through disaster," as George Kennan remarks? How does disaster shape her life and her art?

11. How is the protagonist of *Deborah's Gift* a product of her time? If Deborah were a twenty-first century woman, how would this affect her attitudes and thoughts?

12. Is *Deborah's Gift* a tragic novel? Why or why not?

13. The Author's Note provides the sources for events and characters that were borrowed from history or from other fictional sources. What surprised you? What confirmed your suspicions?

14. We respond to novels out of the wealth of experience in our own lives. What experiences shaped your response to *Deborah's Gift*?

ACKNOWLEDGMENTS

I am grateful to all the kind people who read my pages, listened to me read my pages, and let me tell them the story that ended up on these pages, particularly to fellow writer Anara Guard for her friendship and assistance, practical and profound.

Thanks, as always, to my little sister, Dr. Adair Landborn, first audience for my stories, for caring about Deborah, helping me travel, and keeping me focused on the things that matter. Also to my older sister, Melinda Lightfoot (Sanchez Art Center artist and co-founder of Tangerine Arts), for her feedback on the nuts and bolts of painting and for listening to my difficulties with a loving heart.

In addition, I want to thank Joyce Gold of Joyce Gold History Tours of New York for sharing from her wealth of knowledge about Greenwich Village in the very early 1900's. Thanks also to Marie-Gabrielle Amingo of the Musée Heritage in St. Pierre, Martinique, who gave me valuable insight into the great catastrophe. Any inaccuracies in the text are entirely my own.

Helen Tucker, docent at Crocker Art Museum, read the manuscript of this novel from the art history angle, and I am most grateful for her generosity. Thanks to Gini Grossenbacher for her encouragement and keen eye for detail that helped me polish my rough draft into a finished novel.

Loving thanks are due to Coda and Niki Hale for their ongoing support and to my late husband, Thomas O'Toole, for his steadfast faith in me as a writer.

ABOUT THE AUTHOR

Lois Ann Abraham grew up in the Southwest and attended the University of New Mexico, where she won the Freshman Honors prize one semester and dropped out the next. After a brief but enjoyable stint as a singer-songwriter in Berkeley, she completed her education and taught English at American River College in Sacramento where she still resides with her sisters and cats. She is also the author of *Circus Girl and Other Stories* and *Tina Goes to Heaven.*

www.loisannabraham.com

Also available from New Wind Publishing...

Circus Girl and Other Stories by Lois Ann Abraham

A little girl discovers the power of the creative impulse. A woman remembers her first confusing sexual encounter. An aging flower child travels to Mexico to save her daughter. A baby is born with blue feet. A man ponders his ex-wife's last word. A collection of short stories in which characters thirst for clarity, self-discovery, a new life...

Tina Goes to Heaven by Lois Ann Abraham

An irreverent and madcap coming-of-age novel about a resilient woman's journey to find a place to finally call home. After a successful bank robbery to fund her escape from a sordid life, Tina ends up stranded at a rustic fishing resort in the Sierra Nevada. To stay there and remain safe, she must find a way to make herself indispensable to the proprietor...

Like a Complete Unknown by Anara Guard

In 1970, a girl's life is not her own. Katya Warshawsky runs away from home rather than settle for the narrow life her parents demand. She revels in Chicago's counterculture, plunging into anti-war protests, communal living, and new liberties. But even in this free-wheeling world, she confronts bewildering obstacles. Still, she won't relinquish her dream of becoming an artist or her belief in a better world...

Order from your local bookseller or from
www.NewWindPublishing.com